Erin Kaye was born in Co Antrim in 1966 to a Polish-American father and Anglo-Irish mother. One of five siblings, she was raised as a Catholic, yet attended a Protestant grammar school. In the decade following university she pursued a successful career in finance, before re-inventing herself as a writer. She lives with her husband and two young children on the east coast of Scotland. Both of her previous novels, *Mothers and Daughters* and *Choices*, were bestsellers.

SECOND CHANCES

Roisin Shaw hasn't forgiven the smug Donal Mullan for what he did to her sister Ann-Marie, and she's determined to make him pay for it ... But Donal's perfect marriage to Michelle, daughter of the wealthy McCormicks, isn't all it appears. He's facing the most difficult decision of his life. What will he do? ... Pauline McCormick has had enough of her philandering husband, Noel. When she meets the handsome sculptor, Padraig Flynn, sparks fly and Noel gets a wake-up call. But does it come too late to save his marriage? ... Hearts and marriages are broken, but everyone deserves a second chance. Who will find the happiness they've been searching for?

Books by Erin Kaye
Published by The House of Ulverscroft:

MOTHERS AND DAUGHTERS
CHOICES

ERIN KAYE

SECOND CHANCES

Complete and Unabridged

CHARNWOOD
Leicester

First published in Ireland in 2005

First Charnwood Edition
published 2006

British Library CIP Data

Kaye, Erin, *1966 –*
    Second chances.—Large print ed.—
    Charnwood library series
    1. Love stories 2. Large type books
    I. Title
    823.9′2 [F]

    ISBN 1–84617–276–4

Published by
F. A. Thorpe (Publishing)
Anstey, Leicestershire
Set by Words & Graphics Ltd.
Anstey, Leicestershire
Printed and bound in Great Britain by
T. J. International Ltd., Padstow, Cornwall

This book is printed on acid-free paper

For my eldest son, Ryan

1

Ballyfergus Cottage Hospital was silent and still, except for the faint buzz of the monitor and the pitter-patter of light rain on the window. On the bed, by which Roisin Shaw had kept vigil for the last two hours, lay her elder sister, Ann-Marie, in a deep sedated sleep. In repose, she looked peaceful, like a child asleep, her thin face framed by fine brown hair, dark against the white pillow.

Roisin stroked the back of her sister's hand, tracing with her finger the bones, veins and sinews which were clearly visible — thinking how vulnerable, how ill-equipped for this tough world Ann-Marie was. A wave of tenderness washed over her and she squeezed her eyes shut to ward off tears. For what use would more tears be? To make up for her sister's weakness Roisin, though five years her junior, had to be strong. Her hand brushed against the white bandage wrapped around Ann-Marie's wrist and she withdrew it sharply. A faint spot of rusty blood had seeped through the dressing. Roisin shivered even though the room was oppressively hot.

She looked up and saw her face reflected in the glass partition wall beside Ann-Marie's bed. Her long brown hair was lank and lifeless and the colour drained from her face by the gently pulsating fluorescent light. She glanced across at

1

her mother who sat on the opposite side of the bed. In spite of the trauma she'd endured over the last few hours, Mairead still looked neat and prim in her knee-length skirt and china-blue twin-set. Her eyes were wide open but staring vacantly at the green cellular blanket covering Ann-Marie. The smudges of mascara under each eye looked like dark shadows.

'What are you thinking?' asked Roisin.

Mairead shook her head slowly and let out a long audible sigh. 'I can't believe that she's done it again. If I hadn't called round when I did, God knows . . . it doesn't bear thinking about.'

'The doctors said the cuts weren't that deep, Mum. She's going to be all right.'

'Look at her!' said Mairead sharply. 'Does she look all right to you?'

'I didn't say she looked all right,' replied Roisin, the little hairs on the back of her neck prickling defensively. 'I know you're upset, Mum, but don't take it out on me.'

'I'm sorry, love,' said Mairead flatly. 'I just want to be cross at somebody.'

'So do I,' said Roisin, her voice a whisper.

'Where did I go wrong?' asked Mairead, talking more to herself than Roisin. 'God knows I did the best I could.'

'You're not to blame for this,' said Roisin, 'but I know who is.'

However, Mairead didn't seem to hear her daughter for she continued, 'Maybe someone else could have managed her better. I don't know. All I know is that ever since she was a child I wasn't enough. It was as though she

2

wanted something from me, I never worked out what, and I couldn't give it to her.'

'Don't say that, Mum. You were — you are — a wonderful mother.'

'Not wonderful enough,' said Mairead, ruefully, examining the figure in the bed.

She got up then and came round to Roisin's side of the bed. She put her arm around her daughter and pulled her head in to her chest. It was unbearably comforting. Roisin turned her face towards the warmth of her mother's bosom and wept.

'Oh, Mum, why does she do it?' she said, between sobs. 'She can't truly believe that her life isn't worth living, can she? And if it's a cry for help, like they say, what does she want from us?'

'I don't know the answers to those questions, Roisin, any more than you do,' said Mairead, stroking the back of her daughter's head, 'but I do know one thing.'

'What's that?' said Roisin, drying her eyes and looking up into her mother's face. She searched for a hankie in her pocket, found one and blew her nose.

'Do you know what date it is?' asked Mairead.

'Of course. It's the fifth of May. It was Ann-Marie's birthday yesterday.'

'That's right. Just like the last time she attempted this.'

'And the same date Daddy died,' said Roisin.

Anthony Shaw, Roisin and Ann-Marie's father, had died almost two decades earlier in 1974, on Ann-Marie's eighth birthday.

'Do you still think that Daddy's death has something to do with this?' said Roisin. 'Surely she's got over that by now?'

'Given the circumstances of your father's death, it's not something anyone could easily forget, never mind a child. It certainly affected her very deeply for a long time afterwards. But Ann-Marie was always different, from the day she was born. Sensitive, delicate, easily hurt. And so emotional about everything. Do you remember the time Blossom the rabbit died? She mourned that animal for months.' She paused, then added sadly, 'Maybe nothing I could have done would have made any difference.'

Just then a nurse came into the room and Roisin was glad, for she could not follow where her mother was going with this. Why was she blaming herself?

The nurse said that, given the level of sedation, Ann-Marie would not stir till morning. She told them they might as well go home and get some sleep.

Roisin kissed Ann-Marie on the forehead, Mairead following suit. Then they collected their things and slipped quietly out of the deadened hospital. Instinctively, they pulled their jackets tighter as the chill night air enveloped them.

'You're wrong, you know, Mum,' said Roisin, once they'd reached the car and Mairead was fishing around in her handbag for the keys. 'It's all because of that Donal Mullan.'

Mairead stopped what she was doing and looked up at Roisin in surprise. 'Oh, Roisin, are you still blaming him?' She sighed, then

4

continued to rummage in her bag. 'He hurt her very deeply of course, but Ann-Marie had problems before Donal Mullan came along. Here's the keys! Come on, it's cold. Let's get home.'

But Roisin knew she was right. Donal Mullan had broken Ann-Marie, snapped her in two like a dry twig, and she'd never been the same since. Roisin had been there — she'd witnessed it all. Night after night she'd listened to her sister sobbing into her pillow, inconsolable with grief and disbelief.

Donal Mullan. How she hated him for what he'd done! She'd learnt a few years later that he'd married some vacant-headed bimbo, the daughter of a wealthy businessman. Well, he'd got what he wanted. For all he'd ever talked about was money.

★ ★ ★

In his home in Belfast, twenty-five miles away, Donal Mullan was having a disturbing dream. He dreamt he was at school, except it wasn't school as he remembered it. All the boys wore grey shorts with creases in them like folded paper, knee-high socks, smart navy blazers trimmed in red and blue braid and matching peaked caps. Their black shoes shone like wet roofslates. Donal looked down at his black school trousers, hand-me-downs from an older brother, his washed-out red jumper and scuffed shoes. Suddenly he was surrounded by laughing boys, all pointing at him and shouting 'Mangey

5

Mullan! Mangey Mullan!' He looked around frantically, searching for a means of escape. Four high grey walls enclosed the playground — there was no way out.

Donal woke with a start, his heart beating madly in his chest. He let his head sink into the white goose-down pillow, and concentrated on relaxing all the tensed muscles in his body. Why did he have that stupid dream over and over? The boy in the dream was definitely himself. He recognised the pale grey eyes and mid-brown hair; the fine-featured face with its promise of handsomeness to come, the thin, whippet-like frame that had yet to develop into the body of a sportsman. He'd never been ribbed at school — he'd been accepted the same as everyone else. The feelings of anxiety and inferiority were, however, familiar. He turned his head to look at the clock on the bedside table and the starched cotton pillowcase crinkled in his ear. The finest Egyptian cotton Michelle had said, and Donal pretended to understand the difference between that and any other bed-linen. He looked at the clock — two a.m. He was relieved to be released from the nightmare but he would not sleep now.

The figure beside him on the bed had not stirred. Michelle's breathing was even and deep — the restful sleep of the privileged, thought Donal, undisturbed by fears of any kind. Since she'd told him her news Donal felt differently about her — more protective, guiltier. He leaned up on his elbow and carefully brushed the peroxide strands of hair from her face. They slept with the blinds open and the room was bathed in the city's orange glow. Stripped of make-up and without the benefit of daytime animation, Michelle's features were laid bare. Her prettiness was unmasked — she was plain, unlovely. Slowly, he peeled back the down duvet, light as air, and slipped out of bed. He found his dressing-gown and put it on over his bare flesh. He padded silently across the well-carpeted room, went into the en-suite bathroom, closed the door and pulled the toggle switch for the light over the vanity unit. He urinated into the Philippe Starck toilet, thinking that the room was as big as the sitting-room in the house where he'd grown up.

He closed the bedroom door behind him and crossed the expansive open-plan living area to the kitchen. He did not switch on any lights as the space was illuminated well enough by the amber glare of the city. They rarely closed the curtains, privacy not being an issue on the top floor. He opened the huge silver fridge and took out a bottle of Evian, the best bottled water — apparently. He shoved the door closed with his hip, twisted off the screw top and flung it towards the sink. Then he walked over to the vast sheets of glass that formed two entire walls of the room. In spite of all the safety reassurances they'd received, he was still a little nervous when he stood right up close to the window.

The views from the penthouse apartment, all three thousand square feet of it, were breathtaking. The huge yellow cranes of Harland and Wolfe, in little use these days, loomed in the distance like great sleeping dinosaurs. Far below, the wide curve of the Lagan River was black like ink. Reflections of the security lighting on the other side of the river sparkled like jewels on the water's surface.

At first, Donal had been dubious about moving into the waterfront but, three years on, it was the up-and-coming place. Close to the city centre, millions were being pumped into regeneration. Hotels, prestigious office buildings and luxury apartment blocks were popping up all over the place and a huge entertainment complex was planned. Noel McCormick's shrewd instincts had been proven right. Donal's father-in-law, in the guise of his company, McCormick Limited, was one of the first to develop waterfront properties and he had built, and paid for, this apartment and the furnishings. It had been a wedding present to Michelle and Donal. And it would prove a sound investment — apartments in this building and others were selling for fifty per cent more than they'd cost three years before.

Donal walked slowly around the room, taking swigs of water from the bottle in his hand. He touched the back of the cream sofa, lingering over the grain and extraordinary softness of the Italian leather. Rich luxurious fabric, in reds and golds, woven like tapestry, dressed the windows. Fine pieces of elegant furniture, sourced from all around the world, graced the apartment. And each surface displayed beautiful objects d'art, acquired by Michelle.

Michelle didn't shop like ordinary people. She 'found' things, as though they were lost orphans looking for a home. As though the very notion of money changing hands was distasteful. And yet she knew the price of everything.

There was no doubt about it, Michelle had an eye for style. And yet, Donal felt like a stranger in his own home. Everything was so carefully chosen and placed that he could never quite kick off his shoes and truly relax.

He had dearly wanted to be involved in planning and decorating this, their first home, but somehow he'd become sidelined. He'd once made the mistake of suggesting velvet curtains and Michelle had smiled at him indulgently.

'But, Donal, darling, velvet is so seventies. So naff!' And then she'd laughed.

So he pretended it was woman's work and that he was not interested. But he listened carefully to the discussions Michelle had with her mother and her friends about where they shopped and the names they mentioned. He was learning all the time. He now understood that it was all about subtlety — the watch you wore, the car you drove (not too ostentatious), who tailored your suits, whether your tie was handmade Italian silk. Not for the first time he wondered what in God's name Michelle had seen in him.

Their imminent house move might be a good thing. Maybe he'd be a bit more assertive this time and have some say in things. After all, he'd learnt a lot in the three years they'd been married and he'd developed quite a few expensive tastes of his own.

He would miss being in the city, at the hub of everything, so close to restaurants and cinemas, their private health club and all the places they went to with their fashionable friends. Well, Michelle's friends. Donal hadn't seen any of his friends since he'd married her. In fact he'd dropped them pretty quickly after meeting her — they weren't the sort of people she felt comfortable with and he could see why. They came from a background that was worlds removed from her privileged upbringing. And he hadn't wanted to jeopardise his chances. Though if he'd known how crazy she was about him, he wouldn't have worried. So now they had 'our friends', people Donal hardly knew yet pretended to have some connection with. Friends were people you grew up with, people who knew you better than you knew yourself. Donal was glad he didn't have any true friends, for they'd be able to see into his soul. And he knew it was ugly in there.

He could understand why Michelle wanted to move to Ballyfergus. She wanted to be near her parents. And who was he to say no? What did he understand of these things? What use would he be to her when the time came?

So he carried on as though he was just thrilled with the idea. But their lives were set to change in several ways and it unsettled him. For one thing, every time he thought of Ballyfergus all he could think about was Ann-Marie. Was she still living there? Had she changed? Had she married? Had kids? Was she happy?

He told himself to look on the bright side too. Living in Ballyfergus would throw him much more into the company of Noel McCormick and that could only be a good thing. Noel would get to know him better and realise that he could be an asset to the company. He'd languished long enough in the bank, doing his 'apprenticeship', as Noel had laughingly called it. It was time Noel offered him a senior position within McCormick Limited.

And there was Grainne, his beloved elder sister. She lived in Carrickfergus, not far from Ballyfergus, which meant he would be closer to her than they were currently. She was the only member of his family that he saw much of these days. He must go and see her soon and tell her all their news.

'Donal, darling,' said a voice from behind and Donal froze.

Something round his heart tightened a little.

'What are you doing up at this time?' continued Michelle and he heard the shush of her feet on the rug.

Two capable arms wrapped themselves around him and warm flesh nuzzled into the back of his neck like a puppy. Michelle was a big-framed woman, not fat exactly, but solid and strong.

'Couldn't sleep,' he said. 'I'm just looking at the view.'

'Come to bed, darling,' said Michelle sleepily, 'I miss you,' and she led him back into the bedroom.

* * *

Noel McCormick woke immediately the alarm went off at seven, stretched his arm out and silenced the clock. In the bed beside him his wife

11

Pauline turned over and sighed gently. Noel got out of bed, walked over to the curtains and peeked out. It was a fine Sunday morning in May, dry and still, perfect weather for golf.

'Excellent,' he said and padded into the bathroom.

In the shower he whistled cheerfully to himself. His world was a good place. At the age of sixty-seven, he had achieved more than most people could ever dream of. He was chairman and majority shareholder in the family company, McCormick Limited, one of the biggest and most successful companies in Ireland. He was fit and healthy, had a fine family and all the material things he'd ever wanted. He slapped the little paunch he now carried round his waistline and then held it in. If it wasn't for that, why, he could pass for forty-seven!

But there were two flies in the ointment: the fact that he had no son to inherit the business, and Michelle's choice of husband. Donal he would just have to learn to live with, but the solution to the other problem might just be around the corner . . .

By the time he returned to the bedroom, his silvered hair carefully combed into place, the unmade bed was empty. Pauline had disappeared into her bathroom, which connected directly to her dressing-room. He would not see her now until they met downstairs over breakfast. It was a farce really, sharing a room and a bed, for they led largely separate lives, except where the family was concerned. Still, appearances counted for everything. And people round here had loose tongues. If he and Pauline slept in separate beds, you could bet your bottom dollar half of Ballyfergus would know about it.

Noel walked over to the now opened curtains and gazed out of the tall picture window on the scene below. A vast stretch of lawn, the size of a rugby pitch, sloped gently away from the house. Framed on either side by tall poplars, it led onto a deep tract of woodland that Noel called his 'forest'. To the right of the lawn was a landscaped garden, centred round a large ornamental pond. To the left, the paddock was just visible through the trees. Yvonne, Noel's youngest daughter, now grown up, was probably out there already, tending her beloved horses. Less than a mile away, the town of Ballyfergus was a hazy sprawling mass. Beyond it, a ribbon of bright blue Irish Sea trimmed the land like a piece of braid on the hem of a skirt.

Noel surveyed all that he owned, inhaled the fresh spring air and, with it, a wave of emotion. As it coursed through him, he recognised it as pride and the exhilarating sensation of power. He felt as a feudal lord might have done overseeing his fiefdom — not that he owned Ballyfergus, of course, but he had more money than anyone else in the town. It had not always been so and that made it all the more poignant.

If the old man were alive today Noel wondered what he would make of it all. He'd be damned proud, that's for sure. His father had established McCormick and Sons builders' yard in 1932, two years after Noel was born. At first it was a struggle, but Malachy McCormick, his father, was a bloody hard worker, smart and shrewd. So, in spite of being a Catholic in staunchly Protestant Ballyfergus, he'd done well. But it was Noel who'd transformed the once small family business into a nationally recognised name, with house building, construction, and machinery-hire divisions. And there was nothing wrong in being proud of that.

Downstairs, Pauline was preparing breakfast, setting things out on the kitchen table — bowls, spoons, milk and a basket of croissants. She was elegantly dressed in a navy suit and honey-coloured silk shirt, the same colour as her hair. Slim, well-groomed and classy, Pauline was the perfect wife. A woman Noel was proud to be seen with.

'You're up early,' he observed good-naturedly.

Pauline looked up, flashed him an insincere smile and carried on being busy, the heels of her shoes clip-clipping on the slate floor. 'It's all right for some, swanning off to play golf. Somebody has to get the lunch ready. Or had you forgotten that the whole family's coming today?'

'Of course I hadn't forgotten. I'm looking forward to it,' he replied, sitting down and helping himself to muesli from a bowl on the table.

Sometimes Pauline did nag, but it didn't bother Noel too much. Mostly he just let it wash over him, a strategy he'd devised fairly early on in their marriage.

'Anyway,' he went on, as he poured milk on his muesli, 'I thought Esther was coming in today.'

'She is, but you know what she's like. She

14

doesn't know how to set a luncheon table properly or prepare vegetables with any finesse. I have to watch her like a hawk.' Sighing, she added, 'She's a good enough soul but she has her limitations. I just wish she had a bit more initiative. And I have to go to Mass. Aren't you coming?'

Noel ignored the last remark and said, not for the first time, 'Why don't you just get more help then, if you need it?'

'How often do I have to tell you? It wouldn't make any difference. I'd still have to be supervising all the time, making sure things were done properly. It's bad enough with Esther and the other help, never mind that lazy gardener. Do you know what I caught him doing the other day? Sitting with his feet up in the shed, smoking! On *our* time.' She shook her head and tutted. 'What you never seem to understand is that a house like this doesn't run itself. It takes planning, co-ordination, management.'

'God, Pauline, there you go again! Talking as if you were running an international corporation!' laughed Noel and he took another large spoonful of muesli.

Pauline raised her eyebrows and then continued evenly, 'The difference between you and me, Noel, is that you have people to delegate to. I don't. The buck stops with me. I'd like to see you run this place for a week.' With that she sat down, swept a napkin across her lap and began to eat muesli drenched in natural yoghurt.

Sensing that if he didn't retaliate the matter would be dropped, Noel concentrated on his

15

muesli and they made desultory conversation while they ate. Noel's main objective in his home life was to achieve peace and tranquillity and if that meant biting his tongue occasionally he was quite prepared to do it. Just as long as the boat wasn't rocked.

'So, what do you think of Jeanette's new beau?' he asked eventually.

'I haven't met him but, from what I can see of her, she's crazy about him,' replied Pauline.

'Which one of Joe's sons is he?'

'The youngest, Matt.'

'Hmm. I know it's early days and all — but wouldn't it be a great match? Joe Doherty's son and our Jeanette!'

'Yes, it would. And I don't think she'd be inviting him down here to meet all of us if they weren't serious.'

'I suppose not,' said Noel thoughtfully.

He'd have to see how this Matt Doherty measured up. He had the right pedigree: the son of one of Belfast's top lawyers, privately educated by Christian Brothers, now studying at the same university as Jeanette, where they'd met. Just the sort of material Noel had hoped for in a future son-in-law. In the absence of a son, he'd rather see a son-in-law like Matt Doherty at the helm of McCormick Limited, than sell it to complete strangers. It was time he started making plans for his retirement.

'It'd be a better match than Michelle made anyway,' said Pauline, interrupting his thoughts.

'That wouldn't be hard. I still don't understand what she saw — sees — in Donal

16

Mullan. The guy just grates on my nerves.'

'It's the little things that annoy me,' said Pauline. 'The way he stands with his legs apart and his hands in his pockets. Like a thug. And the way he eats. Have you noticed? It's as though he's never seen food before.'

'I know what you mean.'

'Excuse me,' said Pauline and she got up and carried their bowls to the sink where she stacked them for Esther to deal with later. She wiped her hands on a tea towel and picked up the steaming coffeepot.

'Will you ever forget their wedding day, Noel? I've never been so mortified in my life.'

'And after all the effort we put into keeping those damn Mullans under control. The father was the worst of the lot, getting so drunk.'

Pauline poured coffee into Noel's cup. 'We shouldn't have had a free bar. I did tell you.'

'Hindsight's a wonderful thing, Pauline. How was I to know he'd get plastered within two hours?'

'At least he just collapsed and had to be carried out. Those two sisters of Donal's were by far the worst. What were they called? I remember now — Dympna and Finola. They were fighting like two wildcats. I swear I've never seen women behave like that before or since.'

'I never did find out what that altercation was all about,' said Noel.

'Oh, apparently one of them called the other one fat.'

'And that's enough to start a fight?'

17

'Well, they were drunk. Anything could have set them off. It was disgusting.'

Noel had found the whole experience rather exhilarating, though of course he would never admit that to Pauline. The sight of two buxom women pulling the hair out of each other was rather titillating, in a base kind of way. He reached for a croissant, broke it in two and plastered the broken ends with marmalade.

'You have to laugh though, Pauline. It could have been worse.'

'I can't think how it could possibly have been worse,' said Pauline without a trace of irony.

'It could have happened in Ballyfergus, in front of a lot more people.'

'Mmm. At least we had the sense to keep the wedding small. I had a feeling you know, from the outset, that those Mullans would embarrass us.'

'Me too.'

'Thank goodness there was no evening reception. God knows what would have happened if we'd had one . . . ' said Pauline, her voice trailing off as she imagined all kind of horrors. 'I'm still embarrassed every time I have to go to the Culloden. The manager and staff all act like they don't remember but I'm quite sure they do.'

Noel shook his head, to demonstrate his outrage, and allowed a silence to fall between them, long enough to enable him to change the subject. 'Is Michelle coming today? I thought you said she'd been ill.'

'Oh, nothing serious, just a tummy bug. She

18

phoned last night to say she was feeling better and they'd both be down.'

★ ★ ★

As soon as he laid eyes on him, Donal decided he hated Matt Doherty. He was of average appearance — brown hair, blue eyes, clean-shaven — but turned out immaculately, dressed to impress. He was a student, for God's sake, yet he was wearing a suit that must've cost several hundred pounds. And the shoes looked like Church's. He was standing by the oversized marble fireplace in Noel and Pauline's drawing-room, his chin level with the edge of the mantelpiece.

No expense had been spared in the construc-tion of Glenburn House — ceilings were high, every room was graced with an ornate cornice, and the best oak trimmed every window and door. And, even though the house was only twenty-three years old, Pauline managed to make it feel like a stately home. Michelle had obviously inherited her mother's eye for style. Although their apartment was on a much smaller scale, Donal was always struck by the similarities in décor between it and Glenburn.

Michelle's two sisters were in the room with her parents, who were standing close to Matt, hanging on every word he said. Donal had rarely seen grins so broad on their faces. A little wave of panic temporarily wiped the smile from his face. For he recognised Matt Doherty for what he was: competition.

19

Although Noel McCormick loved his three daughters dearly, he made no secret of the fact that he was a chauvinist. Luckily for him, thought Donal, he had raised three fairly docile daughters who were content to fit into his world view. None of them had any notion of going into the business, and Noel wouldn't have wanted them to. He was extraordinarily old-fashioned that way. It surprised Donal that his daughters accepted it — none of them displayed the driving ambition that appeared to fuel their father. Only Jeanette, the quiet studious one, had gone to university and she was studying something airy-fairy like French (or was it German?) literature.

'Michelle!' shouted Yvonne, and she came lumbering across the room towards them, wearing tweed trousers and a riding jacket. She had no make-up on and looked like she'd just got off a horse, which she probably had. She gave her sister a swift hug, then turned to Donal. 'How's it going, old boy?' she asked and punched him playfully on the arm.

Donal summoned up a smile for her and asked about the horses, Yvonne's favourite subject.

'I've got a new mare. Two years old. Fine beast from Galway. I'm expecting great things from her. I'll take you down to the stables after lunch and let you have a look.'

Pointedly, Donal thought, Jeanette stayed where she was, by Matt's side, and greeted them with a weak smile.

'Don,' said Noel jovially, after he'd greeted

20

Michelle, 'great to see you. How's life in banking, these days? I hope you've not been losing any money recently.'

Michelle froze momentarily by his side and Donal looked at the toes of his shoes. Last year one of his main customers had gone into receivership and he had very nearly been sacked for it. On examination of the company's monthly management accounts, the bank's auditors declared that Donal had not acted soon enough to protect the bank's interests. How he managed to keep his job, God only knew. Not for the first time he wondered if Noel McCormick had had a hand in saving his skin. It had been a hard lesson learnt and not one that Donal appreciated being reminded of.

'Come and meet Jeanette's boyfriend,' continued Noel. 'Great lad. Joe Doherty's son,' he added meaningfully in a whisper and Donal glanced over at Matt, struggling to place him. Noel must mean Doherty of Quigley, Doherty and Reid, the lawyers.

'Oh, goody, we're just in time,' said Michelle, as Esther, her wide girth swathed in a crisp white apron, came into the room carrying a tray of chilled sherries. Though the children had known Esther all their lives, she betrayed no familiarity, just as Pauline expected.

The drinks were handed round and introductions made. Matt shook Donal's hand vigorously, full of confidence and charm.

'I believe you're in banking,' he said politely, and Donal started to tell him about his job in corporate finance. But no sooner had he started than Noel, who'd finished talking to Michelle, interrupted.

'So tell me, Matt, what are you studying at Queen's?'

Matt gave Noel his immediate attention, leaving Donal to trail off in mid-sentence. It was pretty obvious who he was trying to impress.

'Architecture,' he said.

'Jeanette,' cried Noel, barely disguising his glee, 'you're a dark horse! Imagine not telling me he's an architect!'

'Well, not yet,' said Matt hastily. 'I've another year to do. Same as Jeanette.'

Jeanette and Matt beamed at each other then, so obviously in love that it was painful for Donal to watch. He looked away.

'Well, Daddy,' said Yvonne, pausing to knock back her drink in one gulp, 'I'd snap him up if I was you. McCormick Limited could do with some fresh new talent.'

While everyone roared with laughter, Donal noticed that Matt did not take his eyes off Noel.

And, when he'd finished laughing, Noel said to Matt, 'My door's always open, Matt. Don't ever be afraid to knock.'

'Lunch is served,' said Esther and Donal could have sighed with relief. Any more of this and he'd be looking for a sick bowl.

He didn't think things could get any worse, but they did. Once in the dining-room, he realised that no one else had carried their drink through and there was nowhere to put it on the polished mahogany table.

'Just put it on the sideboard,' said Pauline, in the same tone she used to address Esther.

Sheepishly, Donal did as instructed and sat down, crimson with embarrassment. He'd never forged much of a relationship with his mother-in-law. He'd always found her cold and distant and yet, when she spoke to Matt Doherty, you'd think the sun shone out of his very arse.

As lunch progressed through four courses of asparagus soup, roast lamb, dessert and cheese, the conversation centred on mutual acquaintances. Matt's father Joseph and Noel knew each other well — both had yachts moored at Carrickfergus, both were members at Royal Portrush Golf Club. Matt's mother, Theresa, knew Pauline through the many charities in which they were both involved. Other names were mentioned that meant nothing to Donal and, despite attempts to stay in the conversation, he felt increasingly marginalised. Then the conversation moved on to sailing and tennis.

'Do you sail?' asked Matt.

Donal shook his head and said, 'I prefer golf.'

He had a natural aptitude for golf and had picked it up quickly to a level where he could play competently in any company. It was a useful skill in banking, for networking with customers. But sailing and tennis he couldn't master. They were things, he reckoned, that you had to be introduced to young, especially sailing. An accomplished sailor herself, Michelle had tried to teach him once on her father's boat, but he'd just felt clumsy and stupid and he couldn't

23

overcome his fear of water.

'Are you all right, Donal?' asked Michelle softly. 'You're awfully quiet.'

Donal looked at his wife and suddenly remembered a way to shut Matt up. A way to remind Noel who his family were and what he owed them.

'Michelle,' he whispered, 'I think we should tell them now.'

'It's too early,' she hissed. 'We should wait until I'm sixteen weeks.'

'No, it's not. You'll be fine,' he said, patting her on the knee.

She smiled then, took his hand and said, 'You're really excited, aren't you?'

But before he could answer, Jeanette interrupted. 'What are you two whispering about? Do let us in on the secret.'

'Hmm,' said Donal, clearing his throat, 'Michelle and I have some news for you.' Everyone hushed, Michelle squeezed his hand and he went on, 'We're going to have a baby.'

The women around the table, with the exception of Yvonne, gasped. A big smile spread across Noel McCormick's face.

'Oh, Michelle darling,' exclaimed Pauline, 'that's wonderful news!' and she clapped her hands together in a strangely childlike manner.

'Congratulations,' added Noel and he raised his glass in a toast. 'Here's to our first grandchild!'

Everyone started talking at once but Michelle interrupted them again. 'There's more,' she said, and glanced at Donal before going on. 'We're planning to move to Ballyfergus.'

Pauline smiled, obviously pleased. Noel looked into his glass, thinking, calculating.

'Why do you want to do that?' asked Jeanette.

'Now we're starting a family, I — I mean we, thought it would be nice to be near Mummy and Daddy.'

'But won't you miss Belfast and all your friends?' asked Yvonne.

'It's only half an hour in the car,' said Michelle. 'It's not like we're moving to Kerry. Anyway, they all work full-time. None of them have children so I'd be on my own most of the day.'

'You'll be giving up your job then?' asked Noel.

Michelle worked for Marston and Reid, Belfast's premier estate agency. From what she told Donal, all she did all day was drive about in her Audi convertible showing fancy houses to rich people.

'Yes, Daddy,' she replied, with a wry smile. 'I think they'll be able to manage without me.'

'But where will they live, Noel?' said Pauline anxiously, turning to look at her husband.

'We've been looking,' said Donal. 'Prices are much cheaper down here than in Belfast. I'm sure we'll be able to get something suitable.'

Noel was rubbing his chin, his slate-grey eyes narrowed in concentration. 'There's that bit of land down by Walter's place. We've had it for years. Nice views. We've already got planning permission for five executive houses, just never got round to developing it. It shouldn't be a

25

problem getting that altered . . . '

'Oh, Daddy, would you build us a house, *would* you?'

'Hold on a minute, pet, I'd have to look into it. We're coming up to our busiest time of year. And you'd be wanting to move in before the baby's born, wouldn't you?'

Michelle nodded, her face radiant with excitement and expectation.

'And you're going to want a decent-sized family home, not some poky little house.'

'I don't know if we could afford that — ' began Donal.

'Oh, stop worrying about details, Donal,' said Michelle. 'I'm sure we'll be able to work something out — won't we, Daddy?'

★   ★   ★

At last everyone was gone, Yvonne out to the stables to check on the horses, and the rest back to Belfast. Pauline and Noel went back into the drawing-room and sat down with the Sunday papers.

Esther came in with fresh coffee and set the cups down beside their respective armchairs.

'That's me finished in the kitchen, Mrs McCormick,' she said, wiping her hands down her still-clean white apron. 'I'll take Wednesday off, if that's OK.'

'That's fine,' replied Pauline, 'and thanks for coming in on a Sunday, Esther. I really do appreciate it.'

'It's no bother. Sometimes I'd rather have a

day off mid-week, anyway. It means I can go shopping and I like going to the Wednesday market.'

'Is there still a weekly market in Ballyfergus?' asked Pauline, surprised. 'I thought they were dying out.'

'Not this one. It's still going just as strong as when I was a little girl. In fact one or two of the traders are the same ones I remember from way back then. You're from Ballyfergus, Mr McCormick. Don't you remember it?'

'Oh, yes, my mother used to drag us round it every week,' recalled Noel. 'We spent the whole time trying not to step in the dung from the animal market the day before!'

'That's still held too, every Tuesday, though now they make a better job of washing the yard out,' laughed Esther.

'Interesting,' said Pauline, thinking that she never even went to a supermarket these days. She simply wrote lists and got everything delivered or Esther shopped for her. She didn't have time, with all the committees and charities she was involved in, never mind organising dinner parties and entertaining the great and the good. And once Michelle's baby came she wanted to spend as much time with her as she could.

Soon Esther's little Ford Escort was chugging down the drive.

'Well, that was an eventful afternoon,' said Pauline to Noel.

'Sure was,' he agreed, folding up the paper

and setting it on his lap.

'Are you serious about building them a house?'

'Why not? They'll only end up paying over the odds for some bit of rubbish. And I've no plans to do anything with that land. It's too small for the type of projects McCormick does these days.'

'Will it be possible to get it done on time though?'

'It'll get done on time. I'll get the boys on to it first thing Monday morning. And we can pull workmen off other jobs if we have to.'

'It's very generous of you,' said Pauline, thinking that for all his faults Noel was a wonderful father.

'Well, I have my reasons. For one thing, I don't want the child seeing too much of Donal's family. Where is it they live again?'

'Some awful housing estate in West Belfast.'

Noel's puckered his mouth in an expression of distaste. 'Exactly. Also, I don't want my first grandchild to be a stranger to us. And he would be, living twenty-five miles away.'

'Wait a minute, did you say 'he'?' she said incredulously.

'Slip of the tongue,' he replied but Pauline knew it was no such thing.

'What if it's a girl?' she persisted.

'Then I'll love her just the way I love my three daughters.'

It was a point well made, for Noel's affection for his daughters was beyond dispute. They lapsed into silence then and Pauline tried to imagine holding her first grandchild in her arms.

How she hoped it would be a girl, for she'd never get a look in with Noel around if it was a boy. He'd be trying to teach him things and show him things and do all the things he'd never got to do with a son of his own. A little girl he'd just indulge. And then she censored herself for having such selfish thoughts. All that mattered, she reminded herself, was that the baby was fit and healthy, regardless of its sex.

How she yearned for that baby now that it had life! A life born of her flesh, blood of her blood. A child that would carry her genes on to the next generation and the one after that, into infinity. Having her children was the best thing she'd ever done. And yet she was unfulfilled. Always had been, even in the early days of her marriage. Something was lacking in her life, but she didn't know what. She'd once looked to the Church for help to fill the gap, believing her problem to be a spiritual weakness on her part, but she'd found no answers there.

Now that the children were grown and all but Yvonne fled the nest, the emptiness in Pauline's life opened before her like a yawning black hole. To avoid falling into it, she elevated 'busyness' to an art form. She immersed herself in numerous charitable causes of which she was patron, chaired various committees, and attended every first night and every exhibition to which she was invited. She rediscovered a real love of the arts, first instilled in her by her father, and she ran the house with military precision.

Noel had no cause to complain and he didn't. She believed he encouraged her in her various pursuits because it kept her busy and out of his way. And it also helped to keep McCormick Limited in the public eye or, more accurately, in the eye of those who mattered. Noel was such a political animal. Everything he did was calculated and shrewd.

'Matt seems like a sound lad,' said Noel, interrupting her thoughts. 'I just hope that daughter of ours has the sense to hold onto him.'

'Oh, I think she does. Didn't you see the way they were mooning over each other?'

'I suppose we'll have to wait and see. I just hope she doesn't let him slip through her fingers.'

'Why are you so concerned? There's plenty more fish in the sea, Noel.'

'Not like him, there aren't,' he replied impatiently. 'I need to start thinking about retirement planning and, at the moment, there's no one to hand the business on to. Matt Doherty could fit the bill nicely, though he'll need a few years' experience.'

Of course she should have known. Noel had an ulterior motive for everything. He didn't just see a prospective son-in-law in Matt Doherty, he saw an heir to the McCormick empire. Still, to be fair, she shouldn't complain. It was his business acumen and focus that kept them in the grand lifestyle they enjoyed. And if she sometimes had doubts about Noel's business ethics, they were reservations she kept to herself. Her life now was so much grander than anything she'd even imagined growing up in Limavady.

Her father had been a consultant at the

Altnagelvin hospital in Derry and they lived a very comfortable, middle-class life. But Noel's wealth had catapulted Pauline into an even loftier sphere. She made the transition with grace and ease for she had been raised to think of herself as a lady. In fact, she considered herself to be superior to her husband. She came from a long line of educated, cultured professionals — Noel's father left school at fourteen and ran a builder's yard. And in spite of her efforts to erase them, there were still a few working-class edges on Noel.

'You're going to have to do something about Yvonne,' said Noel abruptly.

'Whatever do you mean?' she asked.

'Well, her appearance for one thing. She looks terrible. She's so . . . so unwomanly. Compared to her sisters, she looks like a down-and-out.'

Yvonne could not have looked more different from Michelle and Jeanette. While they used every available means, both natural and chemical, to enhance their appearance, Yvonne rarely looked in a mirror. She even came to the dinner table with dirt under her nails!

'I have tried speaking with her, Noel, but it's like talking to a brick wall. She just doesn't care about these things.'

'No man's going to look at her in her present state.'

'I don't think she cares. She's so wrapped up in her horses and her horsey friends, she wouldn't notice a man if he fell down at her feet.'

'Chance would be a fine thing.'

'I do agree with you, Noel. I too wish she

would take a bit more pride in her appearance. But there are more important things in life than what we look like.'

'Not where a woman's concerned.'

Pauline looked at Noel's furrowed brow, bit her lip and paused before she spoke. 'Maybe she doesn't want a man,' she said carefully, airing a thought that had been taking form, but had not yet crystallised, in her mind.

'Every woman wants a man. Don't be ridiculous,' he replied, closing the subject.

'It's getting dark,' said Pauline.

She got up then and circled the perimeter of the room, unhooking six pairs of tiebacks. Then she found the remote control and pressed buttons on it, switching on lights and closing the curtains.

Noel looked at his watch and said, 'I think I'll pop out to the office for a little while and catch up on some paperwork. I'm all over the place next week.'

'Can't you work from home?' she asked, testing. Noel had a fully fitted office upstairs.

'Afraid not,' he said, standing up and jangling the keys that had already found their way into his pocket. 'I need some papers at the office.'

When she looked closely at Noel, Pauline observed that he'd changed his shirt and his grey hair was neatly parted and combed to one side. If she stood close enough she knew she would smell fresh aftershave. He shifted his weight from one foot to the other, and looked at the clock.

'I'll see you later then,' she said, grudgingly giving him her permission to leave. The muscles on either side of her neck tensed involuntarily.

He needed no further encouragement and practically ran out of the room. She listened to the spring in his step as he crossed the gravel drive towards his Bentley, heard the car door open and the deep clunk as it shut. He drove off at a stately pace, only picking up speed when he was on the drive and well clear of the house.

Not for the first time Pauline tried to understand her emotions. When Noel went to his mistress, she felt a tiny flicker of anger. Or was it sorrow? Sometimes they felt the same. Yet, she told herself, she had no reason to feel either emotion. She and Noel had come to an understanding a long time ago — she should be well used to it by now.

She was a young wife and mother of three, just turned twenty-seven, when she discovered that she was married to an adulterer. How innocent and trusting and unworldly she'd been then, she thought wryly. So ill-equipped by her strict Catholic upbringing for the realities of the world inhabited by Noel McCormick.

She'd found out one Monday morning in June. She'd been doing the laundry, in the days before she had someone to do it for her, and found a small sealed foil packet in the pocket of one of Noel's shirts. She set it aside on the windowsill, humming to herself as she loaded the washing machine and thought about what she would make Noel for dinner that night.

But the strange object bothered her and she returned to the little silver package glinting in the sunlight that streamed through the window.

She turned it over and squeezed it between her fingers. She knew it wasn't a sweet as she'd first thought. Looking closely, she noticed that it bore a code number in black ink and what looked like a sell- or use-by date. Curious now, she carefully ripped open one end of the package. She pulled out a skin-coloured rubbery thing, greasy to the touch. For a few brief moments she thought it was a balloon and then she unrolled it and realised, in spite of her lack of first-hand experience, that it was a condom.

Of course, being good Catholics, she and Noel had never used any form of contraception in the six years they'd been married. There was only one reason Noel would be carrying this around in his pocket and it had nothing to do with her. She dropped it hastily in the bin and scrubbed her hands with soap under the hot tap until they burned pink, her own tears mingling with the steaming water. Everything inside her was spiralling down. It felt like her insides were falling out. Like the bottom was falling out of her world.

'I love you,' Noel said that night when she confronted him. 'You are my wife and you will always come first. This doesn't mean anything.'

'It does to me,' she said, holding onto the back of a kitchen chair because she feared that her shaking legs would not support her.

'Well, it shouldn't. Lots of men . . . well, you know.'

'Have bits on the side?'

'If you want to put it that way.'

'But why, Noel? Is it because I haven't wanted

to?' she said, fighting to hold back tears and retain some shred of dignity.

'It's quite normal. You've only just had a baby and you've the two girls to look after as well,' he said, his voice laden with empathy. 'It must be exhausting.'

'You make it sound as though this is my fault.'

'It's not anyone's fault,' he said smoothly. 'It happens in a lot of marriages.'

'And that makes it all right?' she asked but Noel only raised his right shoulder in the merest hint of a shrug.

'Who is she?' she demanded.

'It doesn't matter. She could be anybody. Nobody.'

'I want you to stop seeing her.'

'I can't do that, Pauline.'

Pauline stared at him for a long time and he held her gaze, bold and unrepentant. And his clear pale grey eyes asked the question: what are you going to do about it?

And then the extent of her vulnerability hit her like a labour pain, leaving her winded and slightly bewildered. She had no career, no income, and no money of her own. As a Catholic, she could not get a divorce. If she walked out, where would she go? How would she survive? How could she bear the shame she would bring on her family and herself? Her daughters would be shunned and reviled by respectable people.

As though he could read her thoughts, Noel said, 'I'll always look after you and the girls, Pauline. I'll see you never want for anything.' He

35

paused then and added, 'If you stay.'

That was the choice she was offered and, right or wrong, that was the one she made.

'I'll need to think about it,' she said meekly, and quietly left the room.

That night in bed Pauline closed up the part of her heart that had loved Noel, put dustsheets over it and locked it away. And she never discussed the matter with him again.

Tears came to her eyes at the memory of that pain, so intense and searing it could never be fully eradicated, but lived, even now, in her breast as a deep enduring ache. But that was all in the past, she told herself crossly, wiping her eyes. Why did it still bother her so, after all this time? Pauline couldn't be sure how long Noel had been with this particular mistress, but instinct told her it had been a while. Did she feel threatened by her?

She told herself to stop it. They'd made their unspoken pact years ago, which worked, in Pauline's mind, along the following lines: she kept house, kept up appearances, and enjoyed a luxurious and privileged lifestyle. She didn't have to have sex with Noel and she pretended that she didn't know about his mistresses. He, in return, ensured that Pauline and his daughters wanted for nothing and carried out his nocturnal activities with the utmost discretion, so ensuring that he caused no scandal.

Did she have the raw end of the deal? No, she told herself firmly, the arrangement suited him and, more importantly, it suited her. There was no need to challenge the status quo.

She put down the newspaper, got up and went upstairs to her study where she worked like mad until she was utterly exhausted and then went to bed. As Pauline closed her eyes she glanced at the clock. It said 12.40 p.m. The place in the bed beside her remained empty.

★   ★   ★

On the way home in the car Michelle could tell that Donal was fuming. He was driving her car too fast, revving the engine like it was a rally car, and it was making her feel sick. She put her hand over her stomach and grimaced. He accelerated all of a sudden and overtook a lorry that was chugging slowly uphill on the shallow incline out of Ballyfergus. On either side of the road, the landscape sped past — undulating fields of vivid green, separated by dark green hedgerows, spread out like a giant patchwork quilt. The landscape Michelle had grown up with and loved.

'Don, will you slow down, please?' she asked.

'What?' he said, distracted.

'Slow down. You're making me feel sick.'

'Sorry,' he said, applied the brake and slowed the car to a more comfortable speed.

If she could read him like she thought she could, then she knew what was bothering him. From the minute the two men had met, she'd sensed that Donal didn't like Jeanette's boyfriend. That was putting it mildly. She'd caught him staring at Matt over the lunch table with a look on his face that suggested he could easily

37

murder him. Why he didn't like Matt was beyond Michelle. She thought he was charming and he hadn't said anything to offend Donal. In fact he'd made several attempts to include him in the conversation. If anybody had been rude it was Donal — he'd hardly said a word all through lunch.

But her husband was a complex character and it wasn't always easy to understand him. He was overly sensitive about his background for one thing and took offence easily, even where none was intended.

'So,' she said, 'what did you think of Matt?'

'Hmm,' he grunted.

'I thought he was lovely. He's funny and sweet and Jeanette's head over heels in love with him. Isn't it lovely to see her happy?'

'Well, I just hope he's not using her.'

'Whatever do you mean?' she said, surprised. Sometimes Donal had a funny way of seeing the world.

'Did you see the way he was wheedling his way into the family, acting all smarmy with your mother and father?'

'Don! I can't believe you said that. He was only being polite. I suppose he was trying to make a good impression as well. But there's nothing wrong with that. If my memory serves me well, I remember you doing exactly the same thing.'

'Your parents didn't fawn over me like they did over Matt Doherty.'

This temporarily silenced Michelle for it was true. Her parents did not approve of Donal and were horrified when she wanted to marry him. She'd thought that over time they'd learn to love him, like she did, but they'd never warmed to him completely. Not the way they'd already done with Matt Doherty. Michelle looked at Donal and bit her lip. It hurt her when he was hurt.

'Didn't you hear your dad practically offer him a job?' said Donal.

'He was only joking. Anyway, I don't think Matt's after anything, Don. His father's Joe Doherty, for heaven's sake!'

'Exactly,' he said sarcastically. 'Do you remember when your dad suggested I take a job with his bankers?'

'Yes. That was good of him to use his influence, wasn't it?'

'He said, joking like, that it was 'an apprenticeship'. What do you think he meant by that?'

'I don't know.'

'I thought he meant that he wanted me to get a good grounding in finance before joining McCormick Limited.'

'He never said anything about giving you a job,' said Michelle quietly. 'Anyway, we have everything we want. You have a great job with the bank. And you have me. Why isn't that enough?'

'Oh, darling, you know I love you,' he said reassuringly, patting her on the forearm, 'but after that receivership last year, my prospects of promotion are slim. And we can't even afford the home we want. Your father's going to bail us out by part-financing a new house. I want to be a legitimate part of the family, earning my keep, not on the outside taking scraps off the table.'

'We're not taking scraps off the table! Daddy wants to build us a house and it's his money. He can do what he likes with it. He wants to do it because he loves me.' She paused and then added, too late she realised, 'Us.'

'Yes, and I appreciate his generosity, Michelle. But can't you see what I mean? It's demeaning for a man to have to look to his father-in-law for financial support. Now if I was a director — '

'A director!' interrupted Michelle. She didn't understand much about limited companies and how they worked, but what made Donal think he had the right to demand a share of the family's fortunes? 'You can't expect Daddy — '

'I'm not saying I'd expect that to start with, but I could work my way up. I'm not expecting something for nothing. I'd prove myself. Show your dad I was worthy.'

Michelle fell silent then and watched the countryside fly by the car window. Happiness, it seemed to her, was always just out of Donal's reach. Why wasn't she, and the baby growing inside her, enough for him? They lived very comfortably, albeit supplemented by the generous allowance Daddy still gave her for personal expenditure. How else could she afford her weekly beauty treatments and shopping trips to London and Paris with her friends? They wanted for nothing. But whatever they had, it was never enough for Donal.

She could see how much this meant to him. She'd never seen him so intense about anything. Perhaps this was the one thing that *would* make him happy. If she could persuade Daddy to give him the chance he so desperately wanted, then maybe he would be satisfied, at last. Maybe then he would love her as much as she loved him. And when the baby came, everything would be perfect.

2

Happy memories engulfed Roisin as soon as she stepped into Sadie Hopkins' hair salon. As a teenager she'd worked here every weekend, washing hair, sweeping up after the stylists and making cups of tea for the customers. The place still smelt of Elnett hairspray and cigarettes, just like she remembered it. It was here, in these humble surroundings, that she'd discovered her vocation in life. Now she too worked in the beauty industry.

A bell tinkled above the door as it closed behind Roisin and Sadie looked up from blow-drying a head of grey-blonde hair. Her face broke into a warm smile that lifted Roisin's spirits. She'd not had much sleep these last few days since Ann-Marie ended up in hospital and everything was beginning to overwhelm her.

'Nearly done, Roisin, love,' shouted Sadie over the noise of the dryer. 'I'll be with you in a minute.'

Roisin sat down on one of the cracked faux-leather seats and flicked through dog-eared copies of *Woman's Realm* and *Woman's Own*. Then she watched Sadie at work, her sinewy arms moving quickly and expertly as she teased and pulled, holding the dryer far too close to the hair. She stood only five foot four inches tall and her short hair was bleached a blonde colour she mixed herself and called, 'Marilyn Monroe'. In her checked overall and flat shoes, she looked more like a cleaning lady than a hair stylist, but her customers loved her. Not for her hairdressing expertise — which was only adequate — but for her basic goodness. Whenever someone was ill or in trouble she was always the first one on the spot with practical help and common-sense advice. Roisin returned to the magazines, found she couldn't concentrate on the words, so looked at pictures of celebrities instead.

But it wasn't long before the whirr of the hairdryer stopped. She glanced up and smiled briefly at the reflection of the woman in the seat. It was Mrs Alexander, the Bank Manager's wife — she nodded back politely at Roisin.

When Mrs Alexander had paid and left the shop, Sadie peeped out through the candy-coloured Venetians, turned the sign on the door to 'Closed', then shut the blinds.

'Listen, Sadie, I'm not keeping you back, am I?'

'Lord, no. The place is dead on a Thursday. Half-day closing, don't you remember — that's why I'm on my own. Maureen's got the day off. Anyway I haven't seen you in a while. Have you come in for a haircut?' She eyed Roisin's head, a pair of sharp scissors ready in her hand.

'No, no,' said Roisin hastily, 'I only came in for a chat.'

'Don't wet yourself. I'm only teasing you,' said Sadie, her little green eyes full of mischief, and she roared with laughter. She threw the scissors down and gave Roisin a big hug. 'Sure I couldn't do hair like that. Far too trendy for me. I don't keep up with the times, don't need to. All my ladies are wearing their hair the same as they did twenty years ago.'

'It's good business though. Giving people what they want.'

'Oh, aye, I do all right. Come on through. You've time for a cup of tea,' she stated rather than asked.

'I'll just make it a quick one, Sadie. I'm on my way to see Ann-Marie.'

'How is she these days?'

'You haven't heard then?'

'Heard what?'

'She's in the hospital. Tried to commit suicide again. But it was a pretty feeble attempt. I don't think she really meant it.'

'Oh, love, I'm sorry,' said Sadie and she hugged Roisin again. 'You do need a cup of tea — you're as white as a ghost. Now, tell me, when did this happen?'

Roisin followed her into the untidy little staffroom behind the shop and talked while Sadie listened. When she'd finished, Sadie gave her a hanky to wipe her eyes and a dose of her homespun wisdom, which was why Roisin had come here in the first place. Sadie was the most down-to-earth, sensible woman that Roisin knew.

'Now, I know you love your sister but you're not her keeper. She's a grown woman and you have to let her live her life.'

'But she needs help. There must be something I can do.'

'Maybe not. Maybe this is something she has

44

to work out on her own. All I'm saying is that you can't let her ruin your life.'

There was a pause during which Sadie extracted a cigarette from the crushed pack of Marlboro Lights lying on the table. She took a slim stainless-steel lighter from her apron pocket, lit the tip of the cigarette and inhaled.

'I was thinking of trying to get a few weeks off work,' said Roisin.

'Whatever for?' said Sadie, pausing to examine Roisin critically, before sliding the lighter back into her pocket.

Roisin shrugged. 'I don't know exactly. Just to be there for her.'

'Get a grip, love. You'll lose your job carrying on like that.'

That possibility hadn't occurred to Roisin and she looked down at her hands folded in her lap and considered it now. She'd have to ask her boss for time off. If she had to, she could always take unpaid leave. If he'd let her.

'I don't understand,' said Sadie softly, interrupting Roisin's thoughts, 'why you feel so responsible for Ann-Marie. It's as though you believe it's your job to make her happy.'

'It was always like that, from when we were children.'

'Like what?'

'Ann-Marie was always the sensitive, delicate one. Mum used to say that she needed protecting from the world in a way that I didn't. You see, I'm stronger than my sister.'

'And what makes you think that it's your job to do this protecting?'

45

Roisin thought hard but could not find an answer to Sadie's question. 'That's just the way it's always been. All I know is that Ann-Marie was with Dad when he died and Mum thinks she's never really got over it. So she has to be treated, well, carefully.'

'It was terrible, love. I remember it well.'

'You see, if I don't look out for her, who's going to do it? She hasn't got anyone else. Just me and Mum.'

'Sometimes we have to learn to look out for ourselves, Roisin. If there's a crutch available, people will lean on it. You might be doing your sister more harm than good.'

'What do you mean?'

'Well, mollycoddling Ann-Marie all the time might not be in her best interests.'

'I don't understand.'

'You're not helping her to be independent. You're teaching her to be dependent.'

'Oh!' said Roisin, shocked. 'I'd never thought of it like that before. But look what's just happened. She obviously can't cope on her own.'

'She might surprise you. Just promise me that you won't take any time off work.'

'OK,' said Roisin reluctantly. 'My boss probably wouldn't let me anyway.'

'Well,' said Sadie, brightening to indicate a change of subject, 'what you need from the look of you is a good night's sleep, love. Are they working you too hard in that salon?'

Roisin worked in one of Belfast's top beauty salons, commuting every day on the train. Her days were long and the work demanding.

'The last few days have been awful, obviously, because of Ann-Marie, but I was pretty whacked before that. It's the travelling that takes it out of you really, getting up so early and getting home late. But I love it. Everything they do is quality. Classy. I'm learning so much.'

'And are you still doing those evening classes at the Tech?'

'Yeah.'

'What're they in again?' asked Sadie, lighting up another cigarette.

Roisin shook her head, suppressed a cough brought on by the smell of the cigarettes, and answered, 'Book keeping and Marketing for Small Businesses.'

'Well,' said Sadie, pausing to exhale a trail of grey smoke, 'I never bothered with any of that stuff and I managed just fine.'

'I know, but things are different now. If I want to have my own salon I need to know about these things.'

'And is that what you want?'

'Oh, yes, one day,' said Roisin, feeling the heat of embarrassment rise in her cheeks. 'I know I'm only twenty-six but you have to have a dream, don't you?'

'You do, love, you do,' said Sadie nodding. 'This was my dream once,' she went on, smiling. 'It's just so long ago I'd forgotten. But I can still recall how I felt the day I got the keys to this place. I felt like the queen bee. I can tell you!'

Roisin looked round the salon and imagined what she would do to it if it were hers. It was in a great location right in the centre of town, up relatively quiet Dunluce Street. You didn't want clients bumping into every Tom, Dick and Harry after eyebrow-shaping, or upper-lip waxing both of which left the skin red and inflamed. There were some things people liked to keep to themselves, especially women like those Roisin had in mind as her future clientele. There was good, free parking close by and the premises themselves had plenty of potential. She'd throw out everything for a start and paint it all white.

'You should have seen how proud Derek was of me. There weren't many women in those days running their own business. Mind you, it was his redundancy money that set me up — but he had faith in me and there's many a husband wouldn't have done what he did.'

Those plastic Venetian blinds would have to go. Pale wood ones would be fine though, and then maybe some wood flooring and big, green plants in white china pots . . .

'He looked after the children as well so I could work. Don't tell me about 'New Men'. My Derek's the original.'

And she would definitely have a no-smoking policy, thought Roisin, staring at the finger of white ash on the end of Sadie's cigarette, about to drop on her lap. Smoking was so eighties.

'Are you listening, Roisin?' said Sadie.

'I'm sorry. I guess I'm just tired. I'd better be going now.'

'Me, too. Derek'll be along in a few minutes.' The cigarette ash landed on Sadie's skirt. She flicked it onto the floor with a quick movement of her wrist, an unconscious reflex action.

48

Roisin stood up and put on her coat.

'Another thing, before you go, Roisin,' said her friend, looking up at her, 'and I'm only saying this because I care about you. I understand what it's like to have ambition. I know it's hard to believe but I felt like you once. But don't let it take over your life. You're only young once. Enjoy it. You don't want to end up an old maid like my sister Mary. Get out there and have a bit of fun too.'

'But I'm happy doing what I'm doing, Sadie.'

'Just don't leave it too late, that's all I'm saying. Don't forget, all the good ones go first.'

* * *

As he drove out of Belfast, Donal decided that he was about to embark on his least favourite customer visit. Patterson Chickens Limited was one of Northern Ireland's most successful indigenous businesses, and one of the bank's most profitable customers. So it was essential that Donal maintained a close, hands-on relationship with them. This required him to feign an enthusiastic interest in all aspects of poultry processing. Patterson Chickens had an enormous processing plant on the outskirts of Coleraine and that is where Donal was destined today.

Tom Patterson met him personally at the factory reception, already attired in blue over-boots, a white coat over his suit and a green hairnet on his head.

Once Donal was similarly dressed, they

commenced a tour of the factory.

'You'll not have seen our new production line working yet,' said Tom, eagerly. 'It's allowed us to increase our production at this site by thirty per cent without increasing staff numbers.'

The bank had recently loaned Patterson two and a half million pounds to finance production upgrades at its various sites across the province. It was Donal's job to ensure that the money, with handsome interest, was recouped as planned.

'The projections show that the capital investment will be paid off over nine years,' he said. 'Now that the line's been running for a few weeks, do you think those forecasts will hold good?'

'If anything we'll exceed them. So long as prices remain stable. We're getting the big volumes from the UK supermarkets but they negotiate a hard deal.'

They had left the warmth and comfort of the office suite for the cold reality of the factory floor.

'This is where it starts,' said Tom, shouting over the sounds of the factory.

As they watched, a lorry loaded with crates of live chickens backed up into the building. Four begloved men stood waiting and, as soon as the lorry had stopped, they each stepped forward and extracted a chicken quickly and expertly. Within seconds the fowls were hanging upside down by their feet on a conveyor system. As it shunted along the first thing they encountered was a stungun, which knocked them out

— within seconds their throats were cut and the life drained out of them. Donal looked away.

He breathed a sigh of relief when it was all over and he was back in his company car, a Rover 620. He couldn't stand the smell of the factory — the noxious odour of warm blood and poultry innards. He opened all the car windows as he drove off, allowing the cool fresh air to cleanse him. The faces of the people who worked there haunted him. They were completely devoid of emotion as they carried out the repetitive, mind-numbing tasks involved in the gutting, cleansing and packaging of poultry.

Soon Donal was on the main road out of Coleraine, tailing a line of slow-moving traffic stuck behind a lorry. There was nothing for it but to sit back and wait. There were few opportunities for overtaking on this stretch of the road and traffic was heavy, probably because it was a Friday afternoon. Students from Coleraine were heading home for the weekend and townies headed in the opposite direction, towards Portrush and Portstewart. He put the car into fourth gear, closed the windows and switched on the radio. The sound of Whitney Houston singing 'I Will Always Love You' filled the car. The music made him remember what true love felt like and sadness enveloped him like fog.

The song was the theme tune from the movie *Bodyguard* starring Whitney and Kevin Costner. He'd gone to see it at the cinema with Michelle just before they got married. A story of doomed love, it made him think then, as it did now, of

51

Ann-Marie. Of course there was no parallel between their stories. Circumstances hadn't forced them apart — he'd chosen to dump Ann-Marie. But if he hadn't, they would probably have been married by now. Instead of Michelle carrying his baby, it would have been Ann-Marie . . .

He told himself to snap out of it. Ann-Marie was history. That was then and this was now. He pressed a button on the dashboard and the music on the radio changed to classical. He forced himself to think of something else.

Like how he wouldn't have to do crappy customer visits like the one he'd just done, once he was working for McCormick Limited. He wished Noel would hurry up and offer him a job. Now the decision to move to Ballyfergus was made, it couldn't come fast enough. The sooner they moved near Noel the better.

At last he reached the M2 and, picking up speed, he glanced at the latest set of Patterson management accounts lying on the passenger seat. He really ought to get back to the office, analyse them, and write up his report of the visit. But after today's gruelling experience he'd no intention of doing so.

He passed a sign for Carrickfergus and decided that it was the perfect opportunity to go and see Grainne. It was only a short detour and he'd been meaning to call and see her for over a week now. Michelle was going out with her girlfriends for a drink after work. He wouldn't be missed.

By the time he pulled up outside his sister's

modern, detached, three-bedroom house, it was nearly six o'clock. At first he thought she wasn't at home, for the car in the driveway — a brand-new silver Mazda MX5 — wasn't one he recognised. Last time he'd seen her, she was driving a beaten-up old Renault.

He gave the car a brief inspection, a little stab of envy, like indigestion, nibbling away at his insides. It had leather seats, alloy wheels and a private registration incorporating her initials — the whole package must've cost her going on fifteen thousand. It was something for a single woman to be able to go out and buy herself a brand-new car just like that.

It wasn't that he begrudged his sister her success — it just reminded him how little he had achieved independently. His father-in-law had given them their home. He had a middle-ranking job with the bank and little prospect of promotion. He was convinced that he'd only kept his job, after that fiasco last year, because of Noel's intervention — Noel was on personal terms with the Chairman and Chief Executive. On his modest salary he couldn't even keep his wife in the lifestyle that she expected.

Approaching Grainne's door, he whistled quietly through his teeth, then rang the bell.

'You've got a new car,' he said, as soon as Grainne opened the door to him, her rich reddish-brown hair in rollers.

'Oh, Donal!' she exclaimed. 'What are you doing here?'

'Nice to see you too,' he replied, pecking her warm cheek and going into the house.

She followed him into the kitchen where she hovered in the doorway. Though she was barefoot and wearing a dressing-gown, her face was heavily made up.

'Look, tell me if this is a bad time? Are you getting ready to go out?' he asked.

'Not till later,' she replied, glancing nervously at the smart chrome clock on the kitchen wall. 'Look, do you mind if I make a quick phone call? Stick the kettle on and I'll be back in a minute.'

He filled the kettle and wondered at his sister's strange behaviour. She must have a boyfriend, he decided. And, at forty-one years old and seven years his senior, it was about time. Grainne had been on her own for too long. Following a short-lived, disastrous marriage in her early twenties to her childhood sweetheart, Kevin Park, she'd never so much as looked at a man. Not as far as Donal knew anyway. But perhaps he didn't know his sister as well as he thought he did . . .

'So who is he?' he said, when she came back into the room looking more relaxed.

'Who?' she said and blushed.

'Never mind. It's none of my business, I suppose,' he said, feigning disinterest, 'but it's good to see you happy, Grainne. After all that's happened . . . well, you deserve it.'

'You mean Kevin?'

'Yes. I thought he'd maybe put you off men for good.'

'Not put me off them, exactly. Just knocked off the rose-tinted glasses. Is that tea ready yet?'

'You mean you don't believe in romance?'

'No, I do,' she said slowly, as though taking time to select her words with care, 'but I'm also a realist. I'm careful to protect my interests. I'm only putting myself first which is what most men do naturally.'

'God help the man who gets you, Grainne! You sound like Germaine Greer.'

'Let's just say that the man in question knows exactly what the score is,' she said finally and crossed her arms over her full chest, her tone of voice indicating that the subject was closed.

Donal found two mugs and poured out the tea, added milk and handed one to his sister. 'So, did you get another promotion?' he asked.

'A promotion? What're you talking about?'

'With the civil service. Cars like that one outside don't grow on trees.'

'Oh, the car,' she said as though it was nothing. 'I decided to treat myself, that's all. I'd been having bother with that old banger.'

'You never said you were thinking of buying a new car,' said Donal. 'I could've fixed you up with a cheap loan through the bank.'

'I didn't need a loan,' she said quickly. 'I mean, I've been saving up. And I saw the car and I just thought — what the hell. It all happened very quickly.'

'I'm telling you, Grainne, it's a wonder you haven't been snapped up. A good-looking woman like you, with your own house, fancy car and a well-paid government job at Belfast City Hall. You're some catch.'

'I'm not a fish,' she said dryly, but not without humour, her green eyes twinkling, 'and I like things the way they are. As far as money goes, I'm just careful.'

Donal raised his eyebrows at this, but she went on, ignoring him.

'I don't go out almost every night on the town like you do,' she said defensively and then, suddenly changing tack, she added, 'Anyway, enough about me. To what do I owe this surprise visit?'

'I was on my way back from Coleraine and thought I'd call in.'

'Carrickfergus isn't on the way back from Coleraine.'

'Do I need an excuse to see my big sis?'

'No, of course you don't,' said Grainne. 'But, seriously, why did you come here?'

He'd come all this way to tell Grainne his news and now he was reluctant to do so. She knew him better than anyone else, even his own mother, for she'd practically reared him as a child. He feared that she could see right through his skin, into the hollow place inside him where his love for Michelle should have been.

He paused, procrastinating, then said, 'Let's go into the lounge, shall we?'

'It's cold tonight even though it is May,' observed Grainne as they entered the room, and she bent over and pressed a switch by the fireplace. Blue and yellow flames leapt immediately into life, lapping round everlasting black coals. They placed their mugs on the coffee-table, then Donal took a seat on the sofa opposite the fire while Grainne sat on the edge of a chair near it, rubbing her hands.

He cleared his throat and tried to sound excited. 'Michelle is, I mean, we are, going to have a baby,' he announced.

'Donal, that's wonderful news! Congratulations! Imagine my wee brother a dad! I can't believe it. Have you told Mam yet?'

'No, you're the first in the family to know.'

She came over to him then, knelt down and gave him a big hug. He felt his body resisting, undeserving. Then she placed her hands on his biceps and looked into his eyes, the way you do with a child when asking it a very important question. 'And how do you feel about it, Donal?'

He dropped his gaze momentarily for he could not bear the searching intensity in her eyes. He steeled himself, then looked up again. 'I'm really pleased,' he said firmly.

Grainne cocked her head to one side. 'Is that all?'

'What d'you mean, 'is that all'? What do you want me to do? Climb onto the roof and shout about it?'

'Some men do feel like that, yes.'

'Well, I'm more reserved. I don't really know what to expect,' he said lamely.

Grainne let go of his arms, stood up and looked at him, then opened her mouth to speak.

But before she could say anything, Donal leapt in with, 'We're moving to Ballyfergus. Michelle wants to be near her family.'

'Oh,' said Grainne, sounding as though she'd suddenly been winded. She paused, thinking, and then went on, 'And how do her parents feel about that?'

'Her mother's delighted.'

'And her dad — Noel, is it? What did he say?'

'Not much. He's going to build a house for us on a bit of land he has out past Killyglen.'

'He must think it's a good idea then,' said Grainne thoughtfully, 'if he's offered to do that.'

'Suppose so. It'll be great though, us being that bit closer,' said Donal, continuing to steer the conversation away from a level of intimacy that he found threatening. 'Why, we'll practically be neighbours. I can pop in and see you more often on my way home from work.'

'I don't know about that!' said Grainne so sharply that it made Donal jump.

There was an awkward pause during which she stared into the fire and her face reddened — though he guessed not from the heat. Then she got up abruptly and moved around the room, busily switching on lights although it was still broad daylight outside.

'I was only joking,' he said, peeved by her response. 'I don't suppose we'll see any more of each other than we do now.'

'No, I'm sorry. I didn't mean to be so short with you,' she said quickly. 'It's just that I've got used to being on my own. I like my — my privacy.'

'Right,' said Donal. 'Look, I'd better be going. I didn't realise the time.'

'Don't be cross with me, Donal. It's nothing personal.'

'If you don't want to see me, Grainne, just say so.'

'You know that's not what I want. All I'm

asking is that you give me a call if you're coming down. That's all. You know I'm always glad to see you.'

She followed him outside and stood in the doorway, watching him while he walked down the drive.

'You know I'm always here for you. No matter what,' she called out after him.

Donal shrugged his shoulders and got into the car. Something wasn't quite right with Grainne. One minute she was giving him the cold shoulder, the next she was his best friend. There was no doubt about it — she'd become decidedly peculiar over the last few years. It was living on your own that did it. Maybe this man she hinted at was just a figment of her imagination. But there was one thing for sure — he wouldn't be making any more surprise visits on his sister. He'd got the message loud and clear.

He tooted the horn, Grainne waved, and he drove off thinking about her simple, uncomplicated life. She lived quietly on an honestly earned living and had only herself to answer to. He, on the other hand, felt like he'd sold his soul for mammon. Had he turned into such a horrible person that even his own sister didn't want to have anything to do with him?

★ ★ ★

It was Wednesday, the day before New Year's Eve and the office was like a morgue. Donal sat with his feet on the desk, scrunched up a sheet of A4 paper in one hand and aimed it at the mini-basketball-hoop suspended over the waste-paper bin. It bounced on the wall and landed on the floor which was littered with evidence of his previous unsuccessful attempts. The door to his room lay wide open but outside, in the corridor, there was little sign of life.

Most staff had taken the three days between Christmas and the New Year off work. So had most of the bank's customers. But Donal had precious little leave left, after taking three foreign holidays earlier in the year. Michelle had been keen to do as much as they could before the baby came. Holidays would never be the same again, she said, not with a howling child in tow.

The secretary came in and dropped a plastic sleeve on his desk.

'There are those reports you wanted typing,' she said, 'and have one of these. If I eat any more I'm going to be sick.'

She held out a huge tub of Quality Street — he chose a green triangle. He peeled off the thin foil wrapper, popped the chocolate in his mouth, crumpled the foil into a tiny ball and threw it at the bin. It cleared the hoop cleanly and hit the bottom of the bin with a satisfying ping.

'Thanks, Mary. I don't know why we bother to open. Who in their right mind would want to come near a bank over Christmas, except to get money out of an autoteller?'

'I know I don't, but we don't make the rules, do we?'

'Indeed we don't,' he said, thinking that he bet

Noel McCormick wasn't working today.

'No word of Michelle yet?'

'Nothing yet. She said she's been getting strange twinges these last few days but I don't know if it's just indigestion.'

'Could be Braxton Hicks contractions,' said Mary knowingly. She was a mother of four and had eight grandchildren. Donal had no idea what she was talking about. 'She's not due till tomorrow, isn't that right? And first babies are often late. You could have a long wait ahead of you.'

Donal thought that he couldn't wait any longer. Michelle had reached a fever pitch of preparation, nagging him to do this, that and the other thing. They'd moved into their new house only four weeks ago and there was still a lot to be done. Noel had built them a fabulous house at cost price — it was far superior to anything they could have bought on the open market for the same money.

But Donal had come home the other day and found her cleaning out brand-new kitchen cupboards! It was totally illogical but he supposed it had something to do with hormones and the nesting instinct. It seemed like she couldn't sit still for a minute. And she was enormous, like a peapod fit to burst.

Time would pass more quickly if he was busy at work, he thought, but the morning dragged so slowly he could've fallen asleep. At lunchtime Jim and Dave from specialist finance called at his door, top buttons undone and silk ties loosened, and rescued him from the terminal boredom.

'Are you coming to the Crown for lunch?' asked Dave.

Donal didn't need to be asked twice. He grabbed his jacket, shrugged it on and strolled out of the office.

'If anyone asks,' he called to Mary over his shoulder, 'I'm on a customer visit.'

'And I'm the Virgin Mary,' retorted Mary and laughed.

Outside it was bitterly cold and a strong northeasterly howled round the buildings and up alleyways. They buttoned their jackets, turned up the lapels, and struggled along Howard Street. Then they rounded the corner onto Great Victoria Street, and pressed on past the ornate Grand Opera House, with its red brickwork and contrasting cream paintwork. They soon came to the Crown, overshadowed on the opposite side of the road by the looming façade of the Europa, infamous as Europe's most bombed hotel. Everyone was trying to move on from the past but labels like that were hard to shake off.

The Crown Liquor Saloon was a preserved Victorian pub owned by the National Trust and run by Bass Ireland. Only in Ireland, thought Donal wryly as he pushed open the door, could a pub achieve museum status. Inside, the atmosphere was warm and friendly and relatively quiet. In summer you couldn't get through the door for tourists packing the place out but now, between Christmas and the New Year, it was mostly locals taking a quiet pint and reading the paper.

They ordered three pints of Guinness and

bowls of Irish stew and sat in one of the little wood-panelled snugs. The soft gas lighting reflected off the stained-glass windows and mirrors giving the place an otherworldly feel. Like stepping back in time.

'Definitely the best place for a pint,' said Donal and the others raised their glasses in agreement.

Nearly three hours and six pints later they emerged. Already it was getting dark and tiny flakes of dry white snow, like dandruff, skittered about in the wind. Fortified with hot food and Guinness, Donal was immune to the cold and walked back to the office laughing and joking with his colleagues.

When they got out of the lift on the third floor Mary met him, flustered with excitement.

'You've to phone home straight away! Michelle's been trying to get you. She thinks she's starting. I didn't know where you'd gone or I'd have come and got you. You must have switched your mobile off.'

The news sobered Donal up in a way the cold air hadn't. He ran along the corridor, picked up the phone and dialled. It rang for ages and then an unfamiliar female voice answered. In his haste he'd dialled their old flat. He quickly ended the call and re-dialled. This time it was answered straightaway.

'Is that you?' panted Michelle's voice on the other end of the phone. 'Where the hell have you been?' He was about to answer when she gasped and said, 'Never mind, never mind! There's definitely something happening. I've been getting

63

contractions on and off for the last couple of hours, but they're getting more frequent now.'

'I'd better come home then,' said Donal quickly as panic set in. He knew there wasn't a lot he could do to help, but he suddenly realised how much he wanted to be part of this baby's birth.

'No, don't do that. Mum's phoned the hospital.'

'She's with you?'

'And Yvonne too.'

'Good,' said Donal, reassured that Michelle was not alone but also feeling slightly excluded. He felt intense protectiveness towards her, the strength of which surprised him.

'What do you want me to do, then?' he asked.

'Meet us at the maternity wing at the Royal. Johnson House. You know where you're going?'

'Yes, yes. It's going to be all right, love,' he whispered into the phone. 'You do know that?'

'I know, I know,' she said, then paused and added, 'Here it comes.'

He heard a sharp intake of breath and a moan, then sobbing into the phone.

'Michelle!'

There were some muffled sounds and Yvonne came onto the line.

'We're just leaving for the hospital now,' she said, in her sensible way. 'Get yourself there as soon as you can.'

Donal drove anxiously through the streets of Belfast, aware that he was over the alcohol limit. He tried to avoid driving with the exaggerated caution that screamed 'drunk driver', straining with all his senses to concentrate on the task in hand. He double-checked every turn, watched out for police cars, and talked himself through every manoeuvre to help him focus on what he was doing. He reached the hospital carpark safely, parked the car and rested his head on the steering wheel.

His head was thumping from the alcohol and from the adrenaline coursing through his body. In a few hours, maybe minutes, he was going to be a dad. Of course he'd known this fact for months but it hadn't felt real, not till now. Would he be up to the job? He knew he had the capacity for great love but the role model he had in his own father wasn't one he'd want to emulate. Not that Patrick Mullan had been a bad father, just a distant figure of authority. His role in the house was that of respected breadwinner and he rarely interacted on any meaningful level with his six children. In many ways, to this day, he remained a stranger to Donal.

Donal took a deep breath, exhaled and got out of the car. He crossed the road and entered the hospital. He found his way to the maternity ward, where a midwife showed him where to wait. He helped himself to several cups of ice-cold water from a dispenser, crumpled up the little paper cone and threw it away. He paced the room several times, loosened his tie and settled down to wait.

Time dragged slowly. The waiting-room was decorated with tawdry tinsel and paper chains that looked like they had seen many Christmases. Outside, the corridor was busy with the sticky sound of rubber soles on lino, like walking on tar. Doors banged, female voices called out unintelligible instructions, and porters pushed full wheelchairs and empty trolleys back and forth. Excited groups of visitors, chattering like birds, came and went.

A full half-hour had passed before Michelle, accompanied by her mother and sister, arrived on the wing. She was in a wheelchair, sitting very erect and holding her enormous belly with both hands. She seemed smaller somehow — shrunken into herself with fear. When she saw Donal she started to cry.

'But it hurts so much,' she said and he knelt down beside her and took her hand.

'It's going to be all right, Michelle. I'm here now. We'll do this together.'

But he felt like a fraud because he knew there was precious little that he could do to help her. However, she stopped crying and smiled. Her blonde hair was lank, strands of it sticking to the side of her face. He reached over and tenderly pushed them off her face with his fingers. She looked so vulnerable Donal wished she didn't have to go through this.

'Now, Mr Mullan,' said a midwife, interrupting, 'we need to get Michelle booked in. Let's get her comfortable and see what's happening. Why don't you wait in here and I'll call you when we're ready?'

She indicated the waiting-room and pushed the wheelchair through a nearby door. Pauline followed with a large holdall, which had been packed, according to all the instructions in the baby books, for weeks. Donal waited impatiently outside with Yvonne.

What the hell was Pauline doing in there? Hadn't they been asked to wait outside? It was typical of Pauline in her authoritative manner to wade in just where she wanted, regardless of the rules or anyone else's feelings. He was the father of the baby — she was only the grandmother.

But the things the McCormicks had done for them — the penthouse flat, the house in Ballyfergus, Michelle's allowance, logged and catalogued in Donal's memory — came to mind. They connected him and Michelle to her parents by an invisible thread. Their relationship was one of dependency — the McCormicks had a controlling interest in their lives. Hence Pauline felt entitled to act like she did and Donal did not feel that he had the right to say no.

It wasn't long before they were allowed in to see Michelle in her private room. She was calmer now, lying on the bed under a crisp white sheet and cream cellular blanket. The room was comfortable but not large with a TV in the corner and pale pink curtains on the windows.

'What's happening?' said Donal to the midwife who was now scribbling things down on a piece of white paper attached to a clipboard.

'Well, the contractions seem to have stopped. That's not unusual, especially in a first pregnancy. But she is partially dilated and her waters have broken so we've called Mr Reid, the consultant, and he's coming in to see you. I'm Christine, by the way. You're doing just fine,' she

67

smiled at Michelle, patted her on the knee and left the room.

Yvonne said, 'I don't know what all the fuss is about. Why can't humans just get on with it like a horse does? Won't the baby come when it's ready to? What's all this about 'starting her'?'

'I'm not a bloody mare,' said Michelle with feeling. 'Will you tell her to shut up, Mum?'

'Yvonne, you're upsetting your sister.'

'But Mum, why should we be any different from other animals? Horses don't need all this carry-on when they foal.'

'Yvonne,' said Donal, raising his voice more than he'd intended, 'I don't think this is helping.'

'What did I say?' she asked, holding the palms of her hands upwards and shrugging her shoulders.

Donal exchanged glances with Pauline who raised her eyes heavenwards.

'Why don't you go and get us all a cup of tea?' said Pauline and, after Yvonne had left the room, added, 'Sometimes I despair of that girl.'

The consultant came in at six thirty to examine Michelle and assure them that everything was OK.

'I would go home and get some sleep if I were you, Mrs McCormick. I don't think this baby's going to come before morning.'

'Now, you'll be attending Michelle personally, won't you, Mr Reid?' asked Pauline, making it clear that was exactly what she expected.

And bloody right too, thought Donal — they were paying an arm and a leg to have this baby privately.

'Rest assured, Mrs McCormick, your daughter will receive the very best of care. You have no need to be concerned on that front.'

Satisfied, Pauline turned to Donal, 'Now you'll let us know if anything happens, Donal, won't you?'

He nodded and she went over to the bed and spoke softly to Michelle.

'Are you going to be OK, love? I can stay if you want me to.'

'I'm OK, Mum. Thanks. I've got Donal.'

For a moment Donal felt like turning round and running out the door. The responsibility of supporting Michelle through the next few hours lay heavily on him. Part of him wanted desperately to be there but part of him was terrified by the prospect.

At last Pauline and Yvonne were persuaded to leave and Donal breathed a sigh of relief. He thought for one awful moment that they intended to be there throughout the entire birth.

They waited all night for the baby to come but it would not. Michelle was put on a drip to restart the contractions and given an injection of pethidine to numb the pain. After that she actually fell asleep between contractions only to be woken again by the next one. In the early hours, Donal dozed in the chair beside her bed, wakened often by Michelle's soft moans and by the intrusions of the night-shift midwife. The effects of the alcohol had long worn off, leaving him feeling dehydrated, filthy and worried that things were not going to plan. Surely it wasn't supposed to take this long or be so difficult?

By mid-morning Michelle was exhausted and the foetal monitor showed that the baby was in some distress. Donal tried to hold her hand, spray her face with Evian, wipe her forehead and give her sips of water. All the things the books said a supportive partner should do. But she pushed him away and shook her head. The pain was now so intense that his ministrations offered no comfort and were merely irritations.

Mr Reid stood on the opposite side of the bed to Donal. He lifted Michelle's hand and held it tightly in his own.

'Now there's nothing to worry about,' said Mr Reid. 'The baby's fine but he wants to come out and I think Michelle has had enough.'

Michelle smiled weakly in agreement.

'So what are you going to do?' asked Donal.

'I think that it would be advisable to carry out a section.'

'A caesarean!' cried Michelle, suddenly animated. 'I don't want one. I want to have this baby myself!'

'I'm sorry, Michelle, but it's just not going to happen,' said Mr Reid. 'You're only six centimetres dilated and I don't think we can wait any longer. This is best for baby and for you. Come on now,' he added briskly, 'I need you to be sensible about this. There's a good girl.'

Michelle swallowed her tears, bit down on her bottom lip and nodded.

'It's OK, love,' said Donal, squeezing her hand and trying to sound calm. Inside he felt like his head was about to burst. He was dizzy with tiredness and hunger — he hadn't been able to eat anything the midwives had kindly offered him at breakfast. What if the baby wasn't all right? What if Michelle died?

A flurry of activity followed, in which Michelle was prepared for theatre. The midwives changed her into a green gown, the anaesthetist appeared briefly, various tests and checks were made, then she was transferred to a trolley and wheeled out of the room. While this was going on, Donal managed to phone her parents and tell them what was happening. Then he followed in the wake of Christine, who was back on duty, and the porter pushing the trolley towards a lift. They didn't ignore him exactly but they knew, and he knew, that this was a drama in which he was little more than an extra.

A theatre nurse helped him scrub down and dress in a hairnet, green gown and overboots, not unlike the garb he wore when he visited Patterson's processing plants. He couldn't stop his hands from shaking.

The nurse touched him lightly on the forearm. 'It's going to be all right, Mr Mullan. This is a very routine operation for us. You have nothing to worry about.'

Suddenly Donal felt the responsibility lifted from his shoulders — someone else was taking over and the relief was instantaneous. He'd never felt so useless in his entire life, not because of anything anyone had said or done, but simply because he could do little more than observe. He followed the nurse into the theatre.

Once the operation was underway, everything calmed down. The operating room was filled with the quiet hum of monitors and Mr Reid's mumbled instructions to the nurses. Everyone seemed relaxed and confident. Perhaps it was going to be all right after all. Donal stood at the head of the bed talking quietly to Michelle, who remained conscious throughout. She too was calm, glad that the pain was over and they would soon have their baby. A green sheet shielded them from full view of the operation, which he had no desire to see. After only a few minutes, he heard a slurping sound and then a small glistening bundle was held aloft for them to see. The baby appeared to be asleep, and then suddenly the room was filled with high-pitched bleating like a lamb.

'Oh, Donal, a baby, our baby,' cried Michelle and he leaned down and kissed her on the forehead.

'I'm so proud of you! I never could have done this.'

'Congratulations! You have a lovely baby girl,' said Mr Reid. 'Now I need to carry on down here and midwife will look after baby for you.'

The baby was taken briefly to the side of the room by Christine, then brought to Michelle wrapped loosely in a white blanket. Donal helped to prop her head up whilst she held the baby in her arms.

'She's beautiful, isn't she?' said Michelle.

The baby's face had been roughly wiped but the little fist that protruded from the blanket, and her head, was smeared with blood and a creamy-white substance, like lard. Her oval-shaped head was covered with light brown hair, wet with moisture. Her eyes were closed and her little mouth opened and shut again like she was trying it out for size.

'She's absolutely gorgeous,' said Donal.

'What a lovely New Year present,' said Christine. 'Now, let's give baby to Dad while we get Mum sorted out, shall we?' and she handed the little bundle to Donal.

He stepped back from the glare of the operating lights into the shadows. For the short time that he held the baby in his arms, time stopped. Everything else around him receded into the background until he was aware only of himself and the weightless life he held in his hands. He looked into the tiny, crumpled face and felt a sense of completeness. A sense of pure joy. Here was something pure and good and unspoilt. For the second time in his life he knew what it was to love unconditionally.

'Mr Mullan? Mr Mullan?'

It was Christine.

'Let me have baby now and I'll take her up to Michelle's room.'

Embarrassed, Donal handed his baby over and flicked the tears from his face.

'She's lovely, isn't she?' said Christine. 'There's no other feeling like it in the world. When you hold your baby for the very first time, it's something special.'

And with that she turned and walked away, leaving him feeling not so foolish after all.

When Donal returned to the maternity wing, Noel and Pauline shot out of the waiting-room and nearly knocked him over.

'We just heard,' said Noel, his face radiant with pride. 'A girl! Isn't that something?' He slapped Donal on the back so hard that he almost fell on his face.

Pauline stood on her tiptoes and peered over Donal's shoulder as though he might be hiding Michelle and the baby behind his back. 'Where are they? Are they all right?'

'Everything's fine. They're on their way up from theatre. But I don't think Michelle will be able to have visitors just yet. She's pretty wiped out.'

'We're not visitors, we're family,' said Pauline firmly.

So eventually they got their way and they saw the baby and Michelle, if only for a few minutes. It was hard for anybody to say no to the McCormicks.

'Her name's Molly Jean,' announced Michelle to her parents and Donal, stroking the infant's cheek with a crooked finger. 'If it's OK with you, Don?'

It was a name they'd more or less agreed on, should the child be a girl. And after what Michelle had just gone through, Donal thought that she could call the child whatever she liked. 'Molly Jean sounds just perfect,' he said.

Then Noel took him outside and gave him the biggest, fattest cigar he'd ever seen. Donal inhaled the hot, mellow smoke and held it in his lungs, savouring the high. Whether it was just a bloody fine cigar, or whether he was suffering from exhaustion he couldn't be sure, but he'd never before felt so elated.

3

1998

Michelle stood in the drawing room in her mother's house and looked at herself in the full-length mirror. The June sun shone brightly through the tall window, cruelly illuminating her reflection perfectly. Dressed in green she looked like an unusually tall, fat leprechaun. She took a swig of champagne. What on earth had possessed Jeanette to put her bridesmaids in emerald green? Strictly speaking though, she wasn't a bridesmaid but Jeanette's matron-of-honour, a title that made her feel many years older than her twenty-five years.

'Darling, you look gorgeous,' cooed Shona, the owner of Elizabeth Rose, Northern Ireland's premier one-off bridal designers.

Michelle looked directly into her narrow slits of eyes and wanted to spit at her. Although in her late forties, she was thin and tall as a telegraph pole with a figure that would look good in anything. 'You really think so?' she said with an edge in her voice that bordered on sarcasm.

'Right. I've had enough,' interrupted Yvonne. 'Get this thing off me!'

She started to pull at the shoulder of her dress, which was identical to Michelle's. She too looked awful in it, maybe even worse than Michelle did. Her face was ruddy from an outdoor life — it was going to take a lot of makeup to make her presentable. Neither woman had the figure, or the colouring, for these dark green sheaths of silk. The bias cut accentuated their wide hips and shoulders and the silky fabric clung to every lump and bump. The strong hue sapped their faces of colour and made Michelle's dyed blonde locks look like straw.

'No, no, darling!' shrieked Shona, then she lowered her voice to a sweet cajole. 'Let me help you, Yvonne. It's a very delicate fabric and must be handled gently.'

She unfastened the buttons on the back of the dress and Yvonne hobbled out of the room, clutching the front of the dress to her chest for modesty's sake. When she returned she was wearing her usual jodhpurs, riding boots and a grubby T-shirt. She flung the dress down in disgust and turned to Jeanette.

'Just so long as you know, I'm only doing this because you're my sister. Now I've got work to do,' she growled and stomped out of the room.

'You'll have to excuse my daughter,' said Pauline, mildly. 'She's finding this all a bit — stressful.'

While no one was looking, Michelle helped herself to another glass of champagne and swallowed it in four gulps. For once her sentiments were entirely in line with Yvonne's. Where they differed, however, was that Yvonne had no aspirations to beauty and didn't give a damn what people thought of her, whereas Michelle did.

'Let me show you,' said Shona, sensing at last that she had rebels on her hands. It was going to take some saleswomanship to convince Michelle and Yvonne to wear these dresses.

She came up behind Michelle, grasped her hair with one hand and twisted it up behind her head like a rope.

'See, once you've got your hair up, it'll look fabulous. And, once you've had the final fitting, the dress will fit like a glove.'

Any tighter, thought Michelle, and you'll be able to see the orange peel on my thighs. How she wished that Lady Diana meringue-style dresses were still fashionable. She'd have looked all right in a dress like that, one that pretty much covered everything up.

'That looks better, Michelle, it really does,' said Jeanette encouragingly. She stood back and regarded Michelle anxiously, her knuckle shoved in her mouth. She looked like she was about to cry.

It couldn't look much worse, thought Michelle, but she bit her tongue. It was Jeanette's wedding and if this was what she wanted her bridesmaids to wear then Michelle would do it, and with a smile on her face.

'Yes, the hair up definitely helps,' she agreed, the only positive thing she could think of to say.

Shona dropped the hank of hair in her hand, with a satisfied air. Jeanette took her fist out of her mouth and smiled.

'I always think that long hair looks better up than down in photographs,' advised Shona. 'It's much more elegant.'

At least her hair would be elegant then, thought Michelle, even if nothing else was. If only she wasn't so fat. She smoothed her hand over the body of the dress and her round, soft belly protruded like a big, green melon. She yawned, tired from the night-time feed that little Molly seemed determined not to give up.

So much for breastfeeding. The midwife, and all the baby books, had assured her that the weight would fall off, that she would get her figure back faster than if she bottle-fed the baby. Well, so far it hadn't worked. Her upper arms were the size of Jeanette's thighs, she had a cleavage like Dolly Parton and a stomach like a big, wet sponge.

Jeanette, the lucky one, had inherited her mother's fine bone structure and slim figure. Michelle and Yvonne, however, took after the women on their father's side of the family. Big and tall, they had a tendency to go to fat at the slightest provocation. Michelle had always battled to keep her weight under control and, up until Molly's birth five months ago, it was a battle she'd won. But the war wasn't over she reminded herself, and she *would* get her figure back. For a start she'd stop feeding the baby, get her into a nursery, stop eating so much (she'd have no excuse for pigging out once she'd stopped breastfeeding) and start doing some serious exercise. She put down the crystal glass and silently resolved not to drink any more. The wedding was still six weeks away. All was not lost.

'What do you think?' she said quietly to her

mother when she was within earshot. Shona and her assistant were busy helping the two other bridesmaids, Adriana and Flora, Jeanette's best friends, into their dresses.

'I think that Jeanette's got her heart set on them and that's what you're going to have to wear,' replied Pauline quietly, avoiding eye contact and sipping thoughtfully at the fizzy pink liquid in her glass. 'It's too late anyway to change them.'

Her mother had a knack of being diplomatic and direct at the same time. So it wasn't just Michelle's imagination — she did look awful.

They watched as Adriana and Flora stood patiently while Shona fussed and pulled at the seams of their dresses. Her assistant, a quiet, unassuming girl, tucked and pinned as instructed, a row of bright pins gripped between her teeth. The wedding would be featured in *Ulster Tatler* and there was pressure on everyone, not least the dress designer, to get it right. A stunning photograph would guarantee her reputation and no doubt gain her lots more customers.

Adriana had pale skin, brown eyes and a mass of short, luscious, black curls. Her neck was long, like a gazelle's, and she must have weighed all of nine stone. Flora was a pretty redhead, with deep brown eyes, brown eyebrows and lashes and a lightly freckled skin. She too was slim. In spite of their very different colouring both girls looked fabulous in emerald green. Both in fact looked like something out of a Northern Ireland Tourist Board advert. All fresh

79

and wholesome and beautiful. Michelle's heart sank.

'Here, have another glass of champers,' said Jeanette, holding out a brimming flute.

Oh stuff it, said Michelle to herself, what difference was one more glass going to make?

'I think I will, sank you. I mean 'thank you',' she said and burped, 'Oops, excuse me.' She giggled and put her hand over her mouth.

'I think you'd better get out of that dress before you spill something on it,' said her mother wisely. 'Turn around.'

Michelle tried not to sway as Pauline undid the many tiny fabric-covered buttons that ran down the back of the dress to the base of her spine. Then she teetered out of the room and across the wide hall to the family sitting-room where she stepped out of the dress and kicked off the green satin high heels. She put on her lovely Marc Jacobs black trouser suit and cream silk shirt — a post-pregnancy present to herself. Shame really, for it wouldn't fit her once she lost weight.

Back in the drawing-room, and freed from the constraints of the tight dress, she started to enjoy herself. Adriana and Flora were now changed into their daytime clothes, which left only Jeanette's dress to fit.

'Now for the bride's dress,' said Shona. 'Are you sure you want everyone to see it?'

'Oh, yes,' said Jeanette. 'I'm not superstitious about these things. Where's the fun in it if you can't share it?'

She went off to change and Adriana turned to

Michelle. 'So, are you planning to go back to work?'

'God no! Not to Marston and Reid anyway. I might do something else though. I don't know.'

She'd worked for the estate agency since 1990, after dipping her toe in several different careers, including banking. That was how she'd met Don — at evening classes for the banking exams. Not that she'd lasted very long at that.

'But don't you miss work?' asked Flora, and Michelle remembered that she was a single, serious-minded career girl, training to be a doctor.

'Well, no. Believe me, looking after a baby is a full-time job,' she replied truthfully. 'More than a full-time job. I'm just thankful that we moved to Ballyfergus when we did. I've hardly been off your doorstep, have I, Mum?'

'And we've loved every minute of it,' said Pauline. 'Babies change so quickly at this age.'

'I really couldn't have managed without you, Mum. Did I tell you that I'm going to stop feeding her? Now she's on solids she doesn't really need it.'

But her mother didn't respond to that and the conversation moved onto the wedding arrangements. Michelle realised that she must have been boring everyone. She looked into her glass, shut up and listened.

'Did you get a band for the evening in the end, Mrs McCormick?' asked Flora.

'Two — one dance band and one ceilidh — so there's something for everyone.'

'And how many guests are coming?' said Adriana.

Pauline popped open another bottle of champagne and replied, 'Three hundred to the chapel and reception, and another seventy at night.'

'Wow,' said Flora. 'It's going to be a hoot. I can't wait!'

'Are there going to be plenty of single men?' asked Adriana, giggling.

'Lots of Matt's nice friends are coming and I don't think many of them are married. Isn't that right, Michelle?'

'Mmm,' she agreed.

She couldn't help but compare Jeanette's very lavish wedding with her own, more modest one, four years ago. Not that her wedding wasn't nice — it was. She'd had a beautiful dress, her two sisters as bridesmaids and the reception was held in the grand Culloden Hotel in Bangor.

But it wasn't on the scale of this one and that hurt her. There was no evening reception for a start and only one hundred guests, the majority of whom came from Donal's side because he had a bigger immediate family. Everyone under the sun was being invited to Jeanette's wedding, or so it seemed — distant relatives, business associates of Noel, Pauline's colleagues from the many charitable causes in which she was involved. In short, all the people that hadn't been invited to her own wedding.

Michelle was sure her parents were making all this fuss over Jeanette's wedding because they simply adored Matt Doherty. And they'd made it pretty clear in various ways that Don didn't come up to their expectations as a son-in-law. His primary fault, as far as Michelle could see, was that as the son of a factory worker from West Belfast he came from the wrong background. And the flaw, being one of birth, was one he could never overcome. Even the fact that he was a Catholic wasn't enough to compensate.

But it wasn't entirely fair to blame her parents about her wedding, she told herself. Hadn't Donal insisted that the wedding take place in Bangor? For some reason he was dead set against having it in Ballyfergus. And that decision had annoyed her parents for, by doing so, he'd taken an element of control out of their hands. So, when it came to footing the bill they talked about keeping it 'low key' and 'intimate'. With the benefit of hindsight, she suspected another reason for their attitude — they did not want their relatives and family friends exposed to the common Mullans. Hence no evening reception.

At the time, she couldn't have cared less where or how they were married — she was so desperate to have Donal that she'd have married him anywhere. Like her sisters, Michelle had been educated at a Catholic boarding school, so few of her friends lived locally anyway. But now she wished she'd dug her heels in. You only got to do it once after all.

But why did Donal dislike Ballyfergus so much? She sensed he had reservations about moving down here from Belfast. He talked about missing the city and their friends, but there was something else, she was sure of it. Something he wasn't telling her.

Just then Jeanette came into the room and everyone gasped. Her dress was made of off-white silk, long and graceful. The high-necked bodice and sleeves were encrusted with beads and pearls. The dress clung to her shapely contours. Her face was radiant with excitement; she looked beautiful.

For the next half-hour everyone admired the finer points of the wedding dress. Shona basked in the reflected glory, while her assistant knelt on the antique Persian rug, pinning the hem.

When Jeanette left the room to take off the dress, Flora turned to Pauline and asked, 'So why did you decide to opt for a marquee instead of a hotel?'

'Oh Flora, dear,' she replied, perched elegantly on an upholstered Georgian armchair, 'you've no idea what the hotels round here are like. There was nowhere nearly big enough and they're all awful anyway. We were left with no option but to have the reception here at Glenburn. And that's when we called in the wedding co-ordinator. It was just too much for me to organise. As it is, it's probably worked out for the best. This way we can ensure the very best food and wine and champagne. The marquee will have carpet and drapes and a wooden floor for dancing, ruched pale green linings and chandeliers,' she counted, the items off on her fingers. 'We'll have a PA system as well. I think there's something very refined about a wedding reception in a marquee, don't you?'

'Now you're all to come here and stay over the night before,' interrupted Jeanette. 'Sheila McCoy and her team will be coming to do our make-up and hair in the morning.'

'All the way from Belfast?' said Adriana.

'We don't have a decent beauty salon or hairdresser's in Ballyfergus,' said Pauline. 'Sometimes I despair living here. But Noel won't move to somewhere more civilised.'

'What, none at all?' said Adriana.

'Well, there are hairdresser's and a beauty salon, but you just wouldn't go there,' said Michelle. 'They're really old and horrible. You'd probably catch some dreadful disease.'

Everyone laughed, then Pauline got up and placed her glass on the high marble mantelpiece and waited for everyone to hush. 'Now, girls, there's a buffet lunch ready in the dining-room if you'd like to come through,' she said and opened the wide door into the hall.

Just then Sybil, Esther's teenage daughter, came in through the door on the opposite side of the room, carrying a screaming Molly. 'I've tried everything, Michelle, but I think she wants you,' shouted Sybil above the child's cries. 'She's just thrown her solids all over the kitchen floor. She's been really good all morning though. Haven't you, pet?'

The baby was in full flow, emptying her lungs in that raging cry peculiar to angry, starving babies.

'Give her here, then,' said Michelle with a sigh. 'There, there, darling!' She pulled up her blouse, unhooked the little flap on her bra and

85

put Molly on her breast. The child latched on and sucked greedily, her shiny blue eyes staring in mute desperation at her mother. Sybil quietly slipped away and Michelle sat on the antique sofa in the now-empty room, holding her baby in her arms. She listened to the chatter and laughter recede down the hall, as the rest of them made their way to the dining-room.

She loved Molly but sometimes it was hard being a mother. Her days of being young, carefree and single were definitely over.

★　★　★

Pauline looked with satisfaction out of her bedroom window at the white structure that now dominated the view from the house. The marquee was huge, a great big rectangle with a smaller one alongside for use by the caterers. It was set back as far as possible, so that drinks could be taken on the lawn in front of the house. It was the grandest one she'd been able to find, brand new this season, with windows affording fine views of the house on one side, and the rolling countryside on the other.

It had taken a team of six men two days to erect and set up. The space was laid out banquet style, each of the ten tables seating thirty and arranged around the polished wood dancefloor. The bar was at the opposite end to the top table. Last night, once the ruched linings, carpet and chandeliers were in place, and the tables laid with linen and silver, it looked fantastic, a real fairytale venue. And just as grand as any of the better hotels.

Much to Yvonne's disgust the paddock was to serve as a carpark. Mike, the gardener, would guide the cars in and direct them where to park. Thank God it hadn't rained overnight and the ground was still rock solid. The cars should do little damage to the grass and the ladies' heels would be saved.

Pauline congratulated herself that she'd left nothing to chance — every detail had been planned, checked and double-checked. Now it was time to relax. Honor McIlvenna, the wedding co-ordinator, was responsible for making the day run on time and dealing with all the last-minute hitches that were sure to arise. Pauline looked down and saw her marching across the grass towards the marquee in a sharp black suit, a mobile phone stuck to her ear. All Pauline had to do was concentrate on making herself as glamorous as possible.

Esther came into the room. 'The hairdresser and make-up people are here,' she said. 'Do you want to get done first? Or the girls?'

'I think I'll get it over and done with. Could you get my outfit ready please?'

'No problem.'

Esther went into the dressing-room and brought out a plastic sheath on a hanger. She removed the plastic and laid a brightly coloured two-piece garment on the embroidered bedspread, with a matching skullcap and high-heeled strappy sandals.

'It's silk isn't it?' she said stroking the fabric,

like the fur of a small pet. 'It's gorgeous, Mrs McCormick, so it is. That Colette Connelly's done you proud.'

'Yes, we're lucky to have such a talented designer on our doorstep, aren't we?'

'You know it's hard to believe she's the same wee lassie who used to help her dad in the fruit and veg shop. And look at your wee Jeanette. I still can't believe she's getting married today. They all grow up though, don't they?'

'They do indeed.'

'Oh, I nearly forgot to tell you,' said Esther just before she closed the bedroom door behind her, 'The bouquets have just been delivered. That McIlvenna woman checked them and says they're fine.'

When her hair and make-up was finished and the master bedroom suite filled with a gaggle of girls, Pauline left them and went downstairs to look at the flowers. They were laid out in the boot room, in shallow brown boxes, with the outside door left ajar to keep them cool. Each bouquet was made from off-white longiflorum lilies complemented by some exotic dark green, waxy foliage, not unlike the flowers she had held on her wedding day.

Pauline picked up the largest of the five bouquets, and held it briefly to her nose. The trumpet-like flowers were opened to perfection, the yellow stamen still firm and waxy. Tomorrow they would turn to turmeric-coloured dust that stained everything and defied every stain-remover known to man.

The smell of the lilies brought back rushing

memories of Pauline's own wedding day. Funny that — how smell was the most evocative sense. She remembered standing in her mother's parlour in a stiff satin dress, sick to the stomach with excitement and apprehension. Her mother fussing and checking as they waited for the cars, the stems of the flowers growing hot and sweaty in her palm. Then stepping into the limousine with Dad, his eyes pricking with tears that would remain unshed. She'd been in love then, the joy and the wonder of it still fresh and raw. Now, viewed from this distance in time, she wondered that she'd ever seen the world through such rose-tinted glasses.

'Are they all right, Mum?' said Jeanette's anxious voice from behind.

Guiltily Pauline replaced the bouquet then turned to smile at her middle daughter. 'They're gorgeous. Here, come and see.'

Jeanette came to stand beside her and Pauline put her arm around her waist. They both wore thick, white towelling robes.

'They are lovely, aren't they, Mum?' she said, then paused and added, 'I'm nervous.'

'Don't be. This is going to be the best day of your life. Allow yourself to enjoy it. Here, let me look at you.'

Jeanette's fair hair was pinned up beautifully in an intricate arrangement of coils and intertwining strands. Her face was heavily made up, too heavily perhaps for such close inspection but the overall effect was one of sophisticated beauty. For a brief moment all Pauline felt was sorrow. Her baby was about to be married.

'You look lovely,' she said, taking her daughter's hands in her own. 'I know you love Matt and he loves you, Jeanette. I wish you all the happiness in the world. And don't forget that I love you.'

Noel came in then and said, 'The carriage will be here for you soon, Pauline.'

'I'm just coming. I only have to put on my dress. You'd better hurry up as well, Jeanette.'

'Shona's getting the others into their dresses first. I'll be last. Wish me luck, then.'

Pauline wasn't surprised to see the crowd outside the church, for this was the biggest wedding Ballyfergus had seen in a long time. And McCormick was such a well-known name around these parts, it was only natural that curiosity brought people out to watch.

Ballyfergus's Catholic Church was a monstrosity of a building in Pauline's opinion. Built in Victorian times it was overly ornate on the outside and oppressive and dark on the inside. Still, she'd made the best of it by swamping the place in flowers. The old arched doorway was framed in white lilies, pale cream ribbon and dark green foliage. Inside, as well as the flowers on the altar, the end of every occupied pew was likewise decorated. And a wonderful floral archway in the same colours had been constructed in front of the altar, under which the happy couple would take their vows. The parish priest had expressed disquiet with these arrangements, deeming them too ostentatious for a religious ceremony, but a substantial donation to the roof fund soon put paid to his objections.

When Pauline and the bridesmaids stepped out of the horse-drawn carriage the crowd clapped loudly and she felt guilty for slating Ballyfergus's townsfolk in the past. She waved and smiled back equally warmly.

* * *

'You sound like the BBC's Royal wedding correspondent,' said Roisin jokingly to her best friend Colette Connelly.

'Believe me, I've heard every detail of this wedding from Pauline McCormick over the past six months. A hundred times,' replied Colette, laughing. 'I could practically recite the guest list.'

They were standing outside the chapel in the warm sunshine, with a small but eager crowd, waiting for the bride and groom to emerge. It was a quarter past four in the afternoon and Roisin was impatient.

'I thought you said the wedding was at three,' she said. 'There's no sign of them yet.'

'That's why I suggested we come down at four. Knowing the McCormicks, the bride was fashionably late and, if most of the guests are Catholics, it'll take forever getting through communion.'

'I only came down to see Pauline McCormick's dress,' said Roisin, lying. Her main motivation for being here — and one which she preferred to keep to herself — was to catch a glimpse of Donal Mullan and, of course, his wife

91

whom she'd never seen in the flesh. 'What's it like then, this creation of yours?'

'Well, it's hard to describe. The inspiration came from some pictures I saw in a book about medieval courtiers. But it doesn't look like a medieval dress. You'll see what I mean — oh, look, here they come!'

The bride and groom appeared in the church doorway. Two women stepped forward from the crowd and threw coloured confetti at them and the crowd gave a small cheer. The photographer snapped away, capturing the impromptu moment. Then they posed for a formal photograph, during which Colette dissected the bride's dress.

'It's all right for what it is,' she said begrudgingly, 'but it lacks originality. It looks like something you could buy off the peg but I know for a fact it's a one-off and cost a bomb. I could have done something really special . . .'

'Oh look, that's Pauline, isn't it?' said Roisin, as a glamorous, petite woman appeared on the church steps. Her hair was perfectly groomed into a shoulder-length strawberry-blonde bob. Her outfit had all the hallmarks of a Colette Connelly creation — too unusual and unique to be the work of anyone else.

It was made from many layers of diaphanous pale-green silk, over-printed with soft pinks and peaches, and it came to just above the knee. The bodice was fitted and boned and criss-crossed with darker green ribbon, showing off her neat figure. Her shoulders were covered with a short bolero style jacket made from the same fabric, and her hat was a skull-cap, again covered with the same material and decorated with two feathers and more of the green ribbon. It should have been too much but it wasn't — all the elements worked perfectly together.

'What do you think?' asked Colette.

'It's fabulous,' said Roisin with genuine admiration.

'She's small, you see, so the idea is to make her appear taller. That's the reason for using the one fabric throughout and for stopping the skirt at the knee. Anything longer and she'd be drowned in it. The figure-hugging bodice gives her body proportion, as does the short jacket.'

'It really is special,' said Roisin. 'You're just amazing Colette. You could design for all the stars!'

'I don't know about that,' said Colette, blushing. 'But Pauline says she'll make sure I get a mention in the *Ulster Tatler*. It's all word of mouth in this business — if people see her wearing one of my outfits, they'll want one too. I only hope they don't think I designed the bridesmaids' dresses as well! Wait 'til you see them.'

The bride and groom inched forward onto the forecourt into the balmy afternoon sun. A fat bee drifted across from the parochial-house garden next door to the church, buzzing sleepily in the late afternoon haze. The garden was separated from the church by a high stone wall and, traditionally, this was where photographs were taken after big occasions.

In the album at home were photographs

marking the religious milestones in Roisin's life. Her christening, First Holy Communion and confirmation were all recorded with a photograph taken in front of the same pampas-grass plant that grew bigger with the passing years. There it was still, towering over the wall like a great triffid.

But the garden obviously wasn't grand enough for the McCormicks, for no-one made any move in that direction. Instead, they started to make painfully slow progress towards the horse-drawn carriages waiting outside the church. The horses shook their heads impatiently, their silver bits and harness clinking like bells.

'Oh, my God, look at the colour of those dresses,' exclaimed Roisin, as two bridesmaids emerged from behind the bride and groom, clothed in bright green satin fabric. She clasped her hand over her mouth and widened her eyes in mock horror at her friend.

'Oh, Roisin, stop it,' giggled Colette. 'They'll see us laughing. I know. They're awful, aren't they?'

'What on earth possessed them?'

'According to Pauline that's what her daughter — the bride, Jeanette — wanted. She tried to talk her out of it but she wouldn't budge. The two bridesmaids,' said Colette, discreetly indicating the heavily built girls now flanking the bride, 'they're her sisters.'

'Oh, yes,' said Roisin, scanning the women keenly, 'I can see the family resemblance — but it looks like Jeanette got the best looks of the three of them.'

'The others have got pretty faces too. If they lost weight they'd look just as good as their sister.'

'Hmm,' said Roisin doubtfully and, unable to suppress her curiosity any longer, she asked, 'Which one's Michelle, then?'

'The blonde one on the right, with her hair up in a 'do'.'

Roisin stared at Michelle Mullan, who was now only a matter of yards away, disliking and pitying the girl at once. So this was what Donal Mullan had chosen over Ann-Marie, she thought bitterly. The plain, overweight girl looked nothing like the glamourous creature she'd been on her wedding day — Roisin had seen a photo of her in a glossy magazine several years ago. It just showed you what professional make-up, hair and good photography could do for a girl.

Because she was scrutinising her so closely Roisin noticed something that the other onlookers probably didn't. In spite of Michelle's broad, radiant smiles for the camera, she looked uncomfortable and self-conscious. She kept pulling at the front of her dress which was revealing more of her ample cleavage than desired, and smoothing the silky fabric over her full hips. How much prettier Ann-Marie was, Roisin thought, and then reminded herself that her sister was better off without him.

The guests started to stream out of the chapel door and down the steps. Roisin's heartbeat quickened as she half-listened to Colette's critique of the women's outfits. Many wore what were obviously very expensive clothes and jewels.

95

Fleetingly, Roisin thought that these women, groomed to within an inch of their lives, were just the sort of clients she had in mind for her beauty salon.

Suddenly she saw the familiar face that she had been searching for in the crowd. She steeled herself, so that she could control the hate, and squinted in the afternoon sunshine for a better view.

It had been many years since she had seen Donal Mullan but Roisin had no difficulty in recognising him. There he was, clear as day. In essentials he had hardly altered at all — his figure was unchanged, his hair was the same colour, and there was no sign of balding. Only now, moving here amongst the great and the good, he carried himself with an air of authority. He held the edges of his grey suit jacket together with the thumb and forefinger of his left hand — like a politician. The suit, and shirt and tie, were quality. Gold cufflinks shone in the sun and an expensive watch flashed on his wrist.

'There's that Donal Mullan,' said Colette with distate.

'Mmm, I see,' said Roisin, nonchantly, not wanting to expose the true extent of her feelings towards him.

'He looks like the cat that got the cream, doesn't he?' The question was rhetorical and Colette merely paused before adding, 'Do you remember that big house McCormick built out at Killyglen?'

Roisin nodded dumbly.

'It was for them, wasn't it? Lucky bugger

falling on his feet like that. And after what he did to your Ann-Marie . . . ' Colette tutted and her voice trailed off. She shook her head at the injustice of Donal's apparent good fortune.

In spite of Roisin's determined resolution to remain impassive, a deeply held reservoir of hate welled up inside her. She looked away, her face flushed with emotion. If Donal glanced her way he'd be sure to spot her amongst the well-wishers — the spite in her would draw his gaze like a magnet.

'Are you feeling OK, Roisin. You've gone a bit pale?' said Colette, her voice full of concern.

'I'm fine, really. Just a bit hot standing about in this sun, I think,' said Roisin. She waved her hand through the stagnant air. 'Look, Colette, I'd better be going.'

'I'll give you a lift.'

'No,' said Roisin hastily, 'I mean, it's all right. I need to pop in and see Ann-Marie on my way home anyway.'

'OK,' said Colette uneasily. 'But what time shall I call for you tonight?'

'I don't know if I'm going to make it. Look, why don't you go on with the others and I'll catch you later. Where will you be?'

'The Ship Inn, probably.'

Roisin walked quickly away, her arms folded protectively around herself. She couldn't tell Colette how the mere sight of Donal Mullan inflamed such terrible anger and bitterness in her. Of course, at the time it happened, she'd told Colette all about him and what he'd done to her sister — how he'd driven her to despair and attempted suicide. But, like Roisin's mother, Colette didn't understand the extent of Donal's treachery. She seemed to think that Ann-Marie must have been inherently unstable, and that she would have attempted suicide anyway. She acknowledged that Donal dumping her had probably tipped Ann-Marie over the edge but she maintained that he wasn't the cause of her problems.

But she was wrong. And because nobody understood, Roisin simply stopped talking about Donal. Her hatred had become a secret that she shared with no-one, not even Ann-Marie.

* * *

To give Pauline her due, she knew how to organise a bash, thought Noel, as he sat at the head table. He set the dessert fork down on the plate and surveyed, with satisfaction, the scene before him. The air was thick with the sound of chatter and the clink of cutlery against china. The catering staff, wearing black, scurried busily round the tables like worker ants, anticipating every need of his guests. The meal, salmon for starters followed by fillet steak and a choice of two desserts, had been exceptionally good. The champagne and wine were superb, with wine waiters so attentive no one was permitted to reach the bottom of their glass. The tables were laid with the finest china and cutlery to rival any five-star hotel and the views of the valley from the marquee were breathtaking. Noel had had reservations about holding the wedding at home, but Pauline's judgement on such matters had, as usual, been proven right. Even the weather was favourable, with the forecast showers failing to materialise.

Jeanette sat three seats away, separated from him by, firstly, Pauline and then her new husband. Her back was turned to him as she conversed with Joe Doherty in the seat to her right, her arm resting on the table. All he could see was the back of her veil and the brown flesh of the arm that protruded from the sleeve of her dress.

Her hand, so slim and delicate, appeared childlike to Noel in spite of the long polished nails, the tips of which looked like they had been dipped, very carefully, in a pot of white paint. A wedding band, shiny and new, nestled against her diamond engagement ring. The garnet birthstone ring that Noel had given her for her eighteenth birthday, and that had for so long graced her middle finger, was gone. Noel bit his lip. He felt just as he had done six years ago at Michelle's wedding — like a little bit of his heart was being slowly ripped out.

Once the tables were cleared, it was time for the speeches. When Noel stood up to make his, he was surprised to discover that his hands were shaking. In spite of his high profile and business success, Noel rarely addressed large audiences. The sheaf of papers on which he had written his speech fluttered like the wings of a disturbed butterfly. He took a deep breath, made a decision and purposefully turned the papers face down on the table.

'I had a speech all carefully planned and thought out,' he said, and swallowed, 'but instead I find that I want to speak to you from the heart.'

A deathly hush spread over the crowd.

'Today my little girl, Jeanette, is getting married and I find my heart is bursting. With joy,' he paused, 'and with sorrow. I know that Matt will make Jeanette happy and it's clear that they love each other very much. But I want you to know, Jeanette, that no father could love his daughter more than I love you. And your sisters.'

Noel glanced at Jeanette who sat with her head craned up at him like a swan, her eyes brimming with tears. She blinked, and two bright droplets toppled over the rim of her eyes and streaked down her cheeks. She dabbed her face with a white napkin and smiled at him.

'And, while it fills my heart with happiness to see you married, I cannot help but feel sadness at losing my little girl to another man. Never forget that I love you, Jeanette . . . ' he said, his voice almost failing him at the last, 'and that I loved you first.'

The marquee erupted with clapping and Noel had to bend his head while he composed himself. When the noise had died down he felt better able to go on.

'Jeanette could not have made a better choice than Matt,' he said in a stronger voice, meaning every word, 'and I am delighted to welcome him into our family.'

This was greeted with a raucous cheer.

Again Noel waited for the noise to die down, and went on, 'This marriage is the wedding not only of two young people very much in love but the cementing of the relationship between our families, a relationship that goes back many years, and I am delighted to welcome Matt's parents, Joe and Doreen, to our family too. Please join me in a toast to the Dohertys!'

Everyone in the room rose to their feet, raised their glasses, took a sip and sat down again. Noel waited while the shuffling and the scraping of chairs died away.

'Now,' he said, when everyone was seated again, 'I'd like to propose a toast to my lovely wife, Pauline, who is entirely responsible for organising this wonderful event today.'

She bobbed her head slightly, blushing, and then looked up at him, her face radiant with happiness. Their eyes met and, for the briefest of moments, Noel remembered the way things had once been between them. Pauline looked like the young girl he'd loved, and married, all those years ago. She held the smile until it became fixed and unnatural and then she lowered her head and faced into the crowd.

Finally, Noel raised a glass of champagne and his guests joined him in toasting the bride and groom. When he sat down he noticed that his palms were sweating and he was glad the formalities were over.

Later on, when the dancing began, Noel enjoyed catching up with friends and family. The combination of copious amounts of champagne, wine and now whisky had mellowed everyone into sentimentality.

'That was a grand speech you made,' said

Noel's younger brother, Tommy, who'd served in the RAF and now ran a successful garden centre outside Antrim. 'It brought tears to my eyes, so it did.'

The group of men around them nodded solemnly, if not altogether soberly, in agreement.

'I love those girls more than life itself,' replied Noel. 'I'd do anything for them.'

'They're lucky lasses so they are,' said someone else. 'They couldn't have a better father.'

Noel became aware of Donal standing on the fringe of the group. Irritated by his silent looming presence, he ignored him. When the conversation turned to another topic, Noel scanned the room for any guests with whom he had not yet conversed. He was not about to let a little drunkenness deter him from fulfilling his duties as host.

As Noel excused himself from the company and broke free of the group, Donal approached him — rather nervously, Noel thought.

'Noel,' he said, 'how's business these days?'

'What?'

'How's business going? I was wondering if — '

'Donal, son,' said Noel, clamping his hand on his son-in-law's shoulder, 'this isn't the time to be talking about business. My daughter's just got married, man.'

Donal blushed.

Noel released his grip and waved him away with his hand. 'Away with you, get yourself a fill of drink and have a bloody good time,' he said dismissively, and he pushed past Donal, the younger man yielding to his force.

On the dance-floor, Noel held Pauline in his arms and they danced properly, their bodies moving fluidly as one. There wasn't much call for it nowadays but Noel was a better-than-average dancer, and women loved to be led on the dancefloor.

'Did I tell you that you look gorgeous today?' said Noel, regarding his wife's face closely. Give or take a few fine wrinkles she was in great shape.

'No,' said Pauline and she flashed a smile at someone over his shoulder.

'Seriously, you look lovely. I was thinking that — '

'Thank you,' said Pauline coolly, deliberately interrupting him.

'Don't be like that, Pauline,' said Noel. 'I'm trying to pay you a compliment. A sincere one.'

'And I've accepted it graciously. Hi there!' she called out at a group of evening guests, from some charity or other, who had just arrived.

'Will you stop doing that?' he said and felt her stiffen in his arms. 'Oh, Pauline why does it always have to be like this? Can't we be . . . friends?'

'You're asking me that?' said Pauline, her voice sour as turned milk. 'You made your choice a long time ago, Noel. And you didn't choose me.'

Ignoring this he said, 'I'd just like us to be closer, Pauline. Sometimes when I think back to the way we used to be . . . well, I think . . . ' Without finishing the sentence he leaned closer aiming to plant a kiss on her lips.

But before he could, she addressed him in a low, even tone, audible to him alone. 'Get your goddamned hands off me, Noel McCormick. You forfeited your right to touch me a long time ago. And if this wasn't my daughter's wedding, I'd knee you right where it hurts.'

She pulled back from him then and said rather formally, 'Thank you for the dance. Now there are some guests just arrived, Noel, and I must go and welcome them.'

Then she turned sharply and left him swaying uncertainly, her heels clicking like claws on the wooden floor. And for the very first time Noel realised that his wife hated him.

★   ★   ★

Roisin approached the twenty-year-old block of flats, not far from her mother's home, where Ann Marie lived. Her neighbours were mainly elderly, house-proud folk, so, though slightly dated, the building was well maintained. Everyone took turns to sweep the stairs and one old lady took it upon herself to polish the glass in the main entrance door every day. Plants and flowers in cheerful pots welcomed approaching visitors and smaller ones stood on the windowsills on each of the four landings. Outside the door to each flat, the owners had personalised their space with doormats, hanging ornaments and plants.

Ann-Marie had used her father's inheritance to buy the flat outright, against her mother's wishes. Roisin's money still lay in the bank safely invested, waiting for the day when she would need it. And Roisin knew exactly what she was going to do with it.

Not that Mairead had objected to the money being used to buy property. Quite the opposite — she viewed the flat in desirable Drumalis Close as a wise and sensible investment. But, after her first suicide attempt, she feared for Ann-Marie living on her own. Would she try and do it again? What if nobody found her in time?

Ironically, it was Mairead's overbearing concern for her daughter that had forced Ann-Marie out of the family home in the first place. She simply couldn't bear living under Mairead's constant, anxious scrutiny.

Roisin pressed the silver intercom button, listened to the loud buzz for a few seconds, then let go. There was no answer, so she waited a few minutes and tried again. Still no answer. She searched in her handbag, found what she was looking for, and opened the main door with one of two keys on a 'Forever Friends' key-ring, a present from Ann-Marie. The two little brown teddy bears on the fob smiled at her, locked forever in a loving embrace.

As she scaled the two flights of steps to Ann-Marie's flat, she quelled her rising appre-hension by telling herself that Ann-Marie was probably out. Or in the bath. Or listening to loud music. But when she reached the door to number three, there was no sound emanating from within. Roisin didn't bother to knock — she opened the door with her key and went straight in. She registered that the flat was a mess — empty soft-drink cans and crisp packets lay on the floor along with discarded magazines and dirty plates. An overflowing, stinking ashtray on the coffee table made the place smell like the inside of a pub the morning after.

Ignoring these, Roisin quickly searched the compact one-bedroom apartment and found Ann-Marie asleep in bed. She pulled back the curtains with a loud swooshing sound but Ann-Marie did not stir. She shook the sleeping figure gently. Her sister's face was hidden under a veil of brown hair.

'Ann-Marie! It's me. Roisin. What are you doing in bed?'

Ann-Marie rolled onto her back and moaned.

'Are you all right?' said Roisin, pulling the hair off her sister's face so she could see her properly. Her eyes were still shut tight.

'Leave me alone,' came the muffled answer.

'All right. I'll make you a cup of tea,' said Roisin, through gritted teeth. 'Get yourself dressed.'

She made the tea in the untidy kitchen, black because there was no milk, and took it in to her sister. She set it on the bedside table and shook Ann-Marie again. This time she pulled the covers back and dragged her bodily into an upright position. Ann-Marie screwed up her eyes and blinked.

'Here's your tea,' said Roisin, thrusting it into her sister's hands. 'Do you have any idea what time it is? Obviously not. It's five in the afternoon. What on earth are you doing in bed?'

'I was tired,' she said squinting. 'Why are you cross with me?'

'I'm not cross with you,' said Roisin the anger towards Donal Mullan leaching from her, 'I'm just worried seeing you like this.' She picked up the bottle of pills that sat on the bedside table and read the label. 'Diazepam! Why are you taking these?'

'It's what the doctor prescribed,' she replied woozily. 'He thought they might help — I've been having trouble sleeping. I think maybe they're too strong. I don't think they agree with me.'

'I don't think you should be taking these, Ann-Marie. Look, I'll come with you to the doctor's next week and see if there isn't something else he can give you. Something less powerful.'

Ann-Marie's eyes were half-closed, the mug of tea still untouched in her hands.

Roisin prised it gently from her grasp and said, 'Why don't you just sleep it off, then?'

She stood and looked down at Ann-Marie and bit her lip. She couldn't leave her alone in this state — she'd just have to stay a while until the drug wore off. So, with time to kill and fuelled by emotion, she set to with vigour on the rest of the flat.

She opened the curtains, blinds and all the windows and soon discovered that the ashtray had been masking an even more noxious smell. Ann-Marie's cat, Bonnie, which must've been locked in all day, had defecated on the bathroom floor. When she checked the poor animal's litter tray it was full to overflowing. Bonnie looked at Roisin with baleful eyes and she said, sighing,

'It's all right, puss, I'll clean it for you.'

If only Donal Mullan could see what he'd done, thought Roisin, as she donned yellow rubber gloves. If only he could see what he'd turned Ann-Marie into. A dysfunctional woman unable to get through life without drugs, unable to hold down a decent job, incapable even of keeping her home clean. She couldn't even look after a bloody cat properly. As if Bonnie could understand her thoughts, she rubbed her body along the leg of Roisin's jeans and meowed. Roisin began the task of cleaning out the litter tray — she used a blue plastic scoop to transfer the soiled litter into a plastic bag. But then, knowing Donal Mullan would he care? No, he'd used Ann-Marie as a stepping-stone on his path through life and shaken her off as easily as dry sand.

Roisin worked so hard and cleaned the flat so thoroughly that she broke into a sweat. But when the work was done and the place looked and smelled clean and fresh, she sat down, exhausted, not by the physical exertion, but by her struggle with grief and rage.

When Ann-Marie surfaced soon after, Roisin made her have a shower while she went down to the corner shop for food, then made her sister something to eat. Afterwards she sat with her as she watched TV, her face blank and motionless as stone.

And then that awful sorrow that she felt so often in the company of Ann-Marie crept over Roisin, a feeling much worse than anger or bitterness. At least with those emotions you felt strong and mad, you felt like you could do something. Sorrow just sapped your energy and made you feel that everything was pointless.

Ann-Marie was thirty-two years old and her life was over before it had begun. She should've been living a life like other women her age. Married with kids or a great career, or both. She'd never even finished the university course that she loved. And here she was on a Saturday night in June, sitting in front of sitcoms and game shows on TV, dressed in an old pair of jogging pants and top. And the sad part was that she was quite happy to do so.

God forgive me, thought Roisin, but Donal Mullan had a lot to answer for, if not in this life, then the next.

4

1998

'Molly! For goodness sake, will you just eat your breakfast and stop throwing it around,' said Michelle in a strained voice, as she knelt down and mopped milk off the floor with a cloth. Molly happily drummed her heels on the back of Michelle's head as she scrabbled around on the floor beneath her highchair.

The kitchen, which was large and rectangle in shape, was fitted at one end with pale-cream units topped with black marble. In the middle of this arrangement stood an island unit and, at the other end of the room, a big weathered oak kitchen table. Michelle walked over to the window and threw the saturated cloth into the sink. Then she counted silently to ten and walked back across the tiled floor to the table.

Sensing her mother's anger, the ten-month-old baby let out a howl of protest and threw a piece of buttered toast in the air. It skimmed the surface of the table, skidded off and landed, buttered side down, on the padded seat cushion next to Donal. He peeled it off and examined the greasy smudge left behind.

'Oh, will you look at that!' said Michelle sharply, the rage bubbling up inside her. 'Christ! As if I've nothing better to do all day than clean up one mess after another. That stain will never come out.'

Molly started to cry.

'Come on, Michelle,' intervened Donal, 'will you calm down? She's only a baby. She doesn't understand.'

He lifted the child out of the highchair and nursed her in his arms. She stopped crying immediately, snuggled against his chest and chewed on a soggy piece of toast. Secure in her father's arms, she eyed her mother reproachfully.

'She understands more than you think,' said Michelle, defending herself but already feeling ashamed of her behaviour.

Donal held the baby-cup full of milk up to Molly's lips. She guzzled happily on the spout and paused to give him a milky smile.

'There's always going to be mess with kids around. Cleaning up after them is part of the job. Look, if you really don't want to be at home all day you could always go back to work.'

'You know I don't want to do that,' said Michelle sulkily.

'It's not as if you're with her all the time anyway,' continued Donal. 'She's in that nursery half the time. I know it's hard work looking after a baby but you can't deny that there's an up-side too.'

'I know,' said Michelle grudgingly.

'How would you like to swap places with me, Michelle? I hardly see my own daughter.'

Instantly Michelle felt like a whinging moan. Much as Molly got on her nerves sometimes, she wouldn't have given up the chance to stay at home and raise her for anything. Poor Donal hardly saw her, sometimes for days on end. By the time he got home from work she was often fast asleep. The first thing he did as soon as he got through the door at night was rush up to see her, asleep or not. If she were awake, he'd lie down on the floor beside her cot and hold her little hand through the bars until she drifted off to sleep. Sometimes he'd fall asleep too and Michelle would find him there on the floor snoring away.

'Here, give her to me,' she said. 'You'll get your shirt and tie all dirty.' She kissed Molly on the nose and settled her on her lap. 'I'm sorry, pet,' she said to her. 'But you just have no idea what it's like, Don. I don't get a minute's peace when she's around. Sometimes she drives me mad. And you've never around to help.'

'I can't help that,' said Donal, sweeping the crumbs off the table with a cupped hand into the palm of the other. He dropped the crumbs into a used bowl.

'You seem to be doing a lot of late nights these days,' observed Michelle. She took a sip of coffee from the white mug on the table and ticked off a mental checklist of the things she had to do today.

'That's corporate life for you, Michelle. If it's not working late on some deal, it's entertaining customers. It's the same for everybody these days. I don't know what happened to the life of leisure we were all promised for the nineties. As far as I can see, everybody's on a hamster wheel and it's going faster and faster.'

'Poor you,' said Michelle and she got up and tousled Donal's hair. A little shiver of love went down her spine.

'Hey, you're going to wreck my hair,' he said, only half-joking, and Michelle laughed.

'You're worse than a woman sometimes,' she said teasing, as he patted down the section of hair she'd ruffled. 'Anyway, shouldn't you be going?'

'In a minute. I can go in a bit late for once. There's something I want to talk you about first. I didn't get a chance last night because of that Institute dinner.'

'Give me a minute, would you? I need to change this nappy first.'

When she returned, Michelle put Molly down on the floor and extracted a few toys from the toy box in the corner.

Donal said, 'I've been thinking, Shell, about the job and the hours I'm working. I hardly see anything of Molly. And I'm not really enjoying the work anyway.'

Fearing where Donal was going with this, Michelle said, 'Well, as you say, everyone's in the same boat. It'll pass and things will quieten down again.'

'It's more than that though. You know how much I'd love to work for McCormick Limited. I'm fed up waiting for your father to give me a job. He said it would stand me in good stead to get a grounding in finance. Well, I've done that — I'm nearly thirty-five. I've been patient for six years — I can't wait any longer. I've decided I'm going to ask him outright.'

Michelle listened with as dispassionate an expression as she could muster. 'Ask him outright,' she repeated, buying herself time to think. He must, under no circumstances, be allowed to do this.

'That's right. What do you think?'

'I think,' she said slowly, 'that Dad doesn't like mixing business and family.'

'That's nonsense! The business *is* family. And what about Matt Doherty?'

'Well, he's a trained architect.'

What she really wanted to say but couldn't, because it would wound Donal too deeply, was that Noel was grooming Matt as his successor. There just wasn't room for another son-in-law in the business.

'What's that got to do with anything?' said Donal, sounding like a spoilt child. 'He's not designing houses now, is he? He's head of the machinery hire division.'

Molly whacked Michelle on the legs with a rattle, providing a welcome distraction.

'Careful darling,' she said. 'Oh, look at that nose!'

She pulled a tissue from the box on the table and wiped Molly's nose. Foremost in her mind was a conversation she'd had with her father when she was in the early stages of pregnancy with Molly. It was a memory so painful to Michelle that she'd pushed it to the back of her mind and rarely brought it out for close examination.

But her father's words were as clear to her now as they had been that wet afternoon in May.

114

She'd called at his office, late on a Friday afternoon, not long after the Sunday lunch where Jeanette had first introduced Matt to the family. On Don's behalf, she'd asked her father to give him a job. His response had horrified her.

'Give him a job? You must be joking! Just like him to send his wife to do the asking for him. You know your mother and I didn't approve of your marrying Donal Mullan. We never thought he was good enough. But we made the best of it. Put on a brave face for your sake because you had your heart set on him and you were too headstrong to be persuaded otherwise. Well, you got what you wanted, Michelle. But if you think I've any intention of involving the likes of him in my business, you've got another thing coming. Not in a million years. You knew what you were doing when you married him.'

Sharing any of that conversation with Donal was completely out of the question. She had been deeply hurt — Donal would be devastated.

'Look, Donal, I can't talk any more right now. I have to get Molly to nursery or I'll be late for my beauty treatments. I need to be in Ballymena for half nine.'

She put Molly's coat on her, and carried her out the back door and through the early-autumn chill towards the waiting Range Rover. The first yellow leaves skittered in circles round the U-shaped enclosure created by the house and the adjoining hedge.

'It's ridiculous you going all that way to get your nails done,' said Donal, following her outside.

'Nails and toes and St Tropez tan. I only go once a week and, anyway, do you want me to end up looking like the women round Ballyfergus? By the state of them, I'd say half of them haven't looked in a mirror in years. I hear someone's supposed to be opening a new salon in Ballyfergus though. Can't come fast enough.'

She opened the back door of the car and strapped Molly into the car seat. Then she walked round to the driver's side, where Donal was standing a few feet from the car. In her one-inch-heeled boots they were of equal height. She reached into the car, took out her Versace sunglasses, and paused before putting them on.

'What we were talking about before,' she said.

Donal nodded.

'Promise me you won't do anything rash. Let's talk about it some more over the weekend. OK?' Donal shrugged his shoulders, which she took to mean assent. She put on her sunglasses, kissed him on the lips and said, 'You know I love you.'

'I love you too.'

Donal went round to Molly's side of the car, spoke with her for a few seconds and kissed her goodbye.

'Bye, hon!' shouted Michelle through the open car window, as the wheels of the big car crunched over the gravel. 'And cheer up. It's Friday!'

Michelle's smile faded as soon as she was out of sight of Donal. She'd have to put her thinking cap on if she were to succeed in dissuading him from approaching her father. Why couldn't he just be happy with things the way they were?

Donal watched, hands in pocket, as a shower of gravel flew up from the wheels of the Range Rover and it disappeared down the one-lane drive that led to the main road.

Matt Doherty. Everyone liked him — he was personable, smart, confident, good crack. And how Donal hated his guts!

Was it because of Matt that he wanted this so much? He only knew that he yearned for acceptance and acknowledgement from the McCormicks because he always felt inferior around them. Whether they intended to make him feel inadequate, he never quite knew. Michelle said he imagined things — the slights, the subtle put-downs — but he wasn't so sure.

And deep down he felt that he hadn't got his just reward for marrying Michelle. If he'd married her purely because he loved her, he'd be made up. He had a great house, a beautiful daughter, a reasonably well-paid job, wonderful holidays, and a smart car to drive. What more could any sane man want? But that was the nature of want, wasn't it? Once a desire was satisfied, it was human nature to seek out another one. Was anyone ever truly satisfied?

He kicked the gravel with the toe of his black brogue, checked the time by his watch and went inside. He collected his jacket and briefcase, and left the house. There was no need to lock the door as Joan, the daily help, had just arrived. He waved to her and got in his car.

The first thing he did once he'd joined the

main road was switch off his mobile. The hour-long drive to work would give him plenty of time to think. Michelle's attitude puzzled him. They might disagree on minor issues but on big-picture topics she was always very support-ive, deferring to his judgement and experience.

Maybe she had some hang-up about him working with her father. Maybe McCormick Limited had taken over her life as a child. Perhaps she didn't want to be reliant on the family business. But why? Nothing was guaran-teed in corporate life — he could lose his job tomorrow. And surely, working for McCormick Limited he'd have more job security? Noel would hardly sack his son-in-law. No, he thought, dismissing Michelle's reticence, she had nothing to fear; it would be the best move he could make. And Noel wasn't a mind-reader — if Donal didn't make it clear what he wanted, how was he ever going to get it? He decided there and then to surprise Michelle. He'd go and see her father today. Get the business over and done with and deliver the good news to her tonight.

With the decision made, Donal was impatient to see Noel. Should he phone his secretary and make an appointment? No, that was too formal, too business-like. He wanted to keep this low-key, friendly — he didn't want to look desperate. A more casual approach was called for. It would be better if he simply dropped by on his way home from work — he was family after all. OK, McCormick Limited offices weren't exactly on his way home, but near enough. Of course, Noel might be out on business or left the office early for a game of golf, but he'd just have to take that chance. He put his foot on the accelerator and pulled into the outside lane as the car made the sweeping descent into Belfast City on the M2.

As the day progressed, Donal became increasingly anxious about the forthcoming visit to Noel. It would be the most important interview of his career to date. If he played his cards right it could lead to a place on the board, shares in the company — he might even become Managing Director one day. And then his current bosses would be bowing and scraping to him.

He found it difficult to concentrate on the lending reports he had to write and the customer calls he had to make. The day passed slowly and with very little achieved. At three thirty in the afternoon he locked his desk and shoved the unfinished reports into his hand-tooled Italian leather briefcase, a present from Michelle.

'You're off early,' said Mary. 'Playing golf?'

'Chance would be a fine thing. But I don't get off that easily,' he said defensively, lifting the briefcase up and showing it to Mary, a dead weight in his arms. Part of the corporate game was to convince everyone that you were working harder and longer hours than everyone else. It wouldn't do to admit to skiving off early.

'I've a pile of reports in here to do over the weekend,' he continued, 'but I want to see Molly before she's asleep. For a change.'

'Well, you have a nice weekend,' said Mary,

pleasantly. 'Anything planned?'

'An engagement party on Saturday night — some old school-friend of Michelle's — and golf on Sunday morning. And you?'

'Oh the usual, all the family'll visit at some point over the weekend. I'll see you Monday morning then, bright-eyed and bushy-tailed as always.'

'Have a good one, Mary.'

He would miss Mary when he was gone. And the camaraderie amongst the men. But that was all. Where he was headed for, he wouldn't be looking back.

It was late afternoon when he pulled into the carpark at McCormick Limited headquarters just outside Ballyfergus. When he removed his hands from the leather steering wheel, they were damp with sweat. He wiped them on his trouser legs and checked his face in the driver's visor mirror. His skin was shiny with grease, or was it sweat? He couldn't tell. Why was he so nervous all of a sudden?

He rummaged in the glove-compartment until he found a box of facial wipes Michelle had bought him for Christmas last year. He'd called them 'poncy' at the time, and laughed at the notion of ever using them. But today called for drastic action.

He cleaned his face and hands, combed his hair and sat with the car door open for several minutes, to let the cool air circulate. Then he felt in control again.

He took several deep breaths as he approached the glass and steel building, rehearsing in his mind, as he had done all day, what he would say to Noel and what his likely response might be. Naturally he'd have some reservations, given Donal's chequered history with the bank, but everyone deserved a second chance. He was family after all.

And then, just as he opened the door to the building, Matt came through it, sharply dressed in a black suit and carrying a briefcase.

'Donal! What a surprise,' said Matt, with his salesman's grin, clearly surprised to see Donal acting as McCormick's unpaid doorman.

'Hi, Matt. Good to see you,' said Donal and he shook his rival's hand.

'So,' said Matt, still standing in the doorway, 'what brings you to these parts?'

'I was just passing . . . ' he began and then, realising how lame that sounded, changed tack, 'I have some business here.'

'Business here?' repeated Matt, making it sound like a question.

'With Noel,' said Donal and he could have kicked himself. He was giving too much away. None of it had anything to do with Matt Doherty. No, that wasn't true — it had everything to do with him.

Just then, to Donal's relief, three women who looked like cleaners tried to exit through the door and Matt was forced to move out of their way. The women threw friendly greetings at Matt and he exchanged banter with them as though he'd been here for two decades not two minutes.

'Look, I'll let you get on,' said Donal. 'Catch you later.'

And before Matt could engage him in further conversation, Donal slipped inside the building. He paused to compose himself once again, the encounter with Matt having unnerved him, then pressed the button for the lift.

Silently the escalator made its way to the third floor where Michelle had told him Noel had his office. It wasn't hard to find. He simply followed the corridor to the end and there was Noel, behind a glass wall, talking on the phone. He hadn't seen Donal approach. Donal stood still, unsure what to do next, certain that the beat of his heart was audible — it was to him anyway.

'Can I help you?' said a voice to his left and he jumped. A navy-suited, middle-aged woman with sallow skin and auburn hair sat behind a desk in a recess. He hadn't noticed her on his approach as his entire attention was fixed on Noel.

'I'd like to have a word with Mr McCormick if I may.'

'I'm sorry, I didn't catch your name? Do you have an appointment?' said the woman who was obviously Noel's secretary. Pointedly she ran the nib of her pen down a column in a large diary that sat on her desk, peering at the entries through her bifocals. Then she rose from her seat.

Clearly this lady was one of a breed of proprietorial secretaries who defended access to their boss like a lioness protecting her young. She'd come round to the front of the desk now, a fixed smile on her face. He wondered what she intended to do next. Strong-arm him out of the office?

'My name is Donal Mullan. And no, I don't have an appointment.'

She stopped, startled, and waited for him to continue. Obviously it was heresy to expect to see Mr McCormick without prior arrangement. Perhaps he'd made a mistake in dropping by like this. But it was too late now to retreat. So he ploughed on.

'I'm Noel's son-in-law. I just dropped by . . . '

'Is everything all right out here, Ann?' interrupted Noel's voice and Donal swivelled round to meet his eyes.

'Donal. What a — a surprise. It's all right, Ann. Come on in,' he said, indicating for Donal to follow him.

Donal flashed a small but triumphant smile in Ann's direction and followed Noel into his office. It was almost as though Noel had been expecting the visit. Had Michelle forewarned him? Once inside, Noel shut the door behind Donal and, strangely, closed the steel-coloured blinds, shutting out Ann's inquisitive gaze.

'Have a seat,' said Noel, and went and sat behind his large oak desk.

This left Donal with no option but to sit across from Noel, the desk a barrier between them. Donal glanced longingly at the low black leather chairs arranged around the glass-topped coffee table, a much more suitable venue for the type of chat he had in mind.

'So,' said Noel. 'What can I do for you?'

If he hadn't known Noel better, Donal would have guessed he was nervous. He was hunched over the desk with a deadly serious expression on his face. He fiddled with a black Mont Blanc pen until the lid, with its distinctive snow-cap logo on the end, popped off and landed at Donal's feet. He picked it up and placed it on the desk. Then he cleared his throat.

'Well, I was wondering if there might be well . . . you know . . . an opportunity for me within the business. As you know I have a sound grounding in finance and I really feel that I have something to offer McCormick Limited.'

Noel seemed to relax then, his tensed shoulders visibly lowering inside his tailored grey suit jacket. That was a good sign. He sat back in the chair, and threw the pen onto the blotting pad in front of him. 'What exactly did you have in mind?'

'I was thinking about finance maybe to start with. I'm not sure exactly,' he said feebly, 'but you would have a better idea where my skills would be most useful. And I'm a fast learner — I'd be keen to understand all aspects of the business.'

'It's difficult just now, Donal. I've got some great guys on the finance side and the way things are going I can't see any vacancies coming up in the near future.'

'But there must be something.'

'I'm sorry, Donal. With the economy the way it is, it's not a time for expanding the business.' Noel folded his arms across his chest.

This wasn't going as smoothly as Donal had hoped. Still, he didn't expect Noel to be a pushover. He was probably testing his mettle to see how serious he was. He decided to try a different tack.

'Well, aren't there any opportunities in other areas, apart from finance?'

'I don't think so, Donal, I really don't.' Noel paused, as though turning something over in his mind, and picked up the pen again. 'You haven't exactly got an unblemished record, you know. You took your eye off the ball with that Semple case, Donal. It cost the bank, and me, dearly.'

'What do you mean it cost you dearly?'

'I had to call in quite a few favours to keep you your job,' said Noel sharply, confirming what Donal had always suspected. 'You must've known that?'

'Yes,' he replied sheepishly, the memory of that unfortunate episode still smarting, 'I guessed as much. And believe me, Noel, I'm grateful to you. But,' he added hastily, 'anyone can make a mistake, can't they? And everyone deserves a second chance.'

Noel sat on, immobile and silent.

'Surely,' Donal went on, 'there must be an opening? I've waited six years.'

Suddenly Noel's face became animated, his brow furrowed in confusion or anger. 'What do you mean, 'waited'? Waited for what? Surely you didn't think — '

'I'm smart, Noel, and I can learn quickly,' interrupted Donal. 'I wouldn't let you down.'

'I've told you that I can't offer you anything. Haven't I made myself clear?' said Noel, and he stabbed the point of the pen in the blotting pad.

'But I'm family . . . '

'You're not family,' snapped Noel, 'you're married to one of my daughters, that's all.'

'So is Matt,' said Donal and immediately regretted it.

'What's Matt got to do with anything?'

'Well, he was only out of college two minutes and you gave him a job. You've never given me the same opportunity.'

'I gave him a job because he's a qualified architect. You're a banker, Donal. What use would you be in a building company?' said Noel, his words stabbing Donal like darts. Noel stood up then, his mouth set in a thin, hard line and walked purposefully towards the door. 'Look, Donal, don't embarrass yourself any further. The answer's no.'

Noel pulled the door handle so hard that the door shuddered in its frame, then held it open for Donal to pass.

Donal got up and walked over to the door. 'Why are you so ... so angry with me?' he asked, partly afraid of, and partly mesmerised by, Noel's wrath. He'd never seen his father-in-law like this before.

'Because I've better things to do all day than sit listening to your whinging,' he growled. 'And I don't have to explain my business decisions to you or anybody else. You just don't know when to give it a rest, do you?'

'What do you mean?'

'Look what I've done for you and Michelle. I build you a dream home. I practically bankroll you. And yet you've the nerve to come in here, badgering me for a job as though it's your

God-given right. You don't even realise when you're well off, do you? My daughter pulled you out of the gutter you came from and you're not even grateful. You still want more.'

'Oh, the truth comes out at last,' said Donal, squaring up to his father-in-law, the anger stinging his eyes like sparks. 'So that's why you can't stand me!'

'I don't know what you mean,' said Noel evenly, but the muscle in the corner of his left eye twitched, belying his composure.

'Oh yes you do. You think that I'm not good enough for your daughter, for the great McCormicks. I saw you at Molly's christening. I saw the way you patronised my family. I saw you give Pauline the 'cut it dead' sign, telling her to get rid of them.' He pulled his finger across his throat just the way he'd seen Noel do the day of the christening. 'You wouldn't treat the Dohertys like that, would you?'

'The Dohertys are old family friends.'

'Well, that's very convenient, isn't it Noel? It gives you the excuse to treat them like royalty and my family like shit.'

'I have nothing more to say to you. And for the avoidance of doubt in future, you, Donal, are no Matt Doherty. Goodbye.'

The anger began to leach from Donal as quickly as it had flared up. There was nothing for him to do but walk out of the room, which he did with as much dignity as he could muster. He heard the door slam shut behind him.

He walked past the secretary, but this time she didn't look up. She sat with her head buried in some papers, pretending she hadn't heard the exchange between the two men. When he was sure he was out of her sight, Donal ran down the flight of stairs beside the lift and burst through the glass door into the open air. Head down, he headed straight for the car, opened the door and got in. He was shaking. His head was swimming. He waited for the nausea to pass.

He'd endured humiliation before. At school, he'd been the last one picked for the football team. In primary school he'd once wet himself and had to be sent home. During his marriage to Michelle he'd been embarrassed on many occasions by her family and friends, due to his ignorance or lack of taste. But nothing had ever come close to the utter mortification he felt now.

He saw things clearly now. Noel McCormick hated his guts — always had done and always would. He and Pauline loathed him because of who he was — the sixth child of an uneducated factory worker from West Belfast. Nothing he could do would redeem him in their eyes. He simply could not make the grade, not now, not ever.

There was absolutely no prospect of a job with McCormick Limited. Noel would rather cut his own throat. Donal was stuck with his dead-end job and his dead-end life. Going nowhere.

Michelle must've known what her father thought of him all along. Why else was she so cagey about him asking her father for a job? Why else did she ask Donal not to do anything rash? Let's chat about it over the weekend, she'd said, no doubt hoping to talk him out of his plan. If only he'd listened to her. Or listened to that nagging, inner voice that had warned him not to do it. He would have saved himself this crushing shame. How could he face Noel or Pauline again with any self-respect?

★ ★ ★

Roisin walked slowly up to the door of Sadie's hair salon and stopped a few feet short of the door, hesitating. A battered 'For Sale' sign hung limply from one nail, threatening to fall down on the head of a passer-by at any minute. Not that many people passing the shop that wet afternoon gave it a second look. The last year and a half had seen a subtle but relentless deterioration in the premises. The coloured blinds had faded to pastel blue, pink and yellow, the big picture window was smeared with grime, and the red paint on the door was peeling off in little flakes, like dry skin.

She told herself not to be nervous — it was only a business transaction and she wasn't doing anything wrong or underhand. She'd offer Sadie the asking price, which was probably more than the shop was worth. Nowhere else had come up for sale that fitted her criteria so well. She wanted somewhere dilapidated that she could completely refit, inside and out. And the location of Sadie's shop was hard to beat.

Still, this meant a lot to Roisin and it was impossible not to be emotional about it. Owning her own beauty salon was what she'd worked for, planned for, dreamt about, for the last decade.

Since leaving school at the age of sixteen, she'd been obsessed by it. With single-minded determination she'd slogged away at those evening classes to gain the knowledge that would enable her to make her dream come true. At twenty-seven she knew she was short on experience but it was now or never. This was her chance and she must grab it.

Roisin swallowed, pushed open the door and went inside. The smoky salon was empty of customers — she had timed her visit with care. The little bell above the door rang out, announcing her arrival, and Sadie came shuffling through from the back of the shop, her hacking cough preceding her.

'Hello, love,' she said, as soon as she could catch her breath. 'What a lovely surprise. I was just about to lock up.'

'It's great to see you, Sadie,' said Roisin, hiding her shock at Sadie's appearance with a big warm smile.

In the space of a couple of months since Roisin had last seen her, Sadie had aged by years. Always thin, she must have weighed little over eight stone and her eyes were surrounded by dark shadows. Her skin had the slack, grey tone of a smoker and was prematurely lined and wrinkled.

'How are you?' asked Roisin.

'I feel like shit,' said Sadie and she coughed for some time, before she could speak again. 'I've only myself to blame,' she said, holding up a lighted cigarette, 'The doctor warned me that these would be the death of me.'

Sadie looked so bad that Roisin thought she might have cancer. And if she didn't have it now that was probably what would get her in the end. She fought back a wave of sadness that threatened to reduce her to tears.

'So what's actually wrong with you, Sadie? That cough, I mean.'

'Bronchitis. I've been on all sorts of antibiotics and they can't seem to shift it.'

'And you're still smoking?' said Roisin, unable to hide her amazement.

'Oh, don't you start,' replied Sadie good-naturedly. 'I get enough of that from Dr Crory. You can't teach an old dog like me new tricks.' She cleared the phlegm from her throat and then continued, 'Anyway, how's life with you? Any men on the go?'

'Oh, Sadie,' laughed Roisin, 'there's more to life than getting a man.'

'So you're not seeing anyone then?'

'No, not at the moment. But that's beside the point. Is that why you're selling up then? Because of the bronchitis.'

'Partly. I'm fifty-nine this November, Roisin, and getting a bit old for this game. I would have retired next year anyway in the natural course of things.'

'Lots of people will be sorry to see you go. Me included. I used to love working here. It brings back lots of happy memories.'

'Oh, love, that's nice of you to say so. But I won't look back. I've enjoyed having this place but it's time for me to move on. I want to see more of David's wee boys. I'm always working and they're growing up so fast. They won't want to have anything to do with their aul Granny in a few years' time.'

Roisin hoped that Sadie was around long enough to enjoy her grandchildren. She bit her lip to stop herself getting emotional.

'Here, come on through and I'll make you a cuppa,' said Sadie.

It wasn't until she was installed in the staffroom with a cup of tea, and they had pretty much exhausted all the local gossip, that Roisin felt able to raise the matter she'd come to discuss.

'Have you had any offers for the place?' she asked.

'Not a sausage. It's on the market as a going concern but I know I've let things get a bit rundown. Nobody's interested in it, not with Billy Jean's opened up down the road.'

Billy Jean's was a trendy new hairdresser's staffed by thin stylists clothed from head to toe in black. It was so popular you could hardly get an appointment.

'I'll be lucky to get an offer for the leasehold premises.'

'Sadie, I've been thinking . . . '

'What, love? More tea?'

Roisin shook her head and went on, 'I've taken all the night classes I can and I've got enough work experience now. At least I think I have. And I have the money. I really think I can make a go of it.'

'Roisin, love, make a go of what? What are you talking about?'

Roisin took a deep breath and plunged on. 'The shop, Sadie. I'd like to buy the shop from you. I want to turn it into a beauty salon. I'll give you a fair price — I don't want you to think that I'm looking for any favours. What do you think?'

'You want to buy this old place?' said Sadie and she let out a raucous laugh, 'I never would have thought. Roisin Shaw, you're some girl, so you are!'

'I'm sure I can make a go of it,' said Roisin, not sure that Sadie entirely approved.

'Oh, I know you can. And I think it's wonderful. I'd rather sell to you than anyone else. But you're going to need a fortune to do this place up.'

Roisin blushed then, for the first thing she intended to do was rip out the entire interior and throw out all of Sadie's old junk. And she didn't want to offend her old friend. 'Well, I was thinking of a modern, minimalist look.'

'I know the sort of thing you mean. White walls and wooden floors and leather sofas. Oh, don't look so surprised. I'm not totally out of touch, you know.' She pointed at a glossy trade magazine lying on the small table. On the front was a photograph of a salon much along the lines of what Roisin envisaged. 'I've plenty of time to read these magazines. Not as many customers these days as I used to have.'

'You wouldn't mind then, if I changed it all?'

'Once it's yours, you can do what you like, love. And with my blessing. But, if you don't mind me asking, where'll you get the money from?'

'Mum set aside Dad's insurance money for Ann-Marie and me.'

'Of course, I'd forgotten.'

'I haven't touched mine yet — you know Ann-Marie bought the flat with hers?'

Sadie nodded.

'With living at home I've managed to save quite a bit over the years and I've applied for a DTI business start-up loan. That should cover everything. I've done all the sums.'

'I'm sure you have,' said Sadie, regarding Roisin with pride. She eased herself out of the chair and continued, 'Well, as you're going to become the new owner, I suppose I should show you around.'

'There's really no need,' said Roisin. Hadn't she dreamed about every nook and cranny in the place and how she would transform it?

'You need to make sure you know what you're getting for your money, love. Rule number one in business — never buy anything without seeing it first. Come on.'

They completed a brief tour of the former butcher's premises, the numerous rooms at the back once used for the butchering and storing of meat and the preparation of pies and sausages. Now they were filled with dusty bits of ancient equipment, half-empty boxes of hair products and broken chairs.

'And what will you call it?' said Sadie, when they stood again in the main salon.

'I'd like to use my own name but I thought Roisin was a bit too Catholic for some people in Ballyfergus.'

Sadie nodded her head slightly to indicate that she understood.

'So I thought I'd call myself Roz and the salon will be 'Beauty by Roz'. What do you think?'

'I like it! I think it's going to be a huge success. I'm so excited for you.' Sadie threw her arms around her young friend and hugged her. 'I wish you all the luck in the world, Roisin. Now, if you ever need my help you let me know. I may not be able to learn new tricks, but I have one or two old ones worth knowing.'

'Thank you for being so understanding, Sadie. You've no idea what this means to me.'

'Oh, I think I do, love, I think I do.' She walked Roisin to the door and squeezed her arm. 'Wait 'til my Derek hears that wee Roisin Shaw's buying the salon. He'll be tickled pink!'

Outside in the street Roisin punched the air with her fist, held her face up to the rain and laughed. People in the street gave her peculiar looks before carrying on with their business.

In a matter of weeks the shop would be hers. Once her and Sadie's solicitors had sorted out the details she would be well on the way to seeing her dream come true.

★ ★ ★

Noel drove the short distance home from the office effing and blinding all the way, the opulent luxury of the Bentley failing, for once, to lull him into a state of relaxation. Damn that Donal Mullan! He'd had a hellish day and Donal's

135

untimely visit to the office had been the final nail in the coffin.

'Damn!' he said out loud and hit the wood and leather steering wheel with the heels of his palms.

He hadn't meant to be so blunt but Donal had pushed him to the limit — he had a nasty habit of getting under your skin. At first, when he saw him standing there in reception, he thought that he'd been rumbled. He thought that Donal had come to confront him about Grainne. But once it was clear that his visit concerned other matters, it didn't make it any less distasteful. In fact, once the fear of discovery had passed, all he'd felt was irritation. Imagine Donal Mullan walking in and practically demanding a job with McCormick Limited! It was bad enough seeing Donal on family occasions — imagine having to see him every day!

The poor bastard. Noel had once admired his ambition — if truth be told, part of him still did. Like Donal, Noel's father had been a man of little education with extraordinary ambition. Maybe, unfairly, that was why he disliked Donal so much — he reminded Noel of his working-class roots, only one generation removed.

By all accounts Donal had had a pretty rough upbringing and, by rights, he should have had limited expectations. But his background never stopped him from seeking ways to better himself. And Noel was convinced that one of the methods he had used was marriage to his daughter. Wasn't today's interview evidence of it? He had a bloody cheek though. After all the things Noel had done for him and Michelle!

Why oh why had his silly daughter fallen for him? Noel remembered the day of her wedding with the distaste he'd come to associate with all things to do with Donal.

The only positive outcome of the whole dreadful day was meeting Grainne. He'd been strongly attracted to her as soon as he set eyes on her in the chapel. He guessed she was one of Donal's sisters because she sat in the same pew as his parents. She wore a severe dark-coloured suit, the top of her ample bosom protruding from the pale pink chiffon blouse underneath. She had the curvaceous, solid body of a sex goddess — strong, shapely legs encased in fine black nylon, killer black heels on her feet. When he finally met her at the line-up at the hotel, he inspected the fingers of her left hand, which clutched a beaded bag — there was no wedding band on her ring finger. The tips of her fingers were painted hot pink. Then, whilst rehearsing the usual welcome courtesies, he looked into her eyes. She held his gaze steadily, her face expressionless, until he had to look away. Everything about her exuded raw sexuality and Noel knew he had to have her.

Immediately after the altercation between Grainne's sisters, everyone was distracted and Noel approached her. With little time to make his move, he knew he would have to be audacious. If she weren't receptive to the idea, fair enough — embarrassment would prevent her from drawing attention to them. And if she told anyone about it later, why, he'd just deny it like he'd done in the past with other women.

'Well?' said Grainne, raising her green eyes to him from beneath the small hat perched on her head. She tilted her head back slightly and blew a trail of grey smoke through her shiny pink lips towards the ceiling.

He stood beside her and watched while Donal's brother and father remonstrated with the two angry sisters.

'I was wondering, Grainne,' he said quietly, 'if you'd like to come out with me some time.'

'I might,' she said without hesitation, mirroring his low tone.

'Here, take this,' he said, and pressed a business card into her palm. 'You can contact me on my mobile any time.'

She put the cigarette between her teeth temporarily while she slipped the card into her purse without so much as looking at it.

'You're not . . . surprised?' he asked.

She removed the cigarette from her mouth. 'Mr McCormick, your reputation precedes you,' she replied icily and walked away, her hips swaying rhythmically.

After that he knew it was a sure thing. She phoned him the very next week and he took her out to dinner where she astounded him by her forthrightness.

'So, what do you want from me?' she asked, once the dessert plates had been cleared away and coffee served.

'Company,' he said. 'Someone to enjoy life with.'

'And you can't do that with your wife?'

'My wife has nothing to do with this. With us,' he replied coolly.

'Fair enough. Do you want me to be your mistress?'

'Yes.'

'Then these are the terms. I think we should meet a few more times like this. Let's find out if we're . . . how shall I put it . . . compatible. Yes, compatible. If it works out, then I'll expect you to take care of me.'

'OK.'

'Come to my flat on Friday night. Here's my address and phone number.' She scribbled the details in a little notebook, ripped off the page and handed it to Noel. 'You won't be disappointed,' she said, stood up abruptly and left the restaurant.

And that was how it had started. At the time he was having unfulfilling sex with a temp who was covering for Ann while she was on extended leave visiting her sick brother in Australia. The girl was young and inexperienced with the lithe, hard body of a greyhound. She was willing to trade sex for a few little niceties that Noel flung her way. But Noel knew the relationship had no future. He needed a woman not a girl. So the young secretary was dispatched with little trouble, her protestations hushed by a minor dent in his bank balance.

A car pulled out in front of Noel and he had to brake hard to avoid hitting it.

'Jesus Christ,' he muttered to himself and

flashed his lights as the car in front accelerated into the gloom.

Noel shook his head. No, Donal had it coming to him. He was a social-climbing little git and he needed to be put in his place. But he was disappointed in the way he'd handled the interview this afternoon. For years, he had been careful to hide his dislike of Donal and he was annoyed with himself for letting his guard slip. He liked to play his cards close to his chest, and letting people know that you hated them was never a good idea. He was quite sure that he would've handled it differently if he hadn't had that visit from the police. Now that had really spooked him.

Earlier, two plainclothes RUC officers had called at the office, exciting Ann's curiosity. If she weren't so damn efficient at her job, he'd have sacked her years ago for her sheer bloody nosiness. Sometimes, though, it came in useful and he could always count on her discretion, a quality Noel valued highly.

The men had asked probing, and uncomfortable, questions about McCormick Limited's vetting procedures for workmen on Army and RUC sites. Someone must have tipped them off. For Noel received immunity from terrorist attacks in exchange for permitting spies to masquerade as bona fide workmen. Much of the public at large thought that the country was well on the way to peace but there were still some rogue elements out there determined to cause trouble. A group had approached him with their 'request' presented in such a manner that made it clear his co-operation was expected. These were people that you simply did not say no to.

As Noel saw it, he was only protecting his interests, his workers and their families. For the contracts had been won and the work had to go on regardless. And he didn't think anything would come of it anyway. The supposed terrorists were a bunch of lunatics — he doubted if they would be capable of mounting an attack on a sweetie shop, never mind an army base.

Noel came within sight of Glenburn and flicked on the indicator. The reassuring mellow tick-tock sound filled the car and he waited for a lorry to pass in the opposite direction before he turned up the lane. Suddenly he changed his mind, checked his rear-view mirror, and continued driving along the road. Thinking of Grainne had induced a stubborn erection. He wasn't ready to go home just yet. He dialled her number on the in-car phone — it was answered almost immediately.

'Hi, it's me,' he said. 'Is it clear?'

'Yes,' said her husky voice on the line.

'I'm just on my way then. See you soon.'

He hung up, switched on the car lights and accelerated into the settling dusk.

5

1999

'I know you've got a lot on your plate, Roisin, but you can't just stop living.'

'I agree with Colette,' chimed in Mairead. 'You can't keep pushing yourself like this. Something's got to give and the rate you're going, it's going to be your sanity.'

'Thanks, Mum,' said Roisin despondently, 'that's just what I needed to hear.'

The three of them were sitting at Mairead's dining-table, drinking white wine. Roisin's head hurt and the wine was making her nauseous. Papers and files bursting with plans, quotes, bills and correspondence relating to the refurbishment of the salon were spread all over the table.

Roisin's was so tired that her eyes stung like she'd been chopping onions. She rubbed them with the heels of her hands until they moistened with tears. She hadn't slept properly in over a month. At first it had been adrenaline keeping her awake at nights, as her dream inched closer to reality. But then things started going wrong and now anxiety was the primary cause of her insomnia.

'I wouldn't have given up work so soon if I'd known it was going to take this long,' she said. 'The workmen have been at it a month and already I'm way behind schedule.'

'You were bound to run into difficulties, Roisin,' said Colette. 'You're doing something you've never done before and it's a steep learning curve. You can't expect it to be plain sailing all the way.'

'Maybe your plan was too ambitious to start with,' said Mairead.

'I don't think so. I think the mistake I made was trying to oversee and co-ordinate the work myself. I should have got a contractor to do the whole project, including managing it. The workmen don't take me seriously and, to tell you the truth, half the time I don't know what they're talking about. The plumber was supposed to come in this week and lay the piping for the central heating and he didn't even bother turning up. He said he was on another job and he'd get to me as soon as he could!'

'Well, does it really matter if the opening's delayed?' asked Colette.

'Yes, it does,' said Roisin, more sharply than she'd intended and she felt awful when Colette winced. 'You see, it's all financial outlay with no return until the salon opens,' she explained. 'I've ordered the furniture, equipment and stock and that has to be paid for before delivery.'

'It'll come together in the end, love, you'll see,' said Mairead gently.

'Oh my God, I hope so,' replied Roisin miserably. 'It's like my dream is turning into a nightmare.' And with that thought she burst into tears. 'I'm sorry,' she blubbered, rested her head on her hands and sobbed. She felt two comforting hands on her back, one rubbing the small of her back in small circular motions, the other one patting her shoulder reassuringly.

'That's right,' said her mother's voice. 'Just you have a good cry.'

Roisin sniffed, raised her head and went on, 'And then the builders ran into problems with the partition I wanted taken down. It turns out that it's a supporting wall and it's going to cost more . . . '

Colette and Mairead glanced at each other knowingly, the way people sometimes do in the company of a small child or a very old person.

'Listen, love,' said Mairead, closing the bulging folder in front of Roisin and sliding it across the table away from her, 'why don't you call it a night? You have to recognise when to stop.'

'Your mum's right, Roisin. Worrying about it isn't going to make any difference to the outcome. Look, why don't you come out tomorrow night? A good laugh'll do you the world of good.'

Roisin sat with her hands between her knees, grateful to hear that it was all right to let go. She thought that if she took her eye off the ball for just one second the whole project would fall apart. She knew her fears were irrational but she was still unable to manage them without help. Thank God for Colette and her mum.

'OK. Maybe a good night out's what I need. This wine is making me dizzy,' she continued, pushing the glass away from her. 'I'm sorry but I'm going to have to go to bed. I'm absolutely exhausted.' She dragged herself onto her feet, holding on to the table and feeling like she was seventy-seven instead of twenty-seven. 'Thank you both. For everything. I couldn't do this without your support, you know.'

The two women nodded and Colette said, 'You go on. I'll sit here a while and finish this glass, then I'll be off. I'll phone you tomorrow. Night, Roisin.'

That night Roisin slept soundly and, in the morning, although nothing had changed, she felt different. The tearful outburst had released much of the tension that had built up over the past four weeks. She realised that she must try to be more relaxed about the salon. As Colette had said, worrying about it wouldn't make one iota of difference to what happened. She promised herself that she would be more business-like, less emotional.

And she allowed herself to look forward to going out. After an early meal, she dry-brushed all over, took a long, hot bath, exfoliated and moisturised, and put a deep conditioning treatment on her hair. Then she styled her hair, dressed with care and carefully applied her make-up. She hadn't felt so good about herself in weeks.

'Listen, Mum,' she said, when she was ready to go out, 'I might be late so you'd better lock the door. I've got my key here.' She dropped it into her black satin evening bag. 'What are you making anyway? Christmas cake?'

'No,' laughed Mairead, letting the sloppy mixture fall off the spoon into a cream pottery bowl. 'Christmas pudding. You'd think you'd know the difference by now!'

'That's your department, Mum. You know I'm no good at baking and cooking!' She took a raisin from the open bag lying on the counter and popped it into her mouth.

'God help the man who gets you, Roisin Shaw!'

Roisin pulled a face at her mother.

'Here, you have to make a wish,' said Mairead and passed the big stainless-steel spoon to Roisin. 'Watch your clothes, mind!'

Roisin closed her eyes tight, stirred the pudding and made her wish, just as she'd done every year of her life since she could remember.

'And I hope it comes true,' said Mairead. 'Now have a good time. I'll see you in the morning.'

Everywhere was busy on a Saturday night. Colette, Roisin and their friends went on a pub-crawl, before heading for the Rugby Club where there was a disco until the early hours. They drank a lot and danced too much and laughed more than was advisable.

'I need the loo,' announced Colette, rising unsteadily to her feet.

'I'll come with you,' shouted Roisin above the din.

The toilets were cool and empty. They stood over the sinks, sobered by the relative calm, and patched up their make-up.

'Do you think your mum would ever remarry?' said Colette.

'Mum? Remarry?' said Roisin and she stopped applying her red lipstick and peered at Colette's reflection in the mirror.

'Don't sound so shocked. It's not unusual for a widow to marry again.' Colette smacked her lips together and dabbed face powder rather haphazardly across her shiny brow and chin.

'It's not that. It's just that I never thought . . . I mean Mum's never looked at a man since Dad. And even before they met I don't think she'd ever had a serious boyfriend. It was a real match made in heaven. I just can't imagine her with someone else. What made you ask?'

'Well, your mum's only fifty-seven and she's lovely. It doesn't seem right that an attractive woman like her should be on her own. I'm sure there are men after her.'

'Hey, that's my mum you're talking about,' joked Roisin and she finished putting on her lipstick. But part of her didn't like what Colette had said. The selfish child in her saw her mother exclusively as an asexual being, with no wants beyond tending home and garden, her job at the local library and continuing to nurture her now-grown daughters. The idea that her mum might desire something beyond that was unsettling, unthinkable even. Changing the subject she asked, 'What do you think of Eric Lawson then? He seems to like you.'

'Oh, Roisin,' said Colette, 'did you see the hair in his ears? And his nose — it's disgusting! Ugh!'

'You'll not be taking him home tonight, then?'

'Oh, my God, imagine what the rest of him's like!' cried Colette and they both collapsed into a fit of giggles.

The next week saw Roisin interviewing for a full-time assistant after placing ads in the local papers and specialised trade magazines. She was disappointed with the response — only four applicants replied.

In the absence of any other options, the interviews were being conducted at home. The first interviewee, being currently unemployed, came during the day. On paper her credentials were OK if a little short on practical work experience. But she was only twenty-one.

When Roisin opened the door she could have closed it again almost immediately. The girl on the front step was a Goth from head to toe, with pale grey eyes peering out from a white face. Her hair was dyed black and stuck out from her head in a matted assortment of short, stiff little ponytails. She had piercings in her nose and eyebrow and dark violet lipstick on her lips.

Roisin went through the motions of the interview, thinking that it was unfair wasting her own time and the girl's. Her boyfriend, who had given her a lift from Ballymoney, waited outside in a beaten-up Mazda.

'So how would you get to Ballyfergus every day?' asked Roisin.

'Dunno,' she said flatly, the notion of transport clearly having not crossed her mind until now. 'Is there a bus?'

When she left Roisin closed the door behind her and threw her application in the bin. Then she retrieved it, reminding herself that the girl deserved the courtesy of a reply, even if it was negative.

She had no more luck with the next one — a middle-aged woman, recently separated from her husband, who hadn't worked in several years. She was a nice lady but her skills, and image, were too outdated to fit in with the kind of cutting-edge treatments Roisin had in mind. And she talked too much about her various health problems, ranging from varicose veins to sinus problems.

Then there was a tall thin girl, about Roisin's age, from Carrickfergus with curly red-blonde hair and lightly freckled skin. She had worked in a couple of good salons in Belfast and was keen and exceptionally well presented. But she was cool, reserved and slightly condescending.

'She seemed like a nice girl,' said Mairead, after the girl had left.

'Mmm.'

'Well, go on then, what's wrong with her?'

'I don't know. We just didn't click. You know the way with some people you just feel that you're on a different wavelength?'

'Well, at the rate you're going you'll be running the salon on your own.'

The final interview was with Katy Keenan who, according to her brief hand-written resume, had gone to the same school as Roisin but a few years ahead of her. She'd worked in London for six years and had recently come back to Ballyfergus.

'Does this name mean anything to you, Mum?' said Roisin.

'"Keenan",' read Mairead. 'What's the address?'

Roisin pointed to the address Katy had given.

'I'm sure that's Joe Keenan's daughter, you know, the newsagent. One of the sons was in your year at school. John, I think it was.'

'Oh, yes, I think I remember him,' said Roisin vaguely, recalling a skinny little boy with socks round his ankles and dirty knees.

'I thought she came back home to get married,' said Mairead thoughtfully.

'Perhaps she's using her maiden name for work.'

Katy turned out to be the answer to Roisin's prayers. Big in personality and stature she was not without glamour and she exuded radiant warmth. She wore a constant smile on her round, smooth face, her wide slash of a mouth carefully lined with liner and the lips brushed with colour. She had plenty of the right experience and had even once manicured the hands of Joan Collins.

After a chat lasting only twenty minutes or so Roisin told her, without hesitation, that she had the job.

'That's fantastic,' she said. 'When do you want me to start?'

'Well, the salon's not going to be open until after Christmas. Probably the end of January. Can you wait that long?' asked Roisin, holding her breath. If Katy didn't say yes she would be well and truly stuck.

'It's perfect,' she replied.

Roisin let out her breath, and grinned broadly.

'I'm getting married at the end of this month,'

explained Katy, glancing at the diamond solitaire on her finger, 'and the house we've bought needs a lot of work done to get it straight.'

'Where is it?'

'Manor Heights.'

This was a relatively new development of semi-detached houses, built on the hills over-looking Ballyfergus.

'It's not brand new but it's only a year old,' added Katy. 'We want to get it decorated before we move in.'

'A winter wedding. That's really romantic,' said Roisin.

'I don't know about that. Mad more like. It's just the way it panned out with work commitments and everything.'

'Well, I wish you lots of luck with the wedding and the house. Now, where can I get in contact with you? There'll be paperwork to fill out for the tax office and, once the salon's in a fit state to be seen, I want to show you around.'

'Just use the address and telephone number I gave you at my parents'. They can always get a message to me. We won't be moving into the new house 'til after the wedding anyway.'

'Well, I think this calls for a celebration, don't you?' said Roisin and she went into the kitchen and got a bottle of wine out of the fridge. Then she sat down with Katy and they talked for hours like old friends.

★   ★   ★

It was hard for Roisin to believe that it was real. She stood inside the freshly completed salon and looked around, taking in every detail. Everything was just the way she'd visualised it, right down to the topiary plants in white china pots and the colour of the hardwood floor. The treatment rooms, though small, were warm and quiet (due to the thick stone walls) with low-level lighting and piped-in music.

She touched the cool glass of the reception desk to reassure herself it wasn't a figment of her imagination and stroked the pale wooden slats of the blinds. She peered between them into the chill of a freezing January day. The blackness outside was studded with squares and rectangles of yellow light pouring out from windows on the other side of the street. Her breath fogged the window until she could hardly see. She rubbed her upper arms, suddenly chilled, and moved away from the window.

Of course she still had to make it a viable business and build a clientele but just standing here in this place was a huge milestone. Especially after all the difficulties she'd experienced over the last three months. Suddenly everything had come together and here she was at last — businesswoman, property owner, employer. It was wonderful and daunting and terrifying. What if she couldn't be a boss? What if the salon couldn't attract any customers? How would she pay the bills and Katy's wages?

She told herself to stop it. Firstly, these things weren't going to happen and secondly, it was out of her hands now. She was committed. The salon would open Monday morning for business and she'd just *have* to make it work.

She went through to the staffroom, now enlarged by knocking through a wall into an old cupboard, and busied herself checking the supplies of drink and nibbles. The little fridge was jam-packed with bottles of beer and wine. Trays containing various finger-foods covered in cling-film lay on every available space, including on the floor under the table. She smiled when she saw them, for each tray was a gift, prepared with the love and support of friends and family.

Taking a box of matches from a drawer beside the sink, Roisin went back to the reception area and lit the rows of tea-lights carefully arranged along the low windowsills at the front of the shop. Then she sat down on the chocolate-brown leather sofa, so luscious she could've taken a bite out of it, and waited for the first guests to arrive.

She wondered what her father would make of this if he could see her now. She remembered a big man, tall as a tree, who'd hugged her against him until the rough fabric of his heavy tweed overcoat made her face itch. She couldn't remember his face or the sound of his voice or whether she loved him or feared him. The image she held of him was, therefore, pieced together largely from the things she'd heard people say about him over the years. He had been kind, good-looking, dark, softly spoken and strong of character — the model husband and father. Or so people said, but people never spoke ill of the dead, did they? So she guessed that the Anthony Shaw she believed in was little more than a one-dimensional caricature of the real man.

Not knowing him, though, didn't make his absence any the less painful. Growing up without a father had left a huge gaping hole in Roisin's life, a space that could not be filled by kind uncles, or Grandad, or anyone else. But tonight, he would be watching over her and she was sure he would be proud.

Someone tapped on the window and Roisin jumped up. She opened the door with a big smile to Mairead, Ann-Marie, Granny and Grandad Shaw, Aunt Veronica and Uncle Paul. Next to arrive were Katy and her husband followed closely by Colette and a group of their friends. Within the hour the reception area and corridor leading to the back rooms were heaving with warm bodies and goodwill.

Roisin had invited a photographer and a reporter from *The Ballyfergus Times* to the launch party. A photograph was taken of Roisin and Katy surrounded by everyone and the reporter interviewed Roisin. Roisin slipped them both twenty-pound vouchers for their wives in the hope that it would ensure a good spread in next week's paper.

Then Roisin cleared her throat and shouted above the din. '*Quiet everyone! Sshh please! Can we have some quiet, please?*'

Uncle Paul took up her cause and bellowed, '*Will you all hush down now! Roisin's got something to say!*' and the room went quiet.

So she stood on one of the low windowsills so everyone could hear and tried to project her voice to the back of the room. She thanked everyone for their help and encouragement in making her dream come true.

'This is the happiest day of my life,' she said, close to tears, and everyone cheered.

'Your dad would've been proud,' whispered Mairead as she gave Roisin a hug. 'I am.'

Then everyone tucked into the food, the party went on into the small hours, and Roisin had never been so happy.

★ ★ ★

The next few months were hard, hard work with much of Roisin's time spent drumming up business through various means. She offered free treatments for competitions in the local papers, ran 'buy one, get one free' offers and open nights when women could try out 'taster sessions' of the treatments. She persuaded the local paper to run an article on the salon and spent long hours handing out leaflets at the supermarket. Eventually it all started to pay off and bookings slowly but steadily increased.

An odd thing happened within a few weeks of opening. Roisin was sitting at the reception desk leafing through various local publications, trying to decide if they were worth placing an advert in, when a blue car pulled up outside and stopped. This caused her to look up, for the road outside the salon had double yellow lines and no one ever parked there.

The car was something big and flash, like a Rolls Royce, all gleaming chrome and ocean-blue bodywork. She watched while a distinguished grey-haired man in a business suit got out, strode purposefully across the pavement and into her salon.

'Good afternoon,' he said with an air of authority, as the door closed behind him. It was Noel McCormick, Donal's father-in-law and Ballyfergus's most famous resident — his face was never out of the papers.

'Hello,' answered Roisin, putting on her best front but wondering what Noel McCormick wanted in a beauty salon.

He stared at her for a few seconds — enough to make Roisin blush and look away — and then said, 'I'd like to buy my wife some vouchers for beauty treatments.'

'Oh, yes,' said Roisin hastily, forgetting about Donal Mullan as she switched into business mode. She gave him a price list, which he examined cursorily with an enigmatic smile on his face. She explained how he could choose a particular treatment as a gift or a general voucher, which his wife could use as she pleased.

'And how's trade?' he asked, as though he hadn't heard a word she'd said.

'Fine.'

'Always difficult to get a new business off the ground, isn't it?'

'Well, yes. It was slow to start with but things are picking up now.'

'You might need a business angel one day.'

'An angel?'

'An investor who puts money into start-ups. Here's my accountant's card. If you ever need financial assistance, I might be able to help.

Strictly business, of course,' he added and flashed her an amused grin. 'The angel takes shares in the business in exchange for capital.'

If he hadn't been old enough to be her father, Roisin could've sworn he was flirting with her. This came as no surprise for he had a terrible reputation as a womaniser. What a creep, she thought. Just the sort of father-in-law Donal Mullan deserved.

'I'm Noel McCormick,' he finally offered and gave her his hand to shake.

She took it and stuttered, 'I know that.' She was so taken aback by his offer that she lost all composure. 'I'm Roz Shaw,' she offered clumsily.

'I know that,' he said, mimicking her graceless reply. 'I'll take three hundred pounds of vouchers, please. That should keep Mrs McCormick going for a while, don't you think?' and he laughed conspiratorially.

By the time he left the shop Roisin's face was the colour of the red varnish on her nails. He'd been trying to make a fool of her and he'd succeeded. Why? Just for fun? Was it normal for a businessman to walk into a place he knew nothing about and offer the owner money? Surely Noel McCormick had far bigger fish to fry than a little beauty salon in backstreet Ballyfergus? But maybe that was how he operated, spotting potential before others did. Perhaps he saw what she saw — that this business was a sound enterprise with a future. And business was business, she told herself firmly. She mustn't let the fact that he was Donal Mullan's father-in-law colour her judgement.

She put the card he'd given her safely inside her briefcase.

The very next week, over the telephone, Pauline McCormick booked a whole series of appointments for the forthcoming month, ranging from an aromatherapy massage to a mud body-wrap, facials, manicures and waxing.

Roisin counted the days to Pauline's first appointment, curious to get a closer look at Donal's mother-in-law. When Pauline arrived Roisin observed her unseen from behind the blinds on the staff-room door and saw that she was prepared to be disappointed. Five minutes early, she perched on the edge of the sofa as though she might catch some dreadful disease from it, her face imperious with disdain. She flicked an imaginary piece of dust off the arm of the couch before resting her elbow on it. Roisin couldn't imagine a woman like her being easily impressed by Donal Mullan's greasy charms.

'Well, here goes, wish me luck,' said Roisin to Katy, who'd just come into the room. 'Pauline McCormick's here.' Knowing how freely clients chatted she wondered if Pauline would let slip any information about Donal. Somehow she doubted it.

'Well, rather you than me. She's one stuck-up cow!' said Katy with feeling, as she pulled on a pair of latex gloves. 'She used to come into the paper shop sometimes when I was working behind the counter. She hardly said two words to me.'

'She was rude to you?'

'Oh, not exactly. Just very proper. Look at her,'

replied Katy, peering through the wooden blinds on the staff room door. 'She's the original ice queen all right. She looks like she's just sucked a lemon,' she said and laughed raucously.

'Katy, keep your voice down! Mrs McCormick and her friends and family could be very valuable clients and it's in my interest, and yours, to secure her goodwill,' said Roisin, amazed at how prim she sounded. In truth, she agreed with Katy's sentiments about Pauline McCormick. And she felt some satisfaction knowing that Donal had to contend with this formidable woman as a mother-in-law.

'Good luck then,' said Katy grudgingly, as she left the room to return to her customer. 'You're going to need it. You'll need a blowtorch to melt that one!'

Roisin smiled thinly. In spite of Pauline's connection with Donal, Roisin meant what she'd said about wanting her as a client. She must be careful not to let her personal dislike for Donal and his family thwart her ambitions. He'd already destroyed Ann-Marie's life — she wasn't about to let him interfere with hers. She looked at her watch. Two minutes to go until Mrs McCormick's scheduled appointment. She opened the staffroom door, took a deep breath and walked briskly into the reception area.

'Good morning, how may I help you?' said Roisin and she waited while Mrs McCormick introduced herself and explained why she was here. Roisin wasn't going to give her the satisfaction of letting her know that she already knew perfectly well who she was.

'I'm Roz. Let me take your coat, Mrs McCormick. Thank you. I'll just pop it in here out of the way. Now, if you'd like to come this way, the treatment room's through here.'

She led the slim, elegant woman into the best room, where the lights had already been dimmed — a fragranced candle perfumed the air and a relaxation tape of sea sounds played unobtrusively in the background. Roisin tried to ignore Mrs McCormick's gaze, ranging critically over the treatment bed, small chair, and shower cubicle squeezed into the corner of the room.

'It's rather cramped isn't it?'

'Not at all. Think of it as cosy. Anyway, size isn't everything. I'm sure you'll find the facilities here quite adequate,' said Roisin brightly.

'Hmm,' said Mrs McCormick.

'I think we'll do the pedicure first, to give the polish time to dry, and then the leg-wax. Would you like a herbal tea? We have fennel, camomile, blackcurrant, lemon and ginger, peppermint — '

'Oh,' said Mrs McCormick, interrupting, 'camomile will do fine, thank you.'

Roisin nodded, settled the client on the bed and left the room, pulling the door shut soundlessly behind her. Then she sprinted the few metres to the staffroom, made the hot drink and returned as quickly as she could.

Mrs McCormick drank her tea and put the empty cup down on the table beside the bed, while Roisin soaked her feet in a basin of warm, soapy water. Then, without so much as a word, Pauline McCormick closed her eyes. The rest of her treatment was carried out in complete

160

silence, a situation not unknown to Roisin, but unusual. Working with someone's body was a highly personal experience and most people either felt the need to converse, to cover their embarrassment, or simply enjoyed a good chat. Though disappointed by the absence of dialogue, Roisin decided to take her cue from Mrs McCormick and did not instigate conversation, which seemed entirely to her client's liking.

As she was leaving, Mrs McCormick said, 'I have a number of bookings over the next few weeks. Would it be possible for you to personally undertake all of these, Roz? I'd be most grateful if you could.'

'Of course,' said Roisin, opening the appointments diary. 'I'll make sure of it.'

'Thank you. And this is for you,' said Mrs McCormick, reaching into her handbag and producing a ten-pound note which she pressed into Roisin's hand.

'I can't take that. It's far too much,' protested Roisin, feeling that the money was tainted by its connection with Donal. She felt unworthy too — she was ashamed of the uncharitable thoughts she'd harboured earlier. Mrs McCormick, while reserved in the extreme, had been perfectly polite.

'Nonsense,' said Mrs McCormick. 'Good morning.'

'Goodbye, Mrs McCormick,' called Roisin as her client's back disappeared out the door, 'and thank you.'

Katy peeked into reception, her arms loaded with fresh towels.

'What a strange lot those McCormicks are,' said Roisin.

'You must have buttered her up well and good to get a tip like that,' observed Katy, staring at the note in Roisin's hand.

'You know, the funny thing is,' said Roisin thoughtfully, spreading the bill out on the desk, 'I hardly said a word to her.'

But she must have made a good impression for very soon afterwards, two of Mrs McCormick's daughters started to patronise the salon. Jeanette, with a body as slim and toned as a gazelle's, came every four weeks for eyebrow-shaping and tinting and leg-waxing. Like her mother, she preferred her treatments to be carried out more or less in silence.

Michelle, however, was the complete opposite of her haughty mother and sister and she came every week. At the outset Roisin was determined to find Michelle spoilt, shallow and obnoxious. A nice girl wouldn't have married a creep like Donal Mullan, she argued to herself. But it wasn't long before Michelle's chatty, warm nature eroded Roisin's preconceptions of her.

On her second visit to the salon, Michelle was lying face down while Roisin applied tanning lotion to the back of her legs. Michelle was a large girl, though not as big as the last time Roisin had seen her at her sister's wedding. And she wasn't exactly fat, for her flesh was firm and hard like her sister's, but there was a lot of her. Though considering she'd had a baby just over a year ago, she wasn't in bad shape — Roisin had seen a lot worse.

Michelle rattled on about the personal lives of celebrities, asking Roisin for her opinion every now and then. Not that she was able to add much to the conversation, as most of the names mentioned by Michelle meant nothing to her.

'Don't you read *Hello!* magazine?' asked Michelle, her voice muffled by the hair that fell over her face.

'Well, no. Not very often,' Roisin answered truthfully, covering Michelle's legs with a towel and removing the one covering her upper torso. 'Only when I'm in the waiting room at the doctor's or the dentist's. And then they're all out of date anyway.' She squeezed more lotion into her palms, rubbed them together briskly, and massaged the liquid vigorously into Michelle's skin.

'Oh, I love reading about celebrities. You know my Don,' continued Michelle, and it took Roisin a few seconds to register that she was talking about Donal, 'he takes the mickey out of me for it. He thinks I'm daft.'

Roisin's hands paused momentarily on Michelle's broad back, thinking of the times he must have touched her there. She shivered a little with revulsion, then resumed her work. Now that the subject of Donal had been raised, it gave Roisin the opportunity to question Michelle about him. And there was one particular piece of information she was after.

'Well, you know what men are like,' she said casually, resuming her task. 'They don't understand.' And then, to keep Michelle on the subject of Donal, she asked, 'What does your

163

husband do, anyway?'

'Oh, didn't I tell you? He's a bank manager. He's in Head Office. Corporate lending. I don't really know what it involves. But he's got some very important clients and he works really hard.'

'And does he play hard too?'

Michelle laughed. 'We both do! Mind you, not so much now that we have Molly.'

'I suppose it's difficult getting a baby-sitter.'

'It's not so much that — it's having to get up the next morning. And Don's not a morning person. Sometimes you think it's just not worth going out. You suffer so much the next day.'

'Sounds hellish. Now, can you turn over, Michelle, while I hold this towel over you and we'll do your front? There, that's it. Careful now.'

Roisin held the towel up and averted her gaze while Michelle rolled onto her back. Then she asked, 'So, had you been married long before Molly was born?'

'Oh yes. We got married in August 1989. We had eight wonderful years of freedom before I got pregnant.' Michelle sighed happily and went on, 'Of course, we didn't appreciate it when we had it. Still, we did have lots of exotic holidays . . . '

'And was it a whirlwind wedding?' interrupted Roisin, steering the conversation towards her end goal. She despised herself for this subterfuge but could not stop until she'd found out what she wanted to know.

'Well, not really,' replied Michelle. 'We knew each other — from the evening classes — for a few months before we got together. Officially, we went out for three-and-a-half years before we got married.'

'Three-and-a-half years,' repeated Roisin, doing a quick mental calculation. That would mean that Donal started dating her in very early 1986 . . .

'We met when Don was working in the student branch at Queen's.'

'You studied at Queen's?' said Roisin, hanging on every word while trying to adopt an air of nonchalance.

'Oh, no,' laughed Michelle. 'I'm far too thick to do anything half as clever as a university degree! No, we were both studying for the banking exams at the time.'

'I didn't know you were a banker,' said Roisin, trying to carry on the conversation in as natural a manner as possible. But her mind was racing.

'No. I'm afraid I didn't last too long at that.' Michelle giggled and added, 'I could never get my sides to balance in accounts. Poor Mr Watt, the accounts teacher, used to despair of me!'

Roisin laughed hollowly with Michelle while her brain processed the information it had just received. Donal dumped Ann-Marie in March 1986 — Roisin remembered it well, because it was just after St Patrick's Day. So her instinct had been right. She'd always suspected that Donal had finished with Ann-Marie because someone better came along. And now she knew it to be true. He'd chosen Michelle over Ann-Marie because of who she was, Roisin was sure of it. She toyed briefly with the notion of sharing this information with Ann-Marie, then decided that it would be unwise. It would hurt her deeply and would serve no purpose. As far as Ann-Marie was concerned Donal was past history.

Now that she had started the ball rolling, Roisin didn't have to say anything to keep Michelle talking about her husband. She lay there and chatted happily about her life with Donal, about the big house they lived in, their frequent holidays, and their busy social life.

And in spite of her hatred for Donal, inflamed even more by the fresh revelation, Roisin found herself hanging on every word, fascinated by the anecdotes Michelle related. She tried to reconcile the suave, sophisticated man of Michelle's description with the Donal Mullan she knew and hated. And she felt jealous. Not of Michelle but of Donal. He'd landed on his feet all right and he didn't deserve it. If only she could find a way to take him down a peg or two . . .

She covered Michelle's torso and moved down to work on her right thigh. And then she felt shame break over her like a wave. Michelle was so open and guileless that Roisin couldn't help but feel deceitful and mean. The girl trusted her with her confidences and all Roisin could think about was spite and revenge.

'You know,' she said, when Michelle had finally fallen silent, 'I thought your dad was very nice when he came in to buy those vouchers.'

'Daddy came in here? All by himself?'

'You sound very surprised.'

'I don't think he's ever bought Mum a present in his life.'

'Really?' said Roisin, moving her hands down to Michelle's right calf.

'I mean, he buys them in the sense that it's his money. But Ann always shops for him.'

Roisin finished Michelle's lower leg, covered it with the towel and started on the other one. 'Who's Ann?'

'His secretary. She's been with him for years and she does everything for him.'

Roisin finished working, and pulled the towel over Michelle's exposed flesh.

'There, that's us done,' she said. 'Now, you just lie there and relax for ten minutes, Michelle, to give that time to dry.'

She went over to the small sink, washed her hands and scrubbed her fingernails thoroughly with a nailbrush. Experience had taught her that even the slightest trace of fake tan would stain her skin brown.

'I'll just pop out for a minute to check if my next client's here. Comfortable? Good. I'll be back shortly,' she said and left the room, shutting the door quietly behind her.

She stood in the hallway and thought hard. It sounded as though Noel McCormick's visit to the salon was uncharacteristic behaviour for him. Had he come here with the intention of chatting her up? He could have seen her photo, and read the news about the new salon, in the papers. And by all accounts he was a desperate flirt. Or was his interest in the business genuine? She didn't know. But one thing was for certain. If she saw him again, which she very much doubted, she would be careful to treat him with reserve.

★ ★ ★

It had been months since Donal's last visit to Glenburn, and he wasn't looking forward to going there today to celebrate the christening of Jeanette and Matt's baby son. Since the blow-up between him and Noel — which Donal had decided to keep to himself — he had avoided the McCormicks where possible, making up excuses to duck out of family get-togethers. When avoidance had, at last, been impossible he'd faced up to them with a mixture of apprehension and dread. But Noel carried on as though nothing was amiss. And Donal could detect no change in Pauline's demeanour either.

This approach confounded Donal for he came from a family where it was considered positively healthy to vent feelings, good or bad. People were always falling out in spectacular fashion, but they were just as easily reconciled with an apology, and grudges were never allowed to fester long enough to cause lasting harm.

'Donal, are you ready to go?' Michelle's voice shouted in to him, where he sat watching Sky Sports in the family room.

'What's the rush, Michelle? We're only going up the road.'

Michelle came and stood in the doorway, irritation radiating from every pore, a small bundle of clothes balled in her hands.

'I know that,' she said, sharply, 'but Mum was

expecting us at twelve thirty. She wants us to sit down for lunch at one o'clock sharp. If Molly hadn't spilled that juice down her front we would've gone straight there from the chapel.'

'Christ, it's a celebration meal, not a bloody military operation,' said Donal testily, thinking of the relaxed, impromptu way the Mullan clan celebrated births and christenings.

'Don't,' said Michelle. She threw the clothes onto the floor, sat down on the sofa beside him, and added softly, 'Don't be so nasty.'

He shoved his foot brutally into a black brogue and tied the lace.

'Don, darling,' she continued, 'what's wrong?'

'Nothing.'

'But there is. I can tell. Won't you tell me what it is?'

Donal stood up, shook his legs so that the fabric of his trousers hung smoothly, and readjusted his tie. He had to wear a bloody suit to work all week — the last thing he wanted to do was wear one on his weekends off.

'I'm just sick of the whole thing. Your family. All this palaver over Jeanette and Matt's baby getting christened.'

'They're not doing any more than they did for Molly.'

'Hmm,' said Donal, determined to find fault regardless. Suddenly he decided to tell her. 'Do you remember last year,' he went on, 'when I said I was going to ask your dad for a job and you talked me out of it?'

Michelle nodded. Donal walked over to the window and looked down at the garden strewn

169

with Molly's outdoor toys.

'You didn't talk me out of it. I went and saw your dad that very afternoon.'

'Oh,' he heard her gasp, 'I see.'

He told her a sanitised version of what had passed between himself and Noel that day. Embarrassment prevented him from telling her how bad it really was.

After a long pause she said, 'Donal, I really think that you're reading too much into it. There could be any number of reasons why Dad couldn't give you a job. You're just being oversensitive.'

'For Christ's sake, Michelle, why are you defending him?' yelled Donal, snapping his head round to face her, where she sat motionless on the edge of the sofa. 'I'm your husband for God's sake! You and I both know what Noel and Pauline think of me. And I'm sick of it. Sick of trying, and failing, to live up to their expectations. And you knew, didn't you? You knew how much your father hated me. That's why you tried to stop me. You knew that he'd never let me into the family firm.'

'No, Don, that's not true,' she protested.

'Why did you try to talk me out of it then?'

Michelle looked down at her hands, working themselves around each other where they lay in her lap. Her face was ashen.

'I thought as much,' he said, flatly.

Michelle looked close to tears when she said, so quietly that he could barely hear her, 'I had no idea you felt like that about my family.'

Just then Molly toddled into the room, a

vision of perfection with her soft, golden curls, dressed in a clean purple velvet dress, white tights and burgundy patent shoes.

'Dada!' she wailed and threw her arms around his legs.

'I don't think she likes you shouting,' said Michelle.

'There, there, pet,' said Donal and he lifted Molly up and buried his face in her fragrant, sweet neck.

'Are you coming or not?' asked Michelle, once Molly had stopped crying and was restored to good humour.

'I suppose so,' said Donal, his anger deflated like a burst balloon. 'Come on.'

When they arrived at Glenburn, Matt's relatives were already assembled in the drawing-room, admiring their first grandchild. The christening robes he still wore from the morning's ceremony dwarfed the baby.

Once everyone's glasses were charged with champagne, Noel proposed a toast to the child.

'Here's to our first grandson, Roger Joseph Doherty,' said Noel, his golf-weathered face radiant with joy. 'And, if I might say so, he's a damn fine looking boy. He obviously takes after his grandfather. On the McCormick side, that is. Sorry, Joe!'

Noel's eyes twinkled with mischief and everyone roared with laughter, except Donal who forced the corners of his mouth into a smile. Naturally Jeanette and Matt had supplied Noel with the grandson and heir he'd always wanted. And, boy, was he grateful!

Donal drained his glass and eyed the spirit decanters on a side table, longing for a proper drink to see him through the afternoon. For he could see it was going to be a long one. Everyone was clucking round the bairn like it was God's gift. At only eight weeks old, the child was a pretty babe but weren't they all at that stage? He glanced down at Molly playing quietly with her doll behind one of the sofas, unnoticed. He had to quell the rage that welled up inside him. He could cope with the McCormick's snubs and put-downs but he could not have Molly ignored like this — that he would not tolerate.

Just when he thought he was about to burst with anger, Matt's mother came over and made a fuss of Molly and she unfolded like a flower under the attention. Donal swallowed and looked away — sometimes his love for Molly was so powerful it hurt.

'I think Roger needs to go for his nap now,' said Jeanette. 'I'll just be a minute.'

'What a clever boy! His timing's perfect,' said Pauline as Jeanette left the room with the baby. 'Lunch is just about to be served. Would everyone like to go through to the dining-room?'

Donal hung back until the rest had left the room, then he shut the door behind them. He opened the whisky decanter and took several large gulps bracing himself as each one went down. Then he put the decanter down, replaced the stopper and wiped his mouth with the back of his hand. That should get him through the rest of this tiresome afternoon.

As soon as the meal was over, Donal excused

himself and slipped outside for a breath of fresh air. The McCormicks and Dohertys were absorbed in a mutual bonding session in the drawing-room and didn't even notice him gone. Michelle had taken Molly upstairs to see Roger, who'd just woken up.

Outside, Donal welcomed the sharp autumnal breeze. He'd had more than his fair share of wine at the meal and his head was throbbing. The late afternoon sun provided little warmth, and he shoved his hands deep into his trouser pockets. He headed first across to the paddock, not caring that his shoes were sticky with mud, and leaned on the gate watching the horses silently graze. Then he wandered aimlessly round the property.

At this point in time Donal reckoned he had never been more miserable. Even the blessing that was Molly wasn't enough to eradicate all that was wrong with his life. He saw now where he'd gone wrong — he had married Michelle for the wrong reasons. He believed at the time that he loved her, not wishing to acknowledge to himself the true motivation for his interest in her. Money and power had always fascinated him — he was drawn to them like a magnet. When he remembered how he'd chosen Michelle over Ann-Marie, he couldn't believe that he'd been such a fool.

It had taken him the best part of the last year or so, since the interview with Noel, to understand himself. He saw that his preoccupation with money came from his mother. As the youngest child in the family by several years,

Donal had spent much time alone with his mother as a small child. From her he learned how his grandfather, Peter Magill, the local vet, had ruined the family through his alcoholism. When he finally drank himself into the grave, it transpired that he'd left the family destitute. At the age of fourteen, Donal's mother had to go out to work in a shoe-shop to keep the wolves from the door. Donal never understood why his mother had married Patrick Mullan, a factory worker with limited prospects. But it was clear to him that she resented the mediocrity of her life, the penny-pinching and the making do.

From her Donal had inherited his abhorrent fear of poverty and a belief that money was the key to contentment. It had taken him all of his thirty-six years, probably half his life, to realise that money had nothing at all to do with happiness.

He peered through the full-length windows that surrounded the swimming-pool attached to the back of the main house. Inside it was dark, the deep blue water glossy and still like wet icing. It looked cold and uninviting but Donal knew that the pool was heated all year round and Noel swam in it every day. Once, a swimming-pool had been high on Donal's list of desirables — now he would have traded everything he had, except Molly, for happiness.

When he'd married Michelle, he'd been intoxicated by the potential for his material advancement. Instead of focusing on the person he was marrying, he'd focused on the family. And now he hated her family. They had rejected him and now he was rejecting them. He no longer had any desire to win their favour; he just wanted out. He did not hate Michelle — he simply didn't love her. She was too insubstantial for him — too much a product of her background and upbringing. Not only had he messed up his own life, he'd done the same to Michelle. And she didn't deserve that. All she'd done was to fall in love with the wrong guy.

The only reason he stayed with Michelle was because of Molly. He had seen Noel McCormick's true colours and he knew that if he walked out on Michelle, Noel would do his damnedest to ensure Donal never saw Molly again. And Donal could not live with that prospect.

Perhaps fate had drawn him to this pool. The deep, calm water was one answer to all his problems. The easiest thing in the world would be to end it here and now. Michelle would get over him — Molly would forget him soon enough. No one would miss him. Donal tried the handle but the door was locked. He turned his back to the building and looked out over the fields to Ballyfergus, a hazy blur in the distance.

One thing was for sure — he couldn't go on living in this emotional void. Something would have to be done.

★ ★ ★

By the autumn the salon was well established and bookings in the run-up to Christmas were looking good. Roisin spent her days on a high, enjoying her work and the sheer pleasure of knowing it was all hers. She loved working with Katy, meeting old and new clients, listening to their life stories and local gossip. And at night she dreamed of her plans for the future and where she could take her concept next. If everything went as well as it had done to date, she'd soon be ready to open a second salon, perhaps in Ballymena or Coleraine.

On the day that she got the phone call she woke up knowing that something was going to go wrong. When she got to work everything appeared normal, only a veil of apprehension coloured her view of the world. When the telephone rang mid-morning she was just saying goodbye to a client. She put her hand on the receiver and paused before picking it up.

'Roisin. It's Mum.'

'What's wrong?'

'It's Ann-Marie. She's done it again.'

In her car on the way to hospital, Roisin felt like her bubble had burst. She tried so hard to leave the past behind but Ann-Marie was incapable of the same. Roisin had overcome her father's death, why couldn't Ann-Marie? But then Roisin hadn't had her heart broken, not like her sister. For Roisin was convinced as ever that her sister's problems stemmed from the past. And Donal Mullan was pivotal in that history.

She recalled the time that Donal Mullan came into their lives. It was 1985 and Ann-Marie had gained a place at Queen's University Belfast to study Environmental Science. Roisin was at the worst possible age — fourteen. She straddled the ungainly divide between childhood and woman-hood, fighting her raging hormones all the way. She had spots on her face, her hair was permanently lank and greasy, she wore a brace to straighten her teeth and glasses for her poor eyesight. She was fat and she hated herself.

She missed her sister terribly. Ann-Marie came home at weekends, out of a sense of duty rather than through choice, Roisin suspected. She sparkled with chatter about the new friends she'd made, the exciting parties they went to, and the boys she'd met. It sounded to Roisin like university was little more than a cover for having a good time and she was filled with envy. Her life in comparison was drab and boring — school, home, school.

Occasionally she was allowed to stay the weekend with Ann-Marie at her digs in Belfast. She shared a draughty old house with five other girls from all over Northern Ireland. Most of the students went home at weekends so often it was just the two of them in the cold, damp three-storey terrace.

They took a bus to the city centre to window-shop and had lunch in Kentucky Fried Chicken. Ann-Marie plastered Roisin's face in make-up and took her around the student haunts, successfully passing her off as a first-year student. She sat with her sister's friends and drank enough fizzy cider to feel tipsy. But the pubs and bars were a little subdued and, everyone said, lacking the frenzied atmosphere of mid-week when all the students were around. Still, it was miles better than being stuck in

Ballyfergus. And she had the added satisfaction of watching her schoolmates go green with envy on Monday morning as she related the weekend's antics to them.

And then one day Ann-Marie came home full of talk about a guy called Donal who worked in the student branch of Bank of Ireland. In fact she talked about little else all that long weekend — it was pretty clear to Roisin that she was head over heels in love with him. When she came home for the Christmas break a few weeks later Ann-Marie was restless — she couldn't wait to get back to university come the beginning of January. When it finally dawned on Roisin that her place in her sister's life was being supplanted by this Donal, she nursed her hurt like a broken arm.

Soon, Ann-Marie stopped coming home every weekend. She had too much studying to do, she said, which Roisin didn't believe for a minute. She was spending her weekends with Donal and that meant that they were sleeping together — Ann-Marie had let slip that he'd stayed the night a few times. If Mum knew she'd kill her! Roisin only hoped that she had the sense not to get herself pregnant.

Finally, Donal was brought down to Ballyfergus for the weekend to meet Ann-Marie's family. She unveiled him like a precious jewel, bursting with pride and the expectation that they would love and adore him. Roisin saw an ordinary bloke with a cheeky grin and wondered what it was about him that had so entranced Ann-Marie.

The first night, while Mairead was making dinner, they sat in the lounge talking.

'Let me tell you about the time I worked in an abattoir,' he said. 'In Paris.'

'Oh, do!' said Roisin, sitting on the floor. 'That must have been horrible. What were you doing in Paris?'

'Oh, it was a while back,' he said vaguely. 'A couple of us went over for the summer to look for work.'

Ann-Marie had obviously heard the story before, for she sank quietly into one of the armchairs, her face radiant with adoration, and said nothing.

'So what did you have to do?'

'Cut up animals. That's what you do in an abattoir,' he said, and Roisin bristled ever so slightly at his patronising tone. 'It was gruesome. The camels, though, they were the worst.'

'Camels? You cut up camels?'

'They were so big you see. It was a real messy job. The French prize their eyeballs.'

'For what.'

'They eat them. They're considered a great delicacy.'

Roisin looked at her feet and plucked fluff from the soles of her socks. She wanted to believe him, but common sense told her that he must have been making it up. She knew that people in the Middle East ate sheeps' eyeballs and that the French ate snails and frog's legs. But not camels' eyeballs. She glanced over at her sister, curled up in the armchair like a contented

179

cat. But her expression showed no signs of incredulity.

'You're having me on,' Roisin said and looked again at her sister for support.

Ann-Marie just smiled.

'No, no, I'm not,' he said earnestly, looking down at her from his perch on the edge of the armchair. 'It's the God's honest truth.'

'You're telling me that you worked in an abattoir in Paris cutting up camels?'

He nodded his head rapidly to affirm his testimony. Then he threw his hands in the air and said with an air of extreme sadness, 'She doesn't believe me, Ann-Marie. She doesn't believe me.'

Then he hung his head in an attitude of dejection. Still Ann-Marie sat on and watched while Roisin hastily sought to retrieve the situation. If what he said was true, and it must be or he was a liar, she had hurt his feelings. He was a guest in their house and it was her responsibility to make him feel comfortable again.

'I never said I didn't believe you,' she said, choosing each word with care. 'It just seems a bit bizarre, that's all.'

He raised his eyes and smiled at her then, triumphantly, as though he'd won an argument or a bet.

'Dinner's ready,' Mairead called from the kitchen and Roisin jumped up straightaway, grateful for the diversion.

Later that night in bed she snuggled into Ann-Marie's back, and pushed her sister's brown hair out of the way. The whole household had bed-hopped to accommodate Donal. Mairead had gone into Roisin's single bed so that the two sisters could sleep in her big double one — she didn't like sharing her bed. And Donal had Ann-Marie's room.

'Ann-Marie,' she whispered.

'What?' said a sleepy voice.

'That stuff about Donal working in an abattoir?'

'Mmm.'

'Was it true?'

Ann-Marie paused before answering. 'Well. What do you think?'

'It wasn't true, was it?'

No answer.

'You knew that, didn't you?' hissed Roisin. 'You sat there and let him tell me all that rubbish, knowing it was all lies. I could tell by your face.'

'Oh, Roisin, don't be so melodramatic. OK, it wasn't true. So what?'

'He lied.'

Ann-Marie sighed heavily. 'It was only a bit of fun. Can't you take a joke?'

'Not when the joke's at my expense,' said Roisin more concerned about the wider implications than her own injured pride. If Donal Mullan was capable of such a barefaced lie then he was capable of anything. And Roisin did not like him one little bit.

At the end of the visit, the two of them dropped their bombshell.

'We're getting engaged, Mrs Shaw,' announced

Donal, playing with Ann-Marie's hand like the keys to a new car.

'Oh,' said Mairead, taken by surprise and unconsciously shaking her head. 'When?'

'Now. Well, as soon as we get the ring.'

Roisin felt sorry for her mum, without a husband to lean on for support. She knew she did not approve because, while she'd been polite and courteous to Donal all weekend, she hadn't warmed to him.

'Well, I suppose congratulations are in order,' Mairead said grudgingly and gave them both a perfunctory kiss on the cheek. 'But it does seem rather soon, don't you think? I mean you've only known each other for a few months and — '

'But we know we're right for each other,' interrupted Ann-Marie. 'Don't we, Donal?'

'You don't have to worry about Ann-Marie,' Donal assured her mother. 'I'll take care of her.'

'So what did you think of him?' Roisin asked her mother after he and Ann-Marie had gone.

'Hmm,' said Mairead, and her eyebrows puckered into a frown.

'You didn't like him, did you?'

Mairead paused to consider her response. She was always straight with Roisin, as though she understood that she could face the truths about life that Ann-Marie couldn't. 'No, I wouldn't go so far as to say that I don't like him. He was well-mannered and funny but I just don't completely trust him. There's something insincere about him. Let me put it this way — in my day we'd have called him a 'lounge lizard'.'

'A 'lounge lizard'? What on earth does that mean?'

'It means he's a real smoothie, with those come-to-bed eyes of his. Laying the charm on thick like honey. It works for some women,' she added implying that she, like Roisin, was immune to his charms.

Then they realised that they'd been so taken by surprise that they'd forgotten to ask the basic questions, like when and where they intended to get married.

Not that it mattered much for no sooner had the word spread to family and friends, than Donal dumped Ann-Marie. Just like that. The engagement had lasted all of four weeks and three days. Karen, one of Ann-Marie's flatmates, phoned to say that Ann-Marie was in a bad way but she wouldn't elaborate or perhaps she simply didn't have the words to describe what was wrong with her.

'Donal Mullan finished with her and apparently she's not taking it too well,' said Mairead, standing with the phone in her hand and the dinner bubbling in pots on the cooker. 'Karen said that she thought I should come and see her. They can't persuade her to get out of bed, or eat, or anything. What should we do, Roisin?'

Karen was one of the more sensible, grounded individuals in the house, not given to over-exaggeration or hysteria. This in itself gave Roisin cause for alarm.

'I think we'd better go and see what's wrong, Mum.'

So that's what they did. They found

Ann-Marie in her bed where she had lain for the last two days. Pale and drawn, she looked for all the world like she was dying of some horrible disease like consumption or tuberculosis.

There were no dramatics, crying or sobbing. She simply lay there like a zombie and wouldn't respond when her mum or Roisin spoke to her.

'How long has she been like this?' said Mairead to Karen.

'Since he told her. He came round on Monday night and split up with her. None of us know the details of what was said for she wouldn't tell us anything. She just stayed in her room and she won't talk to anyone.'

'Well, thank you, Karen,' said Mairead in a composed voice that Roisin knew belied the anguish she felt inside. 'I think we'd better take her home.'

They roused her from the bed, got her dressed and took her down to the car. She didn't resist, nor did she co-operate. Her motor movements were clumsy, like a child learning how to control its body. Her beauty had fallen from her like a veil, leaving stark, hard features devoid of emotion behind.

On the way home in the car Roisin noticed a small gold band on the ring finger of her sister's left hand. In the streetlight that streamed in the window she saw that it contained a very small ruby stone. Ann-Marie touched it, repeatedly, as though checking it was still there and Roisin looked out of the window, choked with tears.

At home Mairead concentrated on persuading Ann-Marie to eat and building up her strength.

This was on the assumption that mental recovery would go hand in hand with physical improvement. Within a few weeks, though still lacklustre and skinny, Ann-Marie insisted on going back to university.

'I can't afford to take any more time off,' she said, briskly. 'The exams are only two months away.'

In discussion with Roisin, her mum said she believed this to be a good sign — Ann-Marie was taking an interest in something other than Donal. Roisin, however, suspected that her sister's true motive was to escape from her mum's remorseless ministrations and her lectures on what a rat Donal Mullan was.

Astonishingly, Ann-Marie vented no spleen against Donal. As for what had caused the break-up, he'd simply fallen out of love with her, Ann-Marie explained. If Roisin had been dumped like that, she'd have been spitting with rage but Ann-Marie remained strangely unemotional. Late at night, however, Roisin could hear her sobbing into her pillow through the thin wall that separated their bedrooms. And she felt helpless and useless for she could do nothing to bring back the old Ann-Marie. Only Donal Mullan, it seemed, had the power to do that and he didn't give a damn about her.

When they saw her off at the train station Ann-Marie didn't look back when she climbed into the carriage. They searched for her at the platform-side windows but she was nowhere to be seen. It was as though the carriage had swallowed her up.

'Well,' said Mairead, as the train pulled away from the station, 'let's hope that she's going to be all right. If I could get my hands on that — that bastard. I'd bloody well kill him!' She stamped her foot on the ground in anger.

Startled though she was by hearing her mother swear, Roisin remained focused on the carriages as they creaked away from the platform. She was filled with a vague sense of uneasiness. She knew Ann-Marie was far from 'all right'. She shouldn't be going back to stay in that house amongst strangers. She started to follow the moving train as it accelerated out of the station, straining on tiptoes to catch a glimpse of her sister within.

She ran beside the train, waved her arms above her head and cried, *'Ann-Marie! Ann-Marie!'* but her voice was lost under the roar of the engine.

'Roisin!' shouted Mairead. 'What are you doing? You're going to get yourself killed. Come on!'

Two days later Ann-Marie attempted suicide by swallowing a bottle of painkillers. Where she'd got them from no one knew. Karen had come home unexpectedly in the afternoon when Ann-Marie had assumed the house would be empty. This in itself suggested some element of planning and serious intent in that she did not expect, nor want, to be found. In the relatives' room at the hospital the doctor spoke to them in hushed tones.

'Luckily, the dose she's taken is insufficient to cause any serious harm,' he said. 'If she'd had enough of them, however, it would have been a different story.'

Mairead let out a little whimpering sound like a frightened puppy. Roisin put her arm round her shoulders.

'Now we're going to release her in a day or two but I'd suggest that she shouldn't be left on her own for a while. A psychiatric doctor will assess her. Mainly we need to satisfy ourselves that she's not a danger to herself or to anyone else before we release her. I'll be writing to her doctor as well and he'll arrange ongoing counselling.'

So Ann-Marie came home to Ballyfergus and that was effectively the end of her university career. She missed the first-year exams that were held in June. Her tutor telephoned several times to ask after her and assured her mother that allowances would be made for her illness on her return to university. While she seemed well enough to take resits at the end of the summer, she made no attempt to study.

'What's the point?' she said. 'What am I going to do with a degree in Environmental Science? It's a waste of time.'

'But Ann-Marie,' argued Roisin, 'what else are you going to do? It's such a waste.'

'You and Mum are like two fishwives. Nag, nag, nag, *nag*, *nag*,' she said, her voice rising to a crescendo, 'all day long.'

'All right, keep your shirt on.'

'Just leave me alone, will you?' said Ann-Marie angrily and went and sat in her room.

6

The first year's trading accounts for 'Beauty by Roz' made impressive reading. Two years ago, if someone had told Roisin that she'd be sitting here today the owner of a successful business, she wouldn't have believed it.

But the figures spoke for themselves. Her takings from the business in the last year were nearly twice what she'd ever earned as an employee. And, after agonising over break-even figures and margins, she'd be able to buy herself a brand new car this spring. The key to it all, of course, had been Dad's insurance money. Though she'd hardly known him in life, indirectly, by his death, he'd given her this wonderful opportunity.

She now had two therapists working for her and the salon was running to capacity most of the time. A healthy percentage of profits already came from product sales and Roisin reckoned there was little scope to increase revenue in this area.

In short, the business had reached its potential and exceeded all of Roisin's expectations. 'Beauty by Roz' had a reputation equal to the best in the province and, thanks to the influence of Pauline McCormick, *Ulster Tatler* had even done an article on the salon, and Roisin, as one of the North's up-and-coming businesswomen.

The question was — what to do next? The premises in Dunluce Street offered no scope for expansion and Roisin did not consider the Ballyfergus market big enough to support a further salon. Katy Keenan, though, had proved herself not only a good friend but perfectly capable of stepping into Roisin's management shoes.

There was a sharp tapping at the window and Colette's pale face peered through the Venetian blinds. Roisin smiled, went to the door and opened it. Colette came inside, rubbing her gloved hands together.

'It's cold out there,' she said, and glanced at the papers on the desk. 'Are you still working?'

'No, not really, I was just looking at the draft annual accounts I got today.'

'And?'

'It's looking good. Far better than I expected. In fact, I was thinking of opening another salon.'

'What, in Ballyfergus?'

'No, I think we've reached saturation point here. I thought maybe Ballymena or Coleraine.'

'Sounds exciting, Roisin. And ambitious.'

'I know. The problem this time would be how to raise the capital. Daddy's money's all spent on this place.'

'How much would you need?'

'It depends on whether I buy or lease the premises, but I'd have to fit it out and invest in equipment and stock. I don't know, I'd need to do some sums.'

'And you'd need to suss out the competition.'

'Mmm,' replied Roisin thoughtfully. 'It's only a thought at the moment. Maybe I'm trying to run before I can walk. Listen, do you still want me to do your eyebrows before we go out?'

'Yes, please.'

Roisin went over to the desk, crammed the papers into her black leather briefcase and shoved it into the recess under the desk. Then, while Colette peeled off her coat, she closed the Venetian blinds, affording them some privacy.

After she'd tinted Colette's fair eyebrows dark brown and shaped them with a pair of precision tweezers, they both freshened up their make-up. In the small staffroom, Roisin changed out of her work clothes — black linen trousers and a matching button-up sleeveless jacket with a mandarin collar. Then she slipped on jeans, high-heeled ankle boots, a bright red top and her black wool pea-coat. She undid her hair from the tight coil on the top of her head and brushed it vigorously.

'Thank God for Saturdays,' she said when she was ready. 'Where'll we go for a drink?'

'How about the Ship? And then maybe we could go on for something to eat later on. Nothing fancy — maybe an Indian?'

'Sounds good to me. Mum's out at her choral group again. She's not expecting me home for a meal.'

'Oh, did I tell you Johnny's joining us for a quick drink?'

Johnny was Colette's elder brother, who lived and worked in Belfast. At one time Colette fancied Roisin and him as a couple but, though

Johnny was likeable and good-looking, he did nothing for Roisin. She sensed he felt the same about her and they remained good friends.

'He might be bringing a mate with him,' she went on, 'Scott somebody or other. He's an accountant too and an old friend of Johnny's from his university days.'

'He's not a geek, is he?' said Roisin remembering that accountants had a reputation as being boring, Johnny being the exception to the rule.

'No, no, no,' laughed Colette, shaking her head, 'I've met him. He's nice. Really.'

Outside, they linked arms and walked slowly through the chill of the early evening, which was unusually calm for March.

'I've been thinking,' said Colette, deliberately. 'You don't think we've left it too late?'

'Too late for what?'

'Do you think we're ever going to meet someone? Or are we going to be left on the shelf?'

'I dunno,' replied Roisin thoughtfully, considering the question that had been bothering her for some time. 'The problem with Ballyfergus is the lack of eligible men. I think we frighten them off, you know.'

'How come?'

'Well, we're successful, independent women with our own businesses. Some men find that threatening.'

'But what about Martin?' said Colette, referring to her last serious boyfriend.

'All he wanted was for you to marry him and

stay at home and have his babies,' Roisin reminded her.

'I couldn't do that. I couldn't give up my job. Not completely.'

'I know. And Jack Magee was the opposite. I think he saw me as a meal ticket — he still hasn't got a decent job, you know. And maybe we're to blame too . . . ' She was remembering Sadie's warning to keep a balance between work and personal life.

'In what way?'

'Well, there's been weeks on end you could hardly get me to go out, I was so tied up with the salon. And sometimes you're not much better when you've got a show on or a deadline to meet. If we're not out there looking, we're not going to meet someone. And sometimes you have to kiss a lot of frogs before you find your prince.'

Colette stopped walking, unlinked her arm from Roisin's and turned to look at her friend.

'You make it sound so, well, ruthless. Whatever happened to romance?'

'I don't mean to sound hard-nosed. It's just that, at our age, you have to be a bit more focused. Do you know what we should do?'

'What?'

'Go out every Friday and Saturday night to lots of different places outside of Ballyfergus so that we're meeting new people all the time.'

'I'm exhausted just thinking about it,' said Colette and laughed, revealing a mouthful of small, creamy-white teeth, 'but I take your point. We're not going to meet the love of our life in the Ship Inn, are we?'

'Exactly,' said Roisin, and added after a pause, 'you know, when you think about it, most of the people we grew up with are married with kids. Some are even onto second marriages.'

'Tricia O'Toole's been married three times,' said Colette ruefully, referring to a girl they'd gone to school with who came from a disadvantaged background.

'Poor Tricia,' said Roisin, shaking her head. 'She's got four kids by three different men and her latest husband is twice her age. And I heard he hits her.'

Colette shivered and shoved her hands deep into the pockets of her coat. 'That's awful,' she said.

Roisin said, 'I've been thinking about getting married and having kids a lot lately, though. Do you think it's got something to with our biological clocks ticking now that that we've turned thirty?'

'God, would you listen to the pair of us! You'll have us applying for our bus pass next. We're only thirty, not forty. We've loads of time yet.'

'Absolutely,' responded Roisin, forcing her voice to sound more positive than she felt.

'And you know,' said Colette, as they reached the door of the Ship Inn, 'lots of people don't get married now until they're well into their thirties.'

Roisin pushed open one of a pair of thin half-glass-panelled doors that guarded the entrance and they went in. They ordered gins and tonics. The Ship was one of the oldest pubs in Ballyfergus with, on the face of it, little to recommend it. With its fake black-leather stools, red carpet and glassy black tables, it was an interior design faux pas from the mid-eighties. Roisin was sure the owners would give their right hands to have it back the way it was before — traditional wood panelling, ancient benches and old oak tables worn hollow with age and use.

However, for some inexplicable reason it was currently popular with the younger crowd, who congregated here on Friday and Saturday nights. In six months or a year, tired of it, they would move on and some other pub would be in vogue for a while, before it too became uncool.

While they waited for their drinks, Roisin became convinced that someone was watching her. She turned her head slightly to the right and caught the eye of a man sitting alone in the corner of the pub. She couldn't help but stare. He was the most gorgeous thing she had ever seen. He had very straight brown hair that flopped over his high forehead, the darkest eyes and lovely olive-toned skin. She realised he was smiling at her. She nodded her head once, almost imperceptibly, in acknowledgement before turning her back on him once more. She was surprised to feel that her cheeks, when she touched them, were hot with embarrassment.

'Oh, there you are,' said Johnny, greeting them at the bar. He wore a suit with a pale blue shirt opened at the collar and the tie removed. 'How are you?' He gave both of them a kiss on the cheek. 'Come on over and meet Scott Johnston.'

He led them in the direction of the gorgeous

creature and Roisin hung back, her stomach churning with desire. She had never felt such a strong physical attraction to a man before. Would his personality prove equal to his looks?

Once the introductions were made, Roisin sat down opposite him and tried to engage in normal conversation. She tried not to stare at the sexy dark hairs on the back of his hands and forearms, visible where he'd rolled up his shirtsleeves. She shifted in her seat and cleared her throat.

'So,' she said, 'do you work with Johnny?'

'God, no,' he laughed, and slapped Johnny on the back. 'We'd never get any work done, would we?'

'We did the same course at uni,' said Johnny, with a grin, 'and I've been trying to get rid of him ever since.'

Roisin did some swift mental calculations. Johnny was three years older than her and Colette. Assuming Scott had gone straight to university from school he would be three years her senior too. Perfect.

'I'm an accountant with Semple and Ross,' continued Scott, ignoring Johnny. 'I've just started with them — this was my first week.'

'Ah, that explains why I've never seen you before,' exclaimed Roisin. 'They're my accountants, you see — Eileen McIlroy does my books.'

'Oh, yes, I've met her. She works part-time, doesn't she?'

'Yes, I think she's got small children,' said Roisin, noticing how emphatically Scott's eyebrows moved when he spoke. 'So are you commuting to Ballyfergus or have you moved here?'

'I'm staying with my parents temporarily until I get somewhere of my own.'

'Your parents?'

'Yes, they live on the Shore Road.' Seeing the surprise on her face he added, 'I'm from Ballyfergus originally.'

'Really?' said Roisin, quite certain that she'd never seen him before in her life.

'Well, I effectively left Ballyfergus after leaving the grammar and going to uni. I haven't been back, except to visit in over — what? Nearly fifteen years. I can't believe it.'

Neither could Roisin. Of course with a name like Scott Johnston she'd known instantly that he was a Protestant. There would have been little opportunity for their paths to cross in Ballyfergus as she attended St Margaret's, a Catholic school for girls. But, still, it was surprising that she'd never even seen him before.

'Johnny tells me that you run your own beauty salon,' said Scott interrupting her thoughts. 'How did you get into that?'

As she told him about her Saturday job as a teenager and how she'd gone on to establish the salon, Roisin found herself relaxing. Scott's interest in her seemed genuine for he listened carefully and asked intelligent questions.

'But how did you know there would be a market in Ballyfergus for this type of salon?'

'Well, firstly you look at the size of the population. Ballyfergus and its hinterland has a population of thirty thousand, which is enough

196

to support a salon. Also, people are more affluent nowadays, especially women, and they like to spend their money on pampering themselves. If you think back only a generation ago, very few women would have used a beauty salon regularly. And I think there's a sense of optimism too, don't you think, since the Good Friday Agreement? It makes people want to live a little.'

'Yes, things are changing for the better. Let's hope it stays that way. But you mentioned that the business had more or less reached capacity. What's next?'

'I'd like to expand one day. Maybe open another salon somewhere else. But that's only a pipe dream at the moment.'

'Well, I take my hat off to you. I really do. I think it's amazing that you've had a goal for all those years and now it's come true. You're living your dream.'

'When you put it like that, yes, I suppose I am. I'm very lucky.'

Johnny went to the bar for more drinks and Colette excused herself to go to the ladies'.

Roisin paused and then asked, cheekily, 'So what's your passion, then? Accountancy?'

'That's only a job. I really enjoy it, but I don't live for it.'

'So what do you live for?'

'Having a good time. Being happy. Making other people happy. And football, of course!'

'That sounds like a good philosophy to have,' said Roisin. 'I think I can be a bit serious sometimes. A bit intense.'

Scott leaned forward and looked deep into her

eyes. 'There's nothing wrong with being intense,' he said, his voice low and husky, and Roisin was glad she was sitting down for her knees turned to jelly.

A fake cough announced Colette's return from the loos.

'Excuse me. Are we going to get a word in edgeways, or are you two going to monopolise each other all night?'

'What's this?' said Johnny, as he set a steel tray, laden with drinks, on the table.

'Sorry,' said Roisin colouring, while Scott took a swig of his fresh pint. 'We were just talking about having a life philosophy.'

'Eat, drink and be merry. That sums up mine,' said Johnny and he patted his stomach. Roisin noticed with surprise that it protruded under his business shirt like an early pregnancy.

Johnny used to have a stomach like a washboard. Roisin sat up straight and held in her tummy. There was no doubt about it, once you were over thirty it was an uphill struggle — the inches crept on stealthily and, once there, they refused to budge. Up until now Roisin had been too busy and lacked the necessary zeal to work out at the gym, but from now on she'd have to be careful . . .

'Speaking of eating,' said Colette, 'we were going to go to the Indian. Do you want to come too?'

After several more rounds of drink, Johnny and Scott joined them as Roisin hoped they would. At the Indian she chose carefully from the menu, avoiding the fattening things like

Chicken Korma and deep-fried starters. All was going well until the main courses came.

'Now, darling,' said the waiter in a thick Indian accent, as he presented her with a sizzling cast-iron platter bearing tandoori lamb pieces, 'the plate. It is very hot. Be careful.'

Gingerly, he positioned the platter, which rested on a charred wooden base, to the right of Roisin's plate. Dishes of rice, side orders, Nan bread and chappatis littered the table and they all tucked in.

'Who's for more wine?' asked Colette.

'Mmm . . . yes, please,' said Roisin as she crumbled a popadom in her mouth, laden with spiced onions.

Colette filled her glass and Roisin remembered, too late, that her breath would reek of onions all night. She took a large drink of wine and decided that she was too drunk to care.

'Lamb anyone?' she said, and lifted the iron platter with both hands. 'Jesus Christ!' she howled as the heat seared the thumb and fingers of her right hand. She released her grip — the plate, and its contents, tumbled onto the brightly patterned red carpet. Somehow, her left hand had escaped injury.

'Oh, God, I'm so sorry,' she gasped to the waiter as he dashed forward to help.

'Never mind that now!' shouted Colette. She leapt from her seat and her napkin slid to the floor. 'Quick, into the toilets!' She grabbed Roisin by the left hand and dragged her away from the table.

'It doesn't feel that bad,' said Roisin, as

Colette held her hand under a running tap.

'That's because the cold water's numbing it. And you're drunk.'

'I am not.'

'You are so. So am I for that matter,' she said and laughed.

'Ouch!' said Roisin, as Colette dabbed her hand indelicately with a paper towel. 'That hurt.'

'It's going to hurt a lot more come the morning,' replied Colette. 'Look, you're blistering already.'

Roisin stared as red welts formed on the tips of her digits, and muttered, 'Shit. Shit. Shit.'

'Cheer up. It's not that bad. They'll be sore for few days but they'll get better.'

'It's not that. What'll Scott think of me?'

'Do you care?'

'I think I do.'

When they returned to the table, all evidence of the accident had been removed. A freshly prepared order of tandoori lamb sat where the other had been, except this time it had, wisely, been transferred to a china plate.

Roisin sat down sheepishly and said, 'I'm sorry about that.'

'What's there to be sorry about?' said Johnny.

'It could have happened to anyone,' agreed Scott. 'But more importantly, did you hurt yourself?'

'It's not too bad,' said Roisin, holding her hand out, palm up, for inspection.

A shiver, like a current of electricity, jolted her whole body when Scott gently took her hand in his. 'Mmm . . . that's gonna be sore,' he said, staring at her fingers and thumb. 'We'd better get you something for that.'

He called over the waiter and requested a pint glass of iced water. When it came he poured half of it into another glass, then rolled up the sleeve of Roisin's top.

'What are you doing?' she said.

'Trust me,' he replied, quite seriously. 'You'll thank me for this in the morning.'

Then he plunged her hand into the water and it wedged there, her fingers pressed against the ice, like dead fish. She sat through the rest of the meal with her hand stuck in the glass, and she'd never felt like such a prat in her life. Discovering that her appetite had suddenly evaporated, the evening looked like a dead loss. After her performance, she considered her chances with Scott well and truly blown.

'Do you want any more wine, Roisin?' said Colette.

'Why the hell not?' replied Roisin, thinking that she might as well get completely plastered.

The rest of the evening was a bit of a blur but it did involve a lot of laughing and giggling. She didn't have to worry about impressing Scott any more so she just had a bloody good laugh. She remembered the ride home in the back of a taxi, and fumbling at the door to get her key in the lock. But after that it was a blank.

★ ★ ★

The throbbing pain in her thumb, index and middle finger of her right hand woke Roisin around seven o'clock. She shuffled into the kitchen where she found a small icepack in the freezer. She didn't know whether to put it on her head or her hand. Opting for the latter, she wrapped it in a tea towel, got back into bed and pressed the damaged digits to the chilly package. The headache took hours to lift, even after two paracetemol, and a very long lie-in. At last Roisin felt well enough to get out of bed and ate some dry brown toast. After her mum had left for Mass she phoned Colette.

'Did I make a complete fool of myself last night?' she asked.

'Mmm . . . I wouldn't say that exactly,' came the diplomatic, sleepy reply, 'but I've never seen you so drunk, Roisin. What got into you?'

'Nerves, I suppose,' she said miserably. 'I did make a fool of myself, didn't I? He'll never want to see me again.'

'Who?'

'Scott.'

'He wants to see you again,' said Colette yawning. 'Don't you remember?'

'Remember what?'

'He asked for your phone number, you twit. You wrote it down for him.'

Now that Colette mentioned it, Roisin did remember scribbling something down on the back of the receipt at the Indian. God, she must've been plastered not to remember that.

'He must think I'm a complete idiot,' she concluded.

'No, he doesn't. He thinks you're great.'

'He does? How do you know?'

'He told Johnny. After the taxi dropped you off they came round to my place for a nightcap. Johnny ended up staying at my flat because he'd missed the last train to Belfast and he was too drunk to drive.'

'So did Scott stay too?'

'No, he went back to his parents' house but I went to bed before he left and overheard them talking in the lounge. That's when he said he thought you were great.'

'He said that?' asked Roisin, desperate for a blow-by-blow account.

'Not in so many words. But he said stuff about how interesting you were and how much he admired what you've done with the salon. Oh, and he thought you were really funny.'

'Funny funny? Or funny ha, ha?'

'He said you were great fun.'

'Tell me exactly what he said.'

'Oh, Roisin, will you stop nagging me!' said Colette good-humouredly. 'I'm going back to bed. I'll speak to you later.'

After that, Roisin's headache miraculously disappeared and the throbbing in her hand became tolerable. She spent the rest of the day mooning around, fantasising about Scott Johnston.

'What's up with you?' said Mum.

'Oh, nothing.'

'You'd better watch those fingers, Roisin. Make sure they don't get infected,' said Mum, examining the blistered skin. 'I hope you weren't drunk last night, girl,' she continued, her tone partly censorious, partly teasing.

'Oh, Mum, give it a rest. I'm a bit old for one of your lectures,' said Roisin, blushing, and she pulled her hand away.

When Scott didn't call that evening Roisin was disappointed. She had a terrible day at work on Monday, juggling clients' appointments between her and Katy. Because of her burnt fingers, Katy had to do all the massages and tanning and anything else it was impossible for Roisin to manage.

When the last client finally left, Roisin rushed home and mentally, if not physically, sat by the phone all night. But he didn't call then, nor the next night or the one after that. By Thursday night she was devastated and gave herself a good talking to.

She'd been acting like a lovesick teenager. Why on earth would Scott Johnston be interested in her anyway? A silly girl — correction, woman — who couldn't hold her drink, or a hot platter. With his good looks and great personality, Scott could have anybody he wanted. Why, girls were probably throwing themselves at him this very minute. Tall, slim ones with bottoms the size of a twelve-year-old and legs that went on forever. What on earth had made her think he'd want her?

She was just coming to terms with this reality, snuggled down on the sofa in front of *Coronation Street* and stuffing her face with Maltesers, when Mum came into the room holding the phone.

'It's for you. Someone called Scott,' she said, passing the handset over to Roisin.

She jumped up, threw the bag of sweets in the bin and ran out into the hall. She looked down at her clothes — old marl grey sweatpants and a baggy jumper that reached down to her knees — and winced. Her reflection in the mirror was so disheartening that she looked away. Her heart pounded in her chest.

'It's Roisin,' she said at last, as casually as she could manage.

'Hi. Look, I'm really sorry I didn't call before now. But I had to go to this conference over the water. Really boring stuff about changes in tax law. I left your number in Ballyfergus by accident and didn't realise until I was on the plane. I just got back tonight and phoned you straightaway.'

'Oh, that's OK,' said Roisin, cool as a cucumber.

They exchanged pleasantries for a bit and then Scott asked, 'So when can I see you? Is this weekend too soon?'

'Let me see,' said Roisin, pretending to consult her social diary by flicking through a copy of the yellow pages lying on the hall table.

'I'm out tomorrow night,' she lied, 'but Saturday would be all right.'

They arranged to meet at the Ship Inn for a drink and then go on for a meal at the Italian.

When they'd said goodbye, she pressed the hang-up button on the phone and put the handset back in its base station. When she looked in the mirror this time, a different girl looked back at her — one full of hope and expectation.

★ ★ ★

The very first thing Scott said when he saw her was, 'Let me see those fingers.'

They were standing under a streetlight at the appointed meeting place just outside the pub. He took her hand gently in his and examined the tips of her fingers where the skin had hardened to shiny discs, like pink plastic.

'Not too bad. I think you'll live,' he said and smiled at her without letting go of her hand. He ran his fingers lightly across her palm, and it felt like the flutter of butterfly wings when you held one in your fist. Shivers tingled up and down Roisin's spine.

They spent a lovely evening getting to know each other, Roisin being careful to drink moderately. They talked well past midnight until they were practically thrown out of the restaurant. Then he drove her home.

He stopped the car outside the house and asked, 'Why do you still live at home?'

Roisin looked at the little bungalow with the outside light, like a watch-fire, left on for her safe return. 'It's a bit odd, I know, living at home at my age. But I like it here and I don't much fancy living alone. My dad died when I was three so Mum's been on her own ever since.'

'I'm sorry,' said Scott.

Roisin shrugged and said, 'It happened a long time ago. I have an older sister, Ann-Marie, but she moved out a few years back. Mum's pretty open-minded about most things and doesn't interfere in my life. And I really like her, you know — she's more like a friend than a mother.'

'I can't wait to get out of the house. My

parents are driving me mad! They mean well, but they treat me like I was thirteen. I'd forgotten what it was like to live with them.'

'Haven't you found anywhere yet?'

'There's a flat coming up for rent this week — the owners have just redecorated it. I'll probably take it and then start looking for somewhere to buy.'

There was a pause and Roisin said, 'Well, then. I suppose I'd better go.'

Scott cleared his throat, leaned over and kissed her chastely on the lips. She put her arm around his neck and kissed him back. Then she hopped quickly out of the car.

They met again the following Wednesday night, by the nursing home on the corner between Main Street and Broadway, a square in the middle of town. Wednesday was late-night opening and shoppers were now scurrying home in the falling dusk.

'Sorry I'm late,' panted Scott, when he finally arrived. 'I got tied up with one of our biggest clients. I've only just managed to get away.'

'I've been waiting here for twenty-five minutes,' said Roisin, full of hurt.

'I know. I tried to phone you on your mobile.'

'Did you?' said Roisin caustically, pulling the phone out of her bag. It was switched off. She hurriedly shoved it back.

What made her say what she said next she would never know. The only explanation she could offer herself, and later Scott, was that she was seized with a pressing sense of urgency. It was as though the potential for this relationship was so great that it had to be said, so that they both understood what was at stake. If it frightened him off then they weren't meant for each other.

'You're the one,' she blurted out.

'The one?'

'For me, I mean. I like you, Scott. I really like you. I don't want you to mess about with me unless you're serious.'

She waited to see what his reaction would be. He did not laugh and deflect her comments, as most men would do when faced with such candour.

'I thought that too,' he said, earnestly. 'As soon as I saw you, I thought the same.'

'I don't want to get hurt.'

'I'm not going to hurt you, Roisin,' he said carefully.

'I'm thirty years old, Scott. I don't have time to waste.'

This time he did laugh. 'Oh, Roisin, you make that pronouncement like reaching thirty is the end of the world. I'm thirty-three and I'm not on a Zimmer-frame yet.'

He took her arm then and they crossed the street towards the Ship. She felt a little foolish.

'You are a peculiar girl, do you know that?' he said and squeezed her arm affectionately.

The evening was wonderful — they talked and talked and then talked some more. Little by little Roisin relaxed until she felt as comfortable in his company as she did in Colette's.

'I'm sorry about earlier,' she said, after several glasses of wine. 'Coming over all serious like that. I don't know what got into me.'

'Well, it did surprise me a little. It's not the sort of thing you expect on a second date.'

Roisin squirmed uncomfortably in her chair.

'But that's what I like about you, Roisin. You're not like anyone I've ever met before.'

He smiled then, a broad grin that made the corners of his eyes crease like a wet cotton blouse straight out of the washing machine. A smile that came from deep within and radiated pure happiness.

They made love that very night, like two randy teenagers, in the back of his car parked down by the harbour — a frenzy of grunting and laughing and limbs in all the wrong places. The windows steamed up and the car rocked as they clambered over each other's bodies, tasting and exploring dark, secret places.

When at last he put on a condom and entered her, it was a moment of pure perfection, like a spiritual awakening. They lay still like that for a few moments, listening to the soft panting of each other's breath, before he moved inside her and she responded with thrusts of her pelvis. She pressed her face against his hairy chest and bit his nipple. He winced with pleasure. She could have consumed him whole. She realised she loved him.

When it was over he pulled off the spent condom and tied the end in a knot. She leaned over and nuzzled her face in his crotch, his penis wet with his own juice. Then he pulled on his underpants and trousers and covered Roisin with his jacket.

'That was great,' he said. 'You're fantastic. And beautiful.'

He stroked the strands of long, damp hair off her face and kissed her forehead.

She sighed and nestled into his chest, not trusting herself to respond for fear of scaring him off with a proclamation of her love. Of course, she knew he loved her too, but perhaps he was not fully aware of it. Yet.

'This is ridiculous,' she said at last. 'Look at the age of us, bonking in a car like two school-kids.'

'I forgot to tell you,' he said. 'I'm getting the keys to my flat next week.'

'Thank God. At least we'll have somewhere to go.'

'Why, are you planning on making a habit of this?' said Scott, teasing.

'You could become a habit. A very bad habit.'

Then she sat astride him and undid the top button of his trousers.

★ ★ ★

When his accountant, Roger Craig, telephoned that morning, Noel smiled to himself. He'd been waiting for this call. He'd known it would come eventually — it was only a question of time. All he'd had to do was wait and she had come to him. And in the end, as he'd anticipated, his offer had proved too tempting to resist.

'What did she say?' he asked.

'She gave me some cock-and-bull story about you giving her my card and telling her to get in touch if she ever needed a business angel.'

'And what did you say?'

'Well, naturally I gave her short shift.'

'Did you now?'

'The only reason I've bothered you is in case she tries to contact you direct. Or calls at your office and makes a scene. She was quite insistent, Noel. She says she wants to open a new beauty salon in Carrickfergus and that she needs an investor.'

'I see.'

'Well, that's all I was calling about. I'll not take up any more of your time.'

'Roger.'

'Yes?'

'I want you to set up a meeting with Roz Shaw. Ask her to send in the financials for 'Beauty by Roz' and plans, budgets and projections for the new salon before the meeting.'

'What?'

'You heard me.'

'But, Noel, this isn't the sort of thing you get involved in.'

'I've decided to diversify.'

'She hasn't been trading for much more than a year. The girl's done all right but she's only a kid. It's her first business — she has virtually no track record. You could be throwing good money away.'

'Roger.'

'Yes, Noel?'

'Set it up.'

Noel put down the receiver without waiting

for a reply and sat back in his chair, thinking. Everything Roger said made sense. But what did he care? He could afford to write the money off if he had to, although something told him that wouldn't be necessary. There was something quite determined about the little lady, and he had every confidence that she would make a success of her next venture.

Noel looked forward to the meeting, which was to be held at his accountant's office. Roisin insisted on bringing her own accountant, Eileen McIlroy from Semple and Ross, with her.

Noel and Roger met early for a pre-meeting brief.

'She has a boyfriend, you know,' said Roger. 'A nice chap that works for Semple and Ross.'

'Really?' said Noel running his eye over the figures for 'Beauty by Roz'. Roger was right, of course. The first year's trading figures were sound enough, but no basis on which to invest thousands of pounds in another start-up.

'Pretty girl. Well, woman,' observed Roger idly, and he peered at Noel over his half-moon glasses.

'Is she?' replied Noel, leafing through the projections for the new salon, perfectly well aware what Roger was getting at. Because it didn't make sense business-wise to Roger, and because Roisin Shaw was a young, attractive woman, he could only come to one conclusion — Noel McCormick was trying to get his leg over.

Or perhaps he believed Roisin was blackmailing Noel for some previous infidelity. Noel laughed inwardly. Neither scenario could be further from the truth, but for once Noel's womanising reputation was an asset. It provided Roger with a satisfactory, if erroneous, explanation for Noel's behaviour. And it meant that he delved no further for his true motivation.

Roisin arrived with her accountant looking every bit the part of the businesswoman in a tailored navy suit and carrying a black leather briefcase. Her dark hair was pulled into a severe bun at the back of her head, adding a certain gravitas to her appearance.

When the pleasantries were dispensed with, they all sat down and Noel asked Roisin to outline her plans. She cleared her throat, glanced nervously at Noel, and then pulled a folder from her bag. She opened it and began to read from a list of bullet points typed on the page. She described her proposal for setting up the new salon in Carrickfergus, and the associated costs.

'It's rather a lot to ask, Miss Shaw,' said Noel, sitting back in his chair with his fingers entwined in his lap.

'Please call me Roz. Yes, I know. But no conventional bank is going to lend me this kind of money. It's high risk.'

'So what security are you offering?'

'Well, there's the lease of the property. And the equipment and stock.'

'All of which would be more or less worthless in the event of closure and a forced sale,' said Noel, testing her mettle.

Roisin glanced at Eileen McIlroy. 'Not necessarily,' she said, and then went on, 'It's true that I can't offer you much in the way of security but I'm going to set up a limited company and you'll get sixty per cent of the shares. Isn't that right, Eileen?'

Eileen nodded.

'Only sixty per cent. You drive a hard bargain, Miss Shaw.'

'OK, you're putting your money in and on paper it looks risky. But I promise you, Mr McCormick, you won't lose a single penny from this deal. It's my livelihood after all. I've a lot at stake here, and I'll work every hour God sends to make this a success. I promise you that.'

'Make it seventy per cent and you have a deal.'

'Sixty-five.'

'Done.'

A warm smile spread across the girl's face then and Noel couldn't help but return it. There was something very disarming about her. And she shared that hunger and ambition that Noel recognised in himself.

'Shake hands on it then,' he said, getting out of his seat.

She stood up, gripped his hand firmly and pumped it with a strength that belied her petite frame.

'Just out of interest, what are you going to call the salon?'

'Why, 'Beauty by Roz' of course. If all goes to plan, one day I'll have a chain of them across the province.'

'You know, I'm quite sure you will,' said Noel.

'You're absolutely mad, Noel,' said Roger, after the two women had left the office. 'You do know that, don't you?'

'Perhaps.'

'Even Eileen McIlroy couldn't believe it! I could see the surprise on her face when you agreed to sixty-five per cent.'

'Roger, I appreciate your help as always. But don't tell me how to run my business. And I won't tell you how to run yours.'

★ ★ ★

'But I want to move in with him, Mum. I love him,' said Roisin firmly, as she stacked the dirty dishes in the dishwasher.

'I don't think it's a good idea. You've only known each other for six months.'

'But he loves me.'

'Why don't you get married, then?'

Roisin slid the plates into the rack and shut the door of the dishwasher. The machine started up, a quiet hum.

'You know he hasn't asked me that,' she replied softly.

'All the more reason not to do it. If there was a wedding in the offing, well, then I might feel differently about it.'

'Is that all you care about? What people think?'

Deliberately Mairead set down the cups she was holding, came over to Roisin and clasped her hands so tightly they almost hurt. 'Roisin, love, you've got that completely wrong. It's the last thing I care about. I just don't want to see you hurt.'

'I won't be. If it doesn't work out, I can always

215

come home, can't I?'

Mairead sighed loudly. 'Life isn't as simple as that, Roisin. You shouldn't move in with someone unless you're both prepared to make a serious commitment to each other.'

'We are.'

'But not marriage?'

'Not at the moment,' said Roisin, folding her arms across her chest. 'You can't stop me, Mum, you know that, don't you?'

'I know I can't stop you. But I wish I could.'

'Well, I've made my decision. I'm moving out on Saturday.'

Saturday arrived much too quickly and, when Roisin found herself in her bedroom packing suitcases, she couldn't quite believe it was happening. Mairead came and stood in the doorway.

'Have you thought about how your grand-mother's going to take this?' she said.

'I think Granny's a lot more liberal-minded than you give her credit for,' replied Roisin. 'And I don't care what people think.'

'Well, what about what I think?'

'You're just being old-fashioned.'

'Roisin,' Mairead said in a more conciliatory tone, 'I've never interfered in your life, have I?'

Roisin shook her head, acknowledging in fairness and despite her anger, that this was true. She continued to fold clothes and throw them rather aggressively into the suitcases.

'I'm really worried that you're taking on too much. You've only just opened the new salon in Carrickfergus and it's taking up all your energy.

This isn't the time to be moving in with someone and all the adjustment that entails. You don't just fall into an intimate relationship. It takes effort and application. No matter how much you love them.'

'The new salon is going like a dream, Mum,' said Roisin, checking the last of the drawers for clothes. 'OK, it's been hard work up until now but the worst is over. It's taken off much faster than the first one did and I've got good staff to support me. Moving in with Scott will make things better, can't you see that? I'll be more settled when I'm with him.' She stood up and looked her mother in the eye. 'You don't like Scott, do you?' she said. 'Is it because he's Presbyterian?'

'I think Scott is great. And he could be a Hindu for all I care. Look, you said that you were looking for a house to buy together. Why don't you at least wait until then?'

Roisin closed the lid of the suitcase firmly and turned to face her mother. 'Mum, I know this is right. If I had any doubts in my mind, any at all, I wouldn't move in with him. Do you remember how you felt about Dad?'

Mairead nodded her head sadly.

'Well, that's how I feel about Scott. You just know, don't you?'

'I can't persuade you then?' said Mairead then, her words more of a statement than a question.

'I've my mind made up. Don't let me go like this. Be happy for me.' Roisin embraced Mairead then and held her until her stiff shoulders relaxed and she returned the hug. 'And you've not to be worrying about me, now. Promise?'

'I'll miss you, love,' said Mairead softly into Roisin's ear. 'I suppose I had to lose you eventually.'

'I'll miss you too, Mum. And you haven't lost me. Ballyfergus isn't exactly a sprawling metropolis! I'm only down the road.'

Roisin packed her car and drove off, the image of her mother standing in the doorway with her pinny on etched in her mind for always.

Scott was waiting for her at the flat, a bottle of champagne on chill.

'Well, how did it go?'

'She's not happy about it. But we parted on good terms,' said Roisin and she let out a long sad sigh. 'She's just worried about me. She doesn't want me to get hurt.'

'It's only natural. But your mother has nothing to worry about,' said Scott, stroking her hair, 'and I'm going to prove it to her. And to you.'

For the first few weeks living together, they were consumed by each other. Outside of work, they rarely looked beyond the confines of their home because everything they needed was there — love, sex, companionship, solace, joy, laughter. Of course the obsession with each other gradually mellowed and, in time, they resumed more normal relations with friends and the outside world. But Roisin had found her soul-mate, and with him a state of inner peace and contentment entirely new to her.

'You know Mum was wrong about us?' she

said to Scott one day when they were unpacking the food shopping.

'In what way?'

'She said that moving in with you would be an added stress when I was so busy already with both salons. She said that it takes time to learn to live together. But she was wrong. It hasn't been like that with us at all. In a way it's as though we've always been together. Moving in with you was the best thing I ever did.'

Scott came over to where she stood, shopping bags strewn about her feet. He put his hands on her arms and looked into her eyes.

'I'm so glad you feel like that, Roisin. It's how I feel too. And I believe it's worked out so well because we were meant to be together. We were born for each other. Maybe it's time we bought that house. What do you think?'

'Yes, I think we should,' said Roisin, well aware that such a move would take their relationship onto another level. 'For one thing, this flat's far too tiny for the two of us. And paying rent really is a waste of money. But it's on one condition.'

'What?'

'We get a cleaner! I'm only just beginning to appreciate all the things Mum did for me when I lived at home. We're both too busy to look after a house as well.'

They visited the show home at Manor Heights the very next day. It was fantastic and, as Roisin wandered from one spacious room to the next, she realised that she wanted this house as much as she'd wanted her first salon. So long as Scott was living in it with her.

As it turned out they were in luck — a house in the style they wanted was nearing completion, although no buyer had yet been found. They put a deposit on it there and then and, legalities permitting, a moving — in date of eight weeks hence was agreed.

They shopped for basic furniture — new sofas, a chest of drawers, dining-table and chairs — and arranged delivery to their new home. Once the building society had accepted their mortgage application, they ordered laminate flooring for the downstairs, cream carpet for the upstairs and arranged for these to be laid the day before they would move in.

Since the opening of her first salon, Roisin had prudently built up a modest pot of savings. She had concealed this when seeking finance from Noel McCormick, believing that she was entitled to her personal nest egg. But the day before the house move, she checked the status of her bank accounts on the Internet and her stomach rolled itself into a tight ball. Her savings, meant for rainy days, had almost disappeared. That night at home, as she and Scott packed up their relatively few belongings, she wondered how to raise the subject of money. In the end, she didn't have to, for Scott gave her the perfect lead-in.

'We're going to have to go on a big shopping spree once we move in,' he said. 'We've hardly got a picture or a pair of curtains to put up.'

'Scott, I don't have any money left,' said Roisin quietly, her stomach knotted with anxiety. 'It's all gone on the furniture.' Everything they'd bought so far had been split fifty-fifty.

'So?'

'I can't expect you to furnish the rest of the house on your own. We'll just have to make do with what we've got for the time being.'

Scott slowly, almost contemplatively, wrapped the flex around the toaster and put it in a big brown box.

'Let's get married,' he said suddenly.

Roisin stopped stacking CDs into a box and looked up at him, not altogether sure if she'd heard correctly. He ran his fingers through his hair, causing it to stick up haphazardly. Dressed in a grubby white T-shirt and baggy blue jeans, he'd never looked more gorgeous.

Roisin's heart stopped momentarily and then started again with a great thud. 'Are you serious?' she said.

'Never more so. What do you say, Roisin?'

'Yes, darling. Yes!' she cried and put her hands up to her face as tears filled her eyes.

Scott came over and put his arm around her shoulder. 'What's wrong, Roisin? Why are you crying?'

'I just can't believe it. Finding you and buying our lovely new home and now this. Is it all right to be this happy? It all seems too good to be true. I keep thinking that something awful's going to happen.'

'Nothing's going to happen to us. Nothing's going to go wrong, baby. You deserve to be happy, Roisin. I love you. Believe that and accept it.'

He kissed her all over the face then, little wet comfort kisses, sweet and soothing.

'I know someone who'll be pleased anyhow,' she said.

'Your mum?'

'How did you guess?' she laughed and pulled his face to hers and kissed him passionately.

'Now, no more talk about money, do you hear me?' said Scott, once he'd extricated himself from her embrace. 'This house is going to be our home and I want it to be perfect. From now on everything we have belongs to both of us.'

'But it's not fair — ' began Roisin, and Scott silenced her by placing his index finger on her lips.

'Don't talk like that, Roisin,' he said, a little frown criss-crossing its way across his brow. 'I really don't want to hear you talking like that again.'

'OK, if that's how you want it to be. If you're sure.'

'I'm sure,' he replied and the tension in Roisin's body subsided.

The next couple of days presented little opportunity to talk about the engagement, even though they'd both taken time off work. Once the few pieces of furniture Scott owned, and the new ones they'd bought, were installed in the house, it still looked bare. So they went shopping for curtains, a coffee table, pictures for the walls and rugs for the laminate floors.

On the second night in their new home in Beeches Court, they were having their evening meal in the kitchen. Roisin took the dirty plates over to the sink and, when she sat down again, a small red jewellery box had appeared in the middle of the table.

'I hope you don't mind,' said Scott. 'I wanted to surprise you.'

He opened the box, removed a ring and slid it onto Roisin's finger. Wordlessly she examined it. Three large diamonds sat proud in a white gold, or maybe platinum, setting.

'You can change it,' he said, hastily. 'I don't want you to keep it if you don't like it.'

'How could I not like it? It's beautiful. I love it.'

'Good, because I love you, Roisin Mary Shaw. And don't you ever forget it.'

'I love you too,' said Roisin, examining with wonder the ring on her finger, 'and I don't think I could ever be happier than I am right now.'

'Well, then,' said Scott eagerly, 'what about a date for the wedding?'

'God, I don't know. A summer wedding would be nice. What do you think?'

'How about August? Then we could go away somewhere nice on honeymoon before the autumn sets in.'

'Mmm, sounds good. We'll have to check with both families first.'

'I know I've just sprung this on you,' said Scott, 'but what sort of wedding do you think we should have? A big one? Small one?'

'Well, I've a small family, Scott. There's really only Mum and Ann-Marie. And Granny and my aunts and uncles, of course.'

'Same here, really.'

In addition to his parents, Scott had one brother, Fraser, three years his senior who was married to Julie. They had one child — a sweet little boy called Oliver.

'But the big issue is where to get married,' said Roisin. 'That might have more impact on the size of the wedding than anything. Depending on where we choose, one side or the other's not going to be too happy. They might even refuse to come.'

'I know. I've given it a lot of thought, Roisin, and whichever way you look at it, getting married in church is going to be a problem. No Presbyterian minister is going to set foot in a Catholic Church, or allow a priest to carry out a ceremony in the kirk, so a joint ceremony isn't going to happen. I'd be happy for a priest to marry us, if they were willing that is, with me not being a Catholic.'

'Oh, Scott that's really, really sweet of you but I can't ask you to do that. Why should we get married in my church and not yours? But I don't much fancy the idea of getting married in the Presbyterian Church either.'

'So what should we do?'

'It'll just have to be the registry office,' said Roisin. 'Let's face it, Scott, neither of us is in any way religious. It'd be hypocritical for either of us to insist on a wedding in our respective churches.'

'I'm cool with that. But would you be happy, Roisin? Most women have a fantasy about a white church wedding, don't they?'

'I'm a big girl now, Scott,' she chided, jokingly. 'I left that fantasy behind in childhood. Anyway I'll still wear a wedding dress and have bridesmaids. The only reason I'd have liked a church wedding would be to please Mum. But I think she'll be so relieved to see us married she won't care where it takes place. What about yours?'

'They'd be happy with that. To be honest they'd be more comfortable there than in a chapel. I don't think either of them has ever been inside a Catholic Church.'

'That's settled then — and if we keep the wedding fairly small, we can afford to have a big party for all our friends in the evening.'

Just then the doorbell rang and Roisin and Scott looked at each other in surprise, not expecting a caller. Roisin opened the door to find Mairead standing, not on the doorstep but on the path, her car on the road and a small inlaid card table beside her. It had belonged to Roisin's maternal grandmother, who was long dead, and had sat for many years in the front room.

'I thought you'd like to have this,' said Mairead, 'As a sort of house-warming present.'

'Oh, Mum, we'd love to! Thank you. Come on in, you'll catch your death standing there. Scott!' she shouted up the hallway. 'Come and see!'

In the living-room they stood and admired the table and Scott said, 'It's really lovely, Mrs Shaw. Thank you. It must mean a lot to you, belonging to your mum as it did.'

'Not as much as my daughter does, Scott,' she said, rather pointedly, though she softened her remark by adding, 'You can call me Mairead if you like.'

'Before I show you round the house, Mum,' said Roisin, glancing at Scott, 'we've something to tell you.'

Scott came over and held her hand.

'You're not pregnant!' gasped Mairead and she put her hand over her mouth and looked at Roisin's stomach.

'Oh, Mum!' said Roisin, laughing to suppress the little wave of irritation that washed over her. She held out her left hand. 'Why do you always suppose the worst? We're engaged.'

'Oh, that's wonderful news! Wonderful news!' cried Mairead. Her whole demeanour changed then and she hugged them both. 'What a fright you gave me there. But when did this happen? Why didn't you tell me?'

'We just did. We only got engaged tonight,' said Roisin, feeling as though her heart wasn't big enough to hold all this happiness.

After they'd sat down and had some tea, Roisin explained the dilemma they had over a church wedding and their decision to get married in registry office.

'Oh,' said Mairead, closing her lips in a tight line over her unspoken objections.

'Don't be like that, Mum,' said Roisin. 'It's either there or nowhere.'

'If you put it like that,' said Mairead, reacting in the pragmatic manner Roisin had anticipated, 'it'll have to do.'

If there was one thing worse in her mother's eyes than a registry wedding, it was no wedding at all.

7

2001

The Shaw sisters, along with Colette, threw themselves into the task of finding suitable wedding and bridesmaid dresses. This provided them with opportunities for several hilarious days out all over the province. They tried on many nice gowns, and many more ghastly ones, but nothing suited.

In a bridal salon in Ballymena, as the trio posed in yet another sea of frothy, overpriced creations, Colette said, 'Look, why don't you let me make your dress and the bridesmaids' too.'

Roisin considered her reflection in the full-length mirror and frowned. She looked like Little Bo Peep. 'Wouldn't it be too much for you?'

'Not at all. It would be my wedding present to you. I'd consult you at every stage of the design so that you could have exactly the dress you want. You'd practically design it yourself.'

'Oh, Colette, would you? I didn't like to ask.'

'I didn't like to offer, in case you didn't want me to.'

'Why wouldn't I want one of your dresses?'

'Oh, I don't know,' she said with a casual shrug of the shoulder. 'Not everyone likes what I do.'

'Oh, Colette, how can you say that? I think

everything you've done is fantastic. I'd be honoured to wear one you made. I just didn't think you'd have the time to do it.'

'Well, I do. So that's it settled then,' said Colette happily, and she added in a low hiss, 'just let me get this monstrosity off.'

Ann-Marie popped her head out of the adjacent changing room, and said with an exasperated sigh, 'Now can we please go home?'

As the day of the wedding approached Roisin brimmed with happiness. One of the main reasons for her joy, Scott aside, was the transformation that Ann-Marie had undergone. It was hard to work out when exactly it had started but, over the last six months or so, she'd gone from being depressed, unreliable and suicidal to something approaching normality. She even had a job now, working part-time as a veterinary nurse in a practice in Victoria Street.

Roisin and Ann-Marie spent the night before the wedding at their mother's house, the hen party having taken place the previous week. Scott, rather inadvisably, was having his stag party that very night, on the eve of the wedding.

Ann-Marie had a bath while Roisin gave herself a French manicure — painting the tips of her nails white over pale pink nail varnish. Katy was coming over in the morning to do their make-up and Sadie to set their hair in old-fashioned rollers. But Roisin thought that you got the best finish with nails when they were allowed to 'set' overnight.

'I hope he's in a fit state for tomorrow,' said Mairead, thoughtfully, referring to Scott.

'He will be,' said Roisin with confidence, switching on a heat lamp positioned over the dining-room table where she sat.

The table was covered with an old beach towel to protect it from damage. She opened a bottle of strong-smelling clear liquid and expertly applied a generous topcoat to each nail. Then she rested her elbows on the table and positioned her upturned hands, fingers bent inwards so that the nails were exposed, some six inches from the light-bulb.

'Ann-Marie seems very cheerful these days, Mum,' she observed. 'Do you have any idea what's happened to change her?'

'I don't know that anything's happened. Maybe she just got better.'

'She seems so much happier to me these days. I've heard her humming to herself, like she's in a little world of her own. Haven't you noticed? And she's taking an interest in her appearance, for the first time in years.' Roisin paused and thought. The subtle changes she had observed in her sister were the same as the ones she'd noticed in herself since falling in love with Scott. 'She hasn't got a boyfriend, has she?'

'Not that I know of,' replied Mairead, taking Roisin's veil out of the box and spreading it out carefully on the sofa. 'Well, whatever it is,' she said, smoothing the folds of the gauzy fabric with the flat of her hand, 'let's hope and pray it lasts. She's a different girl and it's wonderful to see. And if it is a boyfriend I suppose we'll find out soon enough.'

Roisin switched off the lamp, the light died

and she waved her fingers in the air to cool them.

'I'm sorry I gave you a hard time about moving in with Scott,' said Mairead, suddenly. 'You were right about him. You two are made for each other. And I'm very happy to have him as a son-in-law.'

'Thank you for saying that, Mum. It means the world to me. He is wonderful, isn't he?'

The next day at three o'clock a female registrar in a bland but not unpleasant room married Roisin and Scott. Uncle John, Mum's brother, gave Roisin away and Scott was there on time, looking none the worse for the celebrations the night before. Colette had created clinched-waist, knee-length, fifties style gowns for Roisin and her bridesmaids, with cap sleeves and silk neck scarves. The style had been chosen primarily to flatter Roisin's curvy figure, but it looked good on all of them. Roisin's dress was cream, the bridesmaids' dresses a startling shade of royal blue. They carried deep blue and cream rose bouquets — so perfect they looked like they were made of wax.

The ceremony was followed by a meal in a private room at the Marine Hotel for the wedding party, nineteen of them in all. When the meal was over and a few very informal speeches made, they went upstairs to change and then partied into the small hours with family and friends. When Roisin and Scott left the party to go up to their room, Roisin threw her bouquet into the crowd. Colette caught it and both women burst out laughing. The next day Roisin and Scott flew out of Aldergrove airport for two weeks of luxury in the Maldives.

On the plane Roisin leaned against Scott's shoulder and they reflected on the success of their wedding.

'It was perfect,' said Scott. 'Everything was perfect. Just the way I always imagined getting married should be. Fun and relaxed.'

'And romantic,' said Roisin twiddling with the rings on her left hand, still constantly aware of their presence.

'Mmm . . . ' murmured Scott, nuzzling his face into her hair, 'I can't believe I've got you for the rest of my life.'

* * *

One of the things Donal had always despised about Noel McCormick was his womanising. It was a well-known fact round Ballyfergus that he'd had a mistress for years and he visited her several times a week. He couldn't understand how Noel could choose some cheap tart over his beautiful, cultured wife. Once, Donal had disliked Pauline. Now all he felt for her was pity because he was certain she knew about Noel's adultery. He could tell by the clipped way she spoke to Noel, the lack of warmth between them and Pauline's proud bearing, hiding the shame beneath.

Michelle seemed utterly blind to the reality of her parents' marriage. When she talked about their relationship, it was all about how wonderful they were and how much they loved each other and what a great daddy she had. He sometimes wondered if she really believed it, or if she simply didn't want to face up to the unpalatable truth about her father.

Yet Donal was no better than his father-in-law. For here he was, doing the very same thing as Noel — sneaking into another woman's home under the cover of darkness, like a criminal. For adultery was a crime and the innocent victim in this case was Michelle. But he wasn't here to see just any woman, he reminded himself. It was Amy. And he loved her.

He pressed the buzzer and waited impatiently for the door to open. His heart began to race, the way it always did when he was with her. He pictured her serene and beautiful face, her long brown hair, the way the corners of her mouth would turn up in a smile when she saw him. The door opened and there she was.

'Amy!' he cried, almost breathless with desire.

He followed her into the hall, shut the door behind him and put his arms around her waist from behind. He nuzzled his face into her neck, inhaling her scent, her warmth, her spirit.

'Oh God, Amy, how I've missed you!'

She swivelled round inside his embrace and turned her face up at him. Her expression was serious, almost sad. She laid a hand lightly on each of his shoulders.

'I've missed you too, Donal.'

She led him then into the lounge, which was illuminated only by candles, the curtains drawn against the light of an early autumn evening. The air in the room was heavy with the scent of jasmine and sandalwood. Amy picked up a bottle of red wine from the rustic coffee table and, very slowly, poured two glasses. She was wearing no shoes, her toenails were painted bright orange and she had on a flowing skirt of ethnic origin and a long, loose blouse.

Wordlessly, she offered him a glass of wine, sat down on the sofa and stared at him. One of the things he loved most about Amy was her economy with words. She choose them with care, and used them sparingly with the result that everything she said really meant something. Not like the endless chatter that emanated from Michelle's mouth. Immediately Donal felt guilty — it wasn't fair to draw comparisons between the two women. Michelle always came off the worst.

He loosened his tie, sat down beside her and smiled. 'What are you looking at?' he said.

'You.'

'Why?'

'Because I can't remember,' she said flatly. 'When you're not here I can't remember what you look like.'

Her comment stabbed him like a dart — a reproach for not being there always. For being with Michelle and not with her.

'You only saw me on Tuesday,' he joked, making light of her observation.

'I try to,' continued Amy, as though he'd never opened his mouth, 'but I can't.'

'I'll get you a photo.'

She smiled then, trying not to, and said, 'You're making fun of me now.'

'No, I'm not. I'm not,' he laughed, and she thumped him gently on the stomach with a richly embroidered cushion.

Smiling, she put the wine glass to her lips, took a drink and said, 'I don't think it would be a good idea.'

'What?'

'A photo. Somebody might see it.'

'Ah, of course. Not a good idea,' agreed Donal, looking into the wine. There was a long pause and then he added, 'Are you happy, Amy?'

'Happier than I've ever been.'

'I mean happy with the way we are. Meeting like this. Never going out together in public.'

She took her time before replying. 'I accept it,' she said simply. 'I know I can't change it. That, Donal, is up to you.'

'And what do you want me to do, Amy? Do you want me to leave Michelle?'

'Donal, I can't tell you what to do.'

'It's Molly that's keeping me there, you know. If I leave I know I'll hardly get to see her. You've no idea what the McCormicks are like. Noel, especially. He's absolutely ruthless and he hates me.'

'How could anyone hate you?' said Amy, her expression one of bewilderment.

'Oh, believe me, Noel does,' said Donal, nodding his head emphatically, 'and he'd do everything in his power to make sure Molly never sees me again.'

Amy absorbed all this before she spoke. 'All I know is that you have to follow your heart, Donal. Listen carefully for its whispers. It will

234

tell you what to do.'

'My heart tells me that I love you.'

'I know you do.'

'I need you, Amy,' he said and, as though reading his thoughts, she took the glass out of his hand, set it on the coffee table and led him into the bedroom.

★ ★ ★

During one of his regular morning calls to say that he loved her, Scott told Roisin that she was a new aunt.

'Julie had the baby late last night. A wee girl. Fraser just phoned.'

'Are they both well?'

'Yes. I think she had a tough enough time but they're coming home today.'

'God, they don't hang about, do they? Gone are the days when you got to lie around in hospital for a week.'

'That's the NHS for you. Anyway I can't see Julie lying around in bed for a day, never mind a week.'

'No,' laughed Roisin, 'she'd end up running the ward.'

After she'd put the phone down Roisin thought about her sister-in-law. Julie was an extraordinary woman. Physically petite, with a short blonde bob and intelligent blue eyes, her stature belied her inner strength. She was a powerful, strong-minded and extremely capable person. She was also rather serious and, despite Roisin's best efforts, the two sisters-in-law had not formed much of a friendship. They just didn't seem to have anything in common. From little things that Julie had said over the course of their acquaintance, Roisin surmised that she considered Roisin's profession to be rather lightweight and frivolous. Julie was an optometrist and planned to go back to work when the new baby was three months old, just as she had done with her first child.

Scott and Roisin called to see their new niece the next night armed with presents. For the baby they brought a heart-shaped pink balloon, and an exquisite designer dress, matching tights and jacket. For Oliver, a Thomas the Tank train and a jigsaw.

Julie sat on the sofa holding the baby while Oliver, dressed in his pyjamas, watched a video. She opened the baby present with one hand — the infant was latched onto her breast, feeding. The child was wearing some sort of sack-like nightdress, made from natural coloured cotton, probably organic, knowing Julie.

'So,' said Scott when they'd admired the newborn and paid sufficient attention to Oliver, 'have you decided on a name yet?'

'Ruby,' replied Fraser, offering a glass of whisky to Scott and Roisin.

'What a lovely name!' said Roisin, taking the drink.

They toasted the new baby and took a slug of whiskey, so strong it nearly winded Roisin.

'Thank you for all these lovely presents,' said Julie, looking into the box of clothes. 'They're very — pretty. But you won't mind if I have to change them, will you? Perhaps for something more . . . ' she held the frilly skirt up and examined it with undisguised horror, 'practical.' She folded the garment and put it back in the box.

Roisin smiled inwardly. Of course the dainty dress wasn't to Julie's taste — she should've known. But Julie was always direct and open, regardless of whether or not she hurt other people's feelings.

'Not at all,' she said, pleasantly. 'You just get whatever you want.'

In one swift, practised movement Julie removed Ruby, now sated with milk, from her nipple. She pulled the baggy rugby shirt over her breast and thrust the baby at Roisin saying, 'Would you hold her a minute?'

While the conversation continued around her, Roisin examined the little scrunched-up bundle in her arms. Ruby's head, no bigger than a cantaloupe melon, was still marked and bruised by her difficult birth. Her eyes were closed, two perfect crescents in a blotchy face and the corners of her tiny mouth were turned up in a smile. One arm was raised to the side of her head, the wrinkled fingers clenched in a tight fist. Roisin wiped a little milky dribble from the baby's cheek with her finger, the skin still hot and flushed from contact with her mother's breast.

Then an emotion, something akin to jealousy, took hold and startled Roisin. It was accompanied by a yearning sensation deep inside her — a bit like driving fast over sharp undulations on a country road. Roisin cuddled the baby close and kissed the top of her sweet-smelling head.

So this was what people meant by 'being broody'! It wasn't only an emotional response to holding a newborn — it was a physical desire. Alarmed by the strength of her feelings, Roisin sought to pass the sleeping baby on to someone else.

'Do you want a shot?' she said to Scott. 'You don't realise how heavy she is. At first she seems to weigh nothing and then your arm starts to get sore.'

'Heavy?' said Julie scornfully. 'She's only seven pounds, three ounces. You should see how heavy she is when she's four times the weight and you're walking the floor with her all night. Then you'd know what heavy is!'

'I'd be afraid of hurting her,' said Scott to Roisin, shaking his head cautiously. 'She's so tiny.'

'Well then, rather me than you, Julie,' said Roisin, as she handed Ruby back to her mother, who commandeered her like the master of a ship.

On the way home in the car, Roisin said, 'Did you think Julie was acting a bit strange?'

'In what way?'

'She almost seemed to resent Ruby. Or all the hard work that was going to come her way. If she feels that way about it, why did she have another baby?'

'Mmm,' said Scott.

'What does that mean?'

'Well, let's just say she and Fraser have been

having difficulties. For a start the baby wasn't planned. A bit of a surprise for both of them.'

'How do you know?'

'Fraser told me that the pregnancy was an accident. As for their marriage difficulties, I don't know if Fraser was exaggerating. Maybe it'll all blow over.'

'Why didn't you tell me?'

'I thought it was, you know, private. Their business. But the way they're getting on, I'd say it's going to be hard to conceal. Did you hear Julie speak to Fraser?'

'Now that I think about it, no. She didn't address him directly the whole time we were there. How long's the cold-shoulder treatment been going on?'

'Months.'

'Well, what's wrong between them? Has Fraser been having an affair?'

'Fraser? No, don't be ridiculous. From what he's told me, and he hasn't told me much, they've just drifted apart. I honestly don't think that Fraser loves her any more. When Julie's not giving him the silent treatment, they're at each other's throats.'

'If that's the way they feel, then they should separate.'

'Easier said than done when there are children involved, Roisin.'

'But it can't be doing little Oliver any good, living in a house were there's shouting and fighting going on. Or Ruby for that matter. Children are very sensitive to these things.'

'I know,' said Scott, as he pulled into their

driveway and switched off the car engine. 'It's a bloody mess.'

'Now I wish you hadn't told me,' said Roisin, miserably, 'I'll not be able to stop worrying about them.'

Things didn't improve between Fraser and Julie because, two months after Ruby's birth, they started going for marriage guidance counselling. And more often than not they dropped the children at Roisin and Scott's for the hour or so that the sessions required. Sometimes Colette called round, ostensibly to give Roisin a hand. But Ruby was very little trouble, sleeping much of the time, feeding greedily and lying awake quietly on her playmat.

'I honestly don't mind doing it,' confided Roisin to Colette one day, 'if it's going to do any good. But I hate the way Julie treats Ruby. You know, I don't think I've heard her use the child's name once. She just says 'her' and 'she'.'

Colette looked at Ruby sleeping peacefully in her car seat and said, 'That's just Julie's way. Don't pay her too much heed. Maybe she's got post-natal depression.'

'I think they're wasting their time anyway,' said Roisin.

'Oh, don't say that, Roisin.'

'It's true. Fraser told Scott that Julie thinks the sessions are a waste of time. She's talking about a divorce.'

'That would be awful. What about the children?'

'I imagine they'd stay with their mother. Poor Fraser'd be devastated.'

They sat in silence for a few moments.

'But listen,' said Roisin cheerfully, determined to break the dreary mood, not least because Oliver would be due back any minute from the corner shop with Scott, 'what's happening with you these days? Any men in your sights?'

Colette sighed despondently. 'There just aren't any nice men out there, Roisin. They're all married or divorced. You got the last one!'

Roisin tried not to look smug and said, 'Well, the married ones are out of bounds, of course, but what about someone who's divorced?'

'No,' said Colette shaking her head emphatically, 'I don't think so. Not for me.'

'But why ever not?'

'I don't want a guy who's been in a serious relationship with someone else, even if they are divorced.'

'A divorce is pretty final, Colette.'

'Look, half of them have got kids or they're hung up on their previous relationship. I don't want someone who's got a history.'

'But we've all got histories, Colette. What about you and Martin Boyd?'

'Oh, that didn't mean anything.'

'It did at the time.'

'I just don't want to be someone's second choice, that's all.'

'But you wouldn't be. If they're divorced, then that relationship is finished. Over and done with. They've moved on. As for children, most of them live with their mums anyway.'

'I don't want all those complications.'

'Well, all I can say, Colette, is that you're

limiting your options. And you could be missing out on the love of your life.'

★ ★ ★

Roisin swam lengths of Ballyfergus swimming-pool breaststroke, immersing her head fully between each stroke of her arms, pushing forward with her legs. The pool was large, cool and deep, meant for serious swimming. It was here that she'd learnt to swim during weekly lessons with school. She and her classmates had been herded into the icy water every Tuesday afternoon. Arms clamped to their sides, they protested like sheep being forced into a dip. She remembered the sting of the chlorine when the water went up your nose, the chill of the wet tiles underfoot, and the way your ears hurt if you dived to the bottom of the deep end.

One side of the swimming-pool was bordered by the changing rooms and, above these, a massive viewing gallery, built to accommodate at least three hundred people. In all the years Roisin had lived in Ballyfergus, she'd never seen more than a handful of people up there at one time, watching the swimmers below. Tall windows that reached from floor to ceiling surrounded the other three sides of the pool. During the daytime they afforded fine views of the Irish Sea and the harbour mouth, the sea invariably grey-green and, more often than not, the glass lashed with rain.

On this wet autumn night, though, the darkness outside was impenetrable, thick and black as ink. In the early morning a grey blanket of cloud had settled over the town and poured out its contents all day long.

Roisin exhaled slowly through her nose under the water and broke through the surface to take in air through her mouth. Through her goggles everything was tinged with a bluish hue, the rippling water reflected in the blue-black windowpanes. This was how she liked it best — when the weather outside was bleak and inhospitable and the inside brightly lit.

While her subconscious brain was busy controlling the motor movements of her body — telling her when to breathe and when to kick her legs back like a frog — her conscious brain flitted from one thought to the next, fretting and wearying itself with its restlessness. At last it surrendered to the rhythmic, repetitive motion of her body and slowed to a dull, pedestrian pace.

It was then that Roisin's thoughts crystallised, focusing on baby Ruby — the weight of her, the way she squirmed in her arms, stretching and feeling her way in this world. The way she stared at Roisin with those luminescent eyes, innocent and knowing. The way she turned her head and smiled at the sound of her mother's voice.

Mum. Roisin tried the word out for size — testing out in her mind this business of being a mother. She pictured herself with a son, a small boy with straight brown hair. She imagined how he would cling to her possessively, the way little boys do to their mothers. How he would make her the centre of his world, for a time at least. She thought of the responsibility and of the unconditional love. What a great privilege and what a burden — the thought terrified and thrilled her at the same time.

She and Scott had talked in vague terms about having children as something they'd like to do someday. They'd only just moved house and got married — Roisin had just got her feet under the table in the new salon. It was premature, she told herself, to be thinking of babies.

She was the last person to climb out of the pool, self-consciously pulling the edges of her costume over the cheeks of her buttocks as she emerged from the water. Funny that, how swimming costumes always rode up there — they must be designed by men, she thought.

In the shower she reminded herself that she was thirty-two. If she didn't start a family now, when was she going to do it? At thirty-five? Forty? She soaped her legs and noticed how the skin on her knees, in spite of her meticulous personal care and endless moisturising, was starting to loosen in preparation for the sagging that would come with old age. She didn't want to be an old mother, facing retirement before her children were barely out of their teens.

Assuming, of course, that she was fertile and that she and Scott had no problems conceiving. She remembered that she'd read somewhere that a woman's fertility plummeted once over the age of thirty-five. And the incidence of miscarriage increased. Her stomach tightened into a knot — perhaps it was too late already. If there was something wrong with either of them, it could take years to find the cause. She'd stopped taking the Pill in her late twenties, worried about the possible side effects and simply because she didn't believe it was healthy to pump hormones into your body every month. She and Scott had used condoms since they'd met — in theory she could get pregnant straightaway. If Scott was agreeable.

It was nearly half-past ten when she got home. Roisin got ready for bed, put out the lights and got in beside Scott, who'd already turned on his side in preparation for sleep. She found his naked body and moulded hers against the curve of his back. She buried her face in the nape of his neck. But within minutes the heat generated by their naked bodies was so intense that Roisin had to pull away. She rolled onto her back and stared at the pale orange glow on the ceiling — it came from a streetlight twenty yards or so from their bedroom window.

'Scott,' she said into the darkness and waited, 'are you asleep?'

'Hmm,' came the muffled, but distinctly peeved, reply, 'I was. Nearly. But I'm not now.'

'How would you feel if I was pregnant?' she said and the silence seemed to last forever.

Then she heard the rustle of the sheets and, in the halflight, she saw Scott lever himself up onto one elbow. 'Are you?' he asked, in a wide-awake voice.

She wondered what he was thinking and then said, 'No. But if I was how would you feel?'

'I'd be delighted. Naturally.'

He rolled onto his back and she could see his profile against the curtains through which some of the orange light penetrated — his strong aquiline nose, the bushy eyebrows, and the slightly weak chin. How she loved that face!

'Would you though? Would you really?' she questioned.

'Of course I would. What's brought this on, Roisin?' he asked and put his hands behind his head, preparing to listen.

'I was just thinking, that's all. When you're swimming your mind kind of goes into freefall. Your subconscious thoughts come to the surface — things that really matter to you. The important things. And do you know all I could think about?'

'Tell me.'

'All I could think about was little Ruby — how lovely and perfect she is. And how I want a baby of my own,' she blurted out at last, fearful that if she said any more she would burst into tears.

'Oh, Roisin,' he said gently, 'why didn't you tell me that you felt like this before?'

'I didn't know I did. Not clearly. Not until tonight. I don't want to leave it — I mean having children — until we're too old. You're nearly thirty-four, Scott. In just over twenty years' time you'll be nearly retired.'

'I never thought about it in those terms before.'

'Well, it's time you did. Time we both did.'

Scott rolled over then and ducked his head under the covers. He found her breasts and kissed them tenderly.

'What are you doing?' she said, crossly. 'I'm

trying to have a serious discussion with you here.'

He poked his head out from underneath the covers and she could see the wide flash of his smile in the half-light.

'If you want a baby, Roisin, I only know of one way to make one. And it doesn't involve a lot of talking.'

'But it's got to be what you want too,' she said, putting the flat of her palm on his chest, holding him there.

'Of course it is, silly. I want you to have my baby. And I bet it'll be the most beautiful one in the whole wide world.'

'I'm worried though. About the salons. How I'll manage everything during the pregnancy and afterwards.'

'If we want a baby then we'll just have to manage. I'll help you, Roisin — you won't be on your own. You can employ a manager to cover for you while you're off on maternity leave. Women have babies every day and they all manage somehow. Now come here.'

He circled her waist with his arm then and pulled her to him. Reassured by his words of support, she closed her eyes and kissed him on the lips, their bodies entwined in perfect unison.

★ ★ ★

The very day she received the letter in the post about the antenatal classes, Michelle called Roisin at the Carrickfergus salon.

'I was just ringing to see if you're still going to

the antenatal classes,' she said, rubbing the mound of her swollen stomach in a soothing circular motion. 'Did you get your letter from the midwife this morning?'

'No. Maybe. I didn't get a chance to open the post this morning,' said Roisin, 'Oh, could you hold on a minute?'

Michelle heard a loud clunk as though the phone had been set down, then muffled voices, the sound of rustling paper and then Roisin came back on the line.

'Sorry about that, Michelle,' she said. 'It's mad in here at the minute! Now, where were we? Oh, yes, these classes.'

Suddenly Michelle felt rather foolish. With only seven days between their due dates, Michelle felt a bond had developed between her and Roisin. She was looking forward to the classes. She saw them as an opportunity both to get to know Roisin, whom she admired, and to meet other women. Roisin, on the other hand, obviously had more important things on her mind than sitting drinking tea in a stuffy room on a Wednesday afternoon with half-a-dozen pregnant women.

'So, are you still going?' asked Michelle, trying to inject a casual note into her voice.

'Yeah, yeah, I plan to,' said Roisin distractedly.

'Shall I just meet you there, then?' said Michelle.

'OK. Oh, wait a minute, I forgot. I've arranged for the car to go into the garage that day.'

'Nothing serious, I hope.'

'No, no. I went and scraped the bodywork in

the supermarket carpark, that's all.'

'Well, why don't I come and pick you up?'

'I couldn't ask you to come all the way to Carrickfergus.'

'I'll tell you what. Why don't you schedule my weekly appointment in for that Wednesday lunchtime, say one o'clock? Then we can come into Ballyfergus together and — the garage, is it in Ballyfergus?'

'Yes, Robertson's.'

'Right. Then I can drop you off there, or at home.'

'Oh, could you Michelle? That'd be great.'

Michelle hung up and sat and looked at the digital display on the handset for a few seconds, then replaced it in the base unit. The truth was, Michelle had few close friends locally, aside from her sisters. Her best friends from her schooldays were scattered far and wide. She and Donal had moved to Ballyfergus only four weeks before Molly was born — all her antenatal care had been in Belfast so she'd not met any local women that way. And she'd never really clicked with any of the mothers she met through Molly's nursery and then private school. So many of them had high-flying jobs and were always whizzing off to their offices or meetings — they had no time to waste chatting to a stay-at-home mother in the schoolyard.

Michelle glanced at the chrome clock on the kitchen wall and started to prepare Molly's tea. She could hear the blare of the television coming from the family room adjacent to the kitchen where her daughter was watching a video.

It was also true, she thought to herself, that she and Donal had lots of acquaintances and they had a busy social life but sometimes Michelle thought it was, well, superficial. Sometimes she wondered if the people they mixed with really liked her. She wasn't the sharpest tool in the box — she never pretended to be — but even she knew when people were poking fun at her, or patronising her.

She took three fish fingers out of a box in the freezer, placed them on a metal tray and put it in the eye-level oven. Then she got out a loaf of bread, buttered two slices and cut them into triangles.

It was all right Ellen, her best friend, telling her to pop over to London anytime and Louise saying she was always welcome in Dublin. But neither of them had children and children tied you down. While it was lovely to go and see her friends, she could only do so occasionally — she couldn't be disappearing every weekend. And it would be even more difficult when the second baby came along. She loved it when her friends came to stay with her and Donal, but they had busy lives and demanding jobs — they could only manage a long weekend with her once or twice a year.

Michelle opened a tin of beans, spooned some into a glass bowl, dribbling some of the tomato sauce on the kitchen counter as she did so, and zapped them in the microwave.

No, it was what you did on a daily basis that determined the quality of your life — not the high points of weekends away and shopping trips to London. And it was important to have friends you could rely on close at hand.

When the fish fingers were ready she took them out of the oven and put them on a plate along with the buttered bread triangles and baked beans.

'Molly!' she called. 'Your tea's ready.'

Then she got out the gin, which she kept in the fridge along with the tonic water — that way you didn't have to bother with ice cubes — and made herself a very large drink.

The next week, in the car on the way to the Health Centre in Ballyfergus, Michelle and Roisin exchanged small talk.

'So, what are your plans for the business while you're on maternity leave?' asked Michelle.

Roisin told her how she'd planned to employ a manager for the Ballyfergus salon but she'd been unable to find anyone suitable. She'd had to rethink things and was now aiming to work right up until the birth. 'Katy's agreed to manage the Carrick salon,' she said.

'That's good. So what are you going to do about the Ballyfergus salon after the baby is born?'

'I've hired an extra therapist and I'm going to manage it myself. Katy'll help me for the first few weeks after the baby comes.'

'Oh, Roisin, don't underestimate how difficult it is to look after a newborn. It's exhausting and you've hardly time to take a shower, let alone run a business.'

'I really don't have any choice,' said Roisin stiffly. 'Anyway, it's not like I'll be carrying out treatments. It's only the finances, admin and ordering.'

'Yes, of course, I'm sure it'll work out fine,' said Michelle, annoyed with herself for speaking a truth Roisin so plainly didn't want to hear.

'But I'm sure you don't want to listen to me prattling on about work,' said Roisin in a bright, airy tone.

'I do though. I love to listen to you,' said Michelle. 'It's very interesting and, well, it sounds quite glamorous to me.'

Roisin laughed then, rather derisively, and said, 'Believe me, Michelle there's nothing very glamorous about working in the beauty business. It's hard work, long hours and, in the evenings, there's bookkeeping to be done, staff rotas to draw up, stock to be ordered. I think your life must be a lot more glamorous than mine.'

'You'd be surprised. You've got a career, a business of your own. I don't do anything at all,' she said wistfully, 'except look after Molly.'

Her passenger fell silent then — no doubt Roisin perceived her the way she saw herself — as lightweight, frivolous.

'Have you any plans to go back to work, then?' asked Roisin.

'God no!' said Michelle and then she glanced self-consciously at Roisin's profile in the passenger seat. 'Well, I might have done . . . but not now. Not for the time being anyway,' she added, lying. Michelle was keen to impress upon Roisin that she was someone worthy of her friendship. That she had a brain in her head. The truth, though, was that she didn't think she could go back to work. Who would employ her now? It was over six years since she'd worked at the estate agency. And she'd only ever been a glorified gofer anyway. She'd no qualifications to speak of past O-levels, no profession to return to.

'What was it you did before Molly?' asked Roisin.

'I worked in an estate agency.'

'I'm sure you could get a job in one of the estate agencies in Ballyfergus.'

Inside Michelle cringed — she couldn't see herself working out of one of those grotty little offices on Main Street, tramping round sodden hillside farms and poky terraced houses. Michelle had only worked for Marston and Reid because they were a premier firm and Daddy was friends with the director — he'd practically gotten her the job.

'I don't know if I'd want to go back to that,' she said.

'What will you do then. Retrain?' asked Roisin, the presumption in her question being that Michelle would want to do *something*. That she couldn't just do nothing, career-wise, for the rest of her life.

'I don't know,' she replied, vaguely. 'I'll have to give it some serious thought.'

Michelle sat in the antenatal class while the midwife pointed at a poster of a foetus inside the womb and described how the baby moved down the birth canal.

Getting pregnant had been a godsend for Michelle, for she'd found it difficult to fill her days, now that Molly had started school. There were only so many coffee mornings and trips to the shops you could do. With a cleaner to do the housework and the laundry there really wasn't much for Michelle to do round the house. She wasn't keen on cooking either — most of their meals came from the ready-prepared section in Marks and Spencer. And let's face it, thought Michelle, they tasted a lot better than anything she could ever produce.

She found herself focusing on the most mundane matters, escalating them into minor crises. A dripping tap, a broken nail, an oversight on the part of the cleaner — such things could occupy her mind for an entire morning. She prided herself on always being on time for appointments, and keeping the household administration up to date. A bill never lay unpaid, or correspondence unattended to, for more than twenty-four hours. When she related these everyday occupations to Donal she could see his eyes literally glaze over as he took his mind off to another place. She was sure he never really listened to her with full concentration. By his response he confirmed what she had begun to suspect herself — that her life was boring.

Yet all of these activities, however tedious, failed to completely fill her life. When she paused long enough to look into her future she saw it stretched out before her — a series of long, empty days, which she would busy herself trying to fill. She now understood why her mother immersed herself in so much charity work and gardening. Everyone required a purpose in life. Keeping busy made you feel as though you were doing something worthwhile. If you sat idle for too long and thought about things too hard, you could come to the conclusion that your life was unfulfilling. Before she'd got pregnant this time, she'd tried once to explain this to Donal — how she had this fear inside.

'A fear of what exactly?' he'd said.

'I can't explain it very well, Don. It's like I'm worried about what I'm going to do with my life. I sometimes look into the future and all I feel is panic. Do you think I should go out to work?'

'What would you work at, Michelle? You've never stuck at anything. You need application to get exams and qualifications, without which all you'll get is menial work. Take the banking exams — as soon as they got tough, you opted out. Look, why don't you just enjoy being at home with Molly? Sometimes, I really don't understand you, you know. There's lots of women would give their eyeteeth to be in your position — having this lovely lifestyle and not having to go out and work for it.'

Sometimes, when he said things like that, Michelle thought that Donal despised her.

That night at a dinner party at the Lawrences', Donal had joked that a non-working wife was the highest status symbol — the inference being that if your wife could afford not to work, then you were very well paid indeed. He took a swig of wine and settled his elbows on the table, waiting for the reaction such a comment would provoke. Michelle smiled good-naturedly while everyone debated his statement but inside she thought that Donal's comments were hypocritical. Their lifestyle was subsidised by her family — their home gifted by Noel, their holidays too. Twice a year they went to the McCormick family villa in Provence — a free holiday to all intents and purposes. And the cottage in Donegal was available anytime they wanted it.

But now she was having a baby and that more than justified her existence — in fact it would, as she knew, entirely consume her for the first three years. Donal had not been at all keen on trying for another child — infuriatingly, he'd not given her a substantial reason why not. He talked vaguely about having their freedom and living their own lives — whatever that meant. Michelle found his attitude hard to understand — he absolutely adored Molly, he was a model father really. She just knew that he would change his mind when he held another child in his arms — with any luck a boy this time. And so she'd stopped taking the Pill without Donal's consent and, when she got pregnant, blamed it on a bad curry that had given her a stomach upset and made her sick. He'd accepted the news more with resignation than anything else and Michelle had chosen to interpret this as contentment.

'Well, I'm sure you're all ready for a cup of tea,' said Norah Roberts, the health visitor who, along with the midwife, ran the antenatal classes. She went over to a corner of the room and started making tea in pale blue mugs. The classroom atmosphere was broken and the small group relaxed into sociable conversation.

They talked about the experience of being

pregnant, the first-timers absorbing the anecdotes of the experienced mothers like sponges. Michelle remembered being like this too — you tried to face the prospect of motherhood as bravely as you could, armed with all the information the professionals and the textbooks could throw at you. But essentially no-one could really help you — it was something you would, in the end, face alone. Michelle could guess at the fears each woman carried within her breast and all of them were justified.

They were a nice group of women, Michelle thought. Two of them at least seemed friendly, confident types — they'd introduced themselves as Liz and Jayne. The other two women were much younger than the others, quieter and more reserved. They watched and listened and, when they spoke, it was with broad Ballyfergus accents, which enabled Michelle to rule them out as potential friends.

Roisin's car wouldn't be ready until the following morning so Michelle dropped her off in a housing estate she'd never been to before. From the outside Roisin's home looked smart and crisp in the way that brand-new houses do. It looked substantial enough too, with double frontage and a double garage. But it was on an estate all the same — if it hadn't been for Daddy, thought Michelle, with a little shiver she and Donal could have ended up living in a place like this.

'Look, there's Scott! He's waiting at the window,' said Roisin, a smile lighting up her face as she put one foot out of the car door onto the tarmac pathway, eager to be off. 'Bless him,' she said, turning to address Michelle, her eyes radiant with delight. 'You know, he's so excited about this baby — I bet he's come home early to find out how I got on.'

Roisin heaved herself out of the car, in the ungraceful manner of heavily pregnant women. Scott had opened the front door by this stage and was walking down the drive towards the car — a handsome man, dark in colouring like Donal. He had his hands in his trouser pockets and his tie whipped about fiercely in the fresh April breeze.

He greeted Roisin with a long kiss, lifted her hand to his mouth and brushed her knuckles with his lips. He said a few words to her, let go of her hand — reluctantly it seemed to Michelle — and walked over to the car.

'Hi, there,' he said, leaning in, 'I'm Scott.' He extended a hand across the passenger seat and she shook it. His grip was firm and confident — a businessman's handshake.

They exchanged a few pleasantries and then Michelle drove off, watching Scott and Roisin in the rear-view mirror. Scott wrapped his arm protectively around Roisin's shoulder as they walked up the drive to the house and their heads, leaning in towards each other, almost touched. For a moment Michelle felt jealous of their obvious intimacy, of the way Scott treasured Roisin like she was something rare and precious. She couldn't remember a time when Donal rushed home early from work just to see her. Michelle came to the junction, checked for traffic and pulled out onto the main road, feeling more alone and vulnerable than she had done in years.

As she drove home, climbing out of Ballyfergus up towards Killyglen, Michelle acknowledged to herself that she had another motive for wanting this baby. A reason that she was loath to admit, even to herself. Indeed if she was entirely honest with herself, which she preferred not to be, this was the main reason she had got pregnant. Her fervent hope, which she had honed over the past few months until it was almost a belief, was that this baby would narrow, and then close, the gap that had opened between her and Donal like a wound.

She worried that he was falling out of love with her. And she believed that a new baby would secure his love — how could he not love the mother of his baby? A new life, flesh of their flesh, proof of their togetherness — a helpless child that needed a father as much as a mother. For who could walk out on an innocent baby? What man could turn his back on his family?

For a while there last year Michelle had actually feared for Donal's sanity. He'd been so resentful and uncommunicative and bitter — like he hated his life and sometimes, her. His lowest point came round about the time of Roger's christening. She would never forget the conversation they'd had in the house when they'd gone back to change Molly's clothes before going on to her parents'. He'd accused her of keeping things — like what her father thought of Donal — from him. Yes, that was true, but what Donal interpreted as disloyalty was, in fact, the complete opposite. She'd only tried to protect him from hurt and humiliation. She'd only done what any woman would do for the man she loved.

If Molly hadn't come into the room at that precise moment, she wondered what else he would have said. But she was glad the conversation had ended there for something inside of her — an internal warning system — told her to leave it, told her not to draw him out any further. For she feared what he might say. She remembered the hurtful things he'd said about her parents — comments that still stung her. After all her family had done for them, how could he be so ungrateful?

8

From the kitchen window Pauline watched her two grandchildren — Molly now five and Roger three — playing outside in the spring sunshine. Large toys dotted the lawn — a pink kitchen, a playhouse made to resemble a log-house, a sit-on seesaw, a tricycle, scooter and a bike. Noel had had most of the toys delivered to Glenburn the summer Molly was eighteen months old. When Roger was born these were supplemented with a sand-pit in the shape of a frog, a ride-on fire engine and a replica Jaguar pedal car, which neither child could yet operate with their skinny little legs. And, to the side of the house, he'd had a mini-playground erected with swings, a slide, and a climbing frame.

Pauline smiled wryly to herself — the children, ignoring all these expensive toys, were engrossed in playing with plastic buckets and sticks they'd found in the flowerbeds. They'd filled each bucket with mud from the garden borders, bits of grass and dead leaves, a few of which still skittered round the garden from the previous autumn. Still, that summed Noel up — he thought money could buy everything, including people's affections. He'd no reason to believe otherwise — hadn't she allowed herself to be silenced by money? 'Stay with me,' he'd said, 'and I'll see that you and the girls never want for anything.'

Cross with herself for allowing negative thoughts to tarnish such a lovely day, Pauline busied herself in the kitchen. She filled two beakers with orange juice, opened a packet of Party Rings — plain biscuits covered in garish icing, a perennial favourite with small children — and arranged them on a plastic plate. These she set on a large silver tray along with a jug of iced cranberry juice and three tall glasses. Gingerly she carried the tray outside to one of the patio areas that surrounded Glenburn — this one was sheltered from the mild southerly breeze and looked directly onto the area where the children were playing. Michelle and Jeanette sat facing the sun on big wooden chairs, Michelle's huge stomach resting on her thighs. Both women were well wrapped up, for the sun was only warm — in the summer this patio, cleverly designed to make the most of its southfacing aspect and sheltered from the sea breezes, was scorching hot.

Pauline put the tray down on the table, poured the drinks and called the children over. She put their juice cups on a small child-sized wooden table complete with miniature wooden chairs, exact copies of the ones the adults sat on.

'Would you like a biscuit, darlings?' she said, offering the plate and Roger grabbed a handful in each hand with a cheeky grin.

'Now, you know you're only allowed one,' said Jeanette, scolding ineffectually with a smile on her face. She got up and prised all but two of the biscuits out of her child's fist. 'OK you can have two.'

'If he's having two, I want two as well,' said Molly crossly.

'Of course you may have two, darling,' said Pauline, mediating in the way grandparents do. 'Now sit down and have a drink of juice.'

The children sat for all of two minutes while Pauline poured the cranberry juice and passed a glass each to her daughters. After Molly had drunk her juice and Roger had spilt his, inevitably, on the cobbled terrace, the children ran off to play. From where she was seated Pauline watched Molly carry her bucket over to a tap on the wall of the house and fill it. Muddy water lapped over the side of the pail and onto the front of her dress. Roger dragged his bucket, too laden down with mud for him to carry, towards Molly. He grunted and gesticulated until Molly filled his bucket with water as well.

Pauline pretended she hadn't noticed, partly because she was too lazy to get up and intervene and partly because she believed that children should be allowed to do whatever they liked at their grandparents'. Clothes could always be washed. The important thing was that they had only happy memories of being here.

'It's been a while since we've had a May like this,' said Michelle, pushing her sunglasses onto the hair above her brow and turning her face to the sun, eyes closed. 'This is absolutely gorgeous.'

They sipped their drinks and smiled at the perfection around them — the tinkle of children's laughter, the bright spring flowers in

263

the garden and the soft rolling hills of green in the distance.

'What time's your appointment with the midwife?' said Pauline to Michelle.

'I'm seeing Norah at eleven,' said Michelle peering at the watch on her wrist. 'Oh, would you look at the time. I'd better be going. Are you sure you're all right if I leave Molly here, Mum?'

'Of course.'

'Mum,' said Jeanette, 'I was thinking of nipping into town for a few things. Would you mind if I left Roger too?'

'Of course I don't mind. So long as you're both back by two. Eileen Watson's coming over this afternoon to help me draw up the invitation list for the cancer fundraising ball and I've an exhibition to attend tonight up in Belfast.'

'Oh, who is it?'

'Some Irish-American sculptor. Goes by the name of Padraig Flynn — which I presume he's invented to endear him to the locals. OK, girls, if you're going go now before the children notice.'

After her daughters had left Pauline watched the children stir the mud soup with the sticks, absolutely engrossed in what they were doing. The dirty water slopped over the sides of the buckets, soaking their legs and shoes. She wondered what life would have in store for them. What careers they would follow, who they would marry, if they would find happiness. She hoped their parents were wiser in the guidance and coaching of their offspring than she had been.

None of her three daughters were capable of supporting themselves in the lifestyle they expected. Michelle had never excelled academically and flitted from one ill-suited occupation to another before settling down to marriage and motherhood with Donal. Since her graduation in French Literature and marriage to Matt, Jeanette had shown no inclination to forge a career. She'd been happy to sit back and let Matt bring home the bacon — Roger was now over two years old and there was no mention of her going out to work. And although Yvonne was devoted to her horses and appeared to be a fine judge of the beasts, the stables were far short of being a viable business.

In short, Pauline and Noel had failed to instil in their daughters a sense of personal responsibility for their livelihood and welfare. It disappointed Pauline to see them all happy, in various ways, to be dependants. And while she hoped and prayed it would never happen to her daughters, weren't they aware of the number of marriages that ended in divorce these days? If either of their husbands walked out on them, how would they support themselves?

Of course, Pauline was one to talk. Who was she to think of giving advice when she herself was in exactly the same position? It was her unemployability that had given her no choice all those years ago. Faced with Noel's ultimatum — for that was what it was, she saw now — she felt that she had no option but to stay with him.

For many years she believed that she had made the right decision. Now she wasn't so sure. If she'd left Noel she would have found a way to earn money. Somehow. They wouldn't exactly have been destitute — Noel might be a philanderer but he would surely have provided for his children. She could have taken menial work, bar work, any type of work — at least it would have been honest. Her daughters would have grown up understanding the value and honour in hard work. But her snobbery had prevented her from doing that. Her parents wouldn't have welcomed her, a single mother, and her three children into their home. So she would have been reliant on Noel's goodwill, and the State, to keep her and her children fed and clothed. At the time she could think of nothing more horrific.

She realised, of course, that her daughters would never know what she had done for them. She had sacrificed the best part of twenty years of happiness to ensure they had the very best chance life had to offer. They had grown up pampered and spoilt and, given the way they had all turned out, perhaps this hadn't been entirely for the best. But they were all adults now — her job was done.

As she sat in the sun, Pauline looked at the grandchildren she had longed for, and realised that they could never heal the ache within her. She loved and adored them and cherished every moment of their little lives, but she had been wrong to pin all her hopes for happiness on them. She had been wrong to expect them to fill the empty place in her heart.

Children were for giving to, not for taking from. And their childhoods would be short-lived — in a few years they would only come to see their granny under duress and sit in a corner texting their friends. Even the imminent prospect of Michelle's new baby failed to really excite her interest. She was looking forward to the little one, of course, but not with the passion and yearning she had once felt for her first grandchild. Pauline realised she still had a lot more love to give, but not the type you give to children.

'Granny, my feet are cold,' said Molly, standing in front of Pauline, looking in amazement at her shoes.

'And why do you think that might be?' asked Pauline.

Molly shrugged her shoulders and thought hard, biting down on her bottom lip. 'Dunno,' she said at last and Pauline laughed.

'I think it's because your feet are wet, love.'

Roger came over then and stood beside Molly and looked at his feet, mimicking the mannerisms of his older cousin. ''Old, 'old,' he shouted.

'Cold feet?' said Pauline. 'Yes, I think it's time we went inside and got you out of those wet things. And then we'll have something nice for lunch. Let's leave the buckets out here for now, shall we?'

'Out,' repeated Roger, and Pauline took the children gently by the hand, and led them indoors. There was something heartrending about their little hands, curled into hers like soft warm birds. She glanced down in wonder at the little boy at her side, so different from how her daughters had been at this age and from Molly. So much more physical and aggressive and so loud. Pauline allowed herself one small smile. This was what she had denied Noel — a son, the one thing he wanted most in the world. Her revenge for what he had done to her. And it was still, even now, the sweetest thing.

'I want honey sandwiches,' announced Molly. 'Can I have honey sandwiches, Granny? Mummy never allows me. She says I have to eat ham or cheese in my bread.'

'When you're at Granny's house, darling, you can have whatever you want.'

★ ★ ★

The exhibition was busy — the gallery on fashionable Wellington Place in Belfast city centre was spacious but too many people were crammed inside.

Pauline sipped a glass of champagne and looked around. For most of the people here this would only be the first stop on an evening out — several of the men wore black tie. The owner of the gallery, Andrew Whitehead, had chosen his guests well. Pauline recognised the Pattersons of poultry-processing fame, the chief executives of the North's two top banks and their wives, the Hartley-Reids who owned a chain of family clothing stores and many other familiar faces.

'Pauline, darling!' called Bree Patterson, waving to Pauline with one arm while with the other she clung to her portly husband, David, like he was a life raft.

Pauline went over and air-kissed Bree and David. Bree was heavily made up with a turban thing around her head, which made her look like an ageing gypsy. Probably not the look she was aiming for, thought Pauline. She took a sip of champagne to hide the smile that sprang to her lips.

'What do you think of Padraig's work?' gushed Bree. 'Isn't it just sensational? And don't you think Padraig is just divine? That accent is *sooo* sexy.'

She giggled then, like a schoolgirl, and Pauline noticed that her husband was staring off into the middle distance, ignoring her.

'I've only just arrived, Bree,' said Pauline. 'I haven't met the artist yet. Or had a chance to look closely at his work. But I've read that his bronzes are really wonderful.'

'Yes, it's really much too busy in here, isn't it? He's over there somewhere,' said Bree airily and she waved her hand towards the back of the gallery. 'We're just about to head out to dinner. Now, we must get together for lunch soon,' she added by way of a goodbye, kissed the air beside Pauline's ear and was gone.

Pauline smiled to herself. She looked in the direction Bree had indicated and saw Padraig Flynn immediately. He was slouched against a wall, holding court amongst a small group in front of a large bronze statue. He held a half-empty champagne glass by the stem carelessly in his left hand, rolling it round and round between his thumb and forefinger. He wore chino-style trousers, trainers and an open-necked check shirt. He was a strong-featured man — about forty, clean-shaven, tall and blond — but not handsome exactly. However, even from the distance at which she stood, Pauline could sense his magnetism. It was certainly working on the people around him — she was too far away to hear what he was saying but they hung on his every word.

Suddenly Pauline felt a sense of ill will towards him. There was something overly confident about his stance and his careless way of dressing — as though he didn't feel he had to try too hard. As though he had no respect for the good people that had come here tonight to view, and buy, his works. Because of his height, he looked down through hooded eyes as he spoke — Pauline thought she could detect a hint of scorn in his bearing.

As these thoughts passed through her head, inexplicably, he glanced up and caught her eye. They held each other's gaze just for a moment and then Pauline looked away, conscious that she was blushing for the first time in years. No doubt he classed her, in her smart black suit and ivory silk shirt, as another well-heeled potential patron.

Pauline moved about the room, exchanging idle chat with the people she knew. Once the crowd had thinned a little she found herself beside one of the sculptor's pieces — *Girl after a Bath* — a bronze statue about three feet tall of a girl half-draped in a towel. The subject was conventional enough but the execution was exquisite. Pauline could find no fault with the figure. The expression on the face of the pubescent girl was one of surprise, as though she had caught someone spying on her toilet. Her hair appeared wet and Pauline bent down and reached out to touch it.

'Do you like it?' said a deep man's voice in an American accent. Not the mid-Atlantic drawl Pauline had expected but the lazy, languid tone of the Deep South.

She withdrew her hand sharply, and straightened up.

'No,' he said, and took her hand and tenderly placed it on the cold statue again. 'Feel it. That's what it's there for. To be touched and stroked and felt. On the outside . . . and on the inside. In here.' He pressed her hand to his heart.

Pauline coughed and withdrew her hand quickly, casting shooting glances to each side of her to ensure no one was watching. Up close the sculptor was not as young as she had first thought. In fact, in spite of the Robert Redford-type shock of blonde hair and blue eyes, his face was deeply creased from age and too many hours spent in the sun.

'Well,' she said, 'it's . . . I like it.'

'We haven't met,' he stated. 'I'm Padraig Flynn.'

Pauline smiled at this — at a name so unlikely for a man from the southern United Sates that it couldn't possibly be real.

'Pauline McCormick,' she replied, without offering her hand.

'What are you smiling at?' he asked.

'Oh nothing, it's just your name,' she said trying, though not very hard, to keep the scepticism from her voice. 'It's very Irish, isn't it?'

'It should be. My grandfather came from County Cork and my grandmother from County Antrim. All my family have Irish names,' he said seriously, staring at her intently until she had to look away.

'Really,' she said feeling foolish. 'So do you feel at home here?'

'Very,' he said firmly, nodding his head slowly. 'So much so that I've just moved here to live. I feel drawn to the place, as though this is where I'm meant to be. I feel it in my heart.'

It was so American to talk openly about feelings like that, thought Pauline, so unlike the way she had been brought up to behave. Suddenly aware that the gallery was emptying, she decided to change the subject to something with which she felt more comfortable.

'Has it been a successful evening for you?'

'Yeah, I've sold a few pieces,' he replied, flicking a casual glance around the room, as though it didn't matter to him one way or the other. Perhaps he really didn't care — Pauline was beginning to think she'd misjudged him. This was one laid-back guy.

He brought his eyes back to rest on Pauline and said, 'I take commissions, you know. Anytime,' he added and pressed a small card into her hand.

'Thank you,' she said brightly, 'I'll bear that in mind.' She opened her handbag, placed the card inside it and snapped the purse shut. 'Good night.'

She turned and walked briskly outside and got into her car, which she had luckily managed to park right outside the gallery. She put on her seat belt and started the engine. Then she looked into the brightly-lit window of the gallery and there he was, hands in pockets, staring out at her. She stared back for a few moments, the two sheets of glass between them failing to filter the intensity of his gaze.

Pauline put her foot on the accelerator and pulled away from the kerb. Her heart was beating fast, her breathing shallow and she had to grip the leather steering wheel firmly to stop her hands from shaking.

The roads were quiet and she soon made her way out of the city centre and onto the dual carriageway that would take her to Ballyfergus. She drove in the slow lane, at a careful sixty miles an hour, and tried to relax. What was it about that man that had unsettled her so? Why was she acting so out-of-character, so dizzy-headed? She remembered feeling like this many years ago when she was a young girl. The first time had been when she met Seamus McKeown, her first love at the tender age of sixteen, and then again with Noel. What was she doing entertaining such feelings? A sensible woman like her, a mother and grandmother.

At the house the lights were on but no one was home. Pauline remembered that Yvonne had gone out with friends and would not be back, probably, 'til the early hours. She guessed that Noel had gone to his mistress but tonight, rather than feeling resentful, she was grateful. She went upstairs to change into her nightwear, shut the bedroom door and sat on the bed. Before she even took off her high heels she opened her handbag, pulled out the card Padraig Flynn had given her, and examined it. It was a plain business card, black ink on white card, unremarkable. *'Padraig Flynn, Sculptor in Bronze. Commissions taken,'* she read, *'Waterside Cottage, near Ballynahinch, County Antrim.'* There was a telephone number, fax number, website and email address. She put the card to her nose — it smelled of nothing.

She turned the card over — the back of it was blank. Pauline felt suddenly deflated. What had she expected? A love note? She told herself not to be so silly, got up and set the card on the top of the mantelpiece over the fireplace. She looked at her reflection in the over-mantel mirror, trying to see herself as others saw her. The artificial yellow light cast a flattering glow on her face and yet it was plain to see she was a middle-aged woman, albeit well-groomed and fine-featured, but well past her prime. Pauline glanced once more at the card, picked it up and carried it through to her dressing-room where she buried it at the bottom of her underwear drawer. The encounter with Padraig Flynn, however brief, had meant something to Pauline — the card was special. Fleetingly she wondered what secrets Noel had hidden in his dressing-room and then realised that she no longer cared.

After a long and deep sleep, Pauline was still thinking about Padraig Flynn when she got up late the next morning. She was usually up at seven, dressed and groomed and downstairs for breakfast at eight. Today a lethargy hung over her, dulling her senses and slowing her body. There was no sign of Noel — he must have slipped into bed late and left early for the office. He would not have stayed out all night as he was too concerned with appearances to do that.

By the time Pauline came down for breakfast it was half past nine and Esther and Janet, a girl who came in three times a week to help Esther, were already busy cleaning upstairs. Yvonne appeared shortly afterwards, wearing a towelling dressing-gown and slippers, and looking like she'd had too much to drink the night before.

They sat in silence, eating and reading the papers, which Esther always bought for them in town before coming to work. Pauline looked at Yvonne over the top of the *Belfast Telegraph*. Of her three daughters, she was the one that concerned Pauline the most. She showed no inclination to leave home, yet Pauline felt it was time she did. Whilst she lived under her roof, she felt responsible for her in a way that she didn't feel for the others. And, in spite of her cheerful nature and apparent preoccupation with her horses, there was something about Yvonne that bothered Pauline. She detected a deep-seated unhappiness in her youngest daughter. She would not feel her job was done until Yvonne had flown the nest and was happily settled in a life away from Glenburn.

'Yvonne, can I ask you something?'

'Sure, what's on your mind?'

'I, well . . . Yvonne, you can't stay here forever, you know.'

'Why not? Are you and Daddy going somewhere?'

'Don't be so facetious.'

'I'm sorry, Mum. I've got a headache.'

'I just feel you should be thinking of your future.'

'Huh?' said Yvonne, screwing up her features as though the very act of thinking was painful.

'You know, what you're going to do with the rest of your life. Maybe you'd like to get a place of your own. I'm sure your father would help out financially.'

'Why would I want to do that when everything I want is here? And it's right next door to the stables.'

Why indeed, thought Pauline. 'You might want to get married one day?' she persisted. She said it more to see what kind of reaction it would provoke, as she knew her daughter well enough to know that there was little chance of this happening. Men simply didn't figure in Yvonne's life and Pauline was coming to terms with the fact that her daughter would always be a spinster.

'I'm not the marrying type, Mum. I consider it a form of servitude.'

Pauline laughed out loud and said, 'You might be right there. Perhaps you are better off on your own.'

For a moment Yvonne looked like she was going to say something, thought better of it, and closed the conversation by burying her head in the paper.

The telephone rang at ten twenty. It was Barbara Wilson, secretary of the Ulster Society of Women Artists, of which Pauline was president.

'Good morning Barbara,' said Pauline. 'What can I do for you?'

'Are you feeling all right, Pauline?'

'I'm fine, thank you. Why?'

'There's supposed to be a committee meeting this morning at ten o'clock. To discuss the arrangements for the annual exhibition.'

'There is? I completely forgot,' said Pauline, looking at the kitchen clock. 'Where are you meeting?'

'Jane Galway's.'

'Holywood. I could be there by, let me see, eleven fifteen, if I left now.'

'Sorry, we can't wait that long, Pauline. Some of us have other appointments this morning. Look, we'll just carry on without you. I'll send you the minutes.'

'Fine.'

'Look, are you all right, Pauline? You don't sound your usual self.'

'I am feeling a little under the weather. Nothing serious. Just a touch of a cold, I think.'

'Well, you take care of yourself. Bye.'

Pauline replaced the handset slowly. There it was. You busied yourself with this, that and the other thing, convincing yourself that you were so important, so entirely indispensable. And the whole time you were kidding yourself. You weren't even missed — everyone carried on perfectly well without you. Pauline realised with a jolt that no one needed her any more. But she did not feel depressed and worthless — the most common response of middle-aged woman according to popular wisdom. She felt liberated.

'What was that about?' asked Yvonne.

'Oh, nothing. Nothing important,' replied Pauline, and she went and sat in her study for a long time staring out at the lovely view. And thinking.

★ ★ ★

Anthony Scott Johnston, Tony Johnston for short, was born on the night of 10th May 2002, by normal delivery.

'If that was a normal delivery I wouldn't like to experience an abnormal one,' said Roisin to her mother and sister when they visited her the next day. 'I've never experienced pain like it. I swear to God, I thought I was going to die.'

Mairead sat on a hard, grey plastic chair by Roisin's bed in the small ward she shared with three other women. The curtains were drawn around the bed to afford Roisin and her visitors some privacy.

'Have you any stitches?' asked Mairead.

'No, none,' said Roisin, shifting uncomfortably in the bed. She had a sanitary towel like a brick between her legs and her whole body ached like she had a fever.

'You're very lucky.'

'So everyone keeps telling me.'

'You soon forget, Roisin. It doesn't seem

possible now, but in a year or so you'll be struggling to remember the details of his birth.'

'I don't think so, Mum!'

'No, honestly. It's nature's way. Why do you think women go through it a second and a third and even a sixth time?'

Roisin raised her eyebrows in horror and said, 'Because they're completely and absolutely mad?' Mairead smiled and Roisin turned her attention to Ann-Marie who was standing by the window, holding the baby in her arms.

'See the birdies! Aren't they lovely?' Ann-Marie whispered to Tony and the corners of Roisin's mouth turned up in a smile — she didn't have the heart to tell her that the baby could see next to nothing.

'What do you think of your nephew then, Ann-Marie?' she asked.

Ann-Marie turned to face the bed and her whole face was lit by a beaming smile. 'I think he's wonderful. I can't believe how — how absolutely perfect he is. Like a little angel.'

'Five days earlier and he would have shared your birthday with you,' said Mairead.

'And what a lovely birthday present that would have been,' said Ann-Marie delightedly.

Mairead stood up beside her daughter then and both women stared into the face of the newborn, their faces soft with emotion. Mairead pushed back a fold of blanket round the child's face with her hand.

'Do you think he looks like Dad, Mum?' said Roisin.

Mairead glanced very briefly at Roisin and

then stared at Tony again. 'I think,' she said firmly, 'that he looks like you. And Scott.'

'What do you think Dad would make of him if he was here?'

'Your dad would've been over the moon,' said Mairead, relaxing. 'He loved babies, you know. He loved their chubbiness and their laughter. And the smell of them — the sweet, milky smell of tiny babies. He used to go up to babies in their mother's arms and sniff their heads.'

'He never did!' said Ann-Marie, aghast. 'People must have thought he was a nutter.'

'He only did it to the children of people we knew,' laughed Mairead. 'People thought it was sweet. A big man like him being so soft over babies.'

They all fell silent then and Roisin felt sadness mixed with her elation. Death had robbed her father of so much, of so many moments of joy like this one.

'Oh, could you hold him a minute, Mum,' said Ann-Marie, and she handed the sleeping baby to her mother. 'I nearly forgot to give you this, Roisin,' she added.

She reached down to the floor at the bottom of the bed, lifted up a large gift bag and handed it to Roisin — it was covered in little baby bootees and blue tissue paper peeked out from the top. Roisin pulled out the most adorable baby clothes — proper little jeans, a checked shirt and a sleeveless pullover, sleep-suits, fluffy little socks and a pale blue duffle coat.

'It's so sweet, Ann-Marie. Oh, look how tiny the jeans are!' She held the clothes up for her mother to see. 'Aren't they lovely, Mum?' Mairead murmured her approval and Roisin, noticing the designer labels on the clothes, added, 'This is far too much. You can't go spending all your money on Tony.'

'Why not? What else am I going to spend it on? I'm doing more hours at the vet's surgery and I've only myself to look after.'

'Well, it's very, very kind of you,' said Roisin, folding the clothes and placing them inside the gift bag. 'How's the job going anyway?'

'It's great. I'm really enjoying it. I'm doing five mornings a week now, nine 'til one.'

'Would you like to go full-time?'

'Mmm, I don't know. I'm happy with my hours at the moment. It means I have the time to take the courses I need to get fully qualified.'

When Mairead left the room in search of tea, Roisin asked her sister, 'Are you still on medication?'

'No,' said Ann-Marie and she tilted her chin up slightly, an indication of how pleased she was with herself, 'not a thing. I saw Dr Crory last week and he said I don't need to take it any more.'

'I'm so pleased, Ann-Marie. You're doing so well. I'm really proud of you.'

Roisin regarded her sister critically. She still favoured the hippy style of dress from her student days, so different from Roisin's preference for up-to-date sharp tailoring. But at least she now kept her hair clean and wore makeup most of the time. She looked nice. 'You look great and you sound great,' complimented

Roisin. 'You're a different person from the one I knew two years ago.'

'I know,' said Ann-Marie and she blushed.

Just then Tony started to cry and both women turned their heads towards the transparent cot by Roisin's bed. Ann-Marie picked the screaming infant out of the crib and Roisin struggled into a sitting position.

'I'd better try and feed him,' said Roisin. 'He's been asleep for hours and he's probably hungry. Here, give him to me. No, the other side. That's it. Thanks.'

Gingerly she positioned the baby's mouth over her swollen nipple and pressed Tony's face onto her breast, the way she'd been taught by the midwife that morning. She watched for the rhythmic movement of the muscle just below his ear, an indication that he was latched on correctly. Sharp pains shot through her breast and she winced.

Once the pain had subsided and, satisfied that he was suckling properly, Roisin relaxed a little and looked up. Ann-Marie was staring wide-eyed at the baby on her sister's breast.

'You don't have to stay while I'm feeding him,' said Roisin. 'Not if you don't want to.'

'Oh, but I do. It's fascinating. And you never know, one day I might have one of these myself!'

Roisin's eyes widened in surprise. She'd never thought of Ann-Marie with a child, with a family of her own. She reproached herself for pigeon-holing her sister as the old maid of the family.

'Don't look at me like that!' laughed

Ann-Marie. 'I'm not completely over the hill yet, you know. I am only thirty-six!'

Just then Mairead appeared with a small tray laden with three plastic cups of tea which she set down on the bedside table. 'Is he hungry then? Oh look at his wee jaws go! Isn't he adorable?'

Roisin grimaced in pain and wondered if she was the only mother in the world who felt like she'd just gone ten rounds with Mike Tyson.

Three days later Roisin was still in shock.

'You know, your labour and delivery were textbook stuff,' the midwife said as she helped her prepare to leave the hospital, obviously pleased to have attended a fussfree delivery. 'You were made to have babies,' she added with a bright smile on her face.

Outside, at the entrance to the hospital, the midwife handed the car seat, containing Tony, to Scott. 'You'll be back to your old self in no time,' she said to Roisin and patted her kindly on the arm.

So why did Roisin feel as though she was falling off the side of the earth? Why did she feel like her insides had been taken out, put through a mangle, and put back the wrong way? Why had everything changed?

Even Scott seemed different to her. He helped her into the passenger seat, spent a good ten minutes strapping the car seat into the back of the car and drove them home, his face beaming with happiness. Could he not see how she was changed? How their lives and their relationship would never be the same? There were three of them now, two boys for her to divide her love between. The dynamics of their perfect couple-dom had all changed.

'A little boy,' Scott kept saying all the way home. 'Our own wee boy. I can't believe it, Roisin. Can you?'

Roisin turned her head to look at Tony and a sharp pain shot up her neck — every muscle in her body ached. She stared at the wrinkled scrap of life, lost inside a white snowsuit and squashed like a tiny doll into the car seat. How was she going to look after this little creature feeling like this? Feeling like she'd been run over by a ten-ton truck?

'Are you all right?' said Scott and he squeezed her hand in his as they sat in the car outside the house.

No, she wanted to say, I'll never be all right again.

'I'm tired and sore,' she said, looking at the blank windows of the house with apprehension. This was where she would spend most of her days and all her nights for the next four months. Suddenly the prospect terrified her.

'I know, darling,' said Scott. 'I understand,' and she looked deep into his eyes and knew that he hadn't got a clue.

Tony had slept like an angel in the hospital but that night he slept for no more than two hours at a stretch, squawking and screaming to be lifted and fed. Roisin sat up in bed breastfeeding her baby, her breasts throbbing with pain, tears streaming down her face, while Scott slept peacefully beside her. She'd hardly slept at all on the noisy hospital ward, sustained during the previous three nights by wonder at her new baby and the adrenaline pumping through her body. Now she knew what people meant by complete physical and mental exhaustion. After changing Tony's nappy, settling him down to sleep and finally drifting off herself, he would start all over again.

For the first two days Tony's bowels had hardly moved, now he did nothing but shit. Constantly. Day and night. Wet, orange poos that seeped out the side of his nappies and onto his clothing. And then he had to be changed. He screamed when she was giving him a bath, screamed when he was out for a walk in his pram, screamed when he was being held and when he wasn't. The only time he was content was when he was asleep or feeding on her huge inflated breasts. One night she lay in bed full of anger and rage and never slept at all, even when Tony was asleep. There just didn't seem to be any point.

Soon Scott went back to work and Roisin faced the days alone with Tony. She made forays out of the house to buy food at the supermarket and visit the Health Centre where she took Tony every week to be weighed and measured. He screamed everywhere she took him. Roisin undertook these missions with a grim determination, ignoring the stares of people around her and returning home as soon as possible. At least inside the house he wasn't bothering other people. Tony continued to wake four times a night and Roisin learnt to survive every day, permanently angry and irritable, on a few hours' sleep.

'He's just a colicky baby,' the health visitor told her and suggested all sorts of remedies to help. But nothing did.

'Your sister was the same when she was a baby,' said Mairead patting her grandson's back as she held him over her shoulder.

'And you had another one? You had me after this!' said Roisin incredulously.

Mairead shrugged. 'You forget what it's like,' she said.

'I'll never forget this,' said Roisin.

'I know it's hard to believe right now,' said Mairead looking at Roisin with pity, 'but things will get better. By the time he's three months he'll be into a routine. And once he starts on solids it'll be a lot easier on you. You'll see.'

'You mean I've got another two months of this?'

Mairead didn't answer but said instead, 'It's a lovely day. Why don't I take him out for a walk and you lie down and have a rest?'

On the rare moments when Tony was content, or asleep, Roisin rushed about doing housework in her once-pristine home, prepared meals, washed clothes, put them into the tumble-dryer, folded them up and put them away. She no longer ironed unless absolutely necessary. She called into the Ballyfergus salon twice a week but she made no real contribution to the running of the business. If it hadn't have been for Katy taking care of the staffing, admin and ordering, the business would have gone down the pan.

Before she'd had Tony, Roisin had scoffed at the notion that she wouldn't be able to get showered, dressed and out the door by noon. Now, if she managed that much in a day, she considered it a great achievement.

One Saturday morning, three weeks after Tony's birth, he'd just dropped off to sleep and Roisin was preparing to have a shower, shave her legs and generally indulge in as much pampering as she could squeeze into the thirty minutes or so before he woke again. She was brushing the knots out of her hair prior to taking a shower, a bath towel wrapped around her, when Scott came into the bedroom still wearing his dressing-gown.

'Come here,' he whispered and he put his arms round her and kissed her lightly on the head. 'Have I told you today that you're absolutely gorgeous?'

He nuzzled into her neck and she stiffened. She pulled the towel tighter round her gross belly, counting the precious minutes she had left before Tony would wake and demand her attention.

'Can't I have a minute's peace to myself? Is that too much to ask?' she snapped. 'If it's not him, it's you demanding my attention. I'm sick of everybody wanting a part of me.'

She pulled away and walked into the en-suite, not stopping to see what effect her words had on Scott. She was beginning to believe that she would never be normal again. It was the lack of sleep more than anything that affected her — it had turned her into a monster.

When Tony was five weeks old, Colette called round one Sunday afternoon while Scott was out playing golf. It was a beautiful June day so they decided to take Tony out for a walk in his pram. They got him ready and look a leisurely stroll round the estate.

'He's still up half the night,' complained Roisin, jiggling the pram vigorously to try and placate a whinging Tony. 'And Scott! Well, he does try, I'll give him that but he's just useless round the house. By the time I've explained what it is that needs doing and how to do it, I'd be quicker doing it myself. Do you know what he did the other day? Put my silk shirt, the only thing that fits me apart from these horrible maternity clothes, in the tumble-dryer!' Roisin sighed, shook her head and went on, 'He just has absolutely no idea what it's like for me at home all day with this child who just never stops — I swear to God, he spends every waking hour whinging and crying. I never expected it to be like this. It's doing my head in.'

They'd walked the circuit round the estate twice when Roisin realised that Colette hadn't said a word since they'd left the house. Not that she'd had much opportunity — she was too busy being bored to death.

'You think I'm a right bitch, don't you?' said Roisin.

'No, not at all,' said Colette with an audible sigh, and Roisin knew she was lying. 'Look,' continued Colette in an upbeat tone, 'how do you fancy coming out for a meal with me and

Katy? You haven't been out since before Tony was born.'

Roisin looked at her baby in his pram, quiet now while he stared at the fringe on the parasol blowing in the breeze. 'But he needs feeding all the time. And he won't take a bottle. I can't really leave him.'

'Bring him with you. Sure he can sit in his wee car seat, can't you, pet?' she cooed, leaning into the pram. 'We could go somewhere where it's not too noisy or smoky. Like the Marine Hotel.'

'I'm not sure . . . '

'Ach, Roisin, you've got to live a little. It'll do you good to get out. Have a drink and a laugh. It'll cheer you up.'

Colette was right. A night out might help her to calm down a bit. She realised that, though powerless to stop it, she was spiralling out of control.

'Well, OK then,' she said bravely, 'I'll give it a try.'

'That's the spirit. I'll book it for this Friday,' said Colette happily, and she linked arms with Roisin and told her all about her latest commission.

The evening out was a great success. Tony slept most of the time and, when he was awake, they took turns to hold him. It was a relief to talk about something other than babies and Roisin felt herself more relaxed and happy than she had been since Tony's arrival.

Colette dropped Roisin off at her house at eleven o'clock and Roisin glanced up at the bedroom window. The light was still on. As she put her key in the lock, Tony started to grizzle, ready for his next feed. Roisin took him upstairs, and sat on the bed and fed him.

'Did you have a nice night?' said Scott, who was lying in bed reading.

He made no move to touch her or kiss her. And could she blame him? He was probably afraid of getting his head bitten off.

'Mmm, it was lovely. And Tony was really well-behaved.'

'I told you we should have tried that before. Taking him out at night.'

'I was afraid he'd scream the place down,' she said quickly and then added in a more conciliatory tone, 'We can try it again next weekend if you like.' She paused. 'Scott?'

'What?'

'I know I've been horrible since Tony was born but I think I'm over the worst now. I'm sorry if I've been nasty to you. I still love you, you know.'

'And I still love you, you silly sausage,' he said and smiled at her properly for the first time in weeks.

★ ★ ★

Since the antenatal classes had ended, four of the expectant mothers — Roisin, Michelle, Liz and Jayne — had continued to meet every week. Now that their babies were born, the weekly meetings were a lifeline to Roisin. She found that they were the only people to whom she could really talk honestly, the only ones who really understood what she was going through, because they were going through it too.

Prior to the birth of their babies the women had met in coffee shops and cafés but now the practicalities of constant breastfeeding, not to mention continuous nappy changing dictated that they meet in each other's homes. At six weeks — Roisin now defined her life by Tony's age — they were due to meet up at Michelle's for the first time.

Setting off in the car with directions scrawled on a note in the breast pocket of her shirt, Roisin was full of apprehension. She was about to enter Donal's home and the prospect filled her with excitement and dread. She knew he wouldn't be there of course — the men were always at work when the women met up — but still she couldn't stop her heart from racing. She took a few deep breaths and told herself to calm down. Only she knew that this trip to Michelle's home was more than the innocent visit it appeared. All she had to do was stay calm.

As well as her curiosity about Donal, Roisin was keen to see the house itself. At the time of its construction there had been much talk in Ballyfergus about the big mansion Noel McCormick was building for his daughter. Though Roisin had never seen it, she gathered from local gossip that it was impressive.

The directions took her out the Killyglen Road, a couple of miles into the lush green countryside, the hedgerows brimming with summer flowers. Roisin glanced at her gorgeous baby sleeping in his car seat beside her, looking like a little Buddha with his fat little cheeks. She was more optimistic than she had been since the birth — things were definitely getting better.

Michelle's house was set back from the road, hidden behind a copse of conifers. Roisin turned cautiously into the gravel lane signposted 'The Grange' and drove for some fifty yards until a handsome house came into view. It was mock Georgian in style, of substantial proportions with a triple garage set off to the left. In front of the house was a large gravel turning-circle for cars. Roisin parked here beside Liz's Freelander and got out of the car, looking round to take in the scene. With the sun behind her, she took off her sunglasses to admire the beautiful views of the surrounding countryside.

She heard the creak of the huge front door opening and turned around to see Michelle on the doorstep holding her new baby, Sabrina, on her left shoulder. Michelle was dressed stylishly from head-to-toe in black jersey and high-heeled mules. Roisin looked down at her own crumpled linen shirt and trousers and decided she must do something about losing weight so that she could get back into some decent clothes. She wished that she had worn closed-toe mules — she hadn't noticed until now that the varnish on her toenails was chipped and flaking. God, she was a mess!

'Hi, there,' called Michelle, cheerfully. 'Thought it was you, Roz.' Although Michelle knew Roisin's real name by now, she continued to use the shortened version. Roisin didn't mind at all — Roz sounded so much more trendy and cosmopolitan than plain, dreary old 'Roisin'.

'How are you?' asked Michelle as Roisin hobbled to the door, with the heavy car seat bumping off her hips. 'Come on in.'

Roisin followed Michelle into a marble-floored hallway, as big as her dining-room, and then into a very large sitting-room, where Liz was already installed on one of the toffee-coloured leather sofas, feeding her baby. Tony had fallen asleep during the drive over and Roisin deposited him and his car seat in the corner of the room. She sank gratefully into a comfortable leather armchair, pushed her sunglasses off her brow and exchanged small talk with Liz while Michelle went to make tea. She took in her surroundings — the expensive curtains, the solid wood furniture, the luxurious sofas, and the stylish ornaments. Donal sure had done well for himself, she thought with bitterness.

By the time Michelle returned with a tray of steaming mugs and a plate of chocolate biscuits, Jayne had arrived carrying a sleeping baby in a car seat. She sat down beside Roisin.

'That bloody thing is nearly taking the arm off me,' she complained. 'If Alex gets any bigger I'm not going to be able to carry him around in that for much longer.'

'I know,' said Liz. 'They're the most awkward things to carry, aren't they?'

Everyone agreed and then Roisin asked, 'Have any of you tried those baby sleeping-bags?'

'They're great for keeping the baby warm especially in the winter 'cos they can't kick it off like covers,' Liz said.

'Ah, but I've a friend whose baby broke its

arm wearing one of them,' said Michelle and she nodded her head knowingly. 'It got its arm tangled up inside it and rolled onto it.'

Everyone gasped.

The conversation reminded Roisin why these new friends were so important to her — much as her other friends loved her, would they be prepared to spend fifteen minutes discussing the merits of baby sleeping-bags? But right now such things mattered to them. They were all racked with fear and anxiety lest they do something wrong and their little ones come to harm. And they could talk amongst themselves about which brand of nappies was best and what shape of bottle teat to use, without incurring ridicule or feeling like complete and utter bores.

Roisin took a sip of tea and listened to the discussion. Jayne was on her knees changing her baby's nappy and the subject had turned to remedies for nappy rash. Now that she was sitting here in his home, Roisin felt the presence of Donal Mullan all around her. He must have sat right here where she sat now. She shifted uncomfortably in the seat.

She looked at Michelle and tried to imagine the two of them together. They seemed such an unlikely pairing, not least because of their disparate backgrounds. Donal, however, had always aspired to wealth, and she was certain he would have had little difficulty in adjusting to this lifestyle.

There was some noise in the hallway and a lively girl of about five years bounded into the room wearing a uniform of red-and-white checked pinafore, black blazer and white socks. Cute blonde pigtails stuck out on either side of her head. She rushed over to Sabrina, who was lying on a playmat kicking her legs, and kissed her. Then she hauled the baby onto her lap, her head lolling like a rag-doll.

Alarmed, Roisin glanced quickly at Michelle who stood at the door looking down on her two daughters indulgently.

'Careful now, watch her head,' she said without making any move to intervene, and then added, 'This is Molly, girls. Say 'hello', Molly.'

Molly laid her little sister down again and stood up. She looked round the room shyly — her face was the picture of Donal Mullan. 'Hello,' she said gravely, grabbed a biscuit from the plate on the coffee table and ran out of the room.

Yep, thought Roisin, Donal had it made. Two beautiful children, a lovely wife, a high-flying career, wealth and a home Roisin couldn't help but envy. He had it all.

★ ★ ★

Donal stood at the tee-off for the sixth hole on the golf course on one of the most gorgeous summer mornings you could ask for, and all he could think about was what was wrong with his life. The sun beat down on his forearms, birds sang in the trees behind him and there wasn't a breath of wind.

The news of Michelle's pregnancy had devastated him. Until then he hadn't realised that he was working up the courage to leave her. And now that the baby had arrived, a beautiful little girl as sweet and gorgeous as her sister, it would be doubly hard for him to walk out. He certainly couldn't do it while Sabrina was so tiny. He might be a snake-in-the-grass but he wasn't that much of a bastard.

'You're up, mate,' said a voice and Donal jolted.

'Sorry,' he said as the other three golfers watched him walk over to the tee. They were playing a Medal Competition, and he'd been drawn at random with Mark Roberts and John Craig — fifty-something guys he knew socially and sometimes played with at weekends. The third man, Scott Johnston, was younger and relatively new to the club.

He squared up to the tee and tried to concentrate on executing the perfect stroke, the way he'd been shown by the golf professional. He'd wasted a small fortune on lessons trying to improve his game but old habits were hard to break. People who knew about these things said that you should always learn from a professional before setting foot on a golf course. Donal was self-taught and relied primarily on his natural aptitude for golf, but this meant that his game would never rise above the mediocre.

He swung the club and hit the ball with a satisfying 'ping'. But he sliced the ball and it ended up in the rough.

'Hard luck,' said Scott Johnston good-naturedly and Donal shrugged his shoulders.

He resolved to try harder but the situation

didn't improve. By the time they reached the last hole his score was a pitiful ninety-two, even taking into account his high handicap. It was made all the more embarrassing because Scott, with a single-figure handicap, was a very good golfer.

'Thanks for the game,' said Scott and shook Donal's hand.

'Anytime,' replied Donal. 'You're in with a good chance of winning the Medal, Scott. Where did you play before?'

'I was a member of Royal Portrush before moving back down here.'

'It's one of the best links courses I've played,' acknowledged Donal.

Donal fell in beside Alan as they walked from the green towards the nineteenth hole in the clubhouse. 'I don't know what's wrong with me today,' he said. 'That's the worst round I've played in years.'

'Happens that way sometimes,' replied Alan.

Inside the locker room they stowed their clubs, and changed their spikes for casual shoes. They'd been on the course for over four hours, a slow round, and it was pushing on twelve thirty.

'Ready for a drink, chaps?' said Alan, hoisting his trousers halfway up his protruding belly. When he let them go, they slid back down to their former position on his hips.

In the bar they all ordered drinks and then decided to have something to eat. The fare was basic pub grub but hearty and wholesome. They talked about the recent success of the Rules of Golf Quiz Team, plans for the building of a new clubhouse, scheduled improvements to the course and speculated on the winner of the Medal.

Scott proved an amiable lunch companion and Donal learned that he was Ballyfergus born and bred and worked for a local firm of accountants.

'Well, guys,' said Scott as soon as they'd finished eating. 'I'd better be off. The missus'll be wondering where I am.'

Scott stood up and Donal was just thinking that he was well and truly under the thumb when he added, 'We've got a new baby, you see. It's only fair that my wife gets a break.'

Donal looked at the table and felt like a rat. He lingered in the clubhouse as long as possible after every game to avoid going home and facing Michelle.

'Congratulations,' said John. 'I didn't know. When was the baby born?'

'Middle of May. He's nearly eight weeks,' said Scott with pride.

'You two'll have plenty in common then,' said Alan, slapping Donal on the back. 'Don here's got a wee tiddler at home too. 'Bout the same age, isn't she, Don?'

Donal forced a weak smile and said, 'That's right.'

Scott looked at him then with his head tilted to one side, and narrowed his eyes, thinking. 'Your wife's not called Michelle, is she? Michelle Mullan.'

'Yes,' said Donal.

'I met her one night she dropped Roisin off at the house. She was in the same antenatal class. They still meet up every week, don't they?'

Donal was embarrassed to admit that he was unaware of these arrangements as he took little interest in Michelle's daily activities. So he said, 'That's right,' and left it at that.

After Scott had gone, the men ordered more drinks and were joined by two regular drinkers in the club. Donal sat back and listened — soon the voices around him receded into a distant hum and he was lost in his own thoughts.

He thought of Amy with longing and thanked God that she was the way she was. No other woman would've put up with what she'd put up with from him. She bore no ill will towards Michelle and said she understood why he had to stay with her, for the time being at least. But even Amy would only stand for this for so long. Everyone had their breaking point.

They loved each other — they should be together. And it was utter madness for him to stay with a woman he didn't love. In spite of his love for his children, which was fierce and strong, Donal knew he could no longer do it. The time had come to devise an exit strategy from his marriage. He would wait until Michelle was back on top, physically and mentally — he owed her that much — and then he would leave. He set himself a target date — the end of February next year, when Sabrina would be nine months old. She would just be crawling then, saying Ma-Ma and Da-Da and waving goodbye for the first time. A tear leaked out of the corner of Donal's eye — he got up quickly and went to the empty toilets where he sat in a cubicle with the door closed and wept for all the loss to come.

Before Roisin knew it, three months had passed and it was time for her to think about going back to work. Katy had been a saint but it was unfair to expect her to carry the can any longer.

Roisin got into bed wearing a night-time feeding bra and big white cotton knickers. She would miss feeding Tony but she couldn't wait for her breasts, and the rest of her, to get back to their normal size. She longed to feel sexy again and wear the beautiful lingerie she used to favour. Scott lay on his back, naked, and Roisin nestled her head on his shoulder facing the ceiling.

'I wish I didn't have to go back full-time. I wish I didn't have to go back at all,' she said. 'I hate to think of Tony being looked after by strangers.'

'It's a good nursery. He'll be well cared for,' replied Scott and he paused. 'But you don't have to go back full-time, Roisin. You could employ a part-time therapist.'

'I can't,' she sighed. 'The figures don't stack up, Scott. We'll have Tony's nursery fees to meet and the money that I pay a therapist goes straight into my own pocket if I do the work myself. And I know standards have been slipping. I went in the other day and one of the blinds had broken and no one had thought to do anything about it. And the place wasn't as clean as it should have been. It's not Katy's fault — she can't be at both salons at once. I need to be there full-time.'

'Yeah, I suppose you're right,' agreed Scott and they both fell silent. 'Hey,' he said after a few moments had passed, 'did I tell you I met Don Mullan, the husband of that girl in your antenatal class?'

Roisin froze. Hearing Donal's name spring from Scott's lips was disconcerting. 'No, where did you meet him?'

'At the golf club. We played in the Medal together last weekend.'

'What was he like?'

'OK. Nice enough guy. Didn't have a lot to say for himself.'

The Donal Mullan Roisin had known could talk for Ireland although most of what he said was lies. But Roisin said nothing. She had never told Scott the full story of Ann-Marie and Donal Mullan — but not because she had set out to deceive him, simply because she didn't see the point of raking over the sad story again. It was in the past and it was Ann-Marie's story, not hers — why would Scott be interested? All he knew was that Roisin's sister had been jilted when she was young and never really got over it. But now Roisin's life looked set to converge with Donal's and something prevented her from telling Scott the truth.

Scott was such a positive, good-natured person. He was so essentially *good*. Roisin knew he would disapprove of her vendetta against Donal, of the bitterness she carried in her heart. She knew he would think her a lesser person for her inability to forgive. He would see her differently if he knew what she harboured inside

— he would love her less because of it. It was best that she kept this to herself. But there was one small matter she had been avoiding for weeks and now it would have to be faced.

'Michelle asked me if we'd like to come for supper one night,' she said. 'Us and Liz and Jayne and their partners.'

'They're the other two in the group, aren't they?'

'That's right. She's given me a few dates and asked me to get back to her. She thought it would be nice for us all to get together before I go back to work.'

'Hey, that's a really nice thing to do.'

'Michelle is nice. She's really kind.'

'Why didn't you mention it before?'

'Oh,' said Roisin airily, 'I wasn't sure that you'd want to go.'

'I'd love to. I've met Donal now and I'd like to meet the others.'

'OK then,' said Roisin. 'We'll check our diaries tomorrow.'

'Look at the time, love,' said Scott sleepily and he kissed her on the top of her head. 'You'd better get some sleep. You'll be up in a couple of hours with Tony.'

But Roisin's mind was buzzing and, in spite of her tiredness, she knew sleep would evade her for some time. She had put Michelle off twice already about the supper party but, if she rebuffed her a third time, she knew she would hurt her feelings. Roisin had inadvertently mentioned to Michelle that Mairead was desperate to baby-sit, so she couldn't use the lack of a sitter as an excuse. And the four women in the group had become close over the last few months. The next natural stage in their friendship was to involve partners — it couldn't be avoided for much longer. And Roisin had no desire to lose their friendship.

Scott's breathing had deepened and his chest rose and fell in a slow, peaceful rhythm. Roisin gently extricated herself from his left arm and wiggled over to her side of the bed.

At first, she had balked at the idea of meeting Donal face to face. She wasn't sure she could trust herself to be civil and she didn't want to let her guard down in front of Scott or anyone else. She tried to guess what Donal's reaction to seeing her might be and how he'd behave. She reckoned that Donal would keep his mouth shut — after all he must be ashamed of the way he treated Ann-Marie. She wanted to be prepared for everything. But most of all, plain old curiosity got the better of her. She was dying to look into those lying eyes and see what had become of Donal. She wanted to see if he had changed. She wanted him to know that she had the measure of him.

Roisin reached out her left arm and switched off the light.

9

Roisin stood in her walk-in wardrobe and looked at the rails of clothes, virtually none of which fitted. What on earth would she wear to Michelle's? After much rummaging, trying on and discarding, the answer came in a pair of black linen drawstring trousers and matching tunic top. She'd bought them earlier that summer because she was fed up still wearing maternity clothes weeks after Tony was born. She put the clothes on and looked in the mirror. They were OK but not very exciting and far from glamorous.

She should have put more effort into this evening — she should have treated herself to something new. But she'd been so busy getting everything organised for going back to work that she'd not had the time to think about what she'd wear. Not that she hadn't thought about tonight. It was on her mind constantly.

She pulled out her favourite black strappy sandals, put them on and felt much better. She hadn't had time to paint her toenails — she'd just have to hope no one noticed. Her feet were just about the only parts of her body that hadn't changed size due to pregnancy. She tried putting her hair up, then decided to wear it down. Once she'd put on her make-up, she decided she would do.

Just then the doorbell rang, the door opened

immediately and Mairead's voice called up the stairs, 'It's only me.'

'I'll be down in a minute, Mum,' shouted Roisin from the top of the stairs. 'Tony's in the lounge with Scott.'

Roisin laid the linen outfit on the bed along with the shoes and put on her dressing-gown. She looked at the clock — it said six forty-five. She would feed Tony now, a little earlier than usual, and hand him over to her mother, leaving her with forty-five minutes to get herself ready.

After Tony was fed and winded Roisin came upstairs and jumped in the shower for a quick wash. She'd washed her hair that morning knowing that she wouldn't have time to do so tonight. She stepped out of the shower and dried herself roughly, noticing that her belly wasn't quite as spongy as usual. Was it starting to shrink back to normality or was it taut simply because her stomach was tied in knots? In less than an hour she would be face to face with Donal Mullan.

With an eye on the clock, she applied foundation and eye-shadow and put blusher on her cheeks. But when she tried to apply marine blue eyeliner, a job requiring a steady hand, the lines were in all the wrong places. She removed it with a Q-tip and tried again. The giddiness she felt was akin to the feeling she used to get when she was under age and getting ready for a big night out. The thrill then was passing for an eighteen-year-old, drinking alcohol and flirting with men ten years her senior. The thrill tonight was in the unknown — for she could not predict what would happen when she and Donal met. Both situations held an element of danger, albeit of a very different type.

'Are you ready yet, Roisin?' called Scott's voice up the stairs. 'It's gone twenty past eight. They're expecting us at eight thirty, aren't they?'

'Just coming,' said Roisin, and she threw on her clothes, jammed her feet in the sandals and squirted her neck with perfume.

Scott was standing at the bottom of the stairs in his navy chinos and a brown suede jacket with the car keys in his hand.

'I'll just say goodbye,' said Roisin and she popped her head into the lounge. 'We're off now, Mum. Now, you've got Michelle's number and my mobile, haven't you? If there's anything at all, just ring me.'

'Yes, yes,' said Mairead distractedly, rocking Tony gently in her arms, her eyes fixed on his cherubic little face, his dilated pupils gleaming like wet stones.

'He should be ready to go to bed now,' continued Roisin, 'and he might wake up round nine o'clock and grizzle a bit. But don't go into him unless he's really upset. He usually goes over again.'

'Oh, for goodness sake, Roisin, stop fussing. I have raised two children of my own, you know.'

'Sorry, Mum. Here,' she said dropping her evening bag on the floor. 'Let me give him a kiss before I go.'

'Roisin, we need to go!' called Scott's voice from the hall.

'Just coming,' she said loudly over her

shoulder and then more quietly to her mother, 'Give him here a minute.'

She picked the baby up, kissed his little nose and held him upright in her arms against her chest for a few brief seconds. And he vomited all down the front of her top.

'Shit! Shit! Shit!' she shouted and handed Tony back to her mother.

Scott ran into the room. 'What's wrong?'

Roisin turned to face him, her arms held out from her sides, and he saw the puke.

'Oh, Roisin! What did you go and have to pick him up for?'

'How did I know he was going to be sick?' she cried.

The front of Tony's sleep-suit was covered in curdled milk and he had started crying when Roisin thrust him so abruptly into his grandmother's arms.

'You go on upstairs and get yourself sorted,' said Mairead, 'and I'll see to Tony. He'll be all right. He just got a shock, that's all.'

Upstairs in her bedroom, Roisin took off the soiled top and bra and put on clean underwear. Scott stood in the wardrobe going through her clothes and picking out things for her to wear. In trying to help he was only making things worse.

'They don't fit, Scott! None of them fit. Don't you understand?'

'There must be something — '

'There isn't! Don't you hear what I'm saying? Nothing fits!' shouted Roisin and Scott glared at her and walked out of the room.

There was only one thing that wasn't in the

wash that fitted and she would have to wear it — the once-beautiful cream silk shirt that Scott had put in the tumble dryer. She pulled it out of the cupboard and put it on over the trousers. The hem was puckered and the body of the shirt all out of shape. And the combination of linen trousers with a silk shirt didn't work. Now she looked like a middle-aged school secretary with bad dress sense.

'Are you ready?' said Scott. 'You look — '

'Don't, Scott. Don't say it. It doesn't look remotely nice but I'm going to have to wear it. Come on, we're going to be late.' She grabbed a cream silk pashmina from a drawer and flung it round her shoulders.

They drove in silence out to The Grange, Roisin only speaking to give terse directions to Scott. They pulled up outside Michelle's house and Scott switched off the engine. He put his hand out and touched hers — it was balled in a fist on her lap.

'You're shaking, Roisin! I didn't realise you were so upset. Look, I can turn the car around and we can go home right now. Everyone'll understand.'

It wasn't the shirt that bothered Roisin. She looked at the house and toyed with the idea of taking Scott up on his offer. But without the cover of darkness they had been spotted — the front door opened and Michelle came teetering on high heels over the pink gravel towards the car.

'What happened you two?' she said into the passenger window, her breath reeking of wine. 'I was just about to call you.'

'We hadn't factored in Tony puking all over Roisin when she was ready to walk out the door,' said Scott.

'Oh Roz, you poor thing!' said Michelle. She held open the passenger door while Roisin got out of the car. 'What you need is a glass of wine.'

'The answer to all ills,' said Roisin, unable to stop herself from sounding like a sour-faced cow.

'Believe me, it is,' said Michelle with feeling and she linked arms with Roisin and led her towards the house. Scott fell in beside them and he exchanged pleasantries with Michelle, giving Roisin the opportunity to compose herself. She took several deep breaths, forcing the air right down to her diaphragm.

Michelle closed the front door behind them, took Scott's jacket, and asked them what they wanted to drink. Then she said the words Roisin had been dreading. 'Come on into the drawing-room. Everybody's in there.' And she walked through a doorway that led off to the right.

Roisin hung back, willing Scott to go ahead, not sure now that she had the nerve to face Donal.

'After you,' said Scott in his gentlemanly way and Roisin gave him a thin smile and swallowed. She fixed a grin on her face, took a deep breath and walked through the doorway into a big room she'd never seen before. Naively she'd assumed the lounge she'd been in before was the main reception room in the house. Apparently not.

She registered that there were five people

seated in the room — Liz, Jayne, Donal and two men who must be the girls' partners. The corners of her mouth twitched involuntarily and she felt like her legs were about to give way underneath her. She stopped only a few feet short of the doorway, then felt the flat of Scott's hand in the middle of her back, gently propelling her forward into the centre of the enormous room. Everyone stood up for the introductions.

'Don,' said Michelle, touching her husband's arm, 'you know Scott already.' The two men nodded, said their hellos and shook hands. 'And I'd like you to meet Scott's wife, Roz.' Michelle was beaming.

'Nice to meet you,' said Donal mechanically and, to Roisin's surprise, he leaned forward and kissed her lightly on each cheek in the continental way. Where did he learn to do that, thought Roisin? Not in West Belfast. She felt her cheeks redden with embarrassment.

'Nice to meet you too,' she mumbled and looked at her feet.

He took a step back from her then and she risked looking into his face. But he did not meet her gaze — already his attention was turned to something Jayne had said about being able to fit the entire ground floor of her house in this one room. He was laughing in a superior sort of way but not too hard in case it might be read by Jayne and her husband as a slight.

Now that she had the opportunity to examine him up close, she saw that he was hardly changed at all — he still had something of the tousled charm about him that Ann-Marie must've found so attractive. His brown hair was greyed a little at the temples, which gave him more gravitas than his boyish looks would otherwise have commanded. He had retained his slim figure and his pale grey eyes were sunken just a little into his tanned skin. Fine creases appeared at the corners of his eyes when he smiled. He wore cream chinos, brown suede brogues and a pale blue polo shirt, the top two buttons of which were undone. He was, Roisin conceded reluctantly, quite a handsome man.

'Roz,' she heard Michelle say and Roisin turned towards her. 'This,' continued Michelle, gracefully carrying out her role as hostess, 'is Mike, Liz's husband. And this is Jayne's other half, Andy.'

For the next few minutes Roisin turned her attention to the others, grateful for the distraction. Then Michelle went out of the room to fix Scott and Roisin's drinks and they all sat down on the three very large, cream sofas that framed the huge coffee table. The atmosphere was relaxed in spite of people meeting for the first time, everyone eager to make friends and have a good time, everyone slowly realising how precious night outs without children would be from now on. Only Roisin was on edge, watching and listening to Donal carefully, contributing nothing to the conversation herself. He appeared relaxed and comfortable in his role as host — he showed no outward sign of recognising her.

Michelle came in and handed Roisin a very full glass of white wine.

'Here's to having survived the first three months,' she joked.

Everyone laughed, raised their glasses and drank.

'Roz,' said Donal and Roisin nearly jumped out of her seat. 'Oops,' she said, as wine sloshed over the top of her glass and landed with a splash on the sleeve of her shirt.

'I'll get a cloth,' said Michelle.

'There's no need. Really there's not. It's only a tiny drop. Sorry, Don,' she went on, as calmly as she could, and she stared hard into his eyes, 'what were you saying?'

'Michelle tells me that you own two beauty salons,' he said, holding her gaze steadily without so much as a flicker of an eyelid. 'Are you looking forward to going back to work?'

'Yes and no. I'll miss Tony, naturally, but I feel that I need to be there to keep the business on track. And I miss the clients and the girls I work with. You don't realise how much you enjoy the company 'til you're stuck at home all day. The only thing that's kept me sane is this lot,' she went on, anxious to widen the conversation, and she smiled conspiratorially at the women in the room.

'That's right,' said Liz, a little woozily. 'If I hadn't had these three to talk to over the past three months I think I would have gone nuts!'

The women nodded their heads vigorously in agreement and Roisin took a big gulp of wine and stared at Donal. He was either a very good actor or he really didn't know who she was. She drank her wine quickly and felt the tension drain from her body.

While Michelle refilled her glass, Roisin looked about the room, admiring her hosts' taste. If Roisin had thought the other room — which she now realised was the family den — was luxurious, this one was out of this world. The colour scheme was primarily cream with touches of gold and terracotta. From the pale cream rug in the middle of the room, on which the coffee table sat, to the over-sized cream marble fireplace and the burnt-orange silk curtains, everything was of the finest quality. Fragranced candles burned on every surface and, on the coffee table, some floated in a glass bowl of water strewn with amber-coloured rose petals.

She now took the time to focus on the other women, taking in Liz's wacky eastern-influenced turquoise trouser suit and flat pumps. She noted Jayne's tight off-the-shoulders top and figure hugging jeans, not the best choice so soon after giving birth. Then her gaze fell on Michelle and Roisin cringed with embarrassment at her own appearance in comparison to Michelle's.

From the top of her head to the tips of her toes Michelle was perfectly groomed. Her face was well made-up, her lips a perfect bright red and her hair was pulled into a knot on the top of her head. She wore matching bright red varnish on her nails and toes and her tan was too dark to be real — the summer had been a wet one and Roisin knew that the demands of a newborn left no time for sunbathing.

Michelle's figure, like the other women, was still far from her pre-pregnancy size but much better disguised than Roisin's in her top-to-toe black outfit. She wore a sleeveless tank-top — it drew attention to her strong brown shoulders and away from her midriff — and a pair of flattering fluid crepe trousers, with a hipster belt made of interconnecting silver-coloured metal hoops. High heels with a single diamanté stud between her toes finished off the outfit. Her jewellery was understated and classy — large diamond studs and a gold watch, Rolex by the look of it. How did she do it? Maybe, being a second-time mum, she had her act together better than the rest of them.

Roisin looked down at her unpainted toenails, inched forward to the edge of the seat and tucked her feet under the sofa. She curled her fingers round the stem of the wine glass to hide her short unpainted fingernails, and noticed that the back of her hands were dry and chapped — the result of having her hands in water all day washing, wiping and changing nappies. Washing her hair and chucking on some make-up simply wasn't enough to hide her self-neglect. No wonder Donal Mullan had looked right through her — she was a mess. And she hadn't even noticed until tonight. Worst of all, she was a terrible advert for her salons — one look at her and clients would run a mile. Once she was back to work, she told herself firmly, her priorities would have to change.

'Right, I think supper's ready,' said Michelle and everyone got up.

Roisin followed Michelle into the hall. 'The children are very quiet,' she said, marvelling at Michelle's calm efficiency.

'That's because Molly's not here. She's up at Mum's. They've had her all day. And I have a babysitter for Sabrina. You know Esther that works for Mum?'

Roisin shook her head.

'Anyway,' continued Michelle, 'it's her daughter, Sybil. She's absolutely brilliant with her. She's been here since lunchtime. She gives Sabrina bottles and everything. She's upstairs now in the playroom right beside Sabrina's bedroom,' she said, raising her eyes heavenwards. 'This way I don't have to worry about her and I can completely relax. They're on the third floor so we'll not even hear Sabrina if she cries.'

Maybe that was why Michelle looked so good, thought Roisin. Breastfeeding might be best for baby but Roisin wasn't convinced that it was best for mum. It had done nothing to shift the extra weight she'd accumulated during her pregnancy and she constantly felt drained of energy.

Roisin was seated right opposite Michelle at the rectangular table, with Donal between them at the head. The simple supper Michelle had led them to expect turned out to be a feast. Jerusalem artichoke soup for starters, with warm home-made bread, salmon and dill sauce with roasted summer vegetables, salad and new potatoes, and a choice of two home-made desserts, tiramisu and lemon tart. And lots and lots to drink — the Mullans were generous hosts.

The conversation, lubricated by copious amounts of alcohol, was easy and much of it humorous. But in spite of the three glasses of wine Roisin had consumed she felt stone cold sober. Throughout the meal she watched Donal intently, at last coming to the conclusion that he truly did not recognise her. And why should he? When he'd last met her she was a chubby-faced, spotty teenager with short mousy brown hair, that was invariably greasy, and thick glasses. Now the puppy fat was gone, the spots had disappeared, she wore her hair long, the colour enhanced to a rich dark chestnut brown, and the glasses had been replaced long ago by contact lenses. He now knew her as Roz Johnston, not Roisin Shaw.

As this realisation sank in, Roisin felt a mixture of relief and disappointment — an odd combination. She had worked herself up for some sort of confrontation and none had happened. She didn't know whether to be happy or sad. But it left her feeling unsatisfied — cheated somehow.

'Michelle,' she said quietly as the meal came to an end, 'that was absolutely wonderful. Where on earth did you find the time to make all this?'

Michelle looked at Donal, and giggled. 'Well, I have to confess that I had a bit of help.'

'What do you mean, a bit of help?' snorted Donal.

The smile fell from Michelle's face — she looked into her glass, and took a large swig of wine.

Roisin looked from one to the other, seeking

316

an explanation. Had Donal done most of the cooking? Was he annoyed because Michelle wasn't giving him due credit?

'Well,' said Michelle, addressing Roisin, and pointedly ignoring Donal, 'you know Esther that I was telling you about earlier?'

Roisin nodded.

'I borrowed her from Mum for the day.'

'Borrowed?'

'She came over here today instead of going to Mum's and she made most of the food.'

'What do you mean 'most' of it?' interrupted Donal and Roisin could feel the tension between the couple sparkle like static.

'Don,' protested Michelle, 'I made the salad. And the bread.'

'A salad,' repeated Donal, in a derisory tone. He was being so mean to Michelle that Roisin felt suddenly protective of her. 'And if I'm not mistaken,' he continued, cruelly, 'the bread machine made the bread.'

'You should be grateful I didn't cook, Don. I would have poisoned everyone.'

Roisin laughed loudly both to support Michelle and to break the tension.

Donal said, straight-faced, 'She's not joking, you know.'

'Right,' said Michelle, standing up with a big smile on her face. 'Let's have coffee in the drawing room. Don, can you get the after-dinner drinks?'

Something in Michelle's manner suggested that she was used to this kind of treatment from Donal, and Roisin felt sorry for her friend. Scott would never speak to her like that. Was it possible that Michelle and Donal's life, which looked so perfect from the outside, wasn't so flawless after all? What was all this affluence really worth if their marriage was unhappy? But perhaps she was reading too much into the exchange — everyone had their off days.

The men drifted off to examine the contents of Donal's drinks cabinet and the women made for the kitchen. The stood around the coffee machine on the island unit while it fizzed and hissed, black liquid dripping into the jug on the hotplate.

With a cleaner and a cook and practically a bloody live-in nanny as well, it was no wonder Michelle looked so good, thought Roisin. She'd had nothing to do all day but pamper herself! Roisin was envious and relieved at the same time. It let the rest of them off the hook. Michelle wasn't superhuman after all.

'The men all seem to be getting on well,' observed Jayne. 'They've organised a game of golf for next weekend.'

'Doesn't take them long to find an excuse for an afternoon away from the babies,' said Liz, dryly.

'It's good that they're getting on so well, though, isn't it?' said Michelle, disposed as always to see the bright side. 'I think it's nice.'

'Roisin, have you had any luck getting Tony to take the bottle?' said Jayne, changing the subject.

'Yes, thank God. In the end it was Mum who got him to take it just last week. We've just been careful to make sure he gets at least one bottle a day and I've started weaning him off breast-milk and onto formula. He'll be on the bottle full-time by the end of this week.'

'I'll have to start thinking about going back to work soon too,' said Liz, who was a primary school teacher. 'I can't believe I'm more than halfway through my maternity leave.'

'Will you get your exact job back?' said Jayne.

'Yes, they've employed a temporary teacher just for the six months.'

'What about you, Liz?' said Roisin. 'Have you got a date for going back?'

Liz was a paralegal with a local firm of solicitors. 'Same as Jayne. Another couple of months.'

Michelle had fallen quiet and, conscious that the conversation excluded her, Roisin said, 'Michelle, we can't leave you with all this mess to clean up on your own. Why don't we clear the table and get the first load in the dishwasher?'

'Oh, thanks, but there's no need. Sybil's staying overnight and she's going to clean all this up in the morning. She's an absolute gem.'

Of course, thought Roisin, envy rearing its ugly head again — Michelle wouldn't soil her hands clearing up dishes. Roisin sternly told herself not to be so horrible.

When the women came into the drawing-room with the coffee, mugs and a plate of Esther's home-made truffles, the men were talking about cars.

'If you're buying a car with your own cash, as opposed to taking a company car, then depreciation does matter,' said Donal, holding court in front of the empty fireplace. Everyone else was seated. In spite of his legs being planted two feet apart on the cream rug, he swayed slightly unsteadily from side to side. He had a very large brandy glass in his hand, with a small measure of amber liquid in the bottom. He swilled it round, put it briefly to his lips and went on, 'Take Michelle's new Mercedes ML as an example,' he continued. 'It'll hold its value better than my company car, a Rover 75.'

'But that's a fairly luxurious car. Why would the Mercedes hold its value better?' asked Jayne, joining the conversation.

'There's nothing intrinsically wrong with Rovers, but there's a lot of them around,' explained Donal. 'Many are run by fleets which change their cars frequently, so supply exceeds demand.'

Roisin helped Michelle hand round the coffees, thinking that the conversation had taken a boring turn.

'And it's also about image,' added Andy. 'In the executive market, it's the quality marques like Mercedes, BMW and Audi that hold their value. And in the four-by-four market a Mercedes ML is seen as one of the most desirable.'

'That's right, Andy,' said Donal, warming to the theme. 'Let me give you another example. Take the Vauxhall Omega. As soon as it leaves the showroom it starts haemorrhaging its value.'

Roisin looked at Scott who, up 'til now had been actively listening, nodding his head and agreeing with the points made. Now he was perfectly still, a smile fixed on his face, and a mug of coffee held motionless in his hand. Outside in the forecourt sat his pride and joy, a three-year-old Vauxhall Omega.

Scott roused himself and said, 'It depends when you buy it.'

'What do you mean?' said Liz.

'If you buy it after year one, then the original buyer's already taken the hit on the worst of the depreciation. A car like that can be quite a prudent buy. You're basically getting a luxury car at a snip.'

'A poor man's luxury car, Scott,' said Donal. 'A Vauxhall's still a Vauxhall. And who'd be seen dead driving an Omega anyway?'

An uncomfortable ripple of subdued laughter followed Donal's comment and died away quickly. Scott turned the faintest shade of pink and he looked past Donal into the empty fireplace.

'I think that's a matter of opinion,' said Scott quietly, but no one except for Roisin seemed to hear him.

Her stomach tightened and she burned with rage. She could tolerate Donal putting Michelle down, much as it pained her to see, but not Scott. Donal must have seen them arriving in the Omega. How could he be so insensitive? So indefensibly rude? She could imagine how Donal must've looked out the window and laughed to himself when he saw Scott's car.

She was glad now that she hadn't told either Michelle or Scott that she knew Donal from before. She was glad no one knew how much she hated him. She had kept her cards close to her chest and that had been the clever thing to do. Now she was close enough to Donal, through her relationship with Michelle, to plan some sort of revenge on him. But what exactly? She wished she knew something about him that she could use to her advantage — and his detriment.

Donal was drunk — his eyes were shining and Roisin could see beads of sweat on his forehead. For Scott's sake she hoped he and the other men in the room were too drunk to remember much of this conversation. The women would not register much of it, she was sure. They would be as bored by the conversation as she had been — until it became personal.

Scott had bought the Omega shortly after they'd decided to buy the house. She knew his primary motivator at the time was keeping costs down as they had so much to buy for their new home. His accountant's prudence had led him to seek out a second-hand Omega precisely because it depreciated so much in the first year or so.

Roisin looked at Michelle, who was chatting happily to Liz and Jayne about her plans for a forthcoming family holiday in the South of France. Roisin decided that she had not been mistaken about Donal — his behaviour tonight proved that her gut instinct was correct. He was, and always had been, bad news — and he deserved his comeuppance.

And another thought went through her mind — how could Michelle love someone like him? For unless her judgement of people had gone completely, Michelle was a truly nice person. And Donal Mullan was a bastard.

*　*　*

'You should think before you open your mouth in future,' said Michelle to her husband on the Monday night after the dinner party. 'You should've seen the look on Scott and Roz's faces. Then again you were probably too drunk to notice.'

'I'm sorry, all right, I'm sorry,' said Donal raising his hands, palm-upwards, in an exaggerated gesture of apology. 'How was I to know that the guy was driving a bloody Omega? And yes, I was drunk, or I probably wouldn't have said it.'

Donal was standing in the kitchen with his work suit, shirt and tie on. He stuffed a piece of buttered bread into his mouth — a habit that really annoyed Michelle when there was a perfectly good meal waiting for him in the oven. But now wasn't the time to be picking holes in his eating habits. She had much more important things to get sorted.

'Roz is my friend, Don, and it would be nice if you made the effort to get along with Scott.'

'I do get along with him. I think he's an OK guy. Look, Shell, I made a mistake and I said I was sorry. What more do you want me to do?'

'Just don't do it again.'

'Deal.'

'OK.'

Still cross but recognising that she could not ask for a fuller apology than the one Donal had given her, Michelle decided to tackle another sore point.

'Have you given any further thought to coming to the South of France with us, Don?'

'I don't think I can swing the time off work,' he said indistinctly, chewing his food.

'But you've hardly taken any time off this summer! You must be due loads of holidays.'

'It's not the holidays so much as what's happening at work. I've a couple of big deals on the go. I can't just up and go.'

'But I'm not talking about going until the middle of September. That's more than three weeks away.'

'I need more than a few weeks' notice to take time off work.'

Michelle was about to retort that he wasn't the bloody chief executive, just an ordinary employee, but she bit her tongue. If she wanted him to come with her to Provence, then she would have to appeal to his instincts as a father.

'Don't you want to come with us?' she asked.

'Of course. But it's just not possible.'

'The girls will miss you.'

'I'll miss them too but there's nothing I can do about it, Shell. Anyway, should you be taking Molly on holiday during term-time?'

'A week or two off school isn't going to do her any harm. Sabrina was too little to think of going before now. And if I leave it until half-term the weather'll be too cold. As it is, it might be a bit on the chilly side at night. But it won't be the same without you, Don. We haven't had a family holiday this year.'

'We went to Donegal for a week,' he retorted, irritation creeping into his voice.

'That doesn't count. I mean somewhere warm and sunny.'

'I don't know what you want to be taking a four-month-old abroad for anyway,' he said grumpily. 'She might get sunstroke.'

'Don't be silly, Don. It'll be perfect. The weather won't be too hot and the pool's heated. We can stroll into Vence and have croissants for breakfast in the town square. Do you remember the little cobbled streets and the fountain and the quaint old town hall? And the market with peaches and figs as big and juicy as oranges?'

'It's not going to work, Shell . . . '

'I'll be lonely,' she said, changing tack.

'No, you won't,' said Donal, and he laughed. 'Your parents are going too, aren't they? And they still have a housekeeper over there, that lovely lady — what's her name — Dominique? You'll not have to lift a finger and I bet she'll spoil the girls rotten.'

'Yes, I know she will,' said Michelle, and she paused before asking carefully, 'Is it my parents, Don? Is it because of them that you don't want to come? There's plenty of room in the villa. It's not as if we'd be in each other's pockets all the time — '

'Shell,' he interrupted abruptly, and gave her a hard stare, 'I'm sorry but I can't go and that's the end of it. Now I'm going upstairs to get changed out of these clothes.'

He walked out of the room and Michelle followed him as far as the door, her arms folded belligerently across her chest. 'I'll go on my own then. See if I care!' she shouted after him, sounding less like the independent woman she aspired to and more like a petulant child. She desisted from stamping her foot on the kitchen floor but she was seething with frustration.

'Right,' she said to herself and went upstairs to the study on the third floor. She switched on the computer and searched the internet for flights to Nice. When she'd narrowed her search to the best flights dates and times she phoned her parents to confirm the details.

Michelle listened to the muffled sounds of Pauline conferring with Noel and then her mother came back on the line.

'Yes, darling, those sound fine to your father and me. We're both really looking forward to it.'

'Me too. Except Don's not coming.'

'Oh, why ever not?'

'Says he's too busy at work.'

'Never mind,' said Pauline and Michelle was sure she could hear relief in her voice. 'It'll be nice to have a family holiday. Just the three of us and the children.'

'Don is family, Mum.'

'Oh, you know what I mean. Now can you go ahead and book those flights and I'll give you a cheque later?'

'Sure.'

'And I'll phone Dominique and let her know we're coming. I'll ask her to organise a nanny as well — it'd be great if she could get that lovely girl we hired in the summer to look after Roger. I can't remember her name.'

'Anais.'

'Anais. That's right. She was just wonderful with Roger.'

'Sounds great, Mum,' said Michelle without enthusiasm. She hung up, typed her credit-card details into the computer, hesitated briefly before proceeding and then hit the 'Submit' button. The holiday was booked.

Michelle closed down the internet connection and sat staring at the wallpaper on the screen, full of misery. She thought back to when she'd got pregnant with Sabrina — how thrilled she'd been and how hopeful for the future. The cracks in her marriage to Donal had been there then and she'd ignored them. She'd hoped that a new baby would be the cement to fill those cracks and hold the marriage together. But after Sabrina's birth, their relationship had not improved — if anything, it had got worse. Michelle put that down to having a new baby in the house — everyone's nerves were frayed from lack of sleep and sheer exhaustion. But now she could see clearly that her plan had not worked.

She suspected now that Donal hadn't wanted the baby in the first place — sometimes she thought he only stayed with her because of the children. But what would she do if he left her? How could she survive without him? He and the children were her entire life. She thought of Roisin, and Liz and Jayne all going back to their high-powered jobs while she, 'Michelle no-job' stayed at home and played at being a proper mum.

And she couldn't even do that right. She

couldn't wait for Molly to go back to school and Sabrina to start at the nursery. She just wasn't cut out for full-time motherhood. And perhaps Don would have more respect for her if she had a career, but she'd left it too late, hadn't she? She was thirty-five years old. It was too late to start all over again.

Michelle closed down the computer, switched the light off and went to bed, alone.

Three weeks later it was with a sense of foreboding that she set off on two weeks holiday with her parents. Her concerns centred not round where she was going — the villa, in the hills just outside the walled medieval town of Vence was fabulous — but what she was leaving behind.

Two weeks was a long time for Donal to be on his own. What would he do in the evenings? And the weekends? Would he miss her? Michelle was not a believer in the general maxim that absence makes the heart grow fonder. She believed that, in some cases, time apart made people realise that they could live quite happily without their other half. In Donal's case she worried that this might be true.

Michelle held four-month-old Sabrina — who had now fallen asleep after forty minutes of screaming — on her lap and looked out the window of the airplane as it took off from Belfast International Airport. As the plane rose into the clouds the landscape below misted over and then disappeared. Michelle tried to put these negative thoughts out of her mind.

'But why couldn't Daddy get time off work,

Mum?' said Molly, who sat in the seat beside her mother examining the safety card with instructions on what to do in the event of a crash.

'I don't know, love.'

'But I wanted him to come on holiday with us,' said Molly and her bottom lip started to quiver the way it did when she was about to cry.

'I know, love,' said Michelle, 'I did too.' She put her arm round her daughter's slight shoulders, squeezed her and added, brightly, 'But think of all the fun we're going to have on holiday with Granny and Grandpa! You'll be able to swim all day long. And I bet they'll buy you an ice cream every day.'

'Every day,' repeated Molly, her eyes wide with delight. 'Do you really think so?'

'I'm sure of it,' said Michelle firmly, and she wished she could be as positive about everything else in life.

★ ★ ★

After two weeks back at work, Roisin was more exhausted than she had ever thought possible. Tony had settled into the nursery well and she had no concerns on that front, but there was simply no time left for herself. And she was so tired.

On Sunday night after Tony was in bed, she started on her 'night-time routine', as she called it. She set the breakfast table, made up a sandwich lunch for herself, had a shower and washed her hair, laid out Tony's clothes for the next morning, made up his bottles for the following day and packed his bag for nursery. Next she prepared the next night's evening meal — because there would be no time to make it on Monday night, coming in at five-thirty after a long day at work. Lastly, she soaked Tony's soiled clothing from earlier that day in a bucket of disinfectant, and threw a load of wash into the machine. She collapsed into bed at ten thirty.

The alarm went off on Monday morning at six forty-five. Roisin opened her eyes and remembered that it was the first day of another full week back at work. Her heart sank, she shut her eyes briefly, opened them and hauled herself out of bed.

While Scott slept on, she dressed quickly in her work tunic and trousers — new ones, two sizes bigger than before — and made up her face, which she could now do in five minutes flat. Just as she finished applying mascara, she heard whimpering from Tony's room. She went through and picked him up before he was fully awake. She changed his dirty nappy and, while he was half-undressed anyway, swiftly changed him into his daytime clothes — another timesaving trick she'd learnt.

Then she carried him downstairs to the kitchen where she heated his bottle in the microwave, shook it vigorously and gave him his first feed of the day. After winding him, she then mixed a little bit of baby rice with milk and a defrosted cube of pear puree, her eye on the clock the whole time. She fed this to Tony from a small plastic spoon — a painstaking process which resulted in most of the food going on his bib. After changing his bib for a fresh one, she was putting Tony in his bouncy chair when Scott appeared in the doorway in his dressing-gown.

'Morning love,' he said sleepily and kissed Roisin on the head.

'Morning,' she replied absentmindedly, remembering that the nursery had requested more nappies for Tony. She got up and ran upstairs — if she didn't get them now, she'd be sure to forget.

When she came back downstairs, Scott was holding Tony aloft in his arms. He brought Tony's tummy down onto his face and blew a raspberry. Tony giggled delightedly.

'You'll make him sick, Scott,' said Roisin as she poured herself a bowl of cornflakes and milk. She used to have museli but it took too long to chew.

'I'm only having a bit of fun,' said Scott in an irritated voice. 'Can't you relax for a minute?'

'If he's sick, you can change him. I don't have time.' She sat down and began to eat her breakfast, quickly.

Scott sighed and put the baby back in his bouncy chair, where he howled with disappointment.

'See,' said Roisin between mouthfuls, 'it's better if you leave him alone.'

'What kind of a night did you have?' said Scott, ignoring her caustic remark.

'Oh, the usual. Bottle at two o'clock, then he went through 'til seven.'

'That's pretty good, isn't it?' said Scott hopefully.

'Depends who's giving him the bottle,' replied Roisin acidly and she got up and put her bowl and spoon in the dishwasher.

After that, she just had time to brush her teeth, sit Tony on her knee and wrestle him into his tiny, pale-blue duffel coat. Then she picked him up and he promptly deposited a tablespoon of sick on the left shoulder of her tunic. She dabbed at it ineffectually with a clean hankie, glanced at the clock and decided that she would clean it properly when she got to work. Scott had gone upstairs to get dressed — if he'd been in the room she'd have given him a piece of her mind.

She left the house in a foul mood, without saying goodbye. It was only when she caught sight of herself in a mirror at the nursery that she realised she'd forgotten to do her hair. Never mind, she told herself — she'd have time when she got to the salon. She parked in the carpark behind Dunluce Street, ran round to the salon and met Debbie, the therapist she employed full-time, waiting for her on the doorstep of the shop.

'Sorry I'm late again,' gasped Roisin. 'It was Tony . . . ' She registered the stony look on the girl's face and added, 'Never mind. I'll try not to be late tomorrow.'

Once inside Roisin had just put her hair up in an untidy topknot and slapped on some lipstick, when her first client arrived. She checked her face in the mirror, put a smile on her face and said to herself, 'That'll do.'

No sooner had she started to wax the lady's

legs than Debbie appeared at the door of the treatment room.

'Sorry to interrupt,' she smiled at the client and then, addressing Roisin, added in a more urgent tone, 'Can I have a word?'

Roisin's first thought was for Tony. She excused herself, stepped into the hallway and pulled the door closed behind her, ready for Debbie to tell her that the nursery had called.

'Roisin, it looks like you've double-booked. Mrs James is in and she's absolutely adamant that she was booked in for this morning. She said that she made the appointment with you on the phone last Thursday.'

'She can't be. Let me see,' said Roisin and she grabbed the appointments book from Debbie and shuffled through the pages. 'There!' she cried. 'She's booked in for next Monday. Not this Monday. She must've made a mistake.'

Debbie looked at the floor and suddenly Roisin knew what she was thinking — if anyone had made a mistake it was more likely to be Roisin than Mrs James. Roisin blushed — she couldn't be trusted to open up on time, never mind take bookings.

'I'll tell you what,' said Debbie. 'I've got an eyebrow tint and shape in just now.' She glanced at her watch. 'I should be finished in fifteen minutes, long before you.'

Roisin looked out into the reception area where she could see a well-heeled foot tapping the wooden floor impatiently.

'Why don't you explain to Mrs James what's happened,' continued Debbie, 'and ask if she'd mind if I did her instead of you?'

'Won't that make you late for your next appointment?'

Debbie glanced at her watch again. 'Only ten minutes or so. I'll soon catch the time up.'

'That's a good idea, Debbie — thanks,' said Roisin, thinking that things must be bad when a twenty-year-old was better at running the business than she was.

But Mrs James was not so easily manipulated. 'Never mind, dearie,' she said graciously, after she had turned down Debbie's suggestion, 'these things happen. I don't mind waiting until you're finished. I'll just sit here and read until you're ready.'

As a result, Roisin was late for the rest of that morning's appointments. She spent all morning apologising and watching the clock, trying to process her clients as quickly as she could. By the time Pauline McCormick turned up for her appointment at eleven thirty, Roisin had gained some time but was still running nearly half-an-hour late. When she came out to the reception area to greet Mrs McCormick, as chic and stylish as usual, she could tell by her face that she was fuming.

While Roisin prepared herself to do some grovelling she remembered that she had to do the ordering today. They were already running dangerously low on wax — she never used to be this inefficient. She'd hoped to get the ordering done over lunchtime when the salon was closed but now she wouldn't have time. Mrs McCormick's appointment would eat into half her lunch hour. Damn — she'd have to take the paperwork home and deal with it tonight. As if she didn't have enough to do . . .

'I'm terribly sorry I'm late, Mrs McCormick. I was double-booked this morning. I don't know what — '

'Never mind. You're here now,' interrupted Mrs McCormick rudely and she stood up abruptly.

Roisin had to struggle to keep the smile on her face. She reminded herself that Mrs McCormick was a good client — she spent a small fortune on treatments and face and body-care products, and recommended the salon to friends and acquaintances.

'Well, as I say,' said Roisin brightly, trying to keep the irritation out of her voice, 'I am very sorry. It won't happen again.'

Mrs McCormick was about to follow her through to the back of the salon when she stopped and said, 'Won't it?'

'No, today was a one off,' said Roisin as firmly as she could.

Without saying anything, Pauline McCormick passed her gaze over Roisin from top to toe in one seamless, almost imperceptible, flicker of her eyes. Suddenly Roisin felt self-conscious under this woman's swift scrutiny. She put her hand up to her head and touched a hank of hair that had fallen from her hastily arranged hairstyle. She tried to tuck it up with the rest of her hair, but the topknot felt like it was about to fall out altogether. She let it be.

Then she remembered the stain on her left

shoulder — the one she'd meant to sponge out when she got to work. She put her hand up and patted it — the sick was caked on hard. Suddenly she saw herself as Pauline McCormick must be seeing her now. Overweight, ungroomed, her hair and clothes unkempt. In short — a mess.

'I don't mean this unkindly, Roz,' said Pauline McCormick, lowering her voice and octave or two, 'but if you want to keep your clientele you're going to have to run this place a bit more . . . ' her gaze paused momentarily on the sick stain on Roisin's shoulder, 'professionally.'

Roisin's cheeks burned with humiliation. 'It's just . . . it's just since Tony came,' she stammered, pushing a stray hairpin back into her dishevelled hair, 'I've been finding it difficult to — to manage everything.'

As soon as she said it, Roisin realised it was a mistake. If she was expecting Pauline McCormick to make allowances she was very much mistaken.

'We all have to manage,' said Pauline. 'I did it and I had *three* children under the age of five.' She put the emphasis on three as opposed to Roisin's one, thereby implying that Roisin deserved no sympathy.

But I bet you weren't running a business full-time, you old cow, thought Roisin. But before she said something she regretted, she announced briskly, 'Well, I've kept you waiting long enough, Mrs McCormick. Let's go through and get started.'

For the next hour Roisin acted as normally as

possible, thankful that Mrs McCormick preferred silence to conversation — Roisin wasn't sure she could bring herself to speak civilly. Inside she fizzled with anger and her eyes pricked hot with unshed tears. She'd put money on it that Pauline McCormick had never worked a day in her life. And she'd probably had a cook and a cleaner and a nanny as well when her kids were small — just like her daughter!

But, by the time she'd finished the pedicure and started on Mrs McCormick's manicure, Roisin's anger had subsided. Mrs McCormick's comments were hurtful — she realised with humility — because they were true. She wasn't behaving professionally. She couldn't keep it all together — something had to give. This week it was the salon, she feared that next week it might be her sanity.

For she could no longer carry on under such stress. There was just far too much to be done and she couldn't do it all. Roisin couldn't remember the last time she'd laughed. She rarely played with Tony, spending all her time doing, doing, doing. She'd hardly spoken to Scott in the last fortnight and, when she had done, it was usually to bite his head off. And no matter how much she did there was always more to be done. She felt as if she'd spent the last two weeks on a hamster wheel, going faster and faster and faster. And getting nowhere.

At the end of the day, Roisin said goodnight to Debbie and locked up wearily. Now all she had to do was pick up Tony, get him home, fed, bathed, into bed, and have something to eat.

Then she would tackle the paperwork in her briefcase before preparing for tomorrow. The prospect was too hideous to contemplate. Take it one step at a time, she told herself, and she concentrated on the next thing on her mental list of things to do. It was the only way she could carry on.

At the nursery Roisin collected Tony and carried him out to the car in his car seat. She strapped him into the back seat, buried her face in his warm neck and whispered, 'I do love you, you know.' She sniffed back tears and looked into his eyes. He stared back, silent and grave, his black eyes knowing.

Scott arrived home when Roisin was in the middle of spoon-feeding Tony pureed carrot and baby rice.

'Sorry I'm late,' he said. 'I got caught up in a meeting. I'll just pop upstairs and change out of these clothes.'

He came back into the room a few minutes later, and rubbed his hands together briskly.

'Now, what's for dinner? What can I do to help?' He started to prise the metal foil off a shallow dish that was sitting on top of the cooker.

'Leave that alone,' snapped Roisin. 'It's to stay on the macaroni while it's in the oven.'

'How was I to know?' he said and when she didn't answer him he asked, 'Shall I put it in the oven then?'

'If you like.'

'What temperature?'

'Oh for goodness sake, I don't know. Anything.

338

One hundred and sixty degrees. It's only to heat it up.'

'Does anything else need doing?'

'You could set the table and make a salad.'

Scott laid cutlery, place mats and glasses on the kitchen table. He went over to the fridge and opened the door.

'What shall I put in the salad?' he asked, peering into the salad box at the bottom of the fridge. 'There doesn't seem to be much here.'

'Use your imagination, Scott. There's lettuce and carrots that can be grated and . . . oh, don't bother. It's easier if I do it. I'll be just as quick doing it as explaining it to you.'

Scott gave her a long, hard look and then said, changing subject, 'I was speaking to Fraser today.'

'And?'

'He says he and Julie have agreed to separate.'

Roisin paused with the laden spoon in her hand and looked up momentarily at Scott. 'I'm sorry to hear that,' she said. 'But it was bound to happen, wasn't it? The marriage guidance sessions weren't going anywhere. At least this way they can both get on with their lives.'

'He said that they were separating because of 'irrevocable differences'.'

Roisin put a spoonful of food in Tony's mouth. 'What does that mean?'

'That's precisely what I said to Fraser and he wouldn't tell me. He just said they were incompatible and refused to discuss it any further.'

'Maybe he's embarrassed talking to you about his marriage.'

'Perhaps. I just have a feeling that he's keeping something from me, though.'

Roisin got up, rinsed the feeding bowl and spoon under the cold tap and loaded them into the dishwasher. 'I presume he's moving out then and Julie's staying on in the house?'

'Yeah, for the time being. He's got a rented flat sorted out from next week.'

'Well, it's the children I feel most sorry for. It's going to be hard on them, especially Oliver.'

After Roisin had put Tony into bed she came downstairs and threw a salad together as quickly as she could.

'Right. Dinner's ready,' she called to Scott and he came through from the lounge where he'd been watching TV.

They sat down and ate hungrily. Roisin told Scott how she was late for work again and about the double booking and how she hadn't been able to get the ordering done at lunchtime.

'I had to bring the paperwork home,' she explained, between hurried mouthfuls, 'and I'll have to get it done tonight. I can't leave it any longer. What are you planning on doing later on?'

'After I've tidied up the dishes I was thinking of watching the TV. There's a big game on.'

Suddenly the tension inside Roisin uncoiled like a spring.

'How about helping me for a change!' she exploded. 'When was the last time I sat down and watched the TV?'

'But you just said that you had paperwork to do — '

'That's not the point! Can't you see?' she screamed, and she brought her fist down on the table so hard that the plates rattled.

'See what, Roisin?' said Scott angrily. 'I do wish you'd tell me because you're not making any sense.'

'How I do everything round here. How come it's me that makes the meals,' she shouted, poking her chest repeatedly with her index finger, 'me that feeds Tony, washes the bottles, makes them up, packs his bag, baths him and puts him to bed? And then I'm up in the middle of the night with him too. How come I do everything?'

And with that she burst into tears, pushed the half-eaten dinner away and covered her face with her hands. She sobbed uncontrollably for several minutes.

When her cries had eased, Scott asked, 'Are you all right?' His anger had all abated and his voice was gentle, concerned.

She looked up and he handed her a tissue on which she blew her nose and wiped her eyes. 'No,' she wailed. 'I want you to hold me.'

'Come here,' he said and patted his right leg. She got up and went over to him and he pulled her onto his knee.

'I'm just exhausted all the time,' she said, between sniffles. 'I can't carry on like this. And you don't help enough.'

'Steady on a minute, Roisin. Maybe I have

341

been a bit insensitive but every time I try to help you won't let me.'

'That's not true.'

'Yes, it is. Look at tonight. I only asked what to put in the salad and you blew a gasket. You said you'd be quicker to do it yourself. And as far as Tony's concerned you hardly let me near him. Everything I do is wrong. When I did get up with him in the night, you got up too and took him off me.'

'That was before I went back to work.'

'The point is that you make me feel inadequate. I've not been happy these last few weeks either. You make me feel as if I'm useless in the house. Everything I do is wrong. And after a while, well, I just stop trying.'

'I never meant to make you feel like that.'

'Well, you do. And it's the same with Tony. You're so possessive about him. It's like you don't trust me to bath him or feed him, or do anything with him. You act like you're the only person who can do it right.'

'I'm sorry,' said Roisin cringing with embarrassment, for suddenly she saw how irrational her behaviour had become. Everything that Scott said was true. 'I just want everything to be right for him,' she said feebly.

'That's only natural. But even taking him to nursery — you insist on doing that yourself too.'

'But I like to keep an eye on what's happening at the nursery,' said Roisin defensively. 'I talk to the staff when I leave him in and pick him up.'

'And I couldn't do that?'

Roisin pouted her lips and furrowed her brow,

knowing that she was in the wrong.

'You know,' said Scott, 'the most important thing for Tony is that he has a happy mummy. Do you think he cares whether his food is homemade or comes out of a jar? Do you think he cares whether the house is clean or dirty, or his clothes spotless?'

'But it matters to me.'

'Well then, we're going to have to find ways of making it easier.'

'How?'

'Well, for a start, we'll get a cleaner. I feel like we've spent the last two weekends doing nothing but cleaning the house. And we'll get the ironing done as well.'

'OK,' said Roisin brightening. 'What else?'

'I'm not great at cooking,' said Scott, more to himself than to Roisin, 'but how about you show me how to wash, sterilise and make up the bottles? I'll take full responsibility for them.'

'Every day?' said Roisin, her spirits lifting with every suggestion.

Scott nodded. 'Every day. And in the mornings when I'm working in Ballyfergus and I don't have any early meetings, I'll take Tony to nursery. And from now on, we'll take turns getting up with him in the night.'

'But I hear him as soon as he makes a peep. And you sleep right through it.'

'I'll get you earplugs to wear in bed.'

'Earplugs?' repeated Roisin incredulously.

'Yes, why not? I've been thinking about it. If we leave our bedroom door open, and his bedroom door open, I'll hear him eventually, won't I?'

'I suppose so,' said Roisin, finding it hard to assimilate all these novel ideas at once.

'And, as far as getting into work on time goes, why don't you give the keys to Debbie and let her open up?'

'But I — I'm the boss,' said Roisin, thinking that this was one step too far.

'All the more reason. It'd give her a greater sense of responsibility and take the pressure off you.'

'I'm not sure — '

'Roisin, you're going to have to let go. You can't control everything. You have to trust other people. Including me.'

'But I do trust you, Scott.'

'I mean with Tony.'

'Oh,' said Roisin and she felt her cheeks redden.

'So from now on when I'm minding Tony, or feeding Tony or bathing him, I'm in charge and you leave me to it. No interfering.'

Roisin nodded.

'Promise?' he asked.

Roisin took a deep breath and held out a crooked pinkie finger. Scott did the same, they locked fingers and she said, 'I promise.'

'Oh, Roisin,' said Scott and pulled her to him and buried his face in her neck, 'you've no idea how miserable I am when you're miserable. These last few weeks have been awful. I can't bear to see you like this. It's like you've been winding yourself up for the last fortnight and nothing I could do would stop you. And I want us to enjoy Tony, not just think of him in terms of all the work involved.'

'I don't want to continue like this either,' said Roisin and she smiled at him. 'Things are going to get better. I promise.'

Then she lifted Scott's face in her hands and kissed him tenderly on the lips. 'Thank you,' she said. 'Thank you for being the way you are.'

★ ★ ★

Pauline put her foot on the accelerator and sped out of Ballyfergus on the dual carriageway, the automatic gearbox shifting effortlessly through the gears. She held the steering wheel with the palms of her hands, to avoid smudging her nails — another half-an-hour and they should be hard enough to withstand everyday bumps and scrapes.

Pauline glanced at the clock on the dash and her heart beat furiously in her chest. Now she would be late for her meeting with Padraig Flynn. She'd been jittery about the whole thing before and now she was a bag of nerves.

She regretted being so short with Roz Johnston. The poor girl looked completely frazzled, and it was with shame that Pauline remembered exactly what it was like when your first baby came along. Your whole world turned upside down and you thought life would never be normal again. Which it never was, not in quite the same way it had been before. But, when Pauline's children were little, in the days before

Noel made serious money, she'd had no help around the house and she'd never let appearances slip.

Perhaps she had been a little hard on Roz but it needed to be said. The girl was running a business — she would lose customers if she continued to carry on like that. And Pauline had recommended the salon to her friends — it would reflect badly on her if things continued as they were. Still, she resolved to give Roz an extra big tip next time, and an apology.

But then her thoughts returned to Padraig Flynn. Here she was, heading towards his house in the back of beyond, and she didn't know what she was going to do when she got there. She thought back to the telephone conversation that she'd had with him the week before.

'Hello. I'm Pauline McCormick,' she'd begun. 'You probably don't remember me — '

'Of course I remember you,' he'd drawled and she waited for him to go on. 'Petite blonde,' he said at last, and continued as though reading off a list and pausing between each item. 'Black suit. Heels. Cream blouse. Silver Merc. Sceptical.'

'Sceptical?' she said indignantly.

'Yeah, I'd say so,' he said, sounding like he was chewing gum.

'Oh, you mean about your name? Well, I'm sorry about that. It just seemed so unlikely. I thought you'd invented it to make yourself sound more glamorous.'

He laughed long and heartily at this and said at last, 'Mrs McCormick, what can I do for you?'

'I'd like to commission you to do a piece for

my husband. A Christmas present.'

'Do you have anything particular in mind?'

'Well no. I haven't given it that much thought.'

There was a very long pause and Pauline was about to speak again when he said, 'Why don't you come out to my studio at Ballynahinch and we can talk about it? You can see some work-in-progress and look at my portfolio. It might give you some ideas.'

They arranged a date, he gave her directions, said goodbye and Pauline put the phone down. Her hands were shaking — she'd never told so many lies all in one go before. But it was done and there was no going back.

Pauline took the turn-off to the townland of Ballynahinch, a hinterland of Ballymena which had no actual town or village to its centre. Ballynahinch was rich farming land dotted with smallholdings and whitewashed farmhouses. She'd read the scribbled directions to Padraig's house so many times, they were embedded in her memory. It started to rain and the automatic wipers silently erased the raindrops from the windscreen.

All her life Pauline had been passive and acquiescent, especially in affairs of the heart. She'd allowed men to woo her, she'd waited for them to come to her and then she'd made her choice — with hindsight a very poor one. It had not occurred to her, until very recently, that there was an alternative to this strategy — that a woman could be proactive. That she could be the one to actively seek out a partner, that she could decide what she wanted and go for it.

347

She saw the small sign for Waterside Cottage, indicated and turned up a narrow dirt lane, now turned to mud in the steady downpour. The lane brought her to the back of an old stone building, more like a farmhouse than a cottage. A large outbuilding was attached to the structure at one side. She guessed this must house the studio. She parked the car beside a beaten-up blue Land Rover on a roughly gravelled parking bay and turned the engine off. Then she sat in the car with her heart beating against her ribs looking at the black-and-white cows grazing in the field in front. She put her hand on her breast to steady it and found that her nerve had vanished.

What was she doing here? What was she going to say to this man? What on earth did she expect to happen? She pulled down the sun visor and looked at her face in the small rectangular mirror — the face of a woman perilously close to old age. A man like Padraig Flynn could have any woman he wanted. She'd mistaken his purely business interest in her for something else. She imagined what he saw when he looked at her — a well-to-do matron with money to burn.

But it was not too late to turn back before she made a complete fool of herself. Pauline fumbled for the keys in the ignition, found them and was about to switch the engine on again, when a hooded figure appeared from nowhere and tapped on the car window. Pauline nearly screamed. Then she recognised the figure as Padraig. She wound the window halfway down and drops of rain spotted the right sleeve of her cream linen jacket.

'Guess you found the place then,' he said.

'Mmm,' said Pauline, feeling like an idiot. The sooner she got out of here, the better. 'Listen, I — ' she began but Padraig appeared not to hear her.

'We'll talk inside,' he shouted above the din of the raindrops that splashed on the bonnet and roof of the car. Then he opened the door, took her by the arm and helped her out of the car. 'Here,' he said, sheltering her under the raincoat he held aloft over his head. 'Let's get inside.'

They half-ran, half-walked in an ungainly fashion to the front of the house, their hips colliding every few steps. The path was muddy and Pauline's beige suede boots were soon sodden and splashed with mud.

He led her through the front door, into an unremarkable hall and then directed her into a cosy old-fashioned room with a log fire burning in the grate.

'I'll just hang this up, Mrs McCormick,' he shouted to her from the hall where he stood shaking the water off the coat onto the doormat.

'Pauline. My name is Pauline,' she replied and he nodded, hung the coat on a peg and disappeared through another door off the hall.

Pauline pushed the hair out of her eyes and looked around. The room reminded her of a teenager's bedroom — a mishmash of furniture and untidy with clutter but wonderfully lived in all the same. The atmosphere was calm and relaxed — the home of someone at peace with themselves and the world.

The dampness gave the September air an

unseasonal chill and Pauline shivered. She walked across the tattered rug to the rustic fireplace, stone-built with a wrought-iron cradle for the burning logs, and put her hands out to warm them. On a shelf above the fireplace she noticed a photograph of a woman. Young and pretty, she looked into the camera shyly and on her lap was a smiling toddler.

'That's my wife and my daughter,' said Padraig's voice very close to her ear, making her start.

Pauline's heart sank. 'They're lovely. Is your wife here now?'

He took the photograph down and stared at it for a few moments. 'No, she's in the States,' he said slowly, 'we're divorced. She married a real estate agent from Florida.'

'Oh,' said Pauline and her emotions seesawed again. 'That must be hard on your daughter?'

'Louise?' he said and paused before continuing, 'Oh, I don't know. That picture was taken a long time ago. She's nearly sixteen now.'

'Do you see her much?'

'Not as much as I'd like.'

Pauline waited, learning to expect long pauses between his sentences.

'Her mother thinks I'm a bad influence on her,' he said at last.

'So you live here alone?'

'That's right.'

He put the photograph back and took a long time in retracting his arm from the shelf. The soft, brushed cotton of his shirt grazed Pauline's cheek and she could smell him — the lovely raw, honest smell of a man, untainted by aftershave or cologne. She closed her eyes and breathed him in. When she opened them again his face was inches from hers, and she found herself staring up into his piercing blue eyes.

It had been a very long time since Pauline had seen a man look at her the way Padraig Flynn was looking at her now, but there was no mistaking his intent. He desired her. And, to her shock, her own desire awoke from a slumber of many, many years. Her breath came in short, quiet gasps and she felt a throbbing sensation in her groin, as her body responded to the yearning of her mind.

She thought of all the things she should say. The excuses she could make, how she could go through with the charade of commissioning a bronze. She knew that all she had to do was cough and look away, and the moment of danger would pass. But she didn't want it to pass. She wanted it to become something more than just a desire. She wanted to feel again.

So she stood there, listening to her heart pounding in her chest, his breath on her face and her legs ready to buckle under her with the pleasure of it. The rain pattered insistently on the window and the logs cracked and hissed in the fireplace.

'Pauline,' he said at last, his voice a husky rasp and his breath hot on her face, 'did you come here today to commission a statue?'

She swallowed, never taking her eyes off him for a moment and said, 'No.'

'What did you come here for?'

'You.'

She stood there more vulnerable and exposed than she'd ever been and waited. He put his hands gently on her shoulders and rested them there. A shock like a current of electricity bolted through her body. 'Are you sure this is what you want?' he said tenderly and her body ached for him.

She nodded.

'You are beautiful, you know,' he said, running his eyes the length of her, taking her all in.

'No, don't say that. I don't want you to say anything to me that is untrue. Whatever happens between us, I want it to be honest.'

He moved his big hands down to grip her slim upper arms and a furrow appeared between his brows. 'But you are beautiful,' he insisted.

'I was once, Padraig. But you don't have to pretend that this is something it isn't. Let's just enjoy it for what it is.'

'And what is it?'

'Desire. Lust.'

'I hope that it's more than that.'

'Who knows, it may be. But for now let's not kid ourselves that it's anything else.'

He leaned forward then, took her head in his hands and placed the tenderest of kisses on her lips. She closed her eyes and moved her mouth in response, awkwardly at first, so unused to this sort of physical intimacy. But soon her body remembered — her lips softened and she relaxed into the rhythm of the long, slow kiss. For the next few minutes she was aware only of the seamless way their bodies joined — she could not distinguish between their lips or their tongues. They were melting into each other.

Then she felt two hands on her buttocks and a firm squeeze. She pulled away with a jolt, opened her eyes and exclaimed, 'Oh!'

'What's wrong, Pauline? Have you changed your mind, baby?'

She loved the way he called her 'baby'. 'No,' she said, aware that she was shaking, 'it's not that. It's — it's just that it's been a long time for me, Padraig. A very long time.'

'Me too.'

She laughed then, the tension broken and said, 'I doubt it, not compared to me. I mean decades, Padraig, not just last month or last year.'

'Then you've a lot of catching up to do,' he said and grinned and she knew then that she loved him.

'Let's go upstairs,' he said and he led her by the hand up a creaking flight of worn wooden stairs to a small landing and into a small room with a double bed. Besides the bed, the bedroom was simply furnished with a small bedside table, oak chest of drawers and a wooden chair. The bed was made up with an American patchwork bedspread — homely, sweet and wholesome. So incongruous with the adultery she was about to commit under it.

She pushed the thought from her mind, reminding herself that her marriage to Noel was nothing more than a sham. Nothing she could do would hurt it any more than it had already been hurt. The damage was all done — it was nothing more than an empty shell with her and Noel rattling round inside it.

Without any more words passing between them, they began to undress. Padraig took off his shirt first, revealing a strong hairy upper body and, she was relieved to see, a saggy paunch. She removed her jacket and took off her boots. She put the boots under the chair and hung the jacket on the back. When she turned round Padraig was standing naked with his back to the window, an erection poking proudly from a nest of wiry fair hairs. She put her hand to her mouth, blushed, and looked away.

'Will you warm the bed?' she said. 'I'm freezing.'

He got in under the covers and put his hands behind his head, his face suddenly serious, a thatch of blonde hairs under each armpit.

'Don't watch me,' she said. 'It's not a pretty sight.'

'Let me be the judge of that. Please.'

'OK.'

She removed the rest of her clothes quickly then, holding in her stomach and trying not to jiggle the cellulite on the tops of her legs. When she removed her bra, her breasts fell two inches and her nipples pointed at the floor. Instinctively, she covered them with her arms.

'Don't, Pauline. Let me look at you. You've no idea how wonderful you are to look at.'

'My body is — is older now. It's not what you're probably used to. All those young girls you model.'

'Youth is a different kind of beauty. I love the

way your body has been lived in. I love you living in it now. And, in case you hadn't noticed, mine's seen its fair share of mileage.'

She revealed her breasts and stood tall for a few moments, feeling more proud of her body than she had in years.

'Come here,' he whispered and she scurried in under the covers. She inched towards his hot body and lay in his arms, looking into his eyes. The heat under the covers built up quickly and she squirmed with the sheer pleasure of being warm and naked with him.

'Kiss me,' she said and he leaned towards her and she rolled on her back. He planted a powerful, almost savage, kiss on her lips then moved his tongue into her ear, then down her neck, between her breasts, onto her tummy. He probed her belly button and then moved down further, between her legs.

She snapped her legs shut and brought her knees up. 'I'm not sure about this,' she said.

'I am. Trust me. It'll be OK. Try to relax.'

He massaged her stomach with his big rough hand and she lay back on the bed and gave herself up to him. He was good, better than Noel had ever been in this department. He stroked and massaged her most intimate parts with his tongue for a very long time until, at last, she was weeping for him. Her body had not forgotten how good this felt.

Then he was on top of her, the wonderful weight of him pressing down on her, squeezing the breath from her lungs. The desire flaring up in her abdomen. She moaned and thrust her pelvis up towards him.

He lifted himself off her for a moment, his hands on either side of her head. She raised her legs slightly, either side of his hips. Then he looked down at his penis and very, very gently he eased himself inside of her. He shut his eyes in ecstasy. Pauline's initial shock at this most intimate intrusion gave way to waves of pleasure as he moved slowly inside her.

He rolled on his back keeping her impaled on his cock, and lay there inert while she rocked very gently on top of him. She took every pleasure she could from him thinking, for once in her life, only of herself. Thinking only of how much she needed this loving. Then her legs began to ache and she rolled onto her back again. He pounded into her then and they were both moving towards a crescendo. He waited until she came before he withdrew and emptied himself on her belly.

'I forgot to ask,' he panted, 'if it was safe.'

She grabbed a handful of tissues from a box on the bedside table. Fleetingly she wondered if they were placed there for instances such as this. She wiped her stomach and threw the wad of tissue on the floor.

'It's been safe for a long time, Padraig. If I have any more babies it'll be a miracle.'

'Come here,' he said and she nestled contentedly in the crook of his arm.

'Is that what you came here for?'

'I don't know why I came here. I knew I wanted to see you again but I hadn't thought beyond that,' she said and then she lifted her head, looked him in the eye, and said, 'Hey, I hope you don't think I used you.'

He laughed. 'Used me?'

'Just for sex.'

'Well, if you did I have to say I don't mind one little bit, darlin'.'

'I'm serious.'

'So am I.'

'I'd better go,' said Pauline, sitting up suddenly and looking for a clock in the room but there was none.

'Will you come back?'

'If you want me too.'

'Oh, I want you to, baby,' he said and kissed the base of her spine. A shiver ran up her back and she smiled.

'Well, now that I've seen your portfolio,' she said, turning to look at him, 'you'll have to show me your work-in-progress next time.'

Padraig laughed loudly. 'You are some lady!'

10

December 2003

Roisin stood in Michelle's drawing-room, enjoying the buzz of conversation, the blare of loud music coming from the other side of the house and the warm glow induced by alcohol. The Mullans had laid on masses of food and drink and everyone there appeared inebriated, some more than others — it was a great Christmas party. Roisin realised that she'd stood too long talking with Jayne and Liz and now she was desperate for the loo. Since Tony's birth her bladder control had never been the same.

'Hold this a minute, would you?' she said to Liz, and handed her friend a half-empty glass. 'I'm dying for a pee. I can't wait any longer.'

She fought her way through the friendly crowd into the hall, now dominated by a twenty-foot Christmas tree. It was decorated entirely in gold baubles and it rose up into the galleried landing on the second floor. In the doorway to the dining room, crammed with people eating from the buffet, Scott was talking animatedly to Donal — neither of them noticed her. She tried the door of the loo off the hallway. It was locked. She looked up the stairs. There were several bathrooms up there, she remembered, most of the bedrooms being en-suite.

She ran up the stairs and tried the door of the

main bathroom — she'd changed Tony's nappy in there before. But it wouldn't open.

'Someone's in here!' cried a merry female voice from within and Roisin looked around desperately. The urge to urinate was almost unstoppable and she knew she couldn't wait any longer. She ran down the hallway and opened the next door she came to. It was a very large room, the master bedroom she guessed, with a huge king-size bed. Donal and Michelle's? The curtains were drawn and the lights in the room were on, but there didn't seem to be anyone there. She left the door ajar, crossed the plush carpet quickly and tapped on one of the doors that led off the room. No response. She opened it — it was a walk-in wardrobe. She slammed it shut, ran to the next door and this time flung it open without knocking. Thank God — it was the bathroom.

She fumbled for the light cord and pulled. Light flooded the room — she slammed the door behind her and locked it. Then she pulled up her skirt, hauled her tights and pants down and planted herself on the loo. The relief was indescribable.

While her bladder emptied she took in her surroundings. The bathroom, tiled everywhere but for the ceiling, was much bigger than the main one in her house. Beside the toilet were his 'n' hers sinks, a bidet, a bath on a raised plinth and a huge walk-in shower — all white. There was room too for a vanity area with a stool and, Roisin noticed, a set of electronic scales tucked in a corner.

When she'd finished, Roisin washed her hands in one of the sinks and dried them on a soft white towel. She moved over to the vanity area, fluffed up her hair with her fingers and checked her make-up in the mirror — it was still intact.

Then, as she put her hand on the bathroom door handle, she heard muffled voices outside — one of them sounded like Donal's. She paused. She really would prefer not to be caught in here without permission. She strained to hear what was going on but could discern only the noisy sounds of the party. Then the sounds suddenly receded — someone must've closed the bedroom door to the hall. But, had that someone come in or gone out?

Then she heard the creak of someone sitting down heavily, or lying, on the bed. This was most embarrassing. Was it Donal? Or Michelle? Or both? If so, what were they up to? Whoever it was, and whatever they were up to, they would get quite a shock when she suddenly emerged from their bathroom.

Perhaps if she waited a moment or two, they would get up and leave again. Then she heard the distinctive '*pip, pip, pip*' of a number being dialled on a mobile — eleven times in all and Donal's voice saying, 'It's me.'

Oh, now she was eavesdropping on a private call, to make matters worse!

'At home,' Donal was saying. 'It's the night of the big Christmas party Michelle insisted on having. Remember? I told you about it.'

And then she realised what she should have done in the first place — flush the toilet. Of

360

course! The universal signal that there was someone in the bathroom! Followed by noisy washing of hands. She began to tiptoe back to the toilet.

'No, there's so many people here, I'll not be missed. I've come upstairs to the bedroom. I just had to hear your voice.'

Roisin froze and stopped breathing.

'I know, and I love you too, sweetheart. I hate it when we're apart. I absolutely hate it. You've no idea how awful it is having to host this ridiculous party when all I want to do is walk out the door, get in the car and come to you.'

Roisin exhaled slowly through parted lips and took a deep breath. So he was having an affair.

'I don't know, Amy. Maybe tomorrow. No, don't cry, Amy. Please don't cry. I hate this as much as you.'

A pause.

'We'll talk about it when I see you again. I promise. Oh, baby, don't make this any harder for me than it already is.'

Poor Michelle. Poor old, bloody Michelle, downstairs making sure everyone was having a good time while her cheating bastard of a husband was up here sweet-talking his mistress.

'OK. I love you, baby.'

Right here in Michelle's own home, in the bedroom she shared every night with him. How could he?

''Night, darling. Love you. Bye.'

She heard the '*pip*' of the phone as he hung up and she waited with bated breath to see what he would do next. The bed creaked as he got off it and her heart pounded as she imagined him coming towards the bathroom. Quickly and silently she slid the lock closed. If he tried the door, she'd just have to act like she'd not heard anything. But then, to her relief, she heard the noise of the party again — he must've opened the bedroom door — and then it went quiet. She waited, her stomach coiled with tension, listening for further sounds. But there were none — he was gone.

Roisin slid the lock open, and walked quickly to the bedroom door. She popped her head into the hall — there was no sign of Donal. She ran downstairs and joined Liz and Jayne who were now talking to Michelle. Roisin stood amongst them, not listening to a word of the conversation. She sipped at her glass of wine and tried to steady her nerves, while her heart thumped against the wall of her chest. Luckily they were all a little tipsy or they might have noticed her reticence. She watched Michelle's flushed face while she joked with the other girls and she felt sick to the stomach with pity for her.

How could he cheat on Michelle — the trusting loyal wife who thought the sun shone out of his arse? How could he be so deceitful? And then, as the anger gave way to more rational thought, she realised that this was the very thing she'd been waiting for. Now she had a way to exact her revenge. For what he'd done to Ann-Marie, and now, for what he was doing to Michelle.

But she would need more information. She needed to find out more about this woman. An eavesdropped telephone call was hardly evidence — a liar as competent as Donal could easily deny it. And she needed to think through how she would use this information. She did not want to hurt Michelle. Perhaps she could force Donal to drop his mistress by threatening to tell Michelle? After all, if he planned on leaving her, he'd have done it by now. He wanted to have his cake and eat it — well, he wasn't going to get away with it.

First, though, she needed the telephone number he'd just called. It would be stored on his mobile phone. All she had to do was get the phone, press the last-number-dialled button and it would be displayed. Had he left the phone in the room? It was unlikely and anyway, from the speed at which he'd exited the room, she did not think he had taken time to hide it there. He'd taken it with him.

She found Donal in the kitchen talking to a group of people she'd never seen before. The top of a small silver mobile phone protruded from the left breast-pocket of his shirt. She wandered back towards the drawing-room, thinking feverishly of ways to get at the phone.

She'd only taken a few steps when there was a loud crash from the kitchen. She snapped her head round to see what had happened. A bottle of red wine had been knocked over and dark red liquid was splashed all across the terracotta tiles, and up the doors of the cream units. Pieces of green glass were scattered over the floor like jewels. Everyone, except Roisin, stood transfixed.

Nimbly she picked her way across the floor, grabbed a kitchen roll and threw it at Donal.

'Here, Don,' she said, taking charge, and suddenly sober, 'you mop up the wine. I'll pick up the glass.'

He went down on his knees and started to rip pieces of paper off the roll and scatter them on the floor. They absorbed the red liquid like bandages.

'Right, everyone,' shouted Roisin, above the buzz of conversation and the music coming from the drawing-room, 'could you just leave the kitchen for a minute while we get this cleaned up? Thanks.'

Everyone shuffled noisily out into the hall.

'I don't know how that happened,' said Donal, looking at his right hand in bewilderment. 'I went to pick it up and it just slipped out of my fingers.'

'Never mind. We'll have it cleaned up in a jiffy. Hey, watch your mobile. It nearly fell out of your pocket there.'

Donal patted his breast pocket, took out the phone, squinted at it and set it on the kitchen counter above his head. Roisin glanced at it and then at Donal. 'I'll just get a brush and pan,' she said and left the room.

Her heart was pounding but her head was clear. She found the brush and pan in the utility room along with a roll of pedal-bin bags. She ripped one off and came back into the kitchen. Donal was where she'd left him, dabbing ineffectually at the floor with a handful of sodden paper. His mobile phone was still on the counter. Roisin's hands were shaking but she kept her nerve. She went over to the counter, and glanced round quickly — there was no one in the kitchen but the two of them. She turned her back to Donal, and in one lightning-quick movement she snatched the phone off the counter and tucked it into the waistband of her skirt. She pulled her shirt down over the small bump — the phone was still warm from Donal's body heat.

'Here,' she said, holding out an opened bin bag in front of Donal, 'put those wet papers in here.'

Donal obeyed and Roisin ripped more sheets off the roll. She bent down and, with careful sweeping motions, wiped up the rest of the liquid and shards of glass. The phone pressed into her stomach and her face burned with guilt. She was terrified it might fall out onto the floor. There was no way in the world she could explain that away if it happened.

'I'll sweep up the rest of the glass,' she said and stood up.

Donal got up off the floor and watched while she quickly swept the floor, adrenaline coursing through her body.

'We'll need to mop it now,' said Roisin.

Donal scratched his head.

'Try the utility room,' she suggested and he left the room while Roisin put the bin bag in the kitchen bin, dampened a cloth and speedily wiped down the cupboard doors that had been splashed with wine. She was shaking all over now and she could hardly think straight — all she wanted to do now was get out of the house.

When Donal eventually returned with a mop

and bucket, she filled it with hot water, squirted in some floor cleaner and swiftly mopped the floor, while Donal just got in her way.

Just as she finished, Michelle appeared in the doorway to the hall. 'Everything all right in here?' she said, a little woozily. 'Sssomeone said there'd been an accident.'

'I dropped a bottle of wine,' said Donal, 'but Roz has got it all sorted.'

'You helped too,' said Roisin, thinking that now at any moment he was bound to start looking for his phone.

'Not much,' he said. 'I wouldn't have known where to start. I've never seen anyone work so fast! Thanks, Roz.'

'Oh, thank you, Roz, darling! You are a star,' said Michelle and she came over, threw herself at Roisin and gave her a big hug. She smelled of Bacardi, and Roisin, praying that Michelle wouldn't notice the mobile phone, almost buckled under her weight. Suddenly she felt as deceitful as Donal Mullan.

Roisin found Scott in the drawing-room talking to Liz, Jayne, Mike and Andy over the music. She squeezed into the group and waited for an opportunity to catch Scott's attention.

'Scott,' she said quietly, 'I think we should go now.'

'Already?' he said and looked at his watch. It took him a few moments to focus on the dial. 'It's only half eleven!'

'I know but we'll have an early start with Tony. And I'm tired.'

'But we're getting a taxi back to Ballyfergus

with this lot. We've both had too much to drink.'

'I haven't. I can drive. Please, Scott,' she begged.

'OK then,' he replied reluctantly and threw back the rest of his beer in one gulp. He fished in his pocket and handed her his keys.

On the way home in the car, Scott fell asleep and Roisin managed to wrest the mobile phone out of her waistband and into her coat pocket. She shivered with the cold and the fear of discovery. Donal would soon notice his phone missing — if not tonight, then tomorrow morning. Would he associate its absence with her?

It was only when she shut the door of her own house behind her that Roisin started to calm down a little. She took her coat off and hung it on a peg in the hall. Briefly she touched the left-hand side pocket and felt the hard lump of the phone. Thankfully, Scott was too drunk to notice anything odd about her behaviour or the fact that she'd come away from the party without her handbag.

Once Alison, the teenage babysitter who lived three doors down, had gone home, they both went upstairs. Roisin checked Tony, who was fast asleep, and they got ready for bed.

'That was a great party,' murmured Scott into his pillow and he soon started to snore.

Roisin lay beside him, stiff as a corpse, her eyes wide open, calculating how long she would have to lie there before he was in a deep sleep. She'd had no opportunity to examine Donal's mobile phone — she prayed he'd left it switched on. If not, she'd never crack the security code.

After ten minutes, Scott's breathing deepened and Roisin sat up in bed, more alert than she'd ever been. She leaned over and kissed him on the cheek — he never stirred. She crept out of bed, slipped on her dressing-gown and left the room, closing the door gently behind her.

Downstairs she got Donal's mobile out of her coat, picked up a pen and pad from the hall table and locked herself in the downstairs loo. She sat down on the closed loo seat and examined the mobile — it was the same make as her phone, a Nokia, but Donal's was smaller and slimmer. It was still switched on, and the time — 12:57 — was displayed in a little window in the middle of the screen. She steadied herself, pressed the green button and waited. The phone made a little '*peep*' and a list came up, headed '*Dialled Numbers*'.

Roisin read the number at the top of the list, with the pen poised over the paper. Then she stopped breathing — the pen and pad fell out of her hands onto the floor. She looked at the blank wall in front of her and a dozen thoughts shot through her mind simultaneously. She closed her eyes in confusion. So many things to think about at once. So many things to understand. So many questions. She inhaled deeply to stop her head from spinning.

She opened her eyes and looked at the number again, just to be sure. But there was no mistake — the number stored in Donal Mullan's telephone was Ann-Marie Shaw's. She was the last person he'd spoken to tonight. She was the woman he had said he loved. She was his mistress.

How could Ann-Marie be having a sordid, dirty little affair with a man like Donal Mullan? How could her lovely, winsome sister be someone's whore? And of all the men in Ballyfergus, why Donal Mullan? *Especially* Donal Mullan, after what he'd done?

How could this possibly be? How could such a thing have come about without her knowing about it? But of course the signs had been there, if only she had opened her eyes wide enough to see. This love affair must be responsible for the transformation in Ann-Marie. And she thought back to Donal's telephone conversation and remembered that he'd called her 'Amy'. Of course, it should have clicked then. That was his pet name for Ann-Marie — she'd heard him use it a couple of times all those years ago.

Roisin sat on the toilet seat until she grew cold, the desire for revenge that had burned so fiercely in her breast for so long, now entirely extinguished. Some things were better left alone. Some things you were better not knowing. For once you knew them, things could never be the same as before.

Did Donal really love Ann-Marie or was he using her? Was Ann-Marie in love with him? How long had it been going on? Did they have any plans for a future together or was this just a fling? And what about poor Michelle, and her children? What would happen to them?

★ ★ ★

When the last guest left the party, at two o'clock in the morning, Donal could have wept with relief and tiredness. He'd stopped drinking a couple of hours ago, not long after he'd knocked over the bottle of wine, and he felt sober now.

'C'mon, let's have a night-cap,' said Michelle and she led the way boldly into the drawing-room towards the drink cabinet. Donal followed, about to remonstrate with her, when she collapsed on one of the sofas instead.

'Well, darling?' she said, stretching out and kicking off her high heels. 'What d'you think? Was it a success?'

'Everyone seemed to have a good time,' he replied, thinking about the conversation he'd had with Amy. He'd never heard her so upset. Not in the two years that they'd been together.

He patted the pocket of his shirt and was surprised to find it empty. He got up and went into the kitchen looking for his mobile phone amongst the debris of half-eaten food on paper plates, dirty glasses and beer bottles. He could've sworn he'd left the phone on top of the kitchen counter, by the stainless-steel cooker. He'd have to find it before Michelle did — but he would worry about that in the morning. Right now she was too drunk to pick up a phone, never mind retrieve numbers from it.

He went back into the drawing-room and found Michelle fast asleep on the sofa. He picked her up, which was no mean feat, given that she must've weighed nearly the same as him and he staggered up the stairs to the second floor. He kicked open the door to their room, and deposited her on the bed. He paused to recover his strength, covered her with a blanket, and left the room. He stood in the hall biting his knuckles and dithered about what to do.

He wanted to go and see Amy — he was so worried about her. What if she did something silly? What if she tried to harm herself like she'd done before? But if Michelle woke up and he wasn't here, how on earth could he explain his absence? He stood there for some ten minutes, his heart pulling him in one direction and his head in another. In the end his heart won. It was reckless but he very nearly no longer cared. He could not lose Amy a second time.

Fifteen minutes later he was at Ann-Marie's door. He knocked gently at first, not expecting her to hear, wondering if he dared ring the doorbell this late at night and risk waking up the other residents in the block. But, to his surprise, the door opened and she was there, looking as lovely as ever but also more miserable than he'd ever seen her. He stepped inside, she shut the door behind him and he followed her into the bedroom. Without a word passing between them he took off his clothes and got into bed with her. She nestled into his shoulder like a small bird.

They lay there for a few minutes and then Donal asked, 'Are you all right now?'

'Yes.' She paused. 'No,' she said in a quiet voice and then she added, 'I don't think I can live like this any more, Donal. Snatching a few hours, here and there. It's no life. It's a sort of . . . of limbo.'

Donal thought of his two daughters, suddenly

filled with a desperate desire to hold them in his arms, to smother them in kisses and tell them that he loved them. He wished they were here now in the room next door. He wished that they were Ann-Marie's children and that she and he were husband and wife. He wished that he could change everything about his life.

'What do you want me to do, Amy? I can't leave the girls. Molly was heartbroken when I didn't go on holiday with them. She cried for me every night.'

'I'm not asking you to leave them. Or Michelle. I'm asking you to leave me.'

This was so unexpected that Donal was speechless for a moment. Then all he felt was panic.

'But I thought you loved me?' he said, and sat up in bed, full of hurt.

'I do love you,' said Ann-Marie and she sat up too and pulled the bedcovers round her naked body. He could just make out her features in the glow from the street-lamp outside the window. Her eyes were full of sorrow but her expression was resolute.

'How can you say that then?' he demanded.

'Because I can't live like this any more. Maybe you can, Donal — you're a different sort of person from me. But I can't. That's why I'm not asking you to choose. I've made my decision and now you must abide by it.'

'Oh, Jesus,' said Donal and he put his hands over his face and felt tears on his cheeks, wet and cold. He opened his mouth to plead with her, but his throat was tight and he could hardly catch a breath.

When at last he could speak he took her face in his hands and he said, 'No, Ann-Marie, I will *not* leave you.'

She shut her eyes momentarily and then opened them again. A tear rolled out of the corner of her left eye and shimmered down her cheek. She bit her lip.

'I'll never leave you,' he said. 'Not if you asked me to every day for the next fifty years.' Ann-Marie gave him a weary half-smile and he went on, 'You're right, Amy — we can't carry on like this. I promise you that I will leave Michelle. But you have to give me a little more time.'

Then he pulled her to him and held onto her like he was a drowning man and she the only piece of driftwood in a cold, heartless sea.

★ ★ ★

Roisin woke up the next morning at seven o'clock to the sound of Tony's cries. As soon as she remembered what had happened the night before, a wave of misery washed over her. She'd lain awake 'til nearly five o'clock and now she was exhausted. She rolled over and looked at Scott who lay with the covers thrown off his naked body, hugging a pillow. She thought fleetingly about waking him up and telling him the whole story. But what would he think of her when she told him that she'd stolen a phone? And how could she explain why she'd kept so much from him for so long? She dragged herself out of bed, went and got Tony and took him downstairs for his first bottle of the day, followed by breakfast.

She waited 'til ten o'clock, then took Tony upstairs and put him in his playpen with some toys while she took a shower. When she came out of the shower, Scott had pulled the bedcovers over his head to drown out the sound of Tony's shouts and shrieks. She dressed quickly, dried her hair and put on make-up. Then she shook Scott gently.

'Are you awake?' she asked.

'Mmm . . . ' he moaned, not opening his eyes, 'hard not to be with all that racket going on.'

'Don't be so grumpy,' she scolded and put her hand under the covers and squeezed his firm buttock.

He grasped her arm by the wrist and opened his eyes. 'If you keep that up, you'll be in serious trouble — hey, what're you doing dressed?'

'It's nearly eleven o'clock, Scott. I've been up since seven.'

He blinked and peered at the clock.

'Scott,' she said cheerily, 'I've got to go round to Michelle's.'

'What for?' he said and he screwed up his face. 'Ouch, my head hurts.'

'I left my handbag there last night.'

'Can't you go later?'

'No, I want to go now. I'm worried in case someone's taken it — my purse and my credit cards were in it. And I'll pop into the supermarket on my way home and get something for dinner. Can you mind Tony for a bit?'

She pecked him on the cheek, leaned into the playpen to kiss Tony goodbye and left the room. Downstairs she put on her coat, checked Donal's phone was still in the pocket and went outside. She drove straight out to The Grange, practising what she would say when she got there. It was nearly eleven-thirty when she pulled up outside the house but the curtains were still drawn.

She rang the doorbell and waited. Michelle opened the door a few minutes later, wearing grey marl lounge bottoms, a matching vest and black hooded top. She held a large glass of water in her hand.

'Roz,' she mumbled, blinking in the bright winter sunshine. 'C'mon in.'

She stood aside and let Roisin enter. 'I'm not long up. God, would you look at the state of the place.' There were empty beer cans and bottles on the floor and someone had trodden food into the hall carpet.

'I'm sorry to call round so early,' said Roisin, 'but I think I left my handbag here last night. In the kitchen. Great party, by the way.'

'Thanks. Go on through,' said Michelle and she padded behind Roisin into the kitchen where two women were cleaning. They looked up and smiled briefly at Roisin before carrying on with their work.

'I'm sure I left it in here somewhere,' said Roisin. She walked over to the cooker, put her hand in her pocket and felt Donal's phone. Her heartbeat quickened.

'Girls,' said Michelle to the cleaners from the other end of the room, where she'd sat down in a chair by the table, 'you didn't see a handbag anywhere, did you? What colour was it, Roisin?'

'Black. Patent leather with a croc trim.'

Michelle addressed the women again and Roisin turned her back to them, pulled the phone from her pocket and shoved it into the bread-bin.

'Have you seen my mobile?' said Donal's voice and Roisin nearly leapt out of her skin.

She turned around with her hands behind her back and smiled brightly. Donal was standing barefoot in the doorway wearing a navy seersucker dressing-gown, his dark hairy legs protruding below the hem.

'Hi, Donal,' she said.

'Hi, Roz,' he replied absentmindedly, and addressed Michelle again, 'It's really important, Shell. It's got all my work numbers in it. I could've sworn I left it in here last night.'

Michelle got up, stood behind him and rubbed his shoulders. 'It'll turn up Donal. The girls'll find it. Roz's handbag is missing too. Don't worry. Here, sit down and I'll make you some coffee.'

Roisin stood with a smile pasted on her face, marvelling at Donal's audacity, and full of pity for Michelle.

'Is this it, love?' said one of the cleaners, holding up Roisin's handbag.

'Oh, thank you very much!' Smiling broadly, she took the bag. 'Well, I'll be off then! Thank goodness this turned up! Thanks again for a great party.' She turned and walked swiftly to the door. 'I'll let myself out. I'll give you a call later in the week, Michelle!' She scurried to the front door and escaped. Once outside, she ran to the car, jumped in and drove away as fast as she could.

When she pulled up outside Ann-Marie's flat Roisin was shaking with rage. She was angry with Donal for what he was doing to Michelle and Ann-Marie and furious with her sister for being such a fool as to get involved with Donal Mullan again. She was furious, too, that Ann-Marie had not told her about the relationship.

Ann-Marie was surprised to see her sister at her door. 'Roisin! I wasn't expecting you, was I?'

'No,' said Roisin, and she walked into the flat without being invited. She went into the small lounge, sat down on the sofa and looked around her, searching for evidence of Donal Mullan. How many times, she wondered, had he sat in this seat? How many times had they had sex in this flat, on this very sofa?

'Can I get you a cup of tea or something?' said Ann-Marie and Roisin glared at her.

'I know about you and Donal Mullan,' she said.

Ann-Marie's face remained impassive but her left eyelid twitched uncontrollably. 'Ah,' she said, and sat down cross-legged on the floor. 'When did you find out?'

'Last night. I overheard him on the phone to you.'

'I knew he'd get careless one day,' said Ann-Marie.

'Is that it? Is that all you've got to say for

yourself? How long has this been going on?'

'Two years, give or take.'

'But you never told me. It's been going on all this time and you never told me.'

Ann-Marie paused before answering. 'What could I have told you, Roisin? That I was seeing a married man, the husband of one of your clients? And when you and Michelle became friends, telling you was completely out of the question. Imagine the position that would've put you in.'

'Jesus, Ann-Marie, she has two children, one the same age as Tony. How could you? Aren't there plenty of single men out there?'

'They're not Donal,' she said simply.

'But he's married.'

'He is at the moment.'

'And you think he's going to leave his wife and kids for you? You think he's going to give up the fancy house and the holidays to come and live with you — what, here?' Roisin looked around the flat incredulously. 'You must be mad.'

'I don't care where we live or what we have, Roisin, and neither does Donal. Things don't matter. All we care about is that we're together. We love each other.'

'He must be a changed man indeed,' said Roisin bitterly. 'It hasn't occurred to you that he could be using you?'

'Using me? For what?'

'Excitement. Company. Sex.'

'Oh, no,' said Ann-Marie and she laughed, 'Donal loves me.'

'Like the way he loved you before? And then

he dumped you. That sort of love?' Roisin demanded. Her sister remained impassive and, before she could stop herself, Roisin went on, 'Do know why he dumped you? It was so that he could take up with Michelle.'

Pain registered in her sister's face and immediately Roisin regretted being so cruel.

'I didn't know that,' said Ann-Marie quietly, 'but it doesn't really make any difference now.'

'I just don't want to see you hurt, Ann-Marie,' said Roisin, her voice softening. 'Not after the last time. Not after the way he destroyed your life.'

'What do you mean 'destroyed my life'?'

'Well, he broke your heart, didn't he? He's responsible for the way you are. You know, for the problems you've had over the years.'

'Is that what you think?' said Ann-Marie, and she shook her head as she spoke. 'It is true that I was devastated when Donal and I broke up. But I realise now that I was unstable long before he ever came on the scene. A normal person would've been able to cope with a broken relationship, wouldn't they? I've never blamed Donal for my problems. In fact, Donal's been helping me to — to come to terms with things.'

'What 'things'?' said Roisin.

Ann-Marie looked into her lap and paused. 'Dad's death and how I felt responsible for it,' she said quietly.

'What are you talking about, Ann-Marie? How could you be responsible for Dad's death? He was in the wrong place at the wrong time. End of story.'

'Oh, Roisin, you don't know the half of it. It's time you did. Donal says it helps to talk about it, instead of bottling it all up.'

'Well, then,' said Roisin, bristling at the mention of Donal's name, 'tell me. I'm your sister. What did happen that day?'

Ann-Marie took a few moments to compose herself and then she spoke as if relating a child's favourite bedtime story by rote.

'It was my birthday and Dad insisted on taking me up to Belfast on the train for the day. He wanted to buy me my birthday present. I remember wearing this beautiful pink dress and black patent shoes and Mum grumbling about how there was nothing wrong with the shops in Ballyfergus and what did he want to be dragging me all the way into Belfast for. We had a lovely day — I had Dad all to myself for a change. No Mum and no you always demanding his attention. We had fish and chips in one of the department stores and I choose a Barbie doll as my present. We'd left the shop and we were heading back to the train station and I started to cry because I wanted a stupid accessory for the doll. It was a skiing outfit with skis and goggles — I remember it clearly. Eventually Dad gave in and we started to walk back to the shop. And then, five minutes later, the bomb went off. It was a noise like I've never heard before — so loud I thought my ears would burst and the pain inside my head was unbearable. I don't know if I went unconscious or not but the next thing I remember is looking up and seeing Dad lying there beside me on the ground. There was shattered glass all around us. Blood was pumping out of a gash on the side of his head, making a big sticky red circle on the pavement. His eyes were open and he called out my name. 'Ann-Marie,' he said, 'Ann-Marie.' And he held out his hand to me and it was shaking and covered in blood. I remember noticing that the glass on his watch face had fallen out. And then I did something that I will never forgive myself for.'

Ann-Marie paused and swallowed before going on, her voice little more than a whisper. She focused on a point some inches to the left of Roisin's shoulder, remembering.

'I pulled away from him, from the blood that was soaking into the hem of my skirt, and the smell of his fear and the way he clawed at my arm, trying to hold onto me. I curled up in a shop doorway and I started to cry. I couldn't look at him — I was scared of my own father. I put my fingers in my ears to block out the sound of his moans. At last these soldiers came along and I looked across at Dad and he'd stopped moving and wasn't making any sound at all. One of the soldiers touched the side of Dad's neck and closed his eyelids and I knew then that he was dead. Then they took me away and put me in an ambulance.'

Ann-Marie stopped talking, her eyes dry but her face contorted with the effort of controlling her emotions.

'So you see,' she went on when she'd composed herself again, 'Dad wouldn't have died if it hadn't been my birthday. If he hadn't taken me to Belfast that day he'd still be alive. If I hadn't cried to go back to the shop, we'd have been safely on our way home when that bomb went off. And, then when he reached out for me, when he was alone and dying and afraid, I turned my back on him.'

Roisin wiped the tears from her eyes and said, 'Jesus, Ann-Marie, you were only a child. Didn't Mum talk to you about what had happened? Didn't she explain to you about fate? Didn't you get any counselling?'

'No,' said Ann-Marie and she paused and thought. 'You were probably too young to remember, Roisin, but after Dad died Mum never talked about him. It was as though he never existed. I see now that she was trying to cope in the only way she knew how. But I heard her say to someone at the funeral, 'If only he hadn't taken Ann-Marie shopping ... ' She never finished the sentence but I knew that she blamed me for Dad's death. And that's why I felt so guilty.'

Roisin shook her head, unable to speak, while silent tears cascaded down her cheeks. This was the first time she'd heard the full details of her father's agonising death. She'd always imagined that his death was instantaneous, that he hadn't suffered. And, because her father's death was a taboo subject at home, she'd never questioned what it was like for her sister. She'd never understood until now the horror of it all. No wonder Ann-Marie had difficulty coping with everyday life. Not only did she have to live with the memory of that day but she'd borne this terrible guilt for all these years. And it had taken Donal Mullan to help her in a way her own family could not.

'So,' said Ann-Marie after a long time had elapsed and Roisin had dried her tears, 'if you're looking to blame Donal for my problems you're barking up the wrong tree.'

Roisin nodded and said, 'So what's going to happen with you and Donal now?'

'He's going to leave Michelle and move in with me.'

'Oh, God,' said Roisin and she put her hands up to her mouth. 'When?'

'Soon. After Christmas.'

'Has he told her yet?'

Ann-Marie shook her head.

Roisin said, 'The poor cow! She doesn't suspect a thing. I know she doesn't. This'll devastate her. You know that, don't you? She adores him.'

Ann-Marie bowed her head and said, quietly, 'So do I. He doesn't love her, Roisin. He never did.'

'You don't know that,' said Roisin and then she added, 'But wait a minute. Does he know I'm your sister?'

Ann-Marie blushed and shook her head.

'What?' said Roisin.

'I told him that you'd left Ballyfergus.'

'But why?'

'I don't really know. Perhaps because I knew how much you hated him. I didn't want anything to frighten him off. And once I'd told the lie there didn't seem to be any need to correct it. I reckoned your paths would never cross. How was I to know you'd end up befriending his wife and visiting his home?'

'But didn't he recognise me when we met?'

'Apparently not. He told me about a dinner party he and Michelle had after Sabrina was born. He mentioned a woman called Roz but it was obvious that he didn't recognise you.'

'So what did you tell him about me?'

'Oh, I told him you'd gone to Findhorn. It's a sort of hippy community in Scotland. I said you'd gone to find yourself and we haven't heard from you in years.'

If the whole situation wasn't so awful Roisin could have laughed. The notion of her living in a hippy community was the most preposterous thing she'd heard in months.

★ ★ ★

'Where have you been?' said Scott when Roisin finally arrived back home at three thirty without any groceries.

'Scott,' she said, standing in the doorway to the lounge, utterly exhausted by lack of sleep and trauma of the last few hours, 'I'm sorry, but can you mind Tony for a bit longer? I'm going to have to lie down.'

Scott got up off the floor where he'd been playing with Tony and came over to her. 'Roisin, what on earth's wrong?' he said, his voice full of concern. 'Are you sick?'

'Sort of. Look, I can't tell you about it right now. Let me get some sleep. After Tony's down tonight, we'll have a long talk.'

'I don't understand. Is something wrong? Has something happened to you?'

'No, I'm fine. Really. There's nothing wrong with me or us. It's to do with Ann-Marie and — '

Tony started to cry and Scott picked him up. The baby reached out for Roisin and she took him in her arms. He stopped crying.

'Look, it's impossible to talk properly with Tony around,' said Roisin. 'I hardly slept last night and we need to sit down and have a proper talk. I have a lot to tell you.'

'OK,' said Scott, doubtfully, 'you go to bed then and I'll take Tony round to my parents. They'd love to see him.'

Roisin went upstairs and crawled into bed and, as she drifted off to sleep, she heard the sound of Scott's car pulling out of the drive. In spite of the emotional rollercoaster of the last few hours, she slept soundly and was surprised when the sound of Scott giving Tony his bath woke her up. She stumbled from the bedroom to the bathroom door.

'What time is it?' she said, blinking in the bright light.

'About half six,' replied Scott. 'Are you feeling any better?'

'Mmm.'

'Listen, Roisin, there's something to eat downstairs if you want it. It's only pasta and sauce out of a jar. I couldn't think what else to do.'

'It sounds great.'

'Why don't I put Tony to bed while you eat and then we can talk?'

'OK.' Roisin went over to Tony, where he sat supported in a baby bath seat, playing with bubbles. She kissed the top of his wet head and said, 'Night, darling.'

She went downstairs and ate the meal Scott had prepared. Then she looked at the clock on the wall, opened a bottle of white wine and waited for Scott to come downstairs.

'Is he OK?' she asked.

'Fine. He went down like a lamb.' Scott opened the fridge, took out a beer, twisted off the top and said, 'C'mon, let's go and sit in the lounge.'

Roisin followed him, taking the bottle of wine with her, and sat down on the sofa. Scott switched on a lamp and the Christmas-tree lights, filling the room with an incongruous festive glow.

'Now,' he said, settling himself into an armchair, his expression grave, 'are you going to tell me what this is all about?'

Roisin took a very big slug of wine, holding the glass by the stem, and looked at Scott, steeling herself to begin. Her hand was shaking slightly — she put the glass on the table beside her and folded her hands into each other on her lap.

'Roisin?' said Scott.

'I'm thinking,' she said and sighed. 'I don't know where to start.'

'How about at the beginning?'

'OK, then,' said Roisin. She took a deep

breath and launched into the story of Ann-Marie and Donal Mullan — where they met, when they got engaged and how Donal broke off the engagement.

'He was engaged to your sister?' said Scott, his eyes wide with disbelief. 'But why didn't you mention it before? I thought you didn't know Donal before you met him that first time at his house.'

'I can explain but there's a lot to tell you, Scott. Can you let me finish and then ask questions afterwards?'

'OK,' said Scott, and he put one finger over his lips and rested his chin on his thumb.

Roisin told him how Ann-Marie went off the rails after that and how Roisin blamed Donal, and hated him for what he'd done to her sister. She told him how she'd felt when she saw him outside the chapel that day with Colette. She told him she'd befriended Michelle to get close to Donal and that she'd planned one day to avenge her sister.

'I made up my mind to find a way to hurt him that night we all met at Donal and Michelle's for the first time. He was so rude to you.'

'Rude to me?' said Scott, looking at her blankly.

'Yes, don't you remember those cutting things he said about Vauxhall Omegas? I was so angry — it made me hate him even more.'

'Oh, that,' said Scott carelessly. 'Donal's a bit of a car snob but you don't take what he says too seriously. It wasn't meant personally.'

'Well, I took it personally. I was furious. And

then at their Christmas party I couldn't believe my luck when I overheard Donal Mullan talking on his mobile to his mistress.'

'He's having an affair?' said Scott, sitting bolt upright. Roisin nodded and Scott went on, 'You're not planning on telling Michelle, are you?'

'No, I never was. I wanted to make Donal give up his mistress. But I didn't want to hurt Michelle.'

'Is that why you went over there this morning? To confront him.'

'No, I went over to return his phone.' Scott furrowed his eyebrows in confusion and she explained how she'd stolen the phone to get the telephone number of Donal's lover.

'What were you planning on doing with the number?'

'I thought I could find out who it was I heard him speaking to on the phone.'

'And did you?'

'Yes.'

'And?'

Roisin paused before going on. 'It was Ann-Marie.'

'Jesus,' said Scott, and he grasped the ends of the armrests. He was speechless for what seemed like several minutes while he took in, and processed, this information. 'Does anyone else know about this?' he asked at last.

'Not as far as I know.'

'And what are you planning to do now?'

'Well,' said Roisin and she massaged her temples with the tips of her fingers, 'now I'm torn between Michelle and Ann-Marie. I know Michelle would be devastated if Donal left her. But you should have seen Ann-Marie the other night, Scott. She's totally in love with him too. And I just know that it's because of Donal that she's been doing so well. If he were to leave her again . . . well, I don't think she could take it. What I just don't understand is what either of them see in him. And, to be honest, I'm really mad with Ann-Marie. First of all he's a married man and secondly, how could she be so stupid as to get involved with him again, after what he did to her?'

'What a mess,' said Scott, still trying to come to terms with it.

'Scott, I'm sorry I kept all this from you for so long.'

He stared at her hard then, his eyes full of hurt. 'I don't understand why you did, Roisin.'

She looked at the floor and her cheeks reddened as she spoke. 'I didn't want you to know that I was capable of such . . . such hate. I didn't want you to think badly of me. I value your opinion above anyone else's, Scott. And you are such a good person, you would never hate someone the way I hate . . . hated Donal.'

'You don't hate him now?'

'I don't like him, but hate him? No,' she said, shaking her head. 'Not any more. You see when I went to see Ann-Marie today, I found out that Donal wasn't entirely to blame for Ann-Marie's problems. If anything it seems he's helping her.'

She then related the conversation she'd had with Ann-Marie about her father's death.

'So you see,' she said, 'all these years I've been blaming Donal when really he was only partly to blame. But now I know about him and Ann-Marie I don't know what to do about it. I want both Ann-Marie and Michelle to be happy but they both can't be.'

'Don't do anything, Roisin. Believe me it'll come to a head anyway without your intervention. Ballyfergus is too small a town for it to go on undetected forever.'

'I suppose you're right,' said Roisin, miserably. 'I know it's my own fault for snooping, but I just wish now that I didn't know.' She paused then and looked at her husband and thought how much she loved him. 'Scott, do you still love me?'

'Of course.'

'Even after what I've done?'

He paused before answering. 'Yes. I'm hurt that you didn't confide in me but I understand why you did it. I think,' he said slowly, 'that you love your sister very much.'

'And I love you even more,' said Roisin and she got up, went over to him and knelt in front of him. 'And I'm sorry if I hurt you,' she said, unable to stem the tears any longer. 'I'll never do it again.'

★ ★ ★

It was the Saturday before Christmas and panic was beginning to set in. Michelle was far from organised for Christmas and time was running out.

'Molly, I know I promised you we'd go and collect holly but we've got to go shopping. I haven't finished getting everyone's Christmas presents.'

She wiped Sabrina's nose and the baby wiggled furiously on her lap, arched her back and whined.

'I hate shopping,' said Molly firmly, and she stomped her foot, sending a plastic teacup skidding across the wooden floor of the playroom.

'It depends what you're shopping for, darling. If it was sweets or toys you'd want to come, wouldn't you?'

'Can we buy sweets and toys?' said Molly hopefully.

'No,' said Michelle and she sighed. Then she looked at her little girl's miserable face and felt ashamed. What was more important right now? Buying more presents for people who didn't want them (or need them), or spending precious moments with her children, doing things with them that would become their treasure chest of happy memories?

'You're right,' she said brightly. 'Shopping is boring! Let's go and collect some holly.'

Instantly Molly's expression changed. Her face broke into a wide smile — she leapt into the air and ran around the room, waving her hands above her head.

'Yippee!' she shouted. 'We're going to collect holly! We're going to collect holly! Come on, Mum! Hurry up!'

Molly ran through the kitchen and into the

boot room where she sat on the floor and pulled on her shoes, still muddy from her last excursion outdoors. Michelle followed her, sat Sabrina down on the cold tiles, and said, more to herself than the children, 'Now where's that rucksack? I'm going to need it for Sabrina.' She remembered then that Donal had taken the children to the beach the weekend before.

'It must be in Daddy's car. Molly, you keep an eye on Sabrina and I'll nip out and get it. I'll just be a second. And don't forget to put on your scarf and gloves. It's cold outside.'

She opened the back door, shut it behind her and ran across to Donal's car, which was parked by the side of the house. Luckily he'd taken her car to the golf course this morning as there was almost no petrol in his own — he said he didn't have time to stop and get some. She pressed a button on the key-ring and the car unlocked with a resonant clunk.

Michelle lifted the lid of the boot but there was no rucksack there. She frowned, wondering where on earth it could be. She put her hand on the lid ready to slam it shut again when something caught her eye — a small bright package shoved far into the boot of the car, half-hidden under the tartan car blanket.

She pulled it out and, guiltily, examined it. It appeared to be a Christmas present, wrapped in shiny gold paper and carefully tied with thin gold ribbon, curls of the metallic thread cascading down the sides of the small parcel. It must be Donal's present to her, she decided. 'Whatever could it be?' thought Michelle. She hoped Donal hadn't gone and got her something really special — all she'd got him this Christmas was a new golf bag and a cashmere jumper. What did you buy the man who had everything?

She shook the parcel gently. There was no noise and it was too large to contain an item of jewellery . . . unless he'd wrapped it in several layers to confound her. As she replaced it where she'd found it, a small label flipped face-up. 'To my darling Donal. Happy Christmas. From, AM xoxoxox,' it said in a tiny but clearly legible hand.

Michelle stood there quite motionless and blinked her eyes. She read the label again. Then she gently closed the boot and turned her back on the car. She crossed her arms across her stomach, which had started to hurt. The pain rose up her torso into her chest and then her throat so that she felt like she was being strangled. She could hardly breathe. And then she started to cry, whimpering quietly like a wounded animal. After a few moments she heard the sound of Sabrina's cries, wiped the tears from her face and went indoors because she had to. She wished she could have turned and run and never stopped running.

* * *

Michelle rang Roisin's doorbell and prayed that she would be at home. When the door opened she had to hold back tears of relief.

'Hi there! What a nice surprise,' said Roisin with a big smile. 'Are you coming in?'

'Yes, if you don't mind,' said Michelle, pushing past Roisin into the hallway. 'I need to talk to you.' Then she knelt on the floor and started taking the children's outdoor clothes off.

The smile fell from Roisin's face then and she said, 'Michelle, are you all right? You look terrible.'

'Here,' said Michelle, her voice husky with the effort of holding back tears, and she thrust a video of *The Sleeping Beauty* into Roisin's hand. 'Put that on and it'll keep Molly amused.'

Roisin did as she was told and they left Molly glued to the TV eating a pack of Fruit Pastilles.

'I was just making a cup of tea,' said Roisin, walking through to the kitchen. 'Do you want one?'

'OK,' said Michelle, trying to keep it together, and she sat down on a kitchen chair with Sabrina on her lap and waited for Roisin to pour the tea. She felt like she had a fever — she was hot one minute, cold the next and she couldn't stop her left leg from jiggling.

'Where's Tony?' she asked.

'Asleep upstairs,' replied Roisin, 'and Scott's golfing. But you'll know that already. He's playing with Donal.'

Michelle nodded. But as soon as her friend sat down, she was unable to contain herself any longer and she blurted out, 'Don's having an affair.'

Roisin stared at her and said, 'How do you know?'

Michelle told her about the package that she'd found in Donal's car and what was written on the label. 'At first I thought it was for me. And then I saw the label. Can you imagine? I thought he'd gone out and bought me a present but it was from some . . . some other woman.'

The tears came again and this time, in the presence of a sympathetic listener, Michelle allowed them to cascade freely. Roisin took the stunned baby out of her mother's arms and walked her round the room, talking softly and pointing things out in the garden through the window. When Michelle's sobbing had eased she asked, 'But, Michelle, couldn't you be mistaken? It could be from his — his mother?'

'His mother never buys him presents,' she sniffed, 'and anyway her name's Ivy Mullan.'

'Maybe she has a nickname, something beginning with an 'A'?'

'No, Roisin. I wish I could believe that. But no mother would sign a present with her initials. You and I both know it's from a lover.'

Michelle noticed that Roisin's cheeks reddened a little at that. She went on, 'Oh God, I had a feeling, you know. I thought he might leave me. That's why I had Sabrina. I thought another baby would make him stay. I thought she would make us closer — that she would make him love me.'

'Oh, Michelle, I'm so sorry,' said Roisin and Michelle started to cry again.

Unsettled by her mother's behaviour, Sabrina began to cry too. Michelle forced the tears to stop, dabbed her eyes with a scrunched-up tissue, and held out her arms for Sabrina. She put her on her lap and the baby quietened.

'What are you going to do?' said Roisin.

'Why, I'm going to carry on as though I don't know. Maybe it's just a fling and it'll all blow over.'

'But don't you want to know if he loves her or how long it's been going on? Don't you want to confront him?'

'No, definitely not,' said Michelle, with clarity. 'If he knows I know then he'll be forced into choosing between us. And I don't want that. I'm afraid he won't choose me. In fact I'm quite sure he won't.'

'But Michelle, aren't you worth more than that? If he is having an affair, why would you want to stay with him? And look at the state of you. How can you carry on as though you don't know?'

Michelle looked at Roisin, full of amazement that she should ask such questions. Roisin obviously had never loved the way Michelle loved Donal. She stopped sniffling, sat up straight in the chair and composed herself.

'Because I love him,' she said simply, 'and I can't live without him.'

* * *

Roisin chose the moment to visit her mother with care. She called at the house on Monday night when Tony was safely tucked up in bed and she knew her mother would be home alone. She rang the doorbell and waited and looked at the house she'd grown up in with fresh eyes.

Her mother kept the little bungalow spic and

396

span, orderly to the point of obsession. The outside had been freshly painted that summer and the path to the front door, the driveway and the garden were tidy and completely free of debris. Everything was contained and disciplined and sterile.

She thought back to her childhood and remembered how, after Dad's death, they had learned to live with tension in the house. Mairead was all wound up like a mechanical doll, going through the motions of her daily life, but not really being there at all. She lost her temper at the slightest little thing — a muddy footprint on the floor, the toilet seat left up, a book left on the floor. It was like walking on a rocky beach — you had to watch where you put every footstep or you'd slip and fall.

The absence of Roisin's father had left a huge gaping hole in the family. But Roisin now saw that, by not talking about him, they had failed to properly mourn him. As a result his presence haunted their everyday lives. Because they had not fully acknowledged his loss, they had not been able to let him go.

The door opened. 'Roisin, love, what're you doing here?' said Mairead. 'Come on in and I'll put the kettle on. It's good to see you.'

In the kitchen Roisin took off her coat and hung it on the back of a chair. She sat down and her mother said, 'So, how are things?'

'OK,' said Roisin.

Mairead busied herself making tea and Roisin waited until they were both sitting down with steaming mugs in front of them before she spoke again. 'Mum, I want to talk to you about my father.'

'What about him?' said Mairead and the muscle on the side of her neck tensed.

'I've been talking to Ann-Marie and she told me about the day he died. And exactly how he died.'

The tension went out of Mairead's neck, she pursed her lips in a grim line, and waited for Roisin to go on.

'She told me that she felt, she feels, responsible for his death. Did you know that?'

Mairead shook her head.

'You know,' said Roisin, 'all these years I thought that Ann-Marie's problems stemmed solely from what Donal Mullan did to her. But it turns out that there's a lot more to it than that.'

'I could have told you that, Roisin. I tried to, but you wouldn't listen. I was angry at Donal Mullen too at the time he dumped her, but I always knew he wasn't the root cause of her depression. I don't think Ann-Marie ever got over her father's death. What she saw . . . well, it was so horrific I doubt if anyone could ever get over it fully.'

'It's not just that she was there,' said Roisin. 'Did you also know that she thought you blamed her for Dad's death?'

Mairead cradled the mug in both hands and looked at the table. 'It's true. I did, at first. But I knew it was wrong and I tried not to let my feelings show.'

'How could you, Mum? She was only a child!'

'I know. But I wasn't thinking rationally,

Roisin. I was so — so distraught — I wanted to blame someone.'

'Do you still blame her?'

'Lord, no,' she said, shaking her head. 'Those feelings only lasted a few weeks. It was the grief.'

'Have you ever told Ann-Marie that?'

Mairead looked up at Roisin and said, 'I never thought there was need to.'

'Believe me, there is, Mum. She needs to hear it from you.'

Mairead nodded slowly and they sat in silence for a few moments before Roisin spoke again.

'Don't you think that it would've helped to talk about what happened to Dad instead of just clamming up? I mean, Ann-Marie never got any counselling. She had nobody to talk to. And do you know how I found out what had happened to my own father? On my second day at school Lily Reynolds told me that he'd been blown up in a bomb.'

A spark of anger flashed in Mairead's eyes and she leaned across the table and stabbed the air with a pointed finger. 'Don't you try and pin all this on me, Roisin Shaw! I did the best I could. I lost my husband and I had two little girls to bring up. No one wanted to listen to me banging on about the dead. No one wanted to see me wallowing in grief. Everyone told me to be brave, that life has to go on. And that's what I did. For the sake of you and your sister, I tried to carry on the best I could. The only way I could.' Tears crept out of the corners of her hazel eyes and ran down the fine creases in her skin. She pulled a tissue from her right-hand sleeve and wiped her eyes.

'I'm sorry, Mum. I didn't mean to upset you. I'm only trying to help.'

Mairead wiped her nose and looked at her daughter, her anger all spent. 'Our marriage wasn't perfect, Roisin,' she said, softly. 'No marriage is. It starts off wonderfully and then things happen that — that change both of you. But I loved your father as much as I could have loved any man. And when he died, well, it was the end of my world. I can still hardly mention his name it hurts so much.'

Roisin extended her arm and took her mother's hand in her own. 'That's because you've never properly grieved for him. You've never come to terms with the fact that he's gone. It's only by talking about what's happened that you can really move on.'

'Perhaps you're right, Roisin. But what should I do about it?'

'I think you should start by going to see Ann-Marie. You two have a lot to talk about. And then maybe we could all get together sometime soon and you could tell us everything you remember about him.'

It was after eleven o'clock when Roisin embraced her mother in the porch and said goodbye. Mairead clung to her for a few moments and held onto her daughter's hands when she at last pulled away.

'Don't judge me too harshly, Roisin,' she said. 'No-one is perfect. I was an ordinary woman faced with extraordinary circumstances. I never expected life to throw at me what it did.'

'Oh, Mum, I'm not judging you at all. I just want us all to be happy. To be at peace with ourselves and with the past.'

'That's all I want too.'

11

Roisin woke on Christmas morning and lay in bed listening to Tony chattering in the room next door. She smiled when she thought of the presents waiting for him downstairs — she imagined his shrieks of delight as he ripped off the paper, his chubby face punctuated by two deep dimples.

Her mood was lighter than it had been in months. Of course there was still the dilemma of what would happen between Ann-Marie, Michelle and Donal. But, on the positive side, she was no longer keeping secrets from Scott, and her family was on the way to healing its wounds.

She leaned over and whispered in Scott's ear, 'Wake up darling. Happy Christmas.'

He rolled over and pulled her to him and gave her a big, wet kiss. 'Happy Christmas, love,' he said.

'Tony's awake,' said Roisin and she jumped out of bed, and grabbed her dressing-gown, 'C'mon, let's go downstairs and open the presents! And I've got to get the turkey in the oven or it'll never be done in time.'

At lunchtime, Mairead, Ann-Marie, Scott's brother Fraser and his two children arrived — Scott's parents were in Australia spending Christmas with their eldest son, Ian. Roisin cooked the main course, while Ann-Marie brought salmon parcels for starters and Mairead supplied a homemade Christmas pudding. Fraser turned up, nicely dressed in grey slacks and a long-sleeved shirt open at the neck, with a bottle of scotch for Scott and a beautiful bunch of flowers for Roisin.

To Roisin's surprise her first-ever Christmas lunch was good and she was happy to see the four people she loved most — Scott, Tony, Mum and Ann-Marie — around her table, enjoying themselves. And she was glad Fraser was there too with Oliver and little Ruby, now an adorable sixteen-month-old. They would be spending time with their mother and her family later on in the day. In spite of his reserved nature, Fraser's courteous behaviour and good conversation made him a welcome guest. Roisin watched him talking to Ann-Marie and wondered why her sister couldn't fall for a decent bloke like Fraser instead of a rat like Donal Mullan.

After toying with some chipolatas and a roast potato, Oliver went into the lounge followed by his little sister to play with the toys they'd just been given by Scott and Roisin. Scott got up and toasted absent family and wished everyone a happy Christmas. Everyone clinked glasses and took a sip of wine.

'Well, everyone, I've got some news for you,' said Ann-Marie, clearing her throat, and she smiled shyly.

Roisin froze with Tony on her lap. Surely she wasn't going to announce her relationship with Donal now? Not here, not at a lovely family Christmas gathering. She was just about to say something when Ann-Marie beat her to it.

'I've passed my first set of exams. I'm on my way to becoming a fully fledged veterinary nurse.'

Roisin started breathing again — she hadn't realised she'd stopped — and buried her face in Tony's wispy hair. Everyone congratulated Ann-Marie and Roisin looked up and smiled brightly. Only she understood just how completely her sister's new-found enthusiasm for life depended on Donal Mullan. What if he dumped her again? How would she cope then?

She knew then, that when the time came, she would take her sister's side. For two good reasons. Firstly, blood was thicker than water and, whatever she might think of Donal Mullan, she had to support her sister. Secondly, Michelle was made of stronger stuff than Ann-Marie. Both women loved Donal, both said they could not live without him but only in Ann-Marie's case did Roisin believe this to be literally true. Michelle would be devastated, but she would survive. Roisin thought of Michelle's two little girls and sighed inwardly. If only there weren't innocent children involved in this whole sordid affair.

'Have you heard from Mum and Dad today?' asked Fraser, addressing Scott.

'They said they'd try and phone tonight, our time.'

The brothers spoke about their parents for a few minutes and then Mairead stood up.

'Well, I think I'll leave you to talk,' said Mairead good-naturedly, rising from her seat. 'If my sense of smell is anything to go by this little fellow needs his nappy changed.' She lifted Tony out of Roisin's arms and cuddled him. He gurgled delightedly. 'You come upstairs with Gran, little man,' said Mairead, leaving the room, 'and we'll get you into a nice clean nappy.'

'I hope we weren't boring your mum,' said Fraser after Mairead had gone.

'Not at all,' laughed Roisin. 'She'll use any excuse to get her hands on Tony. You watch, she'll be upstairs with him for the next hour.'

Ann-Marie wandered through to the lounge where she sat on the floor beside Oliver and Ruby. They were watching a *Teletubbies* video and within seconds Ruby had climbed onto Ann-Marie's knee.

'How are things between you and Julie then?' Scott asked his brother.

'Fine. Coping well with the situation, considering. We're both trying to make it as easy on the kids as possible.'

'Do you think there's any hope of a reconciliation?' asked Roisin.

'Absolutely not,' said Fraser.

'But you said that you were getting on fine. How can you be so sure that it's all over between you?' argued Scott.

'Scott,' said Fraser and he looked from his brother to his sister-in-law and back again, 'you're going to find out sooner or later, so I suppose you might as well find out from me.'

'Find out what?' said Scott.

'She's moving in with someone. Or rather someone's moving in with her.'

'Oh,' said Scott and he looked at the table.

There was an uncomfortable pause and Roisin said, 'Well, it was bound to happen eventually, wasn't it? One of you meeting someone else?'

'You don't think she's been seeing him all along, do you?' asked Scott.

Fraser shook his head. 'No, I don't think so. Julie may be a lot of things but she's truthful. She would have told me.'

'How do you feel about it then?' asked Roisin gently. 'About another man moving in with the children, I mean.'

Fraser paused, looked up at the ceiling, down at the table and then met, first Roisin's, and then Scott's gaze. 'It's not a man,' he said, flatly. 'It's a woman.'

Roisin and Scott stared at each other. Scott looked horrified, opened his mouth, closed it again and said nothing. It was one of the rare times in Roisin's life when she really didn't know what to say. Julie was gay! She never would have guessed. And yet there had always been something about her that Roisin couldn't quite put her finger on. Despite Roisin's best efforts she'd never been able to forge a close relationship with her sister-in-law. Apart from the children they seemed to have nothing in common. Julie's main passion was horses, something that Roisin knew nothing about. And she seemed totally disinterested in the feminine things that fascinated Roisin.

Fraser coughed and looked at the table. Then he picked up his wineglass and drained it in one gulp. 'To be totally honest about it,' he said, 'I feel relieved.'

'You do?' said Roisin.

'Maybe it's a pathetic macho response but it's as though I've been let off the hook. I really tried to make our marriage work but now I know that nothing I could have done would have made any difference. It's like validation that there's nothing wrong with me as a man. And because her lover is a woman I don't even feel jealous, not like I would've done if it'd been a bloke.'

'Don't you love her any more?' asked Roisin.

Fraser thought for a few moments before answering. 'I care for her — she's the mother of my children after all — but I don't love her. I think I stopped loving her soon after Ruby was born. But I couldn't just walk out and leave her with two kids to raise on her own, could I? The decision to separate was hers and hers alone. I would've stuck it out for the children.'

'Will you get divorced now?' asked Scott.

Fraser shrugged his shoulders. 'I don't see why not. She wants it and it'd let us both get on with our lives. You know, since she told me, we're getting on better than we've done for years. Look, you guys,' said Fraser suddenly changing tone, 'I don't mean to be rude and rush off but I've got to get the kids back to Julie. She's meeting me at her mum and dad's for three o'clock.'

'Of course,' said Roisin, standing up. 'Thanks for coming.'

'No, thank you for having us, Roisin. And Scott. It's been great. The children have had a ball and, well, it's just been really nice to share Christmas with you.'

He embraced them both and Roisin was surprised to find that she had tears in her eyes.

'Oliver, Ruby,' he called into the lounge, 'time to go.'

Oliver put up a wail of protest and Ruby came waddling into the room, grinned at her father, went over to him and put her arms around his legs.

'Here's my little princess,' he said and he picked her up and kissed her on the noise. She smiled, showing small pearl-like teeth.

'Time to go and see Mum,' said Fraser more cheerfully than he'd sounded in months. He took Ruby through to the hallway where he wrested her into her coat and put on his leather jacket. Ann-Marie persuaded Oliver to put on his outdoor things by explaining, very patiently, that he could take the *Teletubbies* video with him to his gran's house.

'Here, Fraser, let me drive you over,' said Roisin.

'I'll be all right. I've just had a couple.'

'No, Fraser,' said Roisin and she looked down at the two children, 'let me. It's not worth it. Not when you've got the kids in the car. Even one glass can be one too many.'

'Yeah, you're right,' he said, following her gaze. He handed her the keys and added, 'Thanks, Roisin.'

Mairead came downstairs with a fragrant Tony in her arms and they all said goodbye. As she shut the door behind her, Roisin heard her mother say to Ann-Marie, 'What a lovely, lovely man.' And Ann-Marie replied thoughtfully, 'Yes. Yes, he is.'

★ ★ ★

In the McCormick household Noel was playing his usual role of jovial host, dispensing bonhomie to his family like medicine.

'Merry Christmas, Donal! Great to see you,' he said, pumping his son-in-law's hand and, Pauline noticed, not really listening to what Donal said in reply. Noel was so insincere, so hypocritical. Pauline didn't like Donal any more than Noel did but she didn't pretend. She treated him civilly but she didn't gush like Noel did.

When everyone — Noel, Pauline, Jeanette, Matt, Michelle, Donal, Yvonne and the grand-children — was assembled in the drawing-room, Noel distributed crystal flutes of champagne and toasted everyone in turn. He came to Pauline and said, 'And lastly, but most importantly, here's to Pauline — a wonderful wife, mother and grandmother. The lynchpin that holds this family together.'

So that's what she was — the crutch that held up Noel's fantasy of the perfect family dynasty. She smiled grimly and her family raised their glasses and said, 'Here, here!'

'Grandpa! Grandpa!' cried Molly, running up to Noel. 'Can you pretend to be a tiger again and chase us? Please!'

'Well, OK,' he replied indulgently and he

placed his glass carefully on the top of a dresser by the door. 'Just one more time and then I think lunch's ready. Is that right, Pauline?'

'That's right,' said Pauline.

She left the room and went to check on the roast potatoes. Christmas lunch was one of the few big meals in the year that she cooked herself completely from scratch, and normally she took great pleasure in it. This year, though, it felt like a chore — she had much more important things on her mind than whether a turkey was cooked or vegetables steamed to the point of perfection. She poked the potatoes with a sharp knife and put them back in the oven for another ten minutes.

For weeks now she had been agonising over what to do — Padraig had asked her to move in with him. He said he loved her, that he would love her always. And she believed him — or rather she wanted to believe him, for her experience with Noel had left her very wary of men. Now the life she led here in Glenburn seemed so false and tawdry compared to the beauty she had experienced, albeit fleetingly, with Padraig. He had little to offer her materially, but one corner of the draughty little farmhouse on that remote hill in County Antrim contained more love than this grand house.

But her romance with Padraig had been such a whirlwind affair. They'd only known each other, what, a couple of months? And here she was contemplating moving in with him. Walking out on nearly forty years of marriage. Was she completely insane? Of course, she was well aware

410

of the silliness that love could induce in women — she only had to look at Michelle to see that. Pauline was infatuated with Padraig and infatuation resulted in poor decisions. She would have to be careful that she made the right one. She pulled an apron over her head and tied it around her waist.

'Everything OK in here, Mum?' asked Jeanette.

'Yes. I think we're just about ready to serve the starter,' said Pauline, lifting the lid on a large soup pot, and looking inside. 'Why don't you get everyone up to the table and then give me a hand with the bowls? It'll be all hands on deck to serve the main course. I'll bring the turkey out to the table for your father to carve but I think I'll serve everything else in here on plates.'

'Pity Esther couldn't come in and do it.'

'I can hardly ask the poor woman to come in on Christmas Day, Jeanette,' said Pauline, opening the top oven door to lift out warm soup bowls. 'She's got a family of her own.'

'I know,' said Jeanette and she shrugged her shoulders, 'but still.'

Jeanette left the room and Pauline wondered at her daughter's selfishness. Then she reminded herself that it was her fault, and Noel's — they'd raised three rather spoilt girls.

Pauline transferred the broth to a tureen and carried it across the hall into the dining-room. Jeanette followed with the warm bowls. Noel said grace and, while Pauline served the soup from a marble-topped dresser, Jeanette went back into the kitchen for two small plastic bowls of fruit salad for Molly and Roger.

While everyone ate and admired Pauline's festive table dressing — gold and frosted fruit — Matt and Noel talked shop.

Pauline noticed that Yvonne was quieter than usual. Over the last few weeks Pauline's senses had suddenly heightened. It was as though she'd been living in some kind of fog and, all of a sudden, it had lifted — she saw her world, and everything in it, in an entirely new light. She examined her youngest daughter again — she was definitely out of sorts. Instead of her usual high spirits, she was flat and lifeless and her brow was furrowed, creating a perfectly vertical crease between her eyebrows. She looked, well, worried.

When the starters were finished and the plates cleared away, she carried the enormous turkey out to the table on a silver platter and set it in front of Noel. She handed him the bone-handled carving knife and fork — a wedding present from one of his distant relatives, she remembered. She stood with her hands folded across her tummy while Noel made a big show of carving the bird, and transferring the meat to a serving dish.

'Don't cut it too thickly,' she warned as he hacked great chunks out of the breast.

'Pauline, dear,' he said and laughed, 'I've been doing this for years. Don't you think I know how to carve a turkey by now?'

Pauline said nothing and thought that most of their conversation was like this these days — each of them taking verbal swipes at the other. When he'd finished carving, she carried the platter back into the kitchen.

Noel certainly needed her, of that there was no doubt. But he needed her in the way he needed a damn fine Personal Assistant at work. Someone to keep his home life ticking over, someone to take care of all the mundane aspects associated with Glenburn so that to him it was purely a place to retreat from the rigours of business life. Noel would never leave her because he had everything just the way he liked it.

Once the main course was served, Pauline pushed the food round her plate and drank glass after glass of red wine. It was useful having the grandchildren here — they provided a distraction so that no one really noticed her. Just as well for she was having difficulty keeping a smile on her face, let alone joining in the conversation.

After Christmas pudding the adults sat around the table drinking coffee and liqueurs while the children ran between the dining-room and the playroom. Sabrina sat and dribbled on her father's lap, while he fed her spoonfuls of whipped cream. Pauline swilled the Rémy Martin brandy around in her glass, and wondered what Padraig was doing now. Some arty friends had invited him over for Christmas Day. Had he told them he had a lover? Did he think about her as much as she thought about him?

'Ahhemm,' said Yvonne, and Pauline looked at her.

Yvonne glanced nervously at the faces around the table. 'I've decided to move out,' she said without preamble, directing the announcement

413

at Noel rather than at her mother.

Pauline put her glass down, held her breath and waited.

'What d'you want to be doing that for?' said Noel. 'Sure there's plenty of room here. Isn't there, Pauline?' He looked at Pauline and she raised her eyebrows, allowing herself to exhale slowly. If Yvonne moved out the final obstacle to her leaving Noel would be removed. Her heart pounded in her chest and her head was dizzy with alcohol and possibilities.

'No, Dad,' said Yvonne firmly and her ruddy cheeks went a deeper shade of pink, 'I've decided.'

Noel's face registered hurt, then annoyance. Pauline wondered if the prospect of living in the house with her alone was behind his reaction.

'What're you thinking of?' asked Matt, pleasantly. 'A flat or a house?'

'A house,' she said. 'It's a house.'

'You have somewhere already?' asked Michelle. 'You're a dark horse, Yvonne.' And then she laughed at her own joke. 'Yvonne and her horses, get it?'

Everyone ignored her. Yvonne looked from her father to her sister and then blurted out, as though she could contain herself no longer, 'Yes. You see, I've . . . I've met someone.'

'Glory be!' cried Pauline and Noel glared at her. She put her hand over her mouth to hide her smirk and said, 'Sorry.' So Yvonne had found herself a man. Wonders would never cease. Now Pauline had no reason, no excuse, to stay here any longer. But was she ready to take the next step and actually leave? How would her family react? What would her friends think? Did she really care?

'Who is it?' asked Michelle, eagerly. 'Do we know him?'

Yvonne cleared her throat and her face went an even deeper shade of red.

'Her name is Julie Whitehead. I met her at the stables. She's currently getting divorced from her husband and she's got two children. I'm going to move in with them.'

The colour drained from Noel's face. He wiped his mouth with his napkin, placed it carefully on the table and rose, very slowly and deliberately, to his feet.

'Yvonne,' he said in the tone he used with the grandchildren when they were naughty, 'I don't want to hear any more of this.' Then he left the room and shut the door quietly behind him.

Michelle, Jeanette and Donal looked at each other, shock written all over their faces.

Then Matt spoke. 'Yvonne,' he said, a half-smile playing on his lips as he glanced nervously from Michelle to Jeanette, 'you're not serious.'

Yvonne glared at him and Pauline threw back her head and laughed a long hearty chuckle. Everyone in the room stared at her, even little Sabrina who seemed to understand the gravity of what had just transpired.

'Mum?' said Yvonne, turning the familiar word into an anxious question.

Pauline looked into her daughter's tense face and replied, 'Oh, don't mind me. I just find your

415

father's reaction hilarious.'

If there was one thing Noel McCormick couldn't stand it was what he termed 'sexual perversion'. Yvonne couldn't have socked it to him any harder.

'You do?' said Yvonne, her expression relaxing into a grateful smile. 'You mean you don't mind?'

Pauline looked at her youngest daughter critically and smiled. How could she not have seen what was so obvious? She'd always known Yvonne was different from her sisters but it had never occurred to her that she was a lesbian. Now everything fell into place and made perfect sense.

'No, Yvonne, I don't mind. Not in the slightest. All I really care about is that you're happy.'

'But what about Dad?' asked Yvonne.

Pauline knew exactly what was going through Noel's mind. The scandal that would follow Yvonne's coming out. The family name dragged through the mud. Everybody sniggering and laughing behind his back. As they would do. This was Northern Ireland, conservative and God-fearing, not LA. And only weeks ago she would have thought exactly the same as he. But that was before she'd met Padraig Flynn.

'I wouldn't worry too much about him, Yvonne. The important thing is that you're true to yourself. And if this is what your heart tells you to do then you should do it. If your father can't come to terms with that, then it's his problem, not yours. Now,' she said, rising somewhat unsteadily to her feet, 'I think it's time we paid a bit of attention to those children. It is Christmas Day after all.'

★ ★ ★

Noel sat on the pale green sofa in the sitting-room off the master bedroom. He stared out the window until the view was eclipsed by darkness and he found himself looking at his own reflection in the black glass. Noel prided himself on his perception — he was rarely taken by surprise. But he had not seen this coming and that really irked him. And he was furious that Christmas Day had been so spectacularly spoiled. For he could not go downstairs and face the family, especially the children, when he was so livid with anger.

There was no bloody way any daughter of his was going to set up home with a dike. He shivered with revulsion. Next thing Yvonne would be wearing men's boots, shaving her head and wearing a ring in her nose. Did Yvonne think that she could bring this woman to Noel's home? Did she think that he'd welcome her into the family? There was no bloody way she'd ever set foot in his house. Or Yvonne, for that matter, if she went ahead with this preposterous plan.

She simply couldn't be permitted to do this. It was completely and utterly out of the question. He would never be able to hold his head up in Ballyfergus again. The McCormick name would become synonymous with sniggers and jokes about lesbians. People would pity him and laugh at him behind his back. No, he simply could not allow it.

Noel told himself to calm down and think logically, rationally. He told himself to apply the acumen that had served him so well in his business life. The secret was to find the weak spot and exploit it.

Yvonne was stubborn, always had been. When she said something she meant it and that worried Noel. She would not be persuaded in the way her sisters could be. He would have to find another angle and the obvious one was her passion — horses. The stables and paddock belonged to Noel. He'd given her the money to buy the horses and he knew that her riding business was not viable without his assistance. Noel paid for and ran her car and, living at home, she had little in the way of other expenses. In short, she could not support herself without him.

He heard the door click open and looked up to find Pauline standing there in the doorway. She'd removed the jacket she'd had on earlier, but was still wearing a coral-coloured roll-neck and elegant cream suede trousers.

'Has everyone gone?' he asked.

'Yes.' She came into the room and flopped into the armchair by the window, placed at a right angle to the sofa on which he sat. 'Well,' she said, with an irritating smirk, 'that was a bit of a surprise, wasn't it?'

'You're drunk, Pauline. And I don't know why you think this is so amusing.'

'I'm not drunk, Noel,' she replied still smiling

but her expression was full of malice.

'I just can't believe it,' he said, ignoring her last comment. 'My own daughter a — a lesbian. How did this happen, Pauline? How did this happen to us?'

'So you're looking for someone to blame?'

'No, I'm not,' he said sharply, 'I'm just trying to understand. She must be confused or — or something.'

'She didn't seem confused to me, Noel. She seemed very sure of herself.'

'Well, whatever,' he said, dismissing her opinion. 'We have to stop her — '

'Do we?' interrupted Pauline and Noel glared at her.

'Of course we do,' he said loudly and he struck the arm of the sofa with his balled fist. 'We can't just let her walk out of here and set up home with some bloody lesbian, can we?' Then he paused and, when she did not reply, continued in a calmer tone, 'And there's only one way I can think of to do that. We'll just have to remind Yvonne who's financing that precious little pastime of hers.'

'Force her to choose, you mean, between the stables and her lover? I wouldn't do that if I were you.'

'Why not?' said Noel, piqued at being challenged. 'Have you a better idea?'

'Yvonne's not like you, Noel. She values people more than material things. She'll choose Julie over the stables.'

'No, she won't,' said Noel, smarting at the way Pauline had so casually introduced the name of

Yvonne's lover into the conversation. He stared at his wife who regarded him severely, her lips pressed together into a thin, even line, and asked, 'So what do you think we should do?'

'Let her go.'

'Don't be ridiculous. She's not going to live with another woman and that's that!'

'You can't stop her.'

'But it's — it's wrong,' said Noel, searching for more ammunition to persuade Pauline. 'It's against the laws of nature and the Church.'

Pauline laughed loudly and said in a playful tone, 'Oh, there's a lot worse things she could be.'

She eyeballed him and Noel shifted uncomfortably in his seat. Her manner was unnerving and he didn't like the tack the conversation was taking.

'Did you know about this before today?' he asked, but she carried on as though he hadn't spoken.

'Let me see,' she said, counting on the fingers of her left hand with her right thumb. 'She could be a murderess, or a junkie, or a thief. Or, if she were married, an adulteress. Any of those things, in my opinion, would be much worse.' She paused then, allowing her words to sink in.

Noel watched his wife warily and did not respond. She was treading on dangerous ground — they never, ever discussed his 'other life' as he called it and he wasn't about to start now. It had nothing to do with Pauline and his life here at Glenburn.

'Well, darling,' she said, brightening all of a

sudden, 'are you out tonight?'

Noel relaxed slightly. This, they both knew, was coded language for 'Are you visiting your mistress tonight?' Noel had been planning to slip out later on to see Grainne on the pretext of visiting an old family friend. But something told him he'd better change his plans. Grainne would be annoyed, but it looked like he had work to do here at home.

'No, I don't think so. Not tonight, love,' he said, hoping that this would placate Pauline. Mind you, he'd better get on the phone to Grainne or he'd have hell to pay . . .

Suddenly Pauline stood up and folded the fingers of each hand into one another as if in prayer. Her entire body vibrated and she clasped her hands together so tightly Noel could see the knuckles whiten. Her expression was grim. Determined.

'What?' he said, wondering what on earth was wrong with her.

'Noel,' she said, her voice shaking with emotion, and she paused.

She was obviously more upset about Yvonne than he'd realised.

She continued, 'I'm leaving you now.'

'OK,' he said, glad that this disconcerting conversation had come to an end, 'We can talk later.'

But she stood her ground and said, 'I don't mean the room, you fool. I mean *you*.'

Noel's eyes darted from left to right, as he tried to take in what he had just heard. He did not believe it. His wife couldn't leave him. It was

421

— it was inconceivable.

'Pardon?' he said.

'I'm leaving you,' repeated Pauline, this time more firmly.

'No, you're not,' he said without thinking.

'Right,' she said, turned and walked into their bedroom.

He sat and listened to the sound of a door opening and things being moved around. She could not be serious. Why would she go? Where would she go? He'd have to sort this out now before she did anything silly.

He went into the bedroom where Pauline was hurriedly stuffing clothes into a small Louis Vuitton suitcase on the bed. It was one of a set he'd bought her for their twenty-fifth wedding anniversary, he remembered, and they'd cost him an arm and a leg. The door to her dressing-room was open, the light was on and clothes were strewn all over the floor.

'Pauline,' he said gently, placing a hand lightly on her arm, 'what's all this about? Have I done something to upset you?'

'Upset me?' she shrieked, and Noel recoiled in surprise. Tears were streaming down her face. 'Have you done something to upset me?' she repeated and she thrust her face into his. She bared her teeth, which were clenched in anger, and her cheeks shuddered with the violence of her emotions. Noel had never seen his wife like this in all their time together.

Suddenly she shook her head, went over to the dresser and swiped a collection of bottles into a bag. This she threw on top of the clothes in the

422

suitcase. 'I can't believe that I've put up with you for all these years!' she shouted. 'That I've allowed you to — to demean me the way you have! I can never forgive you for that. Never!'

She slammed down the lid of the suitcase, ignored the bits of clothing sticking out the sides, and snapped it shut. Then she pulled on her suit jacket.

She really meant it. She was actually going to walk out on him.

'Pauline, I'm sorry,' he said, standing in front of her with his hands held out, palms upwards, 'I never meant to hurt you like this. I — I thought that you accepted things the way they were. I thought that you were happy.'

She never looked at him but wiped the tears from her face with a tissue, threw it in the bin, and said flatly, 'I'm going now.' She waited for him to step aside.

'But you have nowhere to go,' he pointed out, refusing to move.

'You think you know everything, don't you?' she said, her voice calm now but full of scorn. Her right eyelid twitched uncontrollably. 'I'm leaving you for someone else, Noel.'

He felt as though someone had punched him in the chest. The shock left him momentarily speechless. The idea that Pauline could possibly be in a relationship with someone was totally foreign to Noel. She was in her sixties, a grandmother for heaven's sake. She was past sex and all that.

'You don't mean you have a — a lover?' he said.

'Don't sound so surprised, Noel. For my one you've had dozens.'

He shook his head. 'I don't believe you.'

'His name is Padraig Flynn,' she said calmly. 'He's an American sculptor living in Ballynahinch. I met him at an exhibition of his work in Belfast. I've been seeing him for over two months.'

'Sleeping with him?' he asked incredulously.

'No, playing bridge. What do you think? Now please move out of my way Noel.'

He stumbled backwards and she hobbled lopsided out of the room, the suitcase banging off her leg. He watched her petite frame disappear through the doorway and knew that there was no point in pursuing her now. He sat down on the bed, suddenly winded, and looked around the room — at the place on the dresser where her perfumes had sat and the dressing-room floor scattered with clothes. She would be back, he was sure of it. For what would he do without her?

★   ★   ★

Noel lay awake most of the night, at first expecting Pauline to come home and then, as the night wore on, realising with some surprise that she wasn't going to. Pauline was one of the essential cornerstones of his life, without which the whole edifice of his existence would crumble and fall. She was his mask of respectability — the graceful, cultured wife he needed to represent the McCormick name in public life.

He had little appetite or talent for the networking and socialising at which Pauline excelled. For so many years he'd relied on her and now the prospect of a future without her was so beyond his comprehension that he could not even imagine it. She simply had to come home. And he would do whatever it took to make her.

Noel finally fell asleep around five o'clock and woke at ten. He pulled on slacks and a polo shirt, not bothering to wash or have a shower. In the kitchen he ferreted for something to eat, made instant coffee and sat at the table and thought about what he should do.

His first priority, he decided, was damage limitation. He must hide the fact that Pauline was gone until he had a chance to find her and bring her back. The staff were off today and tomorrow. Luckily they had no entertaining planned in their own home until the New Year. The children had made other arrangements for the day — both of his married daughters would be seeing their in-laws. And earlier in the week, Yvonne had told them that she would be spending Boxing Day with some of her horsey friends. In light of her announcement yesterday this would almost certainly mean her lover. The anger flared up at once but Noel told himself he didn't have time for that now. He would deal with Yvonne later — right now it suited him if she was gone all day and all night too, for that matter.

'Dad,' said Yvonne's voice from nowhere and Noel jumped. Hot coffee spilt over the side of the cup in his hand, scalding him.

'Damn!' he said loudly and looked up to see Yvonne in full riding gear standing at the back door.

'I forgot my mobile,' she said icily and she strode across the kitchen and into the hallway, leaving muddy footprints on the slate floor.

Noel thought quickly about what he would tell her regarding Pauline. Yvonne came back into the room a few moments later and stood by the kitchen table.

'Where's Mum?' she asked, and blew her nose with a white tissue.

'She had to go up to Limavady to see your great-aunt Doris. The nursing home phoned this morning to say her condition had deteriorated.'

'Oh, poor old dear,' said Yvonne. She stuffed the tissue into the pocket of her Barbour jacket and furrowed her brow, thinking. 'Mum didn't say goodbye to me,' she said at last.

'She was in a hurry. She looked in the paddock but couldn't see you.' He suddenly remembered Pauline's mobile phone and hoped that she had forgotten to take it with her. Yvonne might well try to contact her that way.

'I must've been exercising Rusty down in the bottom field.' Yvonne walked to the back door, turned and added, 'Are you all right?'

Noel realised that, unwashed and unshaven, he must look a mess. He reminded himself that Yvonne would expect him to be furious with her.

'Of course I'm all right,' he growled. 'Why shouldn't I be?'

Yvonne shrugged her shoulders and went outside, slamming the door loudly behind her.

Noel checked the time by the kitchen clock — it was half eleven. He went over to the kitchen window and peered out. He watched Yvonne's back until she rounded the side of the house and was safely out of sight. Then he picked up the kitchen phone, dialled and waited for someone to answer.

'Hello,' said Joseph Doherty's voice.

'Joe, Hi. It's Noel McCormick.'

They exchanged pleasantries about each other's Christmases and then Noel said, 'Listen, Joe, I'll tell you why I'm ringing. I'm afraid Pauline and I aren't going to make it tonight. Pauline's not feeling too good.'

'I'm very sorry to hear that, Joe. Nothing serious I hope.'

'Oh, no,' said Noel quickly, not wanting to cause any alarm that might prompt further enquiries, 'I think it's just a twenty-four hour tummy bug. She's lying down at the moment.'

'Dear, dear. Might have been the turkey.'

'Could have been.'

'Well, give her all our best, Noel.'

'Will do.'

'And we'll have to get together in the New Year when she's feeling better.'

'That'd be great, Joe. Thanks. Bye.'

Noel put the receiver down, pleased with his strategy so far. When Jeanette got wind of Pauline's phantom 'illness' from the Dohertys she'd be on the phone straight away. He'd just have to say that Pauline was in bed asleep and couldn't be disturbed. Now that he'd covered his wife's tracks for the next twelve hours or so, he could concentrate on finding her. He had the rest of the day to sort out this bloody mess. The initial shock he'd felt when Pauline walked out had turned to a simmering anger. How dare she put him through this?

Upstairs in Pauline's study he found her mobile phone sitting on her desk. He sat in her chair and leafed through the telephone directory. There were over two hundred Flynns in the book but none in Ballynahinch. He phoned the dozen or so with 'P' as an initial anyway, and got most of them at home. He asked for Padraig and, when he got a negative response, he pretended he'd dialled the wrong number. Then he looked at the yellow pages. There were two dozen or so entries under *'Sculptors'* but no-one called Flynn. He tried *'Artists'* — again nothing. Noel threw the tome on the floor, sat back in the seat and surveyed Pauline's tidy desk. Then he rifled through all her drawers, found a card index and thumbed through it. After that he searched the top drawer and found a box of business cards all neatly filed by surname. He examined them all but could find no trace of a Padraig Flynn anywhere.

Around one o'clock he heard Yvonne driving off in her car and he was glad to be left alone to think. How on earth was he to find this guy? He knew nothing about him. Some of Pauline's arty friends like Bree Patterson or Barbara Wilson would know of him but he couldn't start phoning people round on Boxing Day. Even he couldn't think of a plausible explanation for that. He could probably do a search on the Internet but he couldn't work the bloody computer. That was what he paid Anne for.

He thought of where he kept the things that he didn't want Pauline to see. The little gifts Grainne had given him over the years — cuf-flinks, ties, and pens — things he could never, of course, use but kept for reasons he wasn't entirely sure of himself. He got up and walked along the hall to the master bedroom where he went straight to Pauline's dressing-room. He started with the built-in drawers, full of expensive underwear and silk scarves and neatly folded cashmere jumpers. He pulled everything out, drawer by drawer, and stuffed the clothes back in again. It felt peculiar being so close to Pauline's most intimate underthings when he hadn't seen her naked in years.

Above the drawers were two long shelves for shoes and he climbed up on the footstool and quickly checked these. Nothing. On the opposite side of the room was a very large built-in wardrobe with a mirrored door that slid into the wall. He pulled it back and surveyed the well-stocked rails. Pauline had taken virtually nothing with her — another reason Noel was confident she would come back. She'd been making a point, that was all. Though, if he wanted her back, he might be forced to rethink his lifestyle. He was in his seventies and he had begun to tire of Grainne. He could be persuaded to give her up if it meant saving his marriage.

He went through all the leather handbags arranged on shelving to the left-hand side of the wardrobe and then the clothes hanging on coat-hangers. He checked the cabinet in her bathroom but found nothing in there either. When he'd scoured every possible hiding place in the house, Noel accepted defeat and sat down to wait. He looked at his watch. It was six thirty. He realised he was hungry — he hadn't eaten anything since breakfast. In the kitchen he made himself sandwiches of cold ham and turkey and noticed that the breakfast things he and Yvonne had used were still littering the table.

He got himself a beer from the fridge, put the food on a tray and went through to the family room where he ate and drank and watched the Boxing Day TV. What, he finally asked himself, what if she didn't come back? What if she'd really meant what she'd said? His life would fall apart without Pauline. He relied on her to run this house, network on his behalf, and keep the family together. He looked at the crusts of bread on the tray and thought that this would be his future without her — a sad, old man having TV dinners on his own every night. Pauline *was* this house — without her it was just four walls and a roof.

He'd underestimated her. He'd thought she had no option but to stay with him and he'd therefore paid her scant attention. And now he was paying the price for that neglect. He'd been a fool and he desperately needed to talk to someone. There was only one person he could turn to in this crisis — Grainne. She was a woman, she'd understand Pauline's thinking and she was smart too. Maybe she could see an angle to all this that he'd overlooked. He knew one thing for certain now. Pauline wasn't coming back — not of her own volition anyway and he couldn't just sit round here waiting for her to contact him.

He got up abruptly, set the tray on the sofa and turned the TV off. He picked up the phone and dialled Grainne's number. No reply. Damn, she must be out. He hung up. Noel walked into the hall and opened the cupboard where the car keys hung inside on hooks. He stared at the keys to the Bentley, took them off the hook and weighed them in his hand. Long ago he and Grainne had made a pact that he would never call unannounced at her house just in case a member of her family was there. But she was out — there was no one at home. In all likelihood she was at the same family gathering as Donal and Michelle. He decided to drive over to Carrickfergus and wait for her to come home. Whereas earlier in the day he'd craved solitude, now he couldn't stand being in the house alone. He took his Crombie overcoat out of the hall closet, put it on and went out into the crisp, cold night.

★ ★ ★

By tradition the entire Mullan clan descended on Donal's parents' home every Boxing Day afternoon. The little terraced house was heaving with Donal's siblings, their spouses or partners and children, and various aunts and uncles. When he counted them all, it came to twenty-seven adults and the same number of offspring. Children screamed and chased each other up and down the stairs, babies cried, and the house reeked of cheap cigarette smoke and alcohol.

Someone had opened the back door to let some air into the hot, stuffy atmosphere — a cooling breeze wafted into the hall where Donal stood at the bottom of the stairs nursing a glass of straight Bushmills whiskey. Christmas was the one time of year when Patrick Mullan splashed out on brand name spirits — the rest of the time he drank the cheapest blended whiskey available in the local supermarket.

'Right, you lot,' shouted Donal's eldest brother, Patrick, to his sons who were playing on the stairs, 'get back up those stairs and don't be bothering us now.'

'But we want some coke and crisps, Dad,' wailed Seamus, the eldest boy of nine.

'Ach, Paddy, it's Christmas. Leave them be,' said a woman's voice from further down the hall.

'Aye, OK, then,' relented Patrick, his chubby face wet with perspiration. 'Go through and get some but I want you straight back up those stairs, boys. And don't be bothering the girls, do you hear?'

But the two boys had already disappeared into the throng, ignoring their father. Patrick's wife, Orla, came up to him and threw her arms around his neck and kissed him full on the lips.

'How are you, gorgeous?' she said and she clung to him drunkenly.

'All the better for seeing you, my girl,' said Patrick, beaming with pleasure, and he grasped his wife by the buttocks and squeezed.

Donal turned away, both embarrassed by the vulgarity of the display and full of envy. The easy intimacy of his brother and his wife only served to highlight the sterility of Donal's marriage.

Just then Michelle came out of the living-room carrying Sabrina, who was chuckling happily, excited by the noise and all the people. Michelle's face was grim with forbearance and she threw a false smile in Patrick and Orla's direction before bearing down on Donal. Molly, who had followed Michelle out of the lounge, wore the same expression on her face as her mother.

'Don,' hissed Michelle, turning her back on Patrick and Orla, 'I can't stay here any longer. The smoke is disgusting. It's making my eyes water and I'm worried about the effect of passive smoking on the children. I think Sabrina's getting asthma. She's started coughing.'

Sabrina gave her father a big, contented smile and Donal said, 'Don't be ridiculous, Michelle. It's only a bit of smoke and it's only once a year. It's not going to do her any harm.'

'Molly wants to go,' said Michelle flatly and she glared at Donal.

He knelt down and took Molly's hand in his own. She wore an ornate silk party dress in rose pink, all bows and flounces with white tights and black patent shoes. The other children wore everyday play clothes — jeans, leggings, jumpers and long-sleeved T-shirts.

'Do you want to go home?' he asked.

Before Molly could speak Michelle answered

for her. 'The other children have been teasing her.'

'No wonder, dressed like that,' replied Donal under his breath.

'What?' snapped Michelle, her head extended on her neck like a turtle's.

Donal sighed and stood up. 'Nothing,' he mumbled, and then added, 'Look, you go home if you want to. But we've only just got here. I'm not going yet.'

He said goodbye to the children and Michelle opened the front door and went outside without saying goodbye to anyone. Her big Mercedes was parked kerbside, out of place amongst the modest, ageing Fords and Vauxhalls that lined the narrow street. Two youths loitered under a street-light — Donal's father had earlier slipped them a few quid to make sure the hubcaps of the Merc and Donal's BMW weren't nicked. Michelle had insisted that they bring both cars — Sabrina was out of sorts, she'd said, she might have to leave early. Donal could see now that she'd planned her early getaway before they'd even got here. Michelle was a snob. She no more belonged in this world than he belonged in hers.

Donal watched Michelle drive off, then closed the door and drank his whiskey. He moved amongst his family, hoping to recapture the closeness he once had to his brothers and sisters. In the kitchen he stood beside his sister Dympna who was talking animatedly to Patrick.

'So how are you, Dympna?' he asked when there was a suitable pause in the conversation.

'Oh, I was just telling Paddy here about the

state of my house. There's damp on the walls of the kids' bedrooms. The wallpaper's falling off and the boys are complaining about the cold. Barry says he's not going to redecorate until the Council do something about the damp. And I've had a leaking tap in my kitchen these past two months and they still haven't sent a plumber in to fix it.'

'It's a bloody crime the rent they're charging,' chimed in Patrick.

'It is that,' said Dympna firmly. 'I'm on the phone to them every other day and all they say is 'You're on our list, Mrs O'Brien. We'll get to you just as soon as we can!''

'It's terrible so it is,' said Patrick and he took a large swig of whiskey from the glass in his hand.

'And how are things with you, Paddy?' said Donal.

'Been out of work these last eight months, Donal.'

'Grainne said something about that on the phone,' lied Donal vaguely. The fact that such a catastrophic event could have happened without his knowledge only served to highlight the great distance between himself and his siblings.

'I'm down at the job centre every other day but there's nothing to be had, not since Dobbins' closed.' At one time Dobbins', the baker's, had been a big employer in the area. Uncle Jimmy used to bring his sister, Donal's mother, broken Paris Buns from work. Donal remembered watching out for him at the front window and the thrill when he saw his uncle walking up the road all dressed in white with a

435

brown paper bag in his big, floury hands.

Orla came up to ask Patrick something and Dympna's youngest, a girl of four, pulled at her mother's skirt and said, 'Ma, I need a wee.'

'Well, come on before you wet yourself,' said her mother irritably. 'You know where the toilet is by now, Bernadette.' Dympna pushed the child urgently in the direction of the stairs and Donal took his chance to move away.

In the lounge doorway he listened to snippets of conversation and wondered at how far he'd come in the last twenty years. He was amazed that he'd ever once been part of this small, insular world. Of the six Mullan offspring, only Donal and Grainne had moved away — the rest still lived in the community they'd grown up in, all within walking distance of this house. Their concerns reflected the working-class world in which they lived and Donal's lifestyle was as foreign to them as if he lived on Mars. He realised for the first time that he would never belong here again. He put the whiskey glass down on the piano near the door. In spite of the four large drinks he'd consumed Donal felt completely sober. It was as though his mind, predisposed tonight to morose thoughts, was immune to the effects of the alcohol.

'Where's Michelle?' said Grainne's voice in Donal's ear, taking him by surprise.

'She's gone home. Sabrina wasn't too well.'

'She looked all right to me.'

'Well, you know Michelle. She doesn't like the children being in a smoky atmosphere. She says passive smoking is dangerous.'

'So is crossing the road,' said Grainne and she took a long drag on the cigarette in her right hand through perfectly painted red lips. She leaned closer to her brother and said, 'I'm away on home now.'

'I think I'll head too,' said Donal but his sister placed her hand on his chest.

'No, I've been sitting in that room all afternoon,' she said, indicating the lounge. 'You haven't even come in to speak to Ma. Sit down with her for a while. Talk to her,' said Grainne and she gave Donal a gentle shove into the room.

'Donal, how are you, son?' said his mother and she patted the empty place on the sofa beside her. Donal kissed his mother and sat down as directed.

'Now,' she said, 'tell me all about you and Michelle and the girls.'

It was after nine o'clock by the time Donal extricated himself from the party, which was now going full swing with a Karaoke machine one of Donal's nieces had got for Christmas. The children would be in bed when he got home and he'd have to face Michelle's chilly reception. She'd berate him for staying at his parents for so long, leaving her to cope with the children alone.

In the car he drove precisely and with care. He reckoned he must be over the legal limit but he'd never felt so sober in his entire life. He knew that the time had come to make the decision that he'd put off for so long. He thought of his two gorgeous little daughters and his heart ached for the heartbreak he was about to cause them now and for the rest of their lives. He gripped the steering wheel tighter and fought back the tears. He needed to talk to someone who was stronger than he for he felt like he would break under the strain of what he was about to do. He thought of Grainne and her strength and independence. He needed some of that tonight. And she was the only person in whom he could confide.

★ ★ ★

The housing development on which Grainne lived consisted of quiet cul-de-sacs radiating from one big crescent-shaped road, 'The Jewel'. Grainne's house was located on 'The Jewel', in a bend in the road. Some hundred yards or so past her home, on the other side of the street, was the entrance to one of the dead-end streets, Craigieburn Court.

Noel drove slowly past her house, which was in darkness, and noted the absence of her car. He pulled into Craigieburn Court and reversed into his usual parking spot — a two-car bay at the end of the street, which was partly screened from the main road by bushes. He never parked directly outside Grainne's home. He turned off the lights and then the car engine, so as not to attract attention from the nearby houses. From this vantagepoint he could see the front of Grainne's property and it wasn't long before her silver car pulled into the drive. She stepped out onto the driveway, which glistened with ice. The red alarm lights flashed as she locked the vehicle, and she went into the house, alone. Noel waited a few minutes, then got out of his car, locked it, put his hands in his pockets and glanced up and down the street. It was deserted. He walked quickly over to Grainne's house and pressed the doorbell.

She answered it almost immediately, still dressed in high heels and a smart black overcoat. The smile fell from her face when she saw him. 'What're you doing here?' she asked, peering over his shoulder. 'You're not supposed to come here unless you phone first. Here — you'd better come in, quick.'

She stepped aside and he went into the warm hallway, saying, 'I know. I'm sorry to land in on you like this. But I was watching from the car — I knew that you were here alone.'

'What, are you turning into a Peeping Tom, Noel?' said Grainne and she laughed throatily. 'Does watching turn you on?'

'Don't be flippant, Grainne.'

She stopped laughing and said, 'You shouldn't have come here without phoning.'

'I did phone but you didn't answer.'

'I'm just back from my Ma's,' she said and stared at him thoughtfully. 'Why don't you come into the lounge and I'll get you a drink?'

He followed her into the comfortable room. She went over to the window, peered out the Venetian blinds, and then closed the curtains. He watched her switch on the gas fire, take off her coat and throw it on an armchair. She was wearing a tight black skirt and red silk shirt. She went into the kitchen and came back with two gin and tonics. She took a large gulp of her drink and watched while he did the same — it was very strong, just what he needed.

'What's wrong, Noel? You look . . . well, you look bloody awful.'

'It's Pauline,' said Noel and he faltered, not knowing where to begin. 'She's left me,' he said simply and he sat down abruptly on the edge of the sofa.

'Left you?' said Grainne, her voice full of interest. She sat down on the sofa beside him. 'What d'you mean 'left you'?' she said eagerly.

'Exactly what I said,' he replied and he related the whole sorry saga of events that had taken place over the last twenty-four hours. Grainne listened carefully, without interruption, and when he'd finished speaking she said, 'Well, Pauline's certainly turned the cards on you, hasn't she? Who would've thought!' She shook her head and laughed. 'I've got to hand it to you, girl,' she said, raising her glass as though Pauline was in the room with them. 'I never thought you had it in you.'

Noel felt that Grainne's mirth was entirely inappropriate and he moved the conversation on. 'Well, I need her to come home,' he said, sharply, 'preferably before anyone's noticed she's gone. But the thing is I don't know where this sculptor lives.'

'Oh, Noel,' said Grainne, cocking her head to one side and regarding him thoughtfully, 'if you want my opinion, I'd say she's not coming back.'

'Why do you say that?' he asked quickly.

'Because what she's done is so out of character, I'd say she's been thinking about it for a long time. This isn't something she's decided

440

on overnight. Look what she's giving up to be with this man. Her home, status, wealth, not to mention disrupting the entire family. Her daughters might never forgive her.'

'I never thought about it like that,' said Noel, the panic rising. He'd come here for help, for reassurance — not to have his worst fears confirmed.

'So that'll leave an empty place by your side,' mused Grainne, speaking more to herself than to Noel. She stared, unfocused, at a point somewhere beyond his left shoulder.

'I don't follow you,' said Noel, a different kind of panic now enveloping him.

'Well,' she said briskly, refocusing on his face, 'you've said often enough how much you love me, Noel. I want you to promise that you'll marry me when all this settles down. It's my turn to play Lady of the Manor.'

'Don't be ridiculous, Grainne,' said Noel and he stood up and slammed his glass down on a side table. 'I can't do that! Anyway, Pauline'll be back and things will go on the way they are. You've never complained before. You're happy with our arrangement, aren't you?'

'Not when there's something better on offer.'

'There isn't anything better on offer,' he said coldly and then, more reasonably. 'And there's the children to think of. How would they react to you taking their mother's place?'

'Your children are big lumps of adults, Noel. I'm sure they'd be able to cope with me on the scene. And Pauline won't be coming back. You know that as well as I do. Quite frankly, I don't know how she put up with the situation for as long as she did.'

'But what about Donal? You don't want him to find out about us, do you?' said Noel to stall her while his brain searched for a more potent excuse to deflect her.

'He doesn't need to find out about us. Our history. You can court me. Do it properly, up front. Leave it, say, six months from now and then we can start to see each other publicly. I could have moved in by . . . let's see, by next Christmas. There's no shame in living together before we get married. As soon as the divorce comes through . . . '

'There'll be no divorce, Grainne. We're Catholics. Remember?'

'A civil divorce, you eejit. And we'll just get wed in a registry office. Oh, don't look at me like that. That's rich, that is. You coming over all sanctimonious about your marriage when you've been screwing around since practically the day and hour you married Pauline.'

Noel stepped back a few paces and stared at his mistress. His whore. Grainne Mullan his wife? Never! She wasn't the sort of woman he could be seen with in public. There was no doubt about it, she was a fine-looking woman, but common, common as muck. That was part of her attraction as a mistress but never as a wife.

Grainne stood up and went over to the gilded overmantel mirror where she examined her reflection. 'That'll give me time to adapt my image a little,' she said and ran her fingers through her hair and pouted her lips. 'Maybe tone down the hair colouring a bit and wear less make-up. And I'll need lots of new clothes.'

Noel swallowed and counted to ten before he spoke. 'Grainne,' he said, speaking very slowly so that there would be no danger of any misunderstanding, 'it's out of the question. It is completely and absolutely out of the question. I will never marry you.'

She turned on him then, her eyes ablaze with anger and she hissed rather than spoke. 'If you don't promise me, I'll go to the papers! I'll tell them everything about our relationship and how long it's been going on. I'll make up lots of sordid little escapades. And I'll tell them about your little business scams too. Like your pact with terrorists in exchange for immunity for your workers on army bases and the like. I wonder what the authorities would make of that?'

Noel groaned. He'd told her about that? How could he have been so stupid! In all the years he'd been screwing around he'd never indulged in pillow talk. But he'd been with Grainne a long time — nearly ten years. He must've got careless.

'You wouldn't wash all your dirty linen in public, Grainne. What would people think of you?'

'I've a lot less to lose than you Noel. Think about it. If I don't take Pauline's place, someone else will. And she might not be as tolerant of your little bit on the side as Pauline was. And where will that leave me?'

The sound of a car pulling into the driveway made them both freeze. The engine died and Grainne rushed over to the window. She pulled back the curtain and peered through the Venetian blind.

'Oh my God,' she said, 'what the fuck is he doing here?'

★   ★   ★

Outside the night had turned icy cold. Pauline snuggled in closer to Padraig's hairy chest, her head resting on his left arm, and stared into the fire. They lay in the sitting-room on a makeshift bed of layered duvet covers, which served as a mattress, and pillows taken from Padraig's bed. The well-stoked fire provided the only light in the room and it sent out a fierce heat that made Pauline's face glow. Beside them on the floor lay an empty bottle of port and the remains of a supper of cheese and crackers and fruit. Pauline felt reckless and daring — sensations she had never experienced in her youth when she'd been too prim to engage in anything as decadent as this, even with her husband.

The farmhouse was draughty and cold and here Pauline felt so much more in tune with nature than she did in her triple-glazed, centrally heated mansion. The furry animal print throw was sensuous against her naked skin and she was so contented she felt like purring.

'You've no regrets?' said Padraig and guilt crept over Pauline like a shadow.

'No, but I really should phone him.'

'Why? From what you've told me, Pauline, about the way he's been carrying on all these years, you don't owe him a damn thing.'

'No,' she replied slowly, 'but I'm still his wife and I've the children to think of. This is going to come as quite a shock to them.'

He absorbed this and then, after a little time had elapsed said, 'Pauline. You're not going to go back to him, are you?'

Pauline opened her mouth to speak but he put a finger to her lips. 'No,' he said, 'don't answer that. I want to show you something first. Here, let me help you up.'

He stood up then, his naked body glowing in the firelight and held out his hands to her. She took them and he pulled her gently to her feet. The throw fell off her body and she shivered in the cold air.

'Where are we going?' she asked.

'Outside. To the studio.'

'But Padraig, it's absolutely freezing.'

'Here, put this around you,' he said. He picked up the throw that had fallen to the floor and wrapped it across her shoulders. She grasped it in her fists and pulled it tightly against her skin.

'We can't go outside like this,' she said, suddenly aware of her vulnerability. 'We'll catch our death.'

He laughed then and said, 'I don't think we're really going to die. It's not that cold.'

'It's just a saying, Padraig. Don't take it literally.'

Padraig, still smiling, put his hands on her shoulders and guided her through to the hall where he pulled on an overcoat and helped her into a pair of wellington boots before putting a pair on himself. He opened the front door.

'I'm not sure this is a good idea,' said Pauline doubtfully, peering into the absolute blackness outside.

'It'll not take long.' He took a flashlight from the shelf above the coats and led the way. The night was cold but calm and they were at the studio door within seconds. Padraig fumbled with the lock, opened the door and pulled a switch to the left of the door. The room was flooded with bright, yellow light.

Pauline shuffled into the studio behind him and kicked the door shut with her foot. Her breath came in hot white clouds of steam and cold air bellowed up underneath the throw. Padraig stood beside a plinth in the middle of the room on which something stood, shrouded with a white sheet. From the height and shape of the object, Pauline surmised that it was some sort of small statue.

'This is what I wanted to show you,' he said, and he pointed at the mysterious object.

'Go on then,' said Pauline and nodded.

He took an end of the sheet, tugged gently and unveiled a small bronze statue about eighteen inches tall. It was of a naked woman, standing upright, her weight resting on one foot, the other leg cocked slightly.

Pauline shuffled forward a few feet across the dusty floor and looked more closely. 'Padraig!' she gasped and put a furry fist up to her mouth. 'It's me!'

'What do you think of it?' he said and crossed his arms, one resting on the other. He raised an index finger to his lips and watched her.

Pauline examined the statuette, fascinated. Every flaw in her body was perfectly recreated in it — the pendulous breasts, the saggy bottom, and the creases across her stomach. It even had tiny wrinkles at the elbows and knees. But the figurine captured too her still-trim waist, her slender calves and, in her smiling face, her fine bone structure and her loveliness. It was an honest portrayal of a woman past her prime. And yet it was sensuous and it was beautiful.

'My God, Padraig. I can't believe it. It's — it's exquisite,' she said at last and looked at him, tears welling up in her eyes.

He grinned and said, 'I told you that you were beautiful.'

'I can't believe it,' she said, looking at the statue again, and shaking her head.

'I did it for you, Pauline. In honour of you. Because you are the most beautiful thing I've ever had.' He paused then and stared at the figurine for a few seconds before continuing, 'And if you leave me then I will always have this to remind me of what I once had. And lost.'

Tears slid down Pauline's face and she went over to him and looked up into his face and said, 'Oh, Padraig. I'm not going to leave you.'

He looked at her without blinking and said, 'I can't pretend that I haven't had a lot of women in my time. I have and I've loved them all and lived with some of them for a long time. But what we have is special, Pauline. I love you and I want to spend what's left of my life with you.'

'You asked me earlier what my decision was,' said Pauline, fighting back the tears so that she could speak with the gravitas she felt inside. 'I made my decision last night when I left Glenburn. I won't be going back.'

Padraig bowed his head. Pauline opened her arms and enveloped him against her naked skin.

★ ★ ★

By the time he got to the street where Grainne lived, Donal was so preoccupied with his thoughts that he drove right past her house and had to turn into the next cul-de-sac to reverse the car. As he did so his headlights shone on a large blue car tucked into one of the communal parking bays that were situated at the end of every street. It was a Bentley, just like Noel McCormick's. Strange, thought Donal, who around here would have the money to drive a car like that? Then he looked at the numberplate and put his right foot on the brake, sharply. The Bentley bore Noel's private registration, NMK 1. As the car came to a halt he depressed the clutch to the floor with his left foot.

What was Noel's car doing here? Did he know someone who lived in this estate? It didn't seem very likely to Donal. Perhaps someone else had taken his car tonight — Yvonne or Pauline. But if so what would either of them be doing in this area?

Donal frowned, completed the reversing manoeuvre and brought the car to a standstill in Grainne's drive beside his sister's silver Mazda. He got out and looked across the street to where Noel's car was only just visible, almost completely obscured by overhanging branches and bushes. As though care had been taken to conceal it.

Noel had met Grainne once, Donal remembered, at his wedding to Michelle. He looked at the house where lights were on in the hall and the lounge. Was it possible that Noel McCormick was here, visiting his sister? But what on earth for? He shook his head, clearing his brain of these unlikely notions, and pressed the doorbell.

He had to press it once more and wait for several minutes before Grainne opened the door to him. 'Hello, Donal,' she said and a hand shot up to her throat. She came out and stood on the threshold, pulled the door almost closed behind her and crossed her arms. 'What're you doing here?'

'I need to talk to you.'

'What about?'

He sighed and said, 'Everything, Grainne. Me. Michelle. The kids.'

He placed a foot on the doorstep, expecting her to step aside and let him in. But she stood where she was and said, 'Look, it's late, Donal. Why don't we meet up and talk about it tomorrow?'

He raised his head in surprise, looked into her face and said, 'But I need to talk to you now, Grainne. And it's only ten o'clock.'

He felt compelled to share his burden immediately. It was not something that he could sleep on — it was not something that could wait. His entire future and his happiness depended on his next course of action. He found himself suddenly irritated. 'Grainne,' he said in a pained voice, 'this is important to me. I am your brother for God's sake.'

She stared at him and her mouth moved but no sound came out.

'Listen, Grainne. Are you going to leave me standing out here in the cold like a door-to-door salesman?'

She cleared her throat and said, 'Now's not a good time, Donal.'

'Do you have someone with you?' he asked. He stood on his tiptoes and peered over his sister's shoulder. The hallway was empty.

'No,' she said and pulled at the lobe of her right ear.

He stared at her and said, 'I saw Noel McCormick's car parked over there. Is he in here? With you?'

To Donal's amazement she nodded slowly and even in the dim porch light he could see her face turn bright red.

'You'd better come in,' she said softly and bowed her head. He followed her inside, shut the door behind him and went into the lounge. Noel was standing in front of the fire — his hands hung loosely by his sides and his feet were planted firmly, two feet apart, on the rug. He started when he saw Donal, looked at Grainne and said, 'What the . . . ' Then he squared up to Donal, his stance suddenly confrontational.

Donal had never seen him look so dishevelled in all the time he'd known him. His hair was standing up in little grey tufts, he was unshaven and he looked as though he'd dressed in the dark. His overcoat hung open to reveal a red polo shirt teamed with brown slacks.

'What are you doing here?' said Donal, remembering that Jeanette had phoned Michelle earlier to tell her that her mother was ill. 'Shouldn't you be at home with Pauline? I thought she wasn't well.'

Grainne went over and stood beside Noel and linked her arm in his. Noel did not acknowledge her presence — the arm she had attempted to claim still hung limply by his side. Grainne lifted her head and stared at Donal — her chin was tilted slightly upwards, her expression defiant. Donal fought against the comprehension that crept over him. Surely to God not Grainne and Noel McCormick! Please God, don't let this be true!

He swallowed and said, 'You'd better tell me what's going on here.'

'Noel and I,' said Grainne and halted. She glanced at Noel's stony features, took courage from them and went on, 'We are . . . we see each other.'

'What? You and Noel?' he said stupidly.

Grainne nodded and Noel said nothing but continued to stare at Donal. His expression was inscrutable, as always.

'You're Noel's mistress?' Donal asked his sister, because the idea was so preposterous that his brain simply refused to accept it.

'If you want to put it that way. Yes.'

Donal's legs buckled under him and he sat down on the edge of the armchair behind him. His sister was Noel McCormick's whore. It

451

couldn't be true. He didn't want it to be true. He looked at the two of them standing there together and he couldn't help but imagine them in bed together — he averted his eyes and looked at the pale apricot-coloured carpet.

'But when? How?' he said quietly.

'We've been together ten years, Donal,' said Grainne. 'We met at your wedding to Michelle.'

Donal cast his mind back but could remember nothing remarkable about that day — only the embarrassing squabble between his other two sisters. Grainne would have been in her thirties then — young enough to have a second chance. She could have married again, had children, had a fucking life. Instead she'd wasted the last ten years on this tosser.

'So this house and the car — it all came from you,' Donal said, addressing Noel and he had the grace to look embarrassed.

'That's right,' he said and cleared his throat, 'I've been good to your sister, Donal. I've treated her well.'

'Treated her well,' repeated Donal, a flash of anger bringing him to his feet. He leapt over to Noel and grabbed him by the lapel of his expensive coat and spat words into his face. 'You think being your whore is a fucking privilege, don't you? Well, I've had enough of you and your fucking family, Noel! A Mullan isn't good enough to marry your precious daughter. Not good enough to enter the family firm. But a Mullan's plenty good enough when all you want is a good fuck!'

He let go of Noel and shoved him backward

towards the fire. Noel steadied himself by reaching out and grabbing the mantelpiece.

'I've done nothing wrong, Donal,' said Noel coolly. 'Your sister is an adult. She's free to make her own choices about how she lives.'

'And so am I,' retorted Donal. 'I'm leaving Michelle. And guess what? I have a mistress too. So how do you think your precious daughter will feel when she finds out about that?'

Noel's eyelids flickered and the corners of his mouth twitched — otherwise there was no outward sign of distress. But Donal knew from these indicators that he had got him where it hurt. Noel's love for his daughters was his first weakness — the second his love for women. Donal waited for Noel to speak again but he stood there and said nothing. He had the air about him of a man defeated.

'Fuck you Noel,' said Donal and he turned and walked out of the room.

'Donal! Donal! Wait!' cried Grainne and she caught up with him in the hallway and placed a hand on his arm.

'How could you, Grainne?' he said, shaking her off. Before she had time to answer he added, 'I thought that you'd worked for all this. I thought you had a great job with the civil service. What the hell do you do in City Hall?'

'I'm a clerical assistant. I file things and answer the phone.'

Donal shook his head. 'I thought you'd dragged yourself out of the gutter we came from and made something of your life. I idolised you. You were my hero. And then to find out that you're just a — a well-paid prostitute. And Noel McCormick of all the men! Jesus Christ, Grainne,' he said and clenched his fists in rage, 'you could have done so much with your life! Why did you throw it away?'

'You don't know what it was like for me being on my own, after Kevin. I didn't want to get married again. I didn't want to get hurt again. I'm happy with this arrangement. Noel loves me.'

'Don't be such a bloody fool, Grainne,' said Donal and he turned his face to the wall then for he did not want her to see him crying. He wiped the tears away viciously with the sleeve of his coat. 'Move out of my way,' he growled and she did so immediately. If she hadn't he would have pushed her. How could she sink so low? The sister he loved and adored. The woman he was closer to than his own mother. And how could she be so stupid as to believe that Noel McCormick felt anything for her? The man was absolutely ruthless. She would be thrown aside when he no longer had a use for her.

Outside in the car Donal fumbled with the keys and eventually got them in the ignition. He blinked hard several times, trying to focus, and then reversed blindly onto the road. He rammed the gearstick into first gear and drove off as fast as he could, the tyres screeching on the tarmac. There was no one left in the world that he could trust. Except Amy.

12

Noel drove the car home with the realisation that the situation was now out of his control. Donal would go home, tell Michelle about Noel's affair with Grainne, and then it would spread through the rest of the family like wildfire. He should have known that Grainne would pull a stunt like that.

'Get rid of him,' he'd instructed and she'd nodded and gone to answer the door.

The next thing Noel knew Donal was in the room and it was all over. In the face of Noel's intransigence Grainne had used Donal's arrival to expose him, knowing that it supported her ultimate aim. And he knew too that she would have no hesitation in carrying out the rest of her threats.

For the second time in twenty-four hours Noel realised that he had underestimated a woman — Grainne had him well and truly by the balls. But all was not lost, he reminded himself. If he got Pauline to come home Grainne would have to accept the status quo, just as she had done for so many years. In her own way she had a strong sense of morality, and a soft spot for Noel's ever-suffering wife. She would never force him to leave Pauline for her. As for the rest of the family, he would apologise, say he was sorry and promise never to philander again — they would forgive him, he was sure of it. And then everything could carry on as before, although he would have to replace Grainne soon. It would cost him dearly but she had become too dangerous.

It was nearly midnight when he got home. He shut and locked the door wearily, hung up his coat and the car keys and then the phone rang. He looked at the number displayed in the little screen and did not recognise it. He picked up the handset and put the phone to his ear.

'Pauline?' he said.

'Yes, it's me. Where have you been, Noel? I've been trying to get you all night. You weren't answering your mobile.'

'I had to go out. Listen, Pauline, we need to talk.'

'Yes, we do,' she said. 'That's why I'm phoning. I'll come by tomorrow afternoon.'

'Good. That's great. Listen, Pauline, are you all right? I've been worried about you.'

'Really? Well you've no need to worry about me, Noel. I've never been better in my entire life.' She paused then and added, 'What have you told the girls?'

'Nothing. They were all busy doing other things today. They never noticed you were gone.'

'Well, we'll have to put that right. I'll see you tomorrow at two o'clock.'

She hung up and Noel put the phone down, hoping that Pauline's bravado was just a front. She did seem decidedly, well, forthright. But Noel knew he was much more persuasive face-to-face than on the phone. He was still certain he could persuade her to come home.

Upstairs he checked in Yvonne's room but she was not there. He went to bed and thought about his confrontation with Donal Mullan. He remembered what Donal had said about leaving Michelle and wondered if he'd really meant it or if he'd only said it to get back at him. He'd have a bloody nerve to leave Michelle — she was responsible for dragging him out of the gutter and introducing him to a whole new, sophisticated way of life.

Personally Noel would love to see the back of Donal, but Michelle still thought the sun shone out of his arse. And Noel knew that she would be heartbroken if he left her. Noel promised himself that, if Donal Mullan hurt his daughter, he would be his sworn enemy for the rest of his life. With these troubling thoughts swimming round in his mind Noel finally fell asleep.

At precisely two o'clock the next day the doorbell rang and Noel rushed to answer it but Yvonne beat him to it. Pauline was on the doorstep, dressed in the same clothes she'd worn the day before.

'Mum!' said Yvonne, standing back to allow her mother entry. 'How's great-aunt Doris?'

'Pardon?' said Pauline, stepping over the threshold and raising an eyebrow at Noel.

'Did you have to stay overnight?' said Yvonne and, when her mother did not immediately answer, she added, 'And what are you doing ringing the bell, Mum? Did you forget your key?'

'Never mind all that now, Yvonne,' said Noel hastily, stepping between them. 'Your mother and I need to talk. Come on in here, Pauline,

457

please.' He opened the door to the drawing-room, which was little used unless they had company.

Yvonne looked at her father in amazement. 'What's going on?' she asked, but Noel led Pauline into the drawing-room and shut the door in her face.

'Great-aunt Doris, Noel?' said Pauline running a hand over the back of a sofa. 'That's a good one. What did you tell her? That Doris was on her death bed?'

'Something like that,' mumbled Noel and then, more clearly, 'Would you like a drink?'

'It's a bit early for that, Noel,' she replied in a clipped tone.

Noel poured himself a very large scotch. He took a large drink then turned around and said, 'It's good to see you back, Pauline.'

'I'm not back, Noel. I'm visiting.'

Ignoring this remark he said solicitously, 'Here, please. Sit down.'

She perched on the edge of the sofa and said, 'We need to get the children together tonight, on their own without husbands or children. I want to tell them face-to-face before they hear about this from someone else.'

'Steady on, Pauline. I know you feel very — very aggrieved but we need to take a little bit of time over this. We don't want to be rushing into anything. Or do anything we'll regret.'

'I'm not rushing into anything, Noel. And you're wasting your breath if you think you can talk me out of this. I know exactly what I'm doing.'

'It's a big step moving in with someone, Pauline. You've only known this guy, what, for a matter of weeks? You know nothing about his background, his history, his reliability.'

'I know all I need to know, Noel. He loves me.'

Noel's first instinct was to laugh but he resisted in the knowledge that he would completely blow it if he resorted to ridicule. 'But what do you know about his financial position? What sort of a life can he offer you?' he said and cast his gaze pointedly around the room.

'That's why I'm here to see you, Noel. I'm prepared to go quietly if you give me a fair settlement. As soon as the holidays are over I'll get my lawyer to contact yours. It's in both our interests if this is settled amicably. But if you try and pull a fast one on me, Noel, I'll take you to the cleaners.'

Taken by surprise at the speed and animosity with which Pauline was pushing matters along, Noel did not answer at once. When he did at last speak he choose his words carefully.

'Pauline, love,' he said gently, 'have you given any thought to what you'd be giving up? Without my money behind you, you'd soon be dropped by your charities and committees. You'd be a social outcast. And how would you afford the lifestyle you're used to? The clothes and the holidays and all the other expensive trappings?'

'There are more important things in life than money, Noel,' she said sadly. 'Though I don't expect you to understand that. You think you can buy everything including people. But the one thing that really matters can't be bought and that's love. Without love, Noel, everything is meaningless.'

Pauline's words did not make any sense to Noel but he knew that the situation required extreme measures if he was to stand any chance of getting her back. He set his drink down, went over and sat beside her on the sofa. 'I've been a fool,' he said. 'Pauline, I don't want you to leave me. I need you. I know I haven't always treated you right but I can change.'

'But you don't love me,' she said.

'I do, Pauline,' he protested.

'No, I don't think so,' she replied and stared at him so intently that he had to look away. She went on, her voice full of sadness, 'I don't honestly think you're capable of truly loving anyone, Noel, except, of course, your children but that's a different sort of love. You're too self-centred to completely love a woman. And as for all this,' she said glancing round the room, 'well, I don't want it. I'd rather take my chance with Padraig. I just wish I'd had the courage to take this step a long time ago.'

'But you can't, Pauline. What will I do without you?' he said, realising that he was losing the battle.

She smiled and said evenly and without rancour, 'Take comfort in the arms of your mistress. There's nothing stopping you now, Noel. You can see whomever you want, when you want. Though my presence never stopped you doing that before, did it?' Then she leaned towards him and gently laid her left hand on his right cheek. 'We had some good times, Noel,' she whispered, her eyes full of tears and her face so close to his that he could feel her soft breath on his face, 'and we made three wonderful daughters together. I wouldn't change that part for the world.'

He put his hand onto hers and pulled it round to his mouth. He closed his eyes and kissed the palm of her hand. A single tear crept out of the corner of his left eye. Pauline pulled her hand slowly away from his and stood up.

'Now,' she said, the softness gone from her voice, 'I'm going upstairs to get the rest of my things. Then I'll be back at eight o'clock. Are you going to phone the girls or shall I?'

'Please, Pauline. You're making a big mistake.'

'Noel, can't you see that it's over? Now go and make those calls,' she said and left him alone in the room.

At eight o'clock Noel and his three daughters were assembled in the drawing-room waiting for Pauline.

'I hope this isn't going to take long, Dad,' said Michelle, and she looked at her watch. 'I was supposed to be going to a party tonight.'

Noel took a swig of scotch and said nothing. Donal hadn't told Michelle about him and Grainne — yet. He was quite certain of this because Michelle was such a transparent person that, had she known, she would have found it impossible to hide the fact. It was clear too, from her demeanour, that Donal hadn't carried out his threat to leave her either. For the time being at least he didn't have to worry about Michelle.

'Matt and I are supposed to be going out for

461

dinner,' said Jeanette. 'Where's Mum anyway? Is she out somewhere? I thought she wasn't well.'

'What makes you think she's ill?' interjected Yvonne, shaking her head. 'She had to go up and see great-aunt Doris yesterday morning. The nursing home phoned to say that she was bad. Mum only got back at lunchtime today. But she went straight out again with packed suitcases and wouldn't say where she was going.'

'Did she go back up to Limavady to see her aunt?' asked Michelle, directing the question at her father.

'But she couldn't have,' said Jeanette, looking at Noel for confirmation. 'She was in bed sick all day yesterday, wasn't she, Dad? That's why you didn't go to the Dohertys last night, wasn't it?'

Noel's head was thumping. He wished they would all stop whinging like a pack of five-year-olds. 'Girls,' he said and raised his hand in the air to silence them, 'you'll have to be patient. Your mother's not ill and she'd not gone up to Limavady. You'll find out everything when she gets here.'

Just then the doorbell went, everyone looked at Noel and he went out into the hall and let Pauline into the house. Without speaking she took off her coat and, when she handed it to him, he noticed that her whole arm was shaking. She was elegantly dressed as always in a tailored grey trouser suit, heels and pale pink rollneck. She walked towards the drawing-room, pausing briefly before crossing the threshold. Noel draped her coat over the banister, followed her into the drawing-room and shut the door behind him.

★ ★ ★

When she came into the room, Pauline's heart was pounding and the palms of her hands were wet with perspiration. She was met by three perplexed and, in the case of Michelle and Jeanette, rather cross expressions. All three of her daughters were sitting down and, for a few seconds, Pauline hesitated, unsure whether to sit or to stand. Then, deciding that what she had to say was really a formal announcement, she went and stood in front of the empty fireplace. Noel went over to the drinks cabinet, poured himself a drink without offering her one, and stood there watching.

'Hello, Jeanette. Yvonne. Michelle,' she said, looking into the faces of each as she said her name. For a few seconds she was taken aback by the thought that these fully grown women had grown inside her — that she'd given birth to them and nurtured them to adulthood. Each one was a miracle.

'Mum,' said Michelle, in an irritated voice, 'can you please tell us what the hell is going on?'

Pauline cleared her throat and looked at Noel. He folded his arms with a glass of scotch in his right hand, and leaned against the wall.

'Your father and I have decided to separate,' she said, her voice barely audible.

Jeanette said, 'What?'

'Your father and I have decided to separate,'

she repeated, her voice louder and more assured, and Michelle immediately burst into tears. Her other daughters looked at each other — Jeanette's expression was one of horror, while Yvonne sat with her mouth slightly open, staring wide-eyed at her mother.

Pauline went over to Michelle and sat down beside her on the sofa and put her arm around her daughter's broad shoulders. 'There, there, now,' she said, placating her like she did when she was a child, 'it's not the end of the world, Michelle. Here, wipe your nose.' She pulled a tissue from her pocket and offered it to her daughter.

'But you can't, Mum,' said Jeanette, her tone that of a thwarted child.

Pauline looked into Jeanette's face and said, 'You have to understand that it's very complicated, Jeanette. Your father and I haven't been happy for a long time. And now I've met someone that I love and I'm going to live with him.'

'You mean you're leaving Glenburn?' said Jeanette.

'That's right.'

'When?'

'I've already left. I moved out last night and came back for the rest of my things this afternoon.'

'So you never went to see great-aunt Doris?' asked Yvonne.

'No, that was your father's invention,' she said and looked pointedly at Noel.

'But where will you live?' said Jeanette.

'I've told you. With the man I love.'

Jeanette looked embarrassed and glanced at her sisters for support. 'But Mum, what will people think? You can't just run off with . . . with someone.'

'I already have, Jeanette.'

'But who is he? How did you meet?' asked Yvonne.

Pauline told them briefly about Padraig Flynn — how she'd met him and where she would be living. She put four small white business cards down on the table and said, 'That's where I can be contacted.' They all stared at them but nobody touched them.

Suddenly, Michelle, who had remained mute throughout this discussion, leapt to her feet. 'But what about Daddy?' she cried. 'You can't just walk out and leave him here all on his own! He needs you, Mum! We all need you.'

Pauline glanced up at Noel, saw his face redden, and then he went and stood at the patio doors with his back to the room, looking out. Resentment welled up inside her. Noel had killed this marriage, not she, and yet she was the one having to break the bad news, having to take all the blame.

'I think you'll find that your father has all his needs taken care of,' said Pauline tightly.

'What do you mean by that?' said Michelle, defensive on her father's behalf. Pauline glanced at Noel who had turned around to face the room. He looked at her, his eyes full of pleading and her heart softened. She knew that he could not bear to lose the admiration, respect and love

465

of his daughters. If she told them the truth, they might hate him — at the very least they would never look at him in the same light as before. Whether he wanted to come clean to them or not, was his decision, not hers.

'All I'm saying is that you don't need to worry about your father. He's perfectly capable of looking after himself. Aren't you, Noel?'

His lifted his chin slightly to indicate his gratitude that she had not told on him. 'Your mother's right, girls. I'll be OK,' he said in a stoic voice.

Pauline stood up then and said, 'I think I'd better go now and give you all time to think about this. I'll give you a call tomorrow. In spite of what's happened between your father and me, I'm still your mother and I will always be there for you. I love you. And I hope that in time you'll be able to come to terms with this.'

Yvonne came over then and threw her arms around her mother, taking Pauline by surprise, and almost knocking her over. Of all of her children, Yvonne was the least given to public displays of affection. 'Good luck, Mum,' she said, burying her face in Pauline's neck, her voice husky with emotion.

Pauline stoked the back of her daughter's head and swallowed to hold back the tears. 'Thanks, love. You'll come and see me up at the farmhouse, won't you?'

Yvonne pulled back and nodded. 'Of course I will, Mum.'

Pauline glanced over Yvonne's shoulder at the resentful faces of her other two daughters and decided not to ask them the same question. She suspected their responses would not be so forgiving. Time, everyone said, was a great healer, and it was going to take a long time to put things right between Pauline and her daughters.

★ ★ ★

When Michelle got home and found Donal in the family room watching TV she burst into tears again.

'Jesus, Michelle,' he said, rising quickly to his feet, 'what's wrong?'

He switched the TV off using the remote, guided her over to an armchair where she sat down, and patted her arm awkwardly. Fresh waves of tears cascaded down Michelle's cheeks.

'What on earth did your parents tell you?' he asked. 'Has somebody died?'

'No, no, nothing like that,' Michelle managed between tears and Donal thrust a box of tissues in her lap.

'What then?'

'Mum,' said Michelle and she paused to dab her face with a tissue and compose herself, 'Mum's left Dad to go and live with some American sculptor. Can you fucking believe it? A fucking artist? At her age.'

'Oh,' said Donal mildly and he went and sat down on his seat again and rested his chin on his hand, thinking. But Michelle could tell that he was deeply shocked — his face was ghastly white and his eyes darted back and forth across the carpet as if searching for something very tiny that he'd dropped there earlier.

'I can't believe it either,' said Michelle. 'It's just awful, isn't it? Glenburn will never be the same without Mum there. And poor Daddy! How could she do that to him?'

Donal raised an eyebrow at this but said nothing and Michelle continued, 'They've been married for nearly forty years, you know. How can she just walk out on a marriage, on all of us?'

'She's walked out on Noel, not on the rest of you.'

'Well, that's how it feels. Glenburn is our home.'

'I thought this was your home,' observed Donal, without emotion.

'You know what I mean,' said Michelle and she flushed slightly. 'Glenburn is the McCormick family home. We grew up there. It's all I've ever known.'

'Well,' said Donal and he sighed, 'there's always two sides to every story, Michelle. You don't know what's gone on between your parents over the years.'

'And you do?'

Donal shrugged and Michelle said, 'What could Dad have done that's so awful he deserved this? Oh, I know he can be a bit bossy at times and sometimes Mum and Dad bickered but it was never anything serious. Not enough to break up a marriage.'

'Maybe they just fell out of love,' said Donal, and he sat upright all of a sudden and gripped the arms of the chair. The tendons stood out on the back of each hand and the muscles in his jaw tightened, as though he was bracing himself for something.

'I don't believe in falling out of love,' said Michelle carefully and, without giving Donal the opportunity to respond, said, 'I think you love one person and you love them always. No matter what. If you stop loving them then it means that you never truly loved that person in the first place.'

'I . . . think . . . ' said Donal very slowly and then he paused and blinked before going on, 'I think, Michelle, that people change. And when people change, relationships change too. Someone you once thought you loved, well, you find out you don't any more.'

The cold hand of dread gripped Michelle's heart and she tried to close her ears and her mind to what Donal was saying. Surely he wasn't talking about their relationship? She must move the conversation onto safer territory, away from her greatest fear.

'She's gone to live in some godforsaken farmhouse in Ballynahinch,' she said, with forced jocularity, trying desperately to lighten the mood. 'Can you believe it? And she'd the nerve to suggest we should go out there and visit her. She handed out business cards for this Padraig Flynn like she was his flipping agent. If she thinks that I'm — '

'Michelle,' said Donal suddenly, and she stopped talking abruptly and bit her lip, 'there's something I have to tell you.'

She put her hands over her ears. But it wasn't

469

enough to drown out what he said next.

'It's over between us, Michelle. I have to leave. I don't love you.'

'No,' said Michelle in a small, frightened voice and she felt as though she was turning inside out. She put a forefinger in each ear and pulled her elbows together until they were touching, a physical barrier against the onslaught of his hateful words. She closed her eyes and they burned hot and painful, but no tears came. This was beyond crying; this was the end of her world.

'I'm sorry, Michelle,' he said and she curled up in a ball on the sofa and pressed her face against the soft jersey fabric of her trousers, moaning softly, comforting herself. Please God, she prayed, make this not be happening to me!

Then, after some time had passed — seconds or minutes, she could not tell — she felt Donal touch her on the back and he said again, 'I'm sorry. I'm so very, very sorry.'

She unfurled herself, sat upright and looked up at him, anger bubbling up fast like filling a milk bottle with water from a tap.

'Who is she?' she asked and was surprised to hear the words come out in her normal voice, as though she was asking him the identity of a stranger at a party.

There was a short pause before he replied, 'This doesn't have anything to do with anyone else, Michelle. It's to do with us.'

'You're lying,' she said, the image of that odious present in the boot of his car burnt into her memory, 'I know you're lying.'

He sighed and looked at her as if deciding whether to own up or not. He sat down abruptly on the huge leather footstool that served as a coffee table. 'OK, there is someone. I didn't want to tell you because I didn't want to hurt you any more than I had to.'

'That's very fucking big of you, Don,' she spat out, incensed by his patronising manner. 'Well, who is she?'

'Her name's Ann-Marie Shaw — Amy for short. I was engaged to her once, a long time ago. It didn't work out — I was the one that broke it off. But I never stopped thinking about her and, by the time I'd realised that I'd made a mistake, it was too late — we were married and we had Molly. I never knew what happened to her and then one day, out of the blue, I met her in a shop in Ballyfergus, buying a Sunday paper.'

'Save the bloody love story, Don! So she's from Ballyfergus then?'

'That's right.'

'How long has it been going on?'

'Two years.'

Michelle hugged herself and began to shake as memories flooded her mind. It had been going on even while she was pregnant with Sabrina. The birth of their second daughter had been a futile exercise then — their marriage was effectively over even before the child had been conceived. That meant he was been sleeping with both her and this Amy for two years — the thought made Michelle feel physically ill.

'You fucking bastard, Don,' she said and started to cry. 'You married me because of my

471

money, didn't you? Because of who I am.'

'Yes,' said Donal and he looked at the carpet between his knees, 'I think you might be right. I didn't realise it at the time, but now I think it's true.'

Michelle stopped crying, dabbed her eyes and said, 'And this woman. She's 'the one', isn't she? It was never me.'

Donal looked up into her face and nodded sadly, his eyes full of remorse.

'I absolutely fucking hate you, Donal Mullan. I never want to set eyes on you ever again. I can't believe you've done this to me. And what about the children? You're so selfish. You think only of yourself.'

'That's not true. I've thought about what this'll do to the girls every day for the last two years. But I can't go on living a lie, Michelle. It's not fair on either of us.'

'Fuck you!'

'I need to tell you something else, Michelle.'

She glared at him and waited. Nothing he had to say could possibly hurt her more — she was numb with pain.

'Your father's been having an affair with my sister, Grainne, for over ten years. They met at our wedding.'

'Right, that's it, you lying bastard!' shouted Michelle and she leapt to her feet. 'Get out of my house — *now!*' she screamed and she pointed at the door with her arm fully extended. 'Before I call the fucking police.'

He went then, without another word. She heard the front door open and the sound of his car driving off, quickly. Then she sat down on the sofa again and sobbed until she could not cry any more. She dabbed her face with the scrunched-up tissue in her hand and explored the condition of her face with the tips of her fingers. The skin around her eyes was swollen and tender and her cheeks were streaked with the salty residue of her tears.

What motive could Donal possibly have for telling such a dreadful lie about her father? She could think of none. She remembered what her mother had said about her father having 'all his needs taken care of'. Could it possibly be true? No, she absolutely refused to listen to Donal. He was a liar and a cheat and she would not believe a word he said.

★　★　★

The next morning, after a surprisingly sound sleep induced by four glasses of red wine, Michelle awoke to the sound of Sabrina crying. She opened her eyes and saw the empty place where Donal used to sleep and misery settled on her like a fine mist. She hauled herself into an upright position and sat on the edge of the bed. Her head began to pound. She moaned softly, fumbled into a dressing-gown and went and got Sabrina and carried her downstairs.

In the kitchen she hastily transferred a carton of premixed baby formula into a bottle and gave it to the baby who sucked contentedly on the teat. Holding Sabrina in one arm she pulled the contents of the medicine cupboard onto the

473

counter and found the Paracetemol. After swallowing two tablets with a large glass of water she went and sat in the family room and thought.

The first person she wanted to see was her mother but she couldn't drive up to Ballynahinch and land in on Padraig Flynn, not in her present state of mind. And she couldn't unburden her terrible news at Glenburn so soon after her mother had walked out on Dad. He needed protecting from this as long as possible, for it would only be another heartache to add to his own.

'Mum,' said a small voice, and Michelle looked up to find a bleary-eyed Molly standing in the doorway, 'where's Daddy?'

'He had to leave for work very early this morning, love,' said Michelle smoothly.

'But everyone's on holiday,' she replied.

'Not today,' said Michelle firmly and added, 'and he's going to be away for a few days on business.'

'Staying in a hotel?' asked Molly hopefully. She thought this the most exciting experience in the world.

'That's right,' said Michelle and she bent her head over Sabrina, allowing her hair to fall over her face. A tear dropped onto the back of the hand that was holding the bottle. How in the name of God was she to explain to this little girl that her daddy would never be coming home? That he had left her.

Just as she was about to allow herself to dissolve into tears, Michelle suddenly realised, for the very first time, what it truly meant to be a mother. What it meant to put your children before and above yourself. Hastily she wiped the tears from her face and said, 'Oh, I must've got something in my eye. There, it's gone now.' She looked up at Molly and smiled, finding an inner strength that she never knew existed. 'You go through to the kitchen, love, and help yourself to some cereal. I'll be through just as soon as Sabrina's finished her bottle.'

Later that morning Michelle took a phone call from Donal in which he asked after the children but not her. He politely but coolly told her that he would be round at one o'clock to collect some of his things.

When she put the phone down Michelle realised that she had been nurturing the belief that he would come home. All morning she had asked herself, subconsciously, what she would do if he came back. Would she forgive him? Could she have him back after what he'd done? But now that hope was gone. And with the uncertainty gone, beneath the heartbreak there glimmered the tiniest bit of relief. She would no longer have to try to please Donal, she would no longer have to try and make him love her. She could just be herself.

And she was damned if she was going to sit here while Donal riffled through the house, taking away the choicest possessions, which he would later claim were his. He could have it all for all she cared — she didn't want anything that they'd shared together. And she didn't want him upsetting Molly.

She glanced at the kitchen clock and thought quickly. Then she walked through to the family room where Molly was watching cartoons and Sabrina had fallen asleep in her bouncy chair.

'Molly,' she said, 'let's go upstairs and get dressed. We're going to see Auntie Roz!'

Michelle washed and dressed quickly, slapped on some make-up, helped Molly into her clothes and bundled a shocked Sabrina into a snowsuit. Then she left the house, locked it carefully behind her and drove quickly into Ballyfergus, hoping that she didn't meet Donal on the way. But the road to town was deserted and she didn't pass a single car until she reached the outskirts of Ballyfergus.

Roz opened her front door to them with a surprised expression that quickly turned to pleasure.

'Come in,' she said warmly, ushering them indoors, 'come in. What a lovely surprise. Molly, what did Santa give you for Christmas?'

A warm feeling enveloped Michelle as soon as she crossed the threshold. Roz was a good friend completely unconnected with the whole sordid business of her marriage. She was intelligent and practical too. She would be able to help Michelle decide what to do.

'We brought *The Little Mermaid* with us,' said Michelle, with a smile pasted on her face and a voice that sounded remote and disconnected. 'Molly got it for Christmas and she hasn't watched it yet.'

'Can I watch it now, Auntie Roz?' said Molly.

'Of course you can, darling. Let's put it on

right away.' Roisin led Molly into the lounge, inserted the video in the player and Molly sat down on the floor in front of it. 'Now,' said Roisin to Michelle, 'I'll put on the kettle on for us,' and Michelle followed her into the kitchen. Tony was asleep in a playpen in the corner of the room. On the floor were a playmat and some baby toys. Michelle took Sabrina out of her snowsuit and set her on the floor were she played happily with the toys.

'This is a nice surprise,' said Roisin, and she opened a cupboard and took out two mugs.

'Where's Scott?' said Michelle.

'Playing golf, where else?' she said with pretend exasperation.

Michelle got up and closed the kitchen door mindful that, like all children, Molly had peculiarly acute hearing when it came to things you didn't want her to hear.

'Michelle,' said Roz and she glanced at the closed door, 'is everything all right?'

'No, it's not,' said Michelle, surprising herself with her composure. She'd felt this way before — once when a lorry nearly took the side off the Range Rover on a sharp bend and again, only yesterday, when Mum announced that she was leaving Dad. Michelle realised that she was in shock.

Roz was staring at Michelle, waiting for her to speak.

'Don's left me,' she said simply.

'Oh,' said Roisin, and she froze for a moment. 'I'm sorry,' she added, then picked up a packet of biscuits and arranged them, very deliberately, one by one on a plate.

'He left last night,' said Michelle and she told Roz what had passed between her and Donal the night before. 'So,' she continued, 'he admitted that he'd been having an affair for over two years. I presume that's where he's gone now — to *her*. He phoned this morning to say that he was coming over for the rest of his things. I didn't want to be there when he came back. I didn't think you'd mind — '

'God, no, of course not,' said Roisin hastily, dismissing Michelle's concern. 'I'm glad you came here. I really am.'

'I couldn't go up to Glenburn. It's all very — very complicated up there at the moment,' she said with a deep sigh. 'I'll tell you about it another time.'

'Did he tell you who the other woman is?' asked Roisin and she set a plate of chocolate digestive biscuits very gently on the table in front of Michelle.

'Someone called Ann-Marie Shaw. He calls her Amy for short.'

Roisin merely nodded and turned her back to Michelle. She fussed unnecessarily at the teapot, which she'd placed over a small gas flame to stew.

'Roz,' said Michelle, 'you don't seem very surprised?'

Roz turned off the gas and the flame under the teapot died. 'Well,' she said slowly, 'we knew he was having an affair, didn't we?'

'Not for two whole bloody years, I didn't,' said Michelle quickly, her sorrow eclipsed for the time being by a pervading bitterness, 'and I didn't expect him to leave me. I honestly didn't. I must be thick or something for I swear to God that I never noticed anything unusual about his behaviour. Nothing at all.'

As she said it Michelle realised that this wasn't entirely true. For no apparent reason a coolness had developed between her and Donal over the last few months, culminating in a decided chill over Christmas itself. The warning signs had been there — she'd just chosen not to see them.

'You don't think he's coming back then?' said Roz.

'No, I can't see it. He says that he was engaged to this Amy once before,' said Michelle and she found that she had to clear her throat before she could go on. 'He told me that she's the love of his life.'

'Hmm,' said Roz and she sat down at the table and pushed a cup of tea in front of Michelle.

'What's that supposed to mean?' said Michelle.

Roz stared at her then for what seemed like several minutes, even though it was probably no more than ten seconds. But it was enough to make Michelle feel extremely uncomfortable.

'Roz, will you stop staring like that,' she said but Roz appeared not to have heard her.

'You see this woman Donal's been having an affair with,' said Roz.

'Yes.'

'I know who she is.'

'You know Ann-Marie Shaw?'

'That's right,' said Roz and Michelle waited.

'So tell me,' she said impatiently.

Roz paused again before going on. 'She's my sister, Michelle. My elder sister, Ann-Marie Shaw.'

'Your sister?' said Michelle stupidly.

'I must have mentioned her to you before.'

Michelle shook her head and tried to process this information, a sense of betrayal rapidly taking root in her mind.

'You knew about this and you didn't tell me?' she said, a bubble of anger wedged in her throat.

'I've only known about the affair for a matter of weeks — just about as long as you. At your Christmas party I overheard Don talking to a woman on the phone and, from the language he used, I guessed he was having an affair. I found out later that it was my sister.'

'How could you know and not tell me, Roz? I thought you were my friend.'

'I needed time to think about it. I thought I could persuade Don to finish with Ann-Marie. I thought I was protecting you from getting hurt.'

'You'd do that for me?' said Michelle.

'Yes, because I know that you love him,' said Roz and then she added hastily, 'but that's not the only reason. I didn't want Ann-Marie to have anything to do with him. He broke her heart once, you see, and I don't trust him not to do it again.'

'You don't think very much of him, do you?'

'No, I don't. But I care a very great deal about you, Michelle. And I think that you deserve a lot better than Donal Mullan. I'm only sorry that I can't persuade my sister to think that too. I honestly believe that you're better off without him. He's a liar and a cheat.'

'He's still my husband,' said Michelle. Her sense of loyalty to Donal, in spite of all that he'd done, was still intact.

'I don't mean to sound harsh but he is bad news, Michelle. He's not worthy of you. You're good and kind and one of the best people I know. And I just think that you don't need someone who treats you like this. You're worth so much more. You deserve to be loved and cherished and adored just for being you.'

And with these kind words Michelle, at last, started to cry and all the tears she had so successfully held back all morning came tumbling down her cheeks.

'Oh, Michelle,' said Roz softly and she came over and put her arms around her friend's shoulders. Then she knelt down and planted a sisterly kiss on her cheek. 'Do you forgive me for not telling you?'

Michelle nodded and said between sobs, 'Yes. I suppose I do. It's just that so much has happened over the last couple of days — I feel as if my whole world is falling apart, Roz. The only thing keeping me together is the children. I have to keep going for them.'

'Yes, you do. But you're going to need some help. I take it your parents and sisters know what's happened?'

Michelle shook her head miserably. 'No, I haven't told anyone. Until I got that phone call from Don this morning I thought he would come home. But he was so cold and businesslike on the telephone, I knew then that he didn't care

481

about me or the children.'

'Well, you're going to need all the support you can get. I'll do everything I can, of course, but you're going to need your family. Here,' said Roz and she handed the phone to Michelle, 'call your parents now.'

'I can't,' said Michelle and she put the handset down on the table and stared at it.

'Why ever not?'

'It's a long story,' said Michelle, she took a deep breath.

'I'm listening,' said Roz and Michelle told her what had transpired up at Glenburn the previous afternoon.

'Wow,' was all Roz said and then she was silent. After a few moments had passed, she added, 'Well, in spite of that I still think you should tell your mother. Ask her to come down to The Grange and stay for a few days. She'll be down in a flash when she finds out what's happened.'

'I know she would. But I'm so embarrassed.'

'What have you to be embarrassed about?'

'My husband's left me, Roz. Isn't it obvious?'

'No, he hasn't,' said Roz firmly. 'You threw him out, remember?'

'Yes, I did, didn't I?' said Michelle, her confidence slowly creeping back.

'When you found out that he'd been cheating on you?'

'That's right.'

'Well, then. You have nothing to be embarrassed about,' said Roz and she took both of Michelle's hands in her own and stared into her face, her eyes shining and clear. 'Believe me, it doesn't feel like it right now, but one day you will look back at this time and you'll be glad it's happened. For there's someone out there waiting for you, Michelle, someone who will truly love you. It's just a question of finding him.'

And even though her heart was still battered and sore, Michelle found herself slowly nodding in agreement.

★ ★ ★

'Michelle's right,' said Donal, standing in the doorway to Ann-Marie's small bathroom, 'I am a bastard.' She was in the bath immersed in bubbles — only her head was visible, resting on the edge of the bath.

'I think you're being a little hard on yourself,' said Ann-Marie loyally, but Donal knew she was only trying to make him feel better.

Now that he had done what he'd planned and dreamt about for months, he was full of nothing but shame and remorse. He could find no joy in his heart; it only ached for the children he'd left behind. He would not be there when Molly had one of her bad dreams and called out for him in the night. He could no longer lie down on her bed when he came home from work and talk to her until she fell asleep. Sabrina's chubby little face and joyous giggle would not be there to greet him when he came home from work. If he were lucky his contact with the children would be a few brief meetings a month. He would become little more to them than a soft touch for pocket money. In time they'd learn to live without him.

'I know what I've done, Amy. I know what I've given up. And it's terrible ... ' He stopped then for he could not go on. He looked at the beautiful woman in the bath and reminded himself that he'd done it for her. And none of it was Amy's fault. The blame lay entirely with him. He swallowed and fought back the tears.

Amy did not say anything at all and Donal took a long time to compose himself before he went on, 'She'll try to stop me seeing the kids, you know. And Noel McCormick'll back her every inch of the way.'

'Did she say that to you today?' said Amy with mild surprise.

'No, she wasn't even there, up at Glenburn I suppose. She must've gone out just as soon as I phoned to say I was coming round for my things.'

'I see,' said Ann-Marie thoughtfully, and she bent her legs so that her knees broke the surface of the water like two small islands in a sea of froth. 'You can't blame her for being angry, Donal. You can't expect her to be all nicey-nice.' She paused and looked at her knees and said, 'It's the children I feel bad about.'

'But you shouldn't feel bad about anything, Amy,' he said and knelt down by the edge of the bath and stroked her forehead with his thumb. 'None of this is your fault. If I hadn't been such a fool all those years ago I never would've ended up in such a mess.'

'If it hadn't been for me you wouldn't have left her.'

'I like to think that I would've had the courage to do it anyway. It's not right living a lie, is it?' he said, desperate for Amy to validate his actions.

She shook her head, agreeing with him. Then she sat up in the bath. The bubbles slid down her breasts, clung to her nipples for a few seconds and plopped into the bath water. 'I'm getting out now,' she said. 'Would you hand me a towel?'

He held up a large blue bath towel like a windbreak as she stepped out of the bath. She turned her back to him and he wrapped the towel around her shoulders. He put his arms around her and she cocked her head to one side. He leant his cheek against hers, which felt damp from the steamy bath.

'I love you. And hard as all this is, I know I've done the right thing.'

'Me too,' said Ann-Marie and she wriggled around in his embrace until she was facing him, 'You'll never leave me again, will you, Donal?'

'I'll die first,' he said, the fear in her face filling him with shame. 'You must believe me, Amy. I promise I'll never let you go again as long as I live. I know you need me, far more than Michelle thinks she does.'

She went into the bedroom then to put on some clothes and while she was in there the doorbell buzzed. Donal's first instinct was to hide somewhere and then he remembered that his relationship with Ann-Marie was no longer clandestine. Whoever it was would find out about

485

them sooner or later. Now was as good a time as any.

Ann-Marie came out of the bedroom wearing a long loose kaftan, made of amber-coloured linen. Her feet were bare and her hair was still pinned up from the bath. She stood in the middle of the room and looked up the hall, which led directly into the lounge without a doorway between them. Then she looked at Donal.

'You'd better answer it,' he said and he sat down on the sofa, then stood up again. His heartbeat was rapid, chugging like a speeding train, making him feel giddy.

'Are you sure you want to do this?' she said quietly. 'I don't know who it is.'

'It doesn't matter. People need to find out. We might as well get it over and done with.'

He eventually settled on a spot on the sofa where he was out of the direct line of vision from the front door. He strained to listen while he savagely chewed a rag-nail on his left index finger.

He heard muffled greetings of familiarity and then Roz Johnston appeared at the end of the hallway. There was something sheepish in the way Ann-Marie came up and stood beside her.

'Roz?' he said, and looked at Ann-Marie. She averted her eyes and her face appeared slightly flushed — but whether that was the after-effect of the hot bath or embarrassment he couldn't be sure.

'What are you doing here?' he said to Roz, and then realising his rudeness, added hastily, 'I mean, I didn't know that you and Amy were friends.'

'It's Ann-Marie,' said Roz icily and she added, 'and we're not friends.' She said it with such uncharacteristic menace, emphasising the word '*friends*' that Donal knew then that she'd been sent as an ambassador for Michelle.

'You'd better come in and sit down,' he said, feeling suddenly more the master of this little flat than he'd ever been of The Grange.

She sat down on the armchair opposite and Amy came and sat beside him. She found his hand and entwined her fingers in his. Her hand was cold and shaking.

'Well,' he said to Roz, 'I suppose Michelle's told you.'

'Yes, she has,' said Roz, and she shook her head in disapproval.

Then she was quiet for a few moments — obviously she was trying to make this as uncomfortable for him as possible.

'So, why did she ask you to come here?' he said.

'She didn't. I came here because I wanted to talk to you and Ann-Marie.'

'I don't follow,' said Donal.

'I don't like you, Donal Mullan. I never have and I doubt if I ever will. I don't think I can ever forgive you for what you've done to Ann-Marie and now Michelle.'

She was talking as though she knew about Donal and Ann-Marie's history, but how, when she wasn't even a friend of Ann-Marie?

'But,' continued Roz, 'if you're the one

487

Ann-Marie has chosen then I'm prepared to — '

'What Amy does is her business,' he interrupted angrily. 'It's got nothing to do with you, has it, Amy?' and he turned to look at his lover just in time to catch her gesticulating furiously at Roz.

'What's going on, Amy?' he asked.

Ann-Marie bowed her head and looked into her lap. 'It has everything to do with her,' she said softly. 'You see, we're sisters, Donal.'

'What?' said Donal and he glanced, confused, from one woman to the other, 'You're telling me that Roz Johnston is your sister?'

'Don't you remember Roisin? My little sister?'

Donal shook his head in disbelief. He stared at the comely woman opposite, at her dark wavy hair; her straight even teeth and her carefully made-up face. An attractive-looking girl, in spite of her grim expression, and every inch the professional beautician. Then he recalled the overweight, acne-faced teenager called Roisin Shaw whom he'd once known. A girl with greasy hair, thick round spectacles and braces on her teeth. He tried unsuccessfully to reconcile the two images. But when he looked closely at Roz, the similarities between her and Ann-Marie slowly became apparent. They shared the same soft jawline and wide-set eyes separated by a broad nose. Certain he'd been the victim of some kind of deceit, or at the very least a practical joke, his confidence in Amy's love was shaken.

'Amy,' he said warily, not taking his eyes off Roz, 'you heard me talking about Roz. You knew she'd been in my home. Why didn't you say who she was before now?'

'I didn't want anything to scare you off. I thought that if you knew who she was, you might finish with me for fear of being discovered. I couldn't risk losing you a second time.'

Coming from Amy that was entirely believable. But what about Roz? Even as a fourteen-year-old she was smart and more worldy-wise than her elder sister. She must've known who he was before they'd even met. Did she simply go along with Ann-Marie's wishes? Somehow he thought that Roz was more independent-minded than that.

'And you, Roz, why did you pretend not to know me?'

'I had my reasons,' she said tersely, and her face went a deep shade of pink.

'Roisin,' said Ann-Marie, 'you might as well tell us . . . tell Donal the truth. There's no need for secrets now.'

'Very well then. Don't say I didn't warn you,' began Roz eagerly. She stared full on at Donal and she said, 'I hated you for what you did to Ann-Marie. I swore that one day I'd get my revenge on you for ruining her life. When Michelle walked into my life I couldn't believe my luck. I watched and I listened, waiting for the perfect opportunity to hurt you. At last I found out that you were having an affair and I was all set to confront you with the fact. And then I found out that your lover was Ann-Marie.'

'And you said nothing,' said Donal, wondering for how long she'd known.

'Only to Ann-Marie,' said Roisin. 'I told her that she was a fool. That you'd use her and discard her like you'd done before.'

Donal gripped Ann-Marie's hand tighter in his own and wished that he could cover her ears and stop her hearing these hateful, unjust words. Words that could poison her mind against him. 'But you're forgetting one thing, Roz,' said Donal, suppressing the anger that welled up inside him. 'I love your sister.'

Roz laughed unnaturally and said, 'You said you loved her before and you still left her.'

'That was different.'

'Oh, really? How?'

Donal looked into Ann-Marie's face and said, 'I was young and foolish. I didn't realise then that what I had with Amy was the most precious thing in the world.'

Roz snorted derisively but Donal continued to stare at Ann-Marie who returned his gaze through tear-filled eyes. 'It's been a long and painful journey to get here,' he continued, 'and I'm sorry for the pain I've caused everyone. But I know that this is right. That we are meant for each other and everything else is wrong.'

'Like you and Michelle?' said Roz.

Donal sighed, the spell between him and Ann-Marie broken. He looked at Roz's bitter face and said, 'Yes, like me and Michelle.'

'So you dump her the same way you dumped Ann-Marie?'

'Roisin,' said Ann-Marie quietly, but with a steeliness in her voice that Donal had not heard before, 'there's no point going over all this again and again. What's happened has happened. I'm sorry that Michelle and her children have been hurt but nothing Donal can do can change that now. And if you want our relationship to continue then you're going to have to accept that Donal is part of my life now.'

'I'm sorry too, Ann-Marie,' said Roisin and she stood up, 'I'm sorry I came here. Maybe I should've waited until I wasn't so angry. That would have made it more comfortable for you, wouldn't it? Because you two don't want to face up to the reality of what you've done, do you?' She faltered and her voice began to break, 'You've no idea what this has done to Michelle.' She started to cry then and Ann-Marie got up and put her arm around her sister's shoulders.

'Donal,' she said, 'why don't you take a walk to the corner shop and get the paper? Roisin and I need to talk.'

He went out into the hallway, took his coat from the peg behind the door and slipped out quietly, onto the linoleum of the communal landing. He stood there for a few moments wondering what the sisters were saying to each other. Hoping for Amy's sake that, in spite of Roz's loathing for him, they would be reconciled.

Epilogue

July 2004

Noel sat on the sofa in the bedroom at Glenburn and eased his socked right foot into a shiny Oxford toe-cap shoe. He stomped his foot on the carpet, twice, until his heel slipped into the comfortable recess of the shoe. Then he got up, put his toe on the footstool and, with a noisy exhalation of air, tied his laces. He repeated the procedure with the other foot. Next thing he'd be reduced to wearing slip-on loafers because he couldn't do up his own laces.

He looked at his reflection in the ornate antique mirror that adorned the wall by the window. He frowned and adjusted the silk grey-spotted cravat that nestled in the starched butterfly wings of a white shirt. Just like her to select something so ostentatious, so silly, he thought.

He peered at his face for some minutes. There was a fine line between distinguished maturity and old age, the former retaining an attraction for the other sex, the latter not. When had he crossed that line? For the man staring back at him with the high receding white hairline, the first faint liver spot on his forehead and the moist, hooded eyes was careering into old age.

'When did that happen, old boy?' he said to himself and a pair of pale thin lips parted to reveal unnaturally white teeth.

Noel shivered and looked away, reminded suddenly of his mortality. He'd made sound financial provision for his retirement and his succession plan for McCormick's had been a masterstroke. Matt Doherty had taken over seamlessly from Noel and was now the driving force behind the business that he, for so long, had dominated.

But Noel had never truly believed that old age was something that would happen to him. Up until this moment he had believed himself to be immortal. He walked away from the mirror over to the window and stood looking out with his hands in his pockets, thinking. The late morning sun shone down fiercely on the lush gardens, so carefully planned by Pauline all those years ago. Noel sat down abruptly on the sofa to nurse his regret.

He should be looking forward to these twilight years with Pauline by his side. The woman he'd loved, at one time, above all others. He should have realised what a precious commodity she was. What he would give to have her back again, a woman with her style and grace! But more important than these qualities, he saw now, was her integrity, her optimistic outlook on life and a certain naivety which had not diminished with age. He, on the other hand, was a cynic. Her goodness had reflected on him and, without her, he was a lesser person. But he had no chance of winning her back now. She had made a life with Padraig Flynn and from the reports he heard back through the girls, she was happy. Happier than she'd ever been with him.

Everything about this day was wrong. But what was he to do? Fear gripped his heart and squeezed it. He couldn't rattle around in this big house all on his own any more with Esther fussing over him, dowsing him with her well-meant pity and her over-large meals. He'd resisted Grainne's plan to move in, but the house was falling apart. The hall needed painting, the kitchen could do with a refit and the gardener had retired and he couldn't get a decent replacement. He forgot birthdays and anniversaries and only this morning the shower attachment had fallen off and cracked him on the head. What did he know about domestic plumbers and handymen and getting things fixed? What did he know about running a home? He was sick of living alone — he needed someone to manage the house.

His children were loving but they had their own lives to live with little time, it seemed, for him. And he couldn't very well complain about their self-centredness — weren't they simply following their father's example? Pauline had warned him that they were raising selfish children and he'd ignored her.

He thought of his other daughter, Roz Johnston — as far as he knew, the only illegitimate child he'd sired — and allowed himself a moment of self-congratulation. He'd done the right thing by her at least, if not by her mother. With her entrepreneurial flair and business acumen he saw more of himself in her than any of his other children. And he was grateful that he'd had the opportunity to help her. On his death, his shares in the business would pass to her and he would have paid his dues.

The door to the bedroom opened.

'Ah, there you are,' said Grainne and she came in and posed in front of him with her hands on her hips. 'Well, what do you think?' she demanded.

Noel groaned inwardly. He was no expert on women's fashion but he knew that Grainne's attire — a tailored baby pink jacket and skirt with a ludicrously ornate matching hat — was inappropriate. Her skirt was too short for a wedding, her heels were too high and her hosiery too shiny for daywear. He noticed that her open-toed sandals were adorned with tiny diamonté jewels. The only diamonds Pauline ever wore during the day were real ones. Glitz, she used to say, was strictly for evening wear.

'Ach, will you cheer up, Noel?' said Grainne, not appearing to notice that he hadn't answered her question. 'You'd think you were going to a funeral. It is your wedding day after all. And everybody's waiting for us downstairs.' She came over to him then and hauled him off the sofa by the arm.

'Here, you haven't done that right,' she added, scrutinising him, and she fussed at his necktie until he pulled away.

Then she squeezed his arm and, as she led him out onto the landing and down the stairs, she said with conviction, 'Just you wait and see, Noel. We'll be good together, you and me.'

Colette and Fraser's wedding took place in Ballyfergus registry office with a total of forty-eight guests. Colette wore a single-breasted cream linen trouser suit of her own design with long, flared trousers, high wedge heels, a floppy cream hat and a big fake flower pinned to her lapel. Her inspiration was Bianca Jagger in the 1970's. Roisin, as her matron-of-honour and only attendant, wore a similar outfit in fuchsia. Fraser and Scott, the best man, sported matching grey lounge suits with grey silk ties dotted with spots of bright pink.

The wedding party stood with their back to the audience and made their vows to each other and Roisin, standing by her friend's side, blinked hard to stop the tears tumbling down her cheeks and spoiling her make-up. Then the newly-weds kissed, the tension was broken and everyone cheered. Even the female registrar, who performed several weddings every week, beamed in the face of so much optimism and joy.

Everyone rushed forward to kiss the just-marrieds and Roisin felt a familiar tugging sensation on her trouser leg.

'Mummy,' said Tony's small, sweet voice, and she smiled down at her son. He was wearing long tailored navy shorts, white socks, navy sandals and a blue and white checked shirt. He had never looked more adorable.

'Up, up,' he said, holding his chubby little arms high in the air, demanding to be lifted. She discarded the small bouquet of pink and cream roses, scooped him up and held him tight against her. She kissed his soft, warm cheeks again and again while he stared around him, wide-eyed and open-mouthed. She followed his gaze to Donal and Ann-Marie, standing just a little away from the rest of the guests.

They stood facing each other, apparently oblivious to the activity around them, gazing into each other's eyes with their hands locked together. She noticed the tenderness with which Donal caressed the back of Ann-Marie's hand and Roisin acknowledged to herself that her feelings towards him had mellowed. Maybe love did change people. Maybe love had redeemed Donal. And who was she to judge what was right and what was wrong in other people's lives? Something made Donal look up then and his eye caught Roisin's. Embarrassed to be caught spying on such an intimate moment, she blushed and looked away.

Tony squirmed and Roisin set him down and watched him toddle over to Mairead. Her heart lurched with love. Mairead knelt down on one knee to talk to him and Roisin examined the man standing beside her mother. George, a sixty-eight-year-old widower, was solid, grey-haired and had a warm smile and personality. Mairead had met him through the choral society and they had been dating for over a year now. And in that time. Mairead's life had been transformed. They went salsa dancing twice a week at the community centre, saw friends every Saturday night and he was teaching Mairead to play golf. They were even going on holiday together next month. And Mairead was softer somehow than she'd been before. More relaxed and happier than Roisin could ever remember her.

'Ah hem!' said the registrar, above the noise. 'We have another wedding here shortly, so if I could ask you all to please move outside . . .'

Everyone shuffled out into the bright sunshine of the small forecourt, which was festooned with pots and hanging baskets filled with brightly coloured flowers. A few photographs were taken and then everyone headed for the carpark.

'Scott, love,' said Roisin when they were about to leave, 'I'd better nip to the loo. I don't think I can wait. You take Tony to the car and get him strapped in. I'll be there in a minute.'

When she came outside again a small crowd had gathered for the next wedding and Roisin quickly started in the direction of the carpark.

'Roz! Roz!' shouted a familiar voice and Roisin froze in her tracks. She turned to meet Michelle running towards her, dressed in mint-green trousers and a long-line tailored jacket. 'Thought you'd be long gone by the time we got here,' she said, slightly out of breath.

'We were running a bit late. Everyone's gone on to the Marine Hotel. Scott's waiting for me in the car.'

'Well, how did it go?'

'It was lovely, really lovely. They're so happy together. Where are the girls?' said Roisin, looking behind Michelle. The guests were starting to filter into the building.

'They're with Stephen.' Stephen was Michelle's

boyfriend of four months — a decent bloke whom Roisin liked a great deal. He was a lecturer Michelle had met at college where she was taking a course in fashion and design. Although Michelle, so deeply hurt by Donal, was cautious about their relationship he seemed to be mad about her.

'He's just parking the car,' she continued. 'I hopped out when I saw you.'

Just then a smart black limousine pulled up outside the registry office. Roisin caught a glimpse of the occupants. On the back seat, staring out at her was Noel McCormick. Beside him was a woman, her face partially obscured by a very large hat.

'That's them now,' gasped Michelle, excitedly. 'Where the heck is Stephen?'

Noel McCormick got out of the car, followed by a glamorous forty-something woman in an enormous pink hat and a very short skirt. Her face was very heavily made up and she wore a slash of bright pink lipstick. The woman was Grainne Mullan and for a moment Roisin felt pity for Donal. His sister was getting married — he should be here.

'Well, I must dash,' she said to Michelle. 'Scott's waiting for me in the car. Bye, Michelle.' She stood on her toes to kiss Michelle on both cheeks and added, 'You look gorgeous, by the way.'

'You too. Speak soon,' she replied absentmindedly and then she ran to meet Stephen who had just appeared with Molly and Sabrina.

Roisin waved at the children and walked to the carpark thinking that Grainne Mullan seemed an unlikely choice as wife for Noel McCormick. But people had a funny way of surprising you — of doing the most unexpected things. Love and happiness, she had learnt, came in all shapes and sizes.

She got in the car, put on her seat belt and said, 'Scott?'

'What?' he said and turned to look at her.

'Have I told you today that I really, really love you.'

'No.'

'Scott,' she said, staring into his melted chocolate eyes, 'I really, really love you.'

'I know,' he said and they smiled at each other and Roisin knew she was the luckiest woman alive.

CHOICES

Erin Kaye

When Sheila gave birth to Claire she was just sixteen years of age. Persuaded by her family to give the baby up for adoption, this choice would affect her life — and the lives of those she loved — forever. Two decades later, Sheila and her older sister Eileen face heartache. Eileen's cancer has returned and Sheila can no longer live with the decision she made all those years ago. She wants her daughter back. But life is never that straightforward and Sheila's desperate yearning threatens to shatter family relationships. With her entire family in crisis, Sheila takes reckless measures to heal the wounds of the past.

MOTHERS AND DAUGHTERS

Erin Kaye

Catherine Meehan was born into a respect-able working-class Roman Catholic family in Ballyfergus on the coast of Antrim. She is determined to flee the poverty, bigotry and antagonism that shaped her early years . . . Jayne Alexander is infused with the privileges that go with being part of a well-to-do Protestant family. Despite her self-assurance, she has a need for love and yearns for approval . . . From 1959 to 1984, the lives of the Meehan and Alexander families become inextricably linked, in moments of great passion and hatred, as deeply held loyalties are threatened.

GAMES PEOPLE PLAY

Louise Voss

Rachel is a rising tennis star. But does she want success more than she wants a 'real life', and a steady boyfriend like everyone else? . . . Susie is Rachel's mother. All she wants is her partner Billy — but he's left her. Is she brave enough to start again? . . . Gordana is Rachel's grandmother. She has all she ever wanted: health, wealth, and a loving family — or at least she thinks she does . . . Ivan is the link between them all: Rachel's father, Susie's ex-husband, and Gordana's son. Unhappy with his life, nobody is prepared for what happens when he gets arrested, or the changes that it forces on their lives.